THE
BORG
PORTRAIT

T0012438

David Hewson is a former journalist with *The Times*, *Sunday Times* and the *Independent*. He is the author of more than thirty novels, including his Rome-based Nic Costa series which has been published in fifteen languages, his Amsterdam-based series featuring detective Pieter Vos, and the brand-new Venetian mystery series. He has also written three acclaimed adaptations of the Danish TV series, *The Killing*. He lives near Canterbury in Kent.

@david_hewson | davidhewson.com

THE
BORGIA
PORTRAIT

DAVID
HEWSON

CANONGATE

This paperback edition published in Great Britain, the USA and
Canada in 2024 by Canongate Books Ltd,
14 High Street, Edinburgh EH1 1TE

Distributed in the USA by Publishers Group West
and in Canada by Publishers Group Canada

First published in 2023 by Severn House, an imprint of
Canongate Books Ltd, 14 High Street, Edinburgh EH1 1TE

canongate.co.uk

1

British Library Cataloguing-in-Publication Data
A catalogue record for this book is available on
request from the British Library

ISBN 978 1 83885 871 1

Typeset by Palimpsest Book Production Ltd, Falkirk, Stirlingshire

Printed and bound by CPI Group (UK) Ltd, Croydon CR0 4YY

MIX
Paper | Supporting
responsible forestry
FSC
www.fsc.org   FSC® C171272

By the *condottiero*'s fearsome gaze, Il Gobbo writhes naked
in his glassy tomb.

Red marble where the Virgin holds back plague.

Eight great dead lie in holy water.

The hound of the Lord and the lily where water once
ran.

Black marble, saintly, over old bones and the eight-point
star.

In wood the secret fellow sits, by chained and sightless
Fury.

Traitor, not a traitor, nor painter, homeless by the Dolphin
and the Anchor. Loc. Col. Bai. The. MCCCX.

Lady L! You must be left to last. Replace those beautiful
eyes that others may look around and truly find you.

One

The Cursed Palazzo

Venice is never short of stories. Every street has a tale to tell, every stone a ghost. This one began with a face at a first-floor window. A young fellow, pale, stubbly features, gaunt, startled to be seen even for a fleeting second as he dashed away, vanishing behind the cracked and dusty tracery glass. Perhaps a spectre, a phantom, so a few of those around me might have thought. Or just my imagination, sparked by the curious day and the even more curious palazzo where I'd found myself.

Ca' Scacchi was supposed to be abandoned, not a soul living there for the best part of thirty-five years. It looked the part. An eccentric, crooked palace on the Grand Canal in Dorsoduro, between the Guggenheim and Salute, that I'd passed countless times on the vaporetto and always found a fascinating sight. Most other palazzi along this privileged stretch were private mansions, galleries, museums or hotels, smart, expensive, part of the international aspect of Venice that rarely interested me. Not this one. It was narrower than the rest and set at an angle that the city surveyors had begun to find alarming. There was a water gate on the ground floor, leading, I assumed, to the usual storage area customary in fifteenth-century palaces of its type. Above was the *piano nobile*, with long, dusty windows and a balcony. Over that stood another floor, almost as tall, though the windows there were tightly shuttered. Then a final, more modest top level, a place for domestic staff.

Circular glass ornamental windows were spaced along the facade like dead, blind eyes. Three funnel chimneys sat on the shallow terracotta-tiled roof, one of them decidedly wonky. The middle of the front was decorated with marble, pale pink geometric shapes. They framed the fading remains of decorative mosaics depicting a man and woman in medieval costume seated at a chessboard, something that always brought out the cameras among passing tourists. Though how many understood that *scacchi* is Italian for chess, or that, according to the history books, there was supposedly a life-size 'board' for matches with human players in the courtyard behind, I'd no idea. The only ugly element was a black and rusty iron balcony protruding from the second floor on the left, an early nine-teenth-century addition that Ruskin had described in vitriolic terms.

Being unusually ornate and somewhat smaller than the grand buildings around, the place stood out, appearing to my unin-formed eyes quaint, eccentric, the dream of an imaginative child gifted a collection of Renaissance Lego. While I always found Ca' Scacchi raised a puzzled smile and my spirits, most Venetians felt very differently and weren't reluctant to say so. The palace, you see, was cursed. Originally built for a city official under the Doge Giovanni Mocenigo, it had cast a dark and bloody shadow on many who'd come to live beneath its funnel chimneys over half a millennium. Bankruptcies, suicides, unexplained disappearances and at least two murders ran through its five-century history. Brave souls who'd wandered down the narrow dead-end alley that led to its Grand Canal side complained of tormented howls coming from within, spectral apparitions, the rank smell of rotting corpses from time to time, and a sudden chill in temperature even at the height of summer. So many stories had come to gather over the years that it almost appeared a relative to the notorious island of Poveglia across the lagoon, an equally hellish, tormented spot according to local lore. Though a couple of Venetians I knew who'd sailed there once and spent the night in a tent said it was a peaceful spot, undeserving of its reputation.

Ca' Scacchi had remained in the ownership of the family of the same name throughout, sometimes occupied by them, on occasion briefly leased to tenants. Mostly those who paid the Scacchi rent were foreign and ignorant of the palace's history and reputation until they moved in and, perhaps prompted by neighbourhood gossip, began to complain of ghostly visitations, mysterious sounds, odd illnesses and a prevailing atmosphere of doom and depression. When the Scacchis' fortunes began to wane in the 1970s, the palazzo went on the market with an international real estate agent for a while. A Hollywood star, a cinema action hero, who saw it during the film festival almost fell for the agent's patter and stumped up several million dollars, only to pull out after hearing hair-raising stories from a famous Italian director.

After that, the House of Scacchi was visited by tragedy again. The financier father and his wife died when their light aircraft crashed in the Dolomites after taking off from the little Nicelli airfield on the Lido. Another suicide, the authorities suspected, since the weather was fine, the plane was old but in airworthy condition and, when the bankers came to look at the books, the accounts were mired in debt.

Only the infamous tiny palazzo on the Grand Canal remained, after that home to the last Scacchi, a young contessa of a marked and intense beauty, who fell into an odd marriage with an English music mogul from a council house in London's East End. Then, five years later, she vanished too, leaving behind a distraught husband and a young child.

The daughter, Lizzie Hawker, had taken her father's name, not her mother's, and certainly wasn't interested in being called a countess as was her right. She'd made that clear already. Now she stood next to me as if I was the only friend she had in Venice, perhaps the world. Ca' Scacchi, a dusty empty shell for nearly four decades, was to be opened up to the prying eyes of bureaucracy through a court order that would allow the city council to assess its structural integrity.

Like explorers attracted to a newly discovered cavern promising unknown treasures, a motley group had gathered for the occasion. Luca Volpetti, my good friend from the Venice State Archives, had been summoned to check whether there were precious items inside the palazzo that needed to be taken into public care for conservation. He stood to one side, sweating in his pale linen summer suit, crossing himself and slyly making the sign of the horns, a superstitious spell against evil, with a hand behind his back. He wasn't the only one. Even Luigi Ballarin, the city surveyor who had instigated the forced inspection, had discreetly made the same gesture as we walked down the dark alley by the side to assemble in front of the locked iron door that led into the premises.

In the shade of the high palace wall, the heat remained intense. Clouds of black midges hovered in the heavy high summer air. The sound of passing boats large and small echoed off the stained brickwork, along with the occasional cry of a gondolier. Valentina Fabbri, Capitano of the Carabinieri, had arrived with four uniformed officers. They were keeping back a small group of reporters and photographers, making them wait in the main street that ran towards the Guggenheim. One I recognised: Alf Lascelles, an English hack, an upper-class fop of a man who'd caused me no end of grief before.

'Arnold! Arnold!' he cried. 'A word in your shell-like, if I may.'

Lascelles had a direct line into the worst of English tabloids. The last thing Lizzie Hawker needed at that moment. I was minded to turn my back on him, but that rarely worked with his type.

I stepped over. 'There's nothing for you here.'

'Not yet maybe.' He tapped his nose, a man of predictable gestures always. 'But it's coming. I can smell it.'

It was tempting to tell the fellow to bugger off. But he must have heard that a million times, to no avail.

'Arnold?' It was Lizzie.

'Your pretty young boss wants you, Clover,' Lascelles said with a charmless grin. 'Remember what I said.'

I went back to the gathering by the door.

'All this fuss.' Lizzie had a pleasant, steady voice, mildly estu-arial with a slightly exotic inflection, perhaps a trace of her Italian heritage on show. 'What on earth do they think is about to happen? Ghosts and ghoulies flying out of the brickwork?'

'I've no idea. But I thought I saw—'

'Oh,' she snapped, glaring at someone striding down the passageway. 'Not him again.'

Enzo Canale. A man I'd known only by reputation until I came on board what I had come to regard as 'the Scacchi case' the week before. Canale was rarely out of the local papers. One of the wealthiest local figures in the city, which meant he was very rich indeed. Owner of hotels and restaurants, a gallery, retail property in San Marco and one café in the piazza itself. A society man about town with that rather dated sense of style a certain kind of mature Italian male deems fashionable. Now in his early seventies, he was tall, imposing, hefty, with the face of an ageing *roué*, a quick and artificial smile, teeth too white and perfect to be real, hair a thinning combover dyed a uniform shade of black, shiny with grease. There was a navy barathea jacket slung over his left shoulder, sweat marks beneath the arms of his bright pink shirt, heavy sunglasses hiding his demeanour. A fat cigar sat between the stubby fingers of his right hand, a wisp of grey smoke curling round his thick wrist.

'Contessa,' he said with a smile and a nod. 'I trust we're ready to go in.'

'Don't call me that. You're not wanted here.'

That brought a very Italian shrug of his heavy shoulders. 'As I've told you a million times, in reality this property is mine. Your mother wished it so when she offered me that contract before she vanished. Nevertheless, I am prepared to be generous—'

After Alf Lascelles, this was quite enough. 'Signor Canale,' I said, getting myself between the two of them. 'As Miss Hawker has made clear repeatedly, the only conversations she will have on this subject must take place in the presence of lawyers. You can either shut up or I'll have to ask the Carabinieri to make you join the press in the street.'

He took off his sunglasses and looked me up and down, wheezing a little, grinning all the while. It was meant to be intimidating, I imagine, but for the life of me all I could think of was the portly New York extortionist in a white suit who got his comeuppance in *The Godfather* during the festival of San Rocco. A ridiculous comparison, of course, since Canale was no small-time crook but a society figure to be reckoned with. Still, with that image in mind, I found it quite easy to smile back.

Before he could respond, Ballarin, the city surveyor, was over. The two men were clearly close, as we understood from an earlier encounter in the city offices.

'I have every right to be here,' Canale said with a bossy wave of his hand. 'Tell them.'

From the look on his face, I don't think Ballarin enjoyed being treated like one of Canale's lackeys. 'Not now. We can talk later.'

'I'm sure you can,' said Lizzie. 'Don't forget an envelope stuffed with notes.'

I groaned. She was late thirties, a charming woman, quick, intelligent, funny when she wanted to be, rather too candid for her own good. Broke, she said, by way of explaining the fact that she always turned up in ragged, holed jeans and a tatty cheesecloth shirt; not that they failed to suit her. I imagine she got her looks from her Italian mother: dark eyes, dark hair, pale complexion. An eye-catching woman, I knew from the way men looked at the two of us together and seemed to ask themselves: father and daughter? Old man with his young lover? Really? With *him*?

Ballarin scowled, an expression that seemed to fit him well. 'Signora Hawker. I've explained the situation already. We have right of entry. By force if necessary. If you have keys with you, please provide them now, or we will break down that gate.'

Big door. All iron. I wished them luck with that.

There was a noise down the alley. I saw a figure scuttle off towards the street, pushing through the Carabinieri officers there. He glanced back, and it occurred to me that this was the man I'd spotted at the palazzo window. I hadn't imagined it. Someone had been inside the infamous Ca' Scacchi before us. He must surely have clambered over the wall somehow.

'Fine. But not him,' Lizzie said, pointing at Enzo Canale. Then she pulled an ancient ring of keys out of her battered canvas shoulder bag. 'Present from my dad.'

I was still staring after the figure vanishing down the alley when she marched forward, barged her way to the front of the small crowd of workmen with their tools and juggled with the lock.

It took her a while to find the right key. She waved at the men to do the rest. After much cursing, heaving and sweating, the door creaked to one side on ancient, rusty hinges. Then the screeches turned louder, higher, became alive, and were joined by the shrieks of the men around the portico as they leapt back in horror. Behind the iron barrier was a mound of churned earth, alive with writhing bodies.

Lizzie Hawker stepped daintily to one side of the squealing mob of rats fleeing their home behind the long-abandoned doorway into Ca' Scacchi. As the grey swarm raced towards the sewer gratings and the canal, she turned to Luigi Ballarin and smiled.

'Any damage,' she said, 'is down to you.'

Ferragosto. This was my first experience of the annual midsummer holiday since I'd moved to Venice after my wife's death the previous year. I'd looked up the term the moment I heard it. As always in Italy, ancient history came knocking on the door. It originated as the Feriae Augusti two thousand years ago, in honour of the emperor who donated the holiday to the nation and his name to the month. A break from work in the middle of the hottest part of the summer, a time for rest and parties and horse races, Siena's famous Palio dell'Assunta being a modern relic.

Mussolini, determined to paint himself as a Roman emperor reborn, had revived it as an important part of the annual holiday calendar, three days in the middle of August when factories and businesses closed and ordinary Italians enjoyed time off; subsidised trains to the beach and cultural attractions, a break from the drudgery of work. The habit stuck long after he was killed at the end of the war. Come the middle of August, all across the city, shops, bars and restaurants would shut their doors, owners and staff heading to the cool of the mountains or the seaside. The streets were left to those meant to man the fort, along with meandering swarms of sweaty tourists grumbling about the thirty-degree weather, the price of a gelato and the fact most of the places they'd marked on their must-dine lists were shut.

Luca and my Carabinieri friend Valentina Fabbri apart, pretty much everyone I knew in the city had decamped for the breeze of the sands or the cool of the Dolomites. Valentina's husband, Franco, had shuttered his swanky restaurant, Il Pagliaccio, no more than a two-minute walk from Ca' Scacchi, and headed off for a boating holiday in Sardinia with their two kids. If she minded being left in Venice, she didn't show it. As I was to learn very soon, the puzzle around Lizzie Hawker's strange legacy of a semi-derelict palazzo played no small part in that.

I'd been wondering whether I ought to catch a bus to somewhere in the Dolomites myself when Valentina called and asked me to help a fellow Brit in something of a sticky position: unable to speak Italian or comprehend the way officialdom worked, on her own in Venice, short of money, in need of a friendly ear. Lizzie offered to pay me ten euros an hour – when she had the money. I wasn't in a rush. After all, when I heard of her predicament, sheer curiosity took over. I remain at heart an inquisitive professional archivist, a seeker after documents and links throughout history. If I had to sit through tedious meetings with lawyers and Enzo Canale, that was a small price to pay for getting past that iron door into the infamous cursed palazzo.

Naturally, I'd no idea what I'd let myself in for. Which tends to be a recurring theme in my life.

Lizzie was five years old when Lucia Scacchi vanished. That, for the moment, was as much as I knew. She seemed unwilling to elaborate, even if there was much more to say, and of that I was unsure. Enzo Canale had lodged a court case claiming that Lucia had entered into negotiations to sell Ca' Scacchi to him. But they were challenged as fraudulent by Lizzie's father, Chas Hawker, who soon entered into a spiral of financial problems and addiction. And, as Lizzie admitted, the one hard piece of information I'd gleaned, there was a further, seemingly intractable problem to do with the title to the palazzo. While there was a general assumption that Lucia Scacchi had killed herself, no proof, no body had ever emerged. As far as the law was concerned, she remained a missing person. Her husband never applied to the courts to have her declared dead, so the property never passed to him. Canale's lawsuit, like pretty much everything else to do with that fetching little building between the Guggenheim and Salute, was trapped in amber, both legal and practical.

And so the palace rotted until Luigi Ballarin saw fit to intervene on behalf of the council. After all, a historic building like Ca' Scacchi couldn't be allowed to tumble into the Grand Canal. Along with all the rumours about curses, there was intense speculation about what riches the family dynasty had accrued over the years and hidden behind its marble walls. Historically, the Scacchi were much involved in banking and the machinations that led to the rise of the Medici in Florence and the Gonzaga in Mantua, as well as the complex politics that saw the Kingdom of Naples involved in a tug-of-war between the Spanish and the French. Several of its men wore the red hats of Vatican cardinals, one almost gaining the papal tiara at one point, until he was outbribed by a rival supported by the French. Some of its women, almost all famed for their beauty, had married into the finest families in Europe.

It was once one of Italy's most illustrious bloodlines. Now there was just one Scacchi left, a solitary woman with scarcely two pennies to rub together. And she couldn't understand a word of Italian or bear to use the famous family name.

Two

Beneath the Earth

'At least they kept that foul creature out of here,' Lizzie said, taking me to one side as we reached the main palazzo door. 'Now what?'

Luigi Ballarin overheard and came over.

'Now you let us do our work, please. I've turned back Canale, not that he's happy about it. In return—'

'Anybody would think I owned the place.'

He was a stocky fellow with the officious look of a civil servant in a position of some power. 'You don't, I'm afraid. Legally everything is still in the name of your mother.'

She retrieved the keys again and found the one that let us through the heavy wooden door that seemed to be the principal entrance at the side.

Ballarin waited until he realised he wasn't going to get an answer, then returned to his team in the courtyard. The exterior seemed of more interest to him at that moment.

There was no sudden rush of rodents. Just the musty smell of a building that hadn't enjoyed fresh air in three and a half decades. Up a short flight of worn stone steps and we found ourselves in the gloom of what looked like a kitchen that hadn't changed since the Second World War.

The city man had told us he'd had the power restored for his workmen. Lizzie reached for the light switch on the wall. The weak yellow bulbs of two shades in the ceiling came to life. Then she walked over to the sink and turned the tap. There was water too.

The interior buzzed with the same tiny black midges that were everywhere in the Venetian summer, hungrier and more annoying than the occasional mosquito.

'Come on, Arnold. Let me see if I can remember this place.

Not that I've seen it for . . .' She had to think. 'Thirty-four and a bit years.'

I couldn't take my eyes off the courtyard. It was about the size of a tennis court, the wall at the end crumbling – the place where the intruder must have escaped, I imagined. Not that I wanted to complicate matters by mentioning him just then.

Scacchi. Chess. The area was dotted with dead palms in cracked pots, and small flower beds at the edge. But the square at the centre was set up as a giant board, black and white marble paving stones in the familiar pattern. To the left stood the statues of a white king and queen, crooked, leaning against the side wall like stone drunks. To the right, their equivalents in black lay on the hard ground, the king broken in half, the queen with her head off. There was no sign of any other pieces. But then this place was made for human players, and the figures I saw must have been there for decoration. The slabs around the black pair looked distinctly uneven, as if something was struggling to rise out of the earth. An odd thought and I don't know where it came from. The atmosphere, perhaps. Ca' Scacchi was getting to me.

'I was never allowed out there,' Lizzie said in a voice that was quieter than usual. The bluster and bravado she'd shown outside standing up to Enzo Canale was fast retreating.

'Why?'

She looked down at Ballarin's men gathering their tools – drills and shovels and picks. 'Mum said it wasn't safe. Besides, I was five when we gave up on this place. I didn't play chess. Still don't. Let's have a peek around. Then I want to see if Bessie's still there.'

I didn't ask.

We left the kitchen and went into the *piano nõbile* proper, little changed in layout perhaps since the place was built. It was a grand room, long and broad enough to hold a ball. There was fading silk wallpaper with gilt threads on all sides, still a little shiny beneath the grime. Gold-panelled mirrors were placed at irregular intervals, their surfaces now mostly an opaque grey. From the beamed ceiling hung three dusty Murano chandeliers fitted with electric bulbs, ancient wiring snaking through the glass.

Lizzie walked to the windows. Beyond the cracked and uneven prisms, a Number 1 vaporetto edged slowly towards Salute. There were tourists crammed together in the open back. They looked exhausted in the heat. I thought of my late wife, Eleanor, the journeys we'd made under much the same circumstances. How her memory would always remain tied to that particular line since I'd taken the liberty of smuggling a small vase containing her ashes onto one of the vessels. A private, idiotic, sentimental gesture I remained quite proud of.

'Are you all right?' she asked.

'Fine. It's just . . .' What could I say?

'Just you're in Ca' Scacchi.'

She was checking the walls, looking for something. Pale rectangles in places clearly indicated where paintings had once been hung. An empty wooden cabinet with glass doors stood beneath one of them. It looked the kind that might have been used for the display of fancy ceramics.

'I was a child. A child believes that normality is whatever's around them. You've no perspective to see things any other way. Which means this . . .' She stepped across the room and picked up something from the floor. The butt of a hand-rolled cigarette. Large. She sniffed it. 'Weed. Booze. Parties with Dad's muso mates and God knows who else he managed to pick up along the way. That was how the world was. Mine anyway.'

She stopped in front of one of the gaps left by a vanished painting. 'After she disappeared, we left Venice. Dad took me back just once, ages ago. He was broke by then. And broken. We stayed in the dump of a hotel I'm using now. He never let me set foot in this place.'

'I'm sorry.'

That seemed to surprise her. 'Why? What's it to you? He kept me out of it. He was a good dad. He loved me. He'd do anything for me.' She winced. 'Even tried to make me something I wasn't. Could never be.'

'Parents do that sometimes.' Lizzie had never mentioned any of this before.

'Later,' she said, heading for the winding staircase back through the open double doors.

One floor up. The first room we met was a small study with an old-fashioned desk pushed up against the window. An Olivetti portable typewriter sat there covered in cobwebs, thick with dust, a pile of damp, distorted paper by its side. There was a yellowing sheet inserted through the carriage of the machine. One line there in English:

You have my silence now, husband. For the Lady L you know where you must look if you dare.

'What on earth does that mean?'

Lizzie shrugged. 'I don't know. Mum always had some fantasy on the go. She told me she'd once wanted to be a professor at the university. She'd been a history student till she got married. Gave it all up after the plane crash. I imagine she felt she needed someone. Maybe it was true. I've no idea. But she kept writing. Making things up. She used to come in here for hours on end. Said she was going to create some kind of historical fantasy and get it published. One more pipe dream.'

That, I thought, is your father talking, not the memory of a five-year-old. A single cryptic sentence on a page. It didn't sound much like the start of a novel to me.

'And then she was gone. Disappeared. Killed herself.'

'You're sure?'

'Dad spent the rest of his life wishing he'd done something to stop her. He said she went for the wrong drugs. The hard ones. He stayed on the soft mostly. He always seemed to think it was his fault really. He was like that. Responsible, even when it wasn't his fault. While she . . .' A glisten in the eye. 'I didn't really know her except in kind of flashbacks. Nice ones mostly, when they weren't arguing. That's what memory does for you. Sift out the good and erase the bad. If you're lucky. Dad told me plenty later. She hurt him. She hurt me. Suicide. How cowardly can you get?'

Nothing more, and then we were walking back along the corridor to the double doors at the centre of the floor. They had grand golden handles, worn, very old. A musty, airless chamber, almost in darkness, lay ahead. Lizzie marched in, strode to the shuttered windows and opened them. For the first time in three and a half decades, the lagoon sun of August, harsh and unforgiving, streamed through the windows of what I realised immediately had to be Ca' Scacchi's master suite, the owner's bedroom.

Here, the silk wallpaper appeared newer, the chandeliers more modern too, not conversions of old Murano glass to the present. Redecorated, I guessed, not that I knew much about such things. Just that it felt as if someone had revamped the place, perhaps with less money.

A king-size bed stood against the back wall, next to it an open door leading to an en suite with a shower, again modern, what looked like pigeon crap staining the floor. The bathroom window was flapping on its hinges, must have been that way for years. Birds had been nesting above the cupboards around the show-business-style vanity mirror. I shut the window and went back into the bedroom. Lizzie was standing at the foot of the bed, staring at the wall.

There were voices from out back, Ballarin's men talking loudly. Then the sound of something mechanical, a drill, or a pump. Footsteps downstairs too: Luca, I imagined, checking what might be of interest to the authorities inside the palace.

'They didn't like me coming in here. Back in London it was different. I could climb into their bed if I wanted. Never Venice.'

'People want their privacy. Parents even.'

'It wasn't that.' There was a sharpness to her voice just then. 'It was . . .'

She stepped forward and walked to the wall by the canal. Directly opposite the foot of the bed there was what looked like a cabinet, half disguised with the same wallpaper used in the room, and two tiny handles for a pair of small doors.

When she opened it, all we saw was a blank space for a painting long gone.

She slammed the doors shut. 'Sorry. I'm inflicting all my past miseries on you. It's not fair.'

I struggled for something to say, to change the mood. 'If you weren't allowed in here . . .?'

'Bessie,' she said, brightening as I followed her back to the corridor. 'Time to meet my little home.'

A door was open to what looked like a small library at the other end. A place I expected Luca would explore before long. But Lizzie was already headed up the narrow staircase two steps at a time, so I had to follow. At the top there was a sign on the corridor wall, hand-painted, covered with leaping horses, clowns and masked carnival figures dancing together to form the word *Lizzieland*.

It was clear the bedroom at the centre had been turned into a delightful little world for an adored only child. Gone was the rich gold silk wallpaper of the grand chambers below. Here there were cartoon characters running from ceiling to floor, all Italian, the work of her mother, I imagined. Pinocchio, Topo Gigio the mouse, Lupo Alberto, a blue wolf. Toys, puzzles, a few furry animals and some board games were stacked against the wall, covered in grime, the colours faded, too neatly arranged to be the work of a child. A large Mickey Mouse clock, the hands stuck at twenty-five past ten, stood over a double bed with a unicorn-pattern duvet, much faded. Lizzie sat on it, smiling, bounced on the thin divan a couple of times, then ran to the window and straddled, very gently, the piebald rocking horse there. 'This was Bessie,' she said, stroking the creature's golden locks – real hair by the looks of it. I thought there was the start of tears in her eyes, but then she clambered off, complaining that the thing was too big for her as a child and too small now she was an adult.

For a moment, she stood by the windows. I joined her and we looked down on the slow passage of traffic on the water: vaporetti, water taxis, delivery boats, gondolas, and the traghetto crossing from San Marco to Dorsoduro.

'It must have been very special.'

'It was. But we had London too. And America. Money back then. Lots of it. Servants.' A memory returned, I could see it. 'Marisol was the one I remember here. She was quite young, I think. Very sweet. Like a big sister. She looked after me, tidied up, brought me food when the grown-ups were having one of their incessant parties downstairs. Marisol. It means sunflower, so mostly I called her Flower.'

'What happened to her?'

She had to think about that. 'This place was like Piccadilly Circus. People came and went. When Mum vanished, Dad closed it down. Everything. Said I was never to set foot in here again. It really was cursed.' She ran her finger across the dust inside the window and made the shape of a child's happy face, a circle with eyes and a smile. 'Perhaps he was right. He gave Marisol the best reference he could, and she got a job with some rich family out of town. Keeping in touch with people wasn't something he did. Reminders of the past. Not for us.'

By a brightly painted child's desk tucked against the wall was a large framed photo, one she was drawn to slowly, reluctantly. I stood back and looked over her shoulder, not wishing to intrude. The colours had grown darker as they'd faded with age. The word 'Kodachrome' came into my head, and a few bars of an old song.

A portrait of the three of them, frozen in time. Something to be looked at in the years to come so that they might laugh at the memories, wonder at the changes time had wrought, be thankful for the love, the support, the warmth that came with family. Or so one always hoped.

A mother and father on the Lido beach in front of the now decrepit Hôtel des Bains, Lizzie, approaching five, just about recognisable as the woman who stood in front of me. She had the same quizzical, searching eyes, the same slight incline of the head, as if she was trying to peer inside you. Little Lizzie wore a pink bathing suit, oversized heart-shaped sunglasses pushed back over her chestnut hair to meet a bright blue baseball cap worn backwards. The grin I'd seen already, even given the awkwardness of the strange mission that had brought us together. Here she was laughing through very white milk teeth, a gelato cone, chocolate, dripping onto her chest. A happy child, lost in time.

Chas Hawker, Lizzie's father, I knew little of at that point, only that he was what we liked to call a 'self-made man' from East Ham. Which meant, as always, someone from an

impoverished working-class background who had come into
money, nothing more. He stood with that cocky, aggressive
stance I associated with a certain kind of Londoner, a big,
powerful figure, the sort you wouldn't mess with even if he
was wearing an expensive-looking blue linen suit, a scarlet shirt
beneath with a gold chain round his tanned neck. On his head
was a straw panama with a black band, cocked to one side
over wiry ginger hair. The grin he wore was a million miles
from the happy, carefree expression I saw on young Lizzie's
face. Perhaps it was the extended incisors that gave him a
vulpine look, not far off that of Alberto, the cartoon wolf on
Lizzie's wall. There was something possessive about his stance,
his appearance, as if he wished people to notice. To say to
them: this is my family, look at the beauty I own and envy it.

That was my instant response anyway. First impressions can
be deceptive, and it struck me immediately how ridiculous it
was to feel this way over a picture a good three and a half
decades old. A man who'd succumbed to a long illness a few
months before, a beautiful young mother missing, assumed
dead, soon after this must have been taken. It was idiotic to
take sides. Unless I was experiencing some strange, almost
jealous need to protect the woman that child had become, a
curious response brought on by the oddness of the atmosphere
inside Ca' Scacchi. Lizzie had loved her father so much – to
bits, she'd said more than once. Unconditionally, in spite of
his background and, not that I knew anything but the bare
details back then, the faint hint of scandal.

Her mother she'd barely spoken about, and then in only the
vaguely derogatory terms I'd heard in the room below. She
seemed an extraordinarily striking woman, like a model from
some expensive glossy fashion magazine, the very picture of
Italian beauty, leaning to one side, cigarette in her right hand,
gazing at the camera, a serious and searching expression on
her flawless face, very far from a smile. She was thin, perhaps
ill, but it was easy to see she was Lizzie's mother. They had
the same piercing eyes, the same straight, fine brown hair falling
to a slender, slightly elongated neck, looks that made a certain
kind of man turn and stare in the street. That was an innate
beauty, impossible to hide, even if her daughter either seemed

to wish to deny the fact or was unaware there was a gift she'd inherited.

Unlike Lizzie, Lucia Scacchi's attention to her appearance extended to her clothes. Her dress was long, loose on her skinny figure, flowing, ruffled at the neck, her arms bare, the front cut quite low, the hem ending beneath the knees. Tailored very precisely it seemed to me, perhaps made to measure by a designer house. The shiny fabric, silk I imagined, carried a bright floral print of peonies and roses, huge flowers, crimson and yellow and blue, shouty, demonstrative, a statement of individuality and intent, very 1980s. There was class and money here. It seemed Chas Hawker was determined to show it in this portrait of his possessions.

'That dress was one of her favourites,' Lizzie said, placing a finger on the photo. 'Gucci or something. They made it for her when she agreed to go on the catwalk somewhere.' The shrug again. 'She wasn't quite as skinny back then.'

'If she was a countess, then surely you are too.'

'No. I told Canale already. I'm not. I'm Lizzie Hawker. From a terraced house in east London. Besides, there are lots of countesses in Italy, or so Dad told me. No need for any more.'

Her eyes were glassy again. She said something I couldn't hear and walked out of the room. There was an *altana* at the back, a Venetian feature common across the city, a timber terrace with a rail around the edge built against the roof. Before I could say a word, she'd opened the doors and walked out. I followed, concerned about the state of that ancient wood. It looked flimsy, dangerous. Parts of the handrail were close to falling off. Still, the view was breathtaking: the dome of Salute, the open garden of the Guggenheim on the way to the Accademia bridge, the ochre tile roofs of Dorsoduro flowing up and down like scales on a gigantic reptile basking in the summer sun.

There were voices, too, men, three floors below in the courtyard, swarming over the marble paving stones. All working on Ballarin's instructions, surveying, I imagined.

Lizzie stood at the edge of the terrace, leaning on the handrail. I was never good with heights and stayed back a foot or two.

'Marisol and I used to come out here and have picnics while they were partying downstairs. I ought to try to find her. I ought to use her real name. Not a silly thing I invented when I was a kid.'

'Thirty-five years. It's a long time.'

'Bits seem like yesterday.' She looked tired, miserable again. 'If I remember right.'

It was more than voices. There was the sound of work, of men heaving at something, of stones shifting.

'Dammit.' She moved quickly when she wanted, and now she was headed back to the steps. 'They can't dig up this place without asking. I won't allow it.'

I peered over the edge. Sure enough, Ballarin and his men had gathered at the furthest end of the chequered paving stones that formed the giant stone chessboard. They were working next to the shattered forms of the black king and his decapitated queen.

It looked as if they'd found something.

By the time I got downstairs, Lizzie was already deep in a row with Luigi Ballarin. His men had downed tools and were leaning on their handles, amused by the growing spectacle. It was obvious what they'd found. There was an entrance to some kind of subterranean passage, ancient brickwork on both sides, steps green with algae and mould leading down to a solid black iron door, a smaller version of the one that guarded the house. Dark brown earth was scattered round in piles beneath the stone walls. Rats, I thought. This was where they came from before they formed that burrow by the gate.

'*Signora,*' Ballarin said, starting to get mad. 'This building is crooked. We have to investigate. We have to know why.'

Luca Volpetti was standing to one side with our friend from the Carabinieri, Valentina Fabbri. He looked uncomfortable. I thought he'd be busy in the palazzo searching for material of potential interest to the Archives, and said so.

'I looked,' he muttered, staring at the strange discovery in front of us. 'Nothing. All gone.' He didn't sound surprised, which baffled me. Then he uttered a long sigh and stepped forward. 'Our records in the Archives show there was once a Templar hospice on this property.'

'And?' Lizzie asked.

'And there were documents that indicated they built a crypt.'

This was quite a revelation. Everyone knew Venice stood on mud and ancient tree trunks. Excavating that for subterranean lairs couldn't have been easy. There'd been a ridiculous if entertaining Indiana Jones film I'd seen in which the hero had descended into a warren of tunnels supposedly beneath the city, then emerged in Campo San Barnaba, near one of our favourite lunch spots. Luca and I had watched it a while back, roaring with laughter as Harrison Ford appeared from what was, in truth, a hole dug beneath a flagstone, just space for him to crouch in then crawl out. It had never occurred to me the city might hold secrets below the ground.

Ballarin grabbed hold of a large workman's electric lantern, then started on a long diatribe in surveyor-speak covering the dangers subterranean workings might pose not just to Ca' Scacchi but to some of the surrounding buildings too. I couldn't stop looking at those slippery green steps and the door at their foot. The stones were crooked and clearly very old. There was a padlock on a chain, unnecessary for years, I imagined, since the way down from ground level had been covered by the chessboard flagstones.

Lizzie had taken out the huge set of keys that let us into Ca' Scacchi in the first place and was going through them one by one.

'In case you didn't know,' she said, cutting off Ballarin as he began to recite some of the tests his engineers would need to carry out to establish the soundness of the palace foundations, 'there are paintings of this place from three hundred years ago. We even had one once, not that it seems to be inside any more. Ca' Scacchi was leaning to one side back then. Just like it is now. I don't think you need worry.'

He stood his ground. 'I hope not. But I do need to make sure.'

'Fine.' Her mind was made up. 'Me first.' She snatched the lantern from his grasp and was halfway down the steps before anyone could stop her. I pushed through the workmen, elbowed my way past Ballarin and followed.

'There are keys on this ring Dad gave me . . . I don't know.'

She was still shuffling through them. I pointed to the largest: long, simple. The kind you'd use for an outbuilding.

Right first time. She opened the padlock. I removed it, then put my shoulder to the door. The old iron budged a little, and then, with a second, harder try, fell inwards with the same kind of tinny shriek we'd heard earlier from the gate.

Lizzie flashed the beam of the lantern at the shadows ahead and lurched inside.

The smell that greeted us was vile, a stink of tainted soil and something organic.

Then we saw the bones.

Lots of them.

Arranged on both sides of the walls, beneath a ceiling so low we had to stoop down to a floor an inch deep in black water.

The lantern shook in Lizzie's hand as she ran the bright beam around the secret crypt of the Templars hidden beneath the Dorsoduro earth.

'We need to get out of here,' I said, trying to take her arm. 'You have to leave it to them.'

'My place. Not theirs.' All the way down one side the torchlight ran, then along the opposite wall. 'What is this?'

I knew the moment I saw it. There were sites like this in Rome, Paris, other cities too. Cemeteries where the skeletons of the dead had been turned into a form of ghastly decoration. A boneyard of limbs and skulls and ribs lay before us, arranged into gruesome patterns of diamonds, circles, rows of indeterminate joints.

'It's called an ossuary. Please . . .'

She shook herself free of my hand. Ballarin and his crew were behind us, more flashlight beams circling through the charnel house hidden beneath the chequered flagstones of Ca' Scacchi's human chessboard.

Lizzie's light flickered ahead, away from the deathly patterns of the walls to the end of the chamber, a few metres away.

No skeletal remains there. Just the dull glint of a stone cross, rising from a low altar towards the ceiling.

And a shape at the foot of the raised platform above the water. Something that rang a bell.

Before I could say a word, she was shrieking, angry, scared. Stumbling towards it, the lantern beam racing everywhere. Then I saw.

There was a body in front of the altar on which the crucifix stood, the sad, dead pose of it not far from that of a deposed Christ. Withered arms outstretched, bony legs akimbo, partly covered by a dress with a pattern I'd seen minutes earlier on a photograph, still discernible through years of grime and dust.

Peonies and roses, once crimson, yellow and blue.

Lizzie started to scream, a painful, childlike shriek, arms flailing as she stumbled into the ever-lower ceiling, struggling to get to the too-familiar shape ahead of us.

Then came a new noise, the rumble of stones moving, earth shifting. A faint trickle of dust hit my cheek, like hard rain carrying the stench of rotten mud. The trickle soon turned into a flood.

'*Signora*,' Ballarin shouted behind us. 'Come back. This is not safe. I beg—'

All I remember is the sound of the walls, the ceiling, and the cold, dry touch of bones beginning to fall around us, my arm reaching out to find her, clutching at the flimsy cotton of her shirt.

Then dust and darkness consumed everything, and I was choking on the filthy miasma of centuries, feeling the small, dank world beneath the courtyard of Ca' Scacchi begin to tear itself apart.

Three

The Lost Lucrezia

I woke at nine the following morning with an aching head and a sore arm, plasters on my fingers where they'd been clawing at the rubble and earth to reach Lizzie, buried alongside a skeletal corpse beneath the fallen roof of a forgotten Templars' crypt. Life in Venice was so free of violent events, it took me a moment to realise I wasn't still inside a nightmare.

The dust, the dirt, the frantic work of Ballarin's team to reach us. Then a rushed journey in an ambulance boat, blue light flashing, siren screaming, and the emergency department of the Ospedale Civile. It was all too real.

By early that same evening, I was standing outside the hospital built behind the beautiful *campo* of San Giovanni e Paolo, looking at the lagoon stretching over to Murano and the cemetery island of San Michele, trousers and shirt torn, shoes ruined. Lizzie would have to stay in, two nights at least. She'd suffered a blow to the head, and they wanted to check for concussion. We'd been lucky, not that I was allowed to see her.

Valentina and Luca had accompanied us to the hospital and fussed over me as I was discharged. There were, of course, questions to be asked about that strange underground chamber, the body we'd seen there in the same faded floral-print dress I'd spotted on the wall of Ca' Scacchi minutes before the earth caved in on us. But the inevitable enquiries, Valentina insisted, could wait, not least because Ballarin and a police team were still working to clear the debris from the Templars' ossuary and reach the corpse we'd all, for a moment, glimpsed.

Back home in my little apartment near San Pantalon, I ransacked my wardrobe for the few new clothes I'd bought in a sale at OVS on the Lido, then bundled the old, muddy ones into a ball and walked round to the rubbish boat by the bridge

to Campo Santa Margherita and threw the lot into the hold.
The last of the things I'd brought from England in all probability. After that, I walked round to Mamafè for breakfast.
The moment I sat down with a macchiato and a pastry, my
phone buzzed. It was Lizzie, calling to express her outrage that
the hospital wouldn't let her out straight away.

'Also,' she added, to my bafflement, 'how the hell am I
supposed to pay for this? Don't they understand I'm broke?'

'Insurance?'

'Insurance is for other people. Ones with money. More to
the point . . . clothes.'

I was, she said, to go round to her two-star hotel, pick up
the case that was packed already, and bring it to the hospital
for the three o'clock visiting slot. Just as well it was that late.
While I was on the phone, a message came in from Valentina
summoning me to lunch at her old Carabinieri colleague Ugo's
bar, hidden away in Castello. Important, she said. Everything
was at that moment.

'This afternoon, Lizzie. Take it easy. One more night and
you'll be out of there.'

'Dead right,' she said, and that was it.

The hotel was hidden away in a side street close to the
Accademia. There was no one behind the desk when I walked
in. I had to ring a bell and wait a good minute before a
middle-aged woman in a bright blue cleaner's coat emerged
from the back. Local from her accent, and very talkative. My
heart sank when she said Lizzie had settled the bill. I already
had a suspicion about what she had in mind.

'This is down to that wicked place of theirs,' the woman
went on, waving her hands. 'The Scacchi. That horrible
palazzo. Her father used to stay with me all the time until the
poor man got sick. Something wrong with it, he said. As if I
didn't know. He'd never sleep in there, only visit.'

'For what?'

She stared at me. 'I didn't ask. It was his, wasn't it? His
wife, the Scacchi woman, disappearing like that. And now
they say they've found her in some place full of bones.' She
shuddered, a touch theatrically. 'I know it's meant to be historic

or something, but the best thing they could do is to pull the whole damn building down and put something better in its place. Something decent.'

'Such as?'

Her finger jabbed at the velvet wallpaper behind me. 'A hotel. They say Enzo Canale has been trying to buy it for years and do just that. Well, if he knocked it down, he could build something better, couldn't he? Lord knows he has the money. Get rid of all those bones and . . .' Another shudder. 'That poor woman, she must have made Signor Hawker's life a misery.'

'He told you that? About his wife?'

I got a fierce glare. 'He didn't need to. The poor man was dying in front of my eyes, short of money, going in there looking for things.' There was a brief moment of embarrassment, when she realised, I think, she was going too far. 'His memories, I imagine. What other reason could there be? And now his daughter's in the hospital. Here . . .'

The case was small, cheap and quite full.

'And this . . .' The bill, marked *Paid*. 'I gave her the rate I used to charge her father as a regular customer. Very favourable. Wish her well, and for her journey back to England. When does she leave?'

If only I knew. I dodged the question.

'Oh, and please tell her some of the toiletry things she mentioned . . . I couldn't find them. No toothbrush. How could she lose a toothbrush? She's a lovely young woman, but a little like her father. He was forgetful too.'

'I'll buy her one.'

'Well, no matter. It wasn't there. I looked everywhere. I told her to keep her door locked too, not that she listened. The room was quite a mess. Took me a while. No charge.'

I remembered the face I'd seen at the window. 'Perhaps there was an intruder.'

'Here?' Her voice rose. 'No, sir. Impossible.'

The woman had taken ages to emerge from out back. She was, it seemed, both concierge and cleaner at that moment. Perhaps the only employee the little hotel had at any one time.

There was a pharmacy along the way. I bought a couple of

toothbrushes. The case was flimsy and light, even though I presumed everything Lizzie Hawker had with her was inside.

What was she going to do when she walked out of the front doors of the Ospedale Civile, that lovely facade that was once the Scuola di San Marco?

Fly back to London? I didn't think so.

Ugo Abate was approaching seventy, long retired from the Carabinieri, where, as Capitano himself, he'd once taken a young Valentina Fabbri under his wing. As soon as he gave up the uniform, he devoted himself to the dream he'd held for years – running a *bacaro* of his own, a small bar hidden away down a cul-de-sac in the narrow terraces that were once homes for the craftsmen and boatbuilders of the neighbouring Arsenale. Few tourists found their way to Ugo's, and he begged those who did never to mention the place on social media. He was a traditionalist, dedicated to serving inexpensive local wine and *cicchetti* to a clientele of men and women he'd mostly known for years. It was more about the company than money.

A widower with a big belly covered with a stained apron, a benign face ruddy with wine, and a wayward head of silver hair, he now lived alone over his little heaven, happily parked six days a week behind the ancient red wooden counter or carrying plates of home-made snacks to the tables in the tiny courtyard. It amazed me the place was open, since Ugo was surely the kind of Venetian who would follow the habit of Ferragosto year in and year out and shut up shop. But there was a sign on the door, *Aperto*, when I arrived, and he was only too keen to shake my hand and let me in.

He wasn't smiling, which was rare. Valentina and Luca were at a table in the courtyard picking at *baccalà* and *sarde in saor*. They weren't cheery either. It struck me there might be more fallout from the strange events in Ca' Scacchi than I realised.

We were the only customers. Wine, Pinot Grigio from a small vineyard outside Treviso Ugo knew, was on the table already. I took a sip and a slice of ham and waited.

'Your friend's recovering, I gather,' Valentina said eventually. She'd checked with the hospital. It was only to be expected.

'That's good news. You were both very lucky. Charging in after her. It's not like you, Arnold. Being rash.'

'I wasn't rash. I was worried about her. We weren't to know . . .'

'All the same.'

'It's her property. Odd as the situation may be. There were strangers crawling all over it. Lizzie had every right to feel proprietorial.'

She was in her dark navy uniform, very smart as usual, the picture of an elegant but serious Venetian woman going about her business. The look on her face was very much that of an investigating officer.

'I understand. We will need to interview her at some point. If you'd like to come along . . .'

'You asked me to help. I'll be there if she wants me. What's the position with the house?'

She glanced at Luca. On cue, he took up the story. Ballarin's team had dug us out from beneath the collapsed ceiling. Luckily, most of it was dried mud rather than stone. The slabs of the gigantic chessboard had remained in place. They'd rushed the pair of us to the ambulance boat, then, worried the collapse might threaten the integrity of the palazzo itself, set about checking the safety of the property. Ballarin's initial opinion, delivered to the city council and the Carabinieri that morning, was that the palace was in better structural shape than he'd expected. As Lizzie had pointed out the day before, there were paintings of that stretch of the Grand Canal going back centuries, two Canalettos among them, which showed Ca' Scacchi leaning to one side for as long as artists had flocked to Venice. There was no sign of any imminent further movement. All the same, his investigation was a process that might continue for weeks.

'They need to involve her,' I said. 'From what I've heard of the legal situation, with her mother gone, Lizzie inherits. She's a right to be consulted.'

Again that glance between them.

'Her mother's been missing for thirty-five years,' Valentina said. 'In all that time, the father made no effort to have her declared dead. I wonder why.'

An obvious question, one I'd raised gently already.

'I mentioned that to Lizzie. She said he still loved his wife. Still hoped she might come back one day. That she hadn't really killed herself. He was ill. Riddled with financial problems.'

'All the more reason why he might try to sell Ca' Scacchi. Or find a tenant,' said Luca.

This was odd, tiresome. 'There were legal complexities. To do with Canale. He claimed he'd made a down payment as part of a contract to buy Ca' Scacchi. That's all I know. Ask Lizzie.'

Ugo came over. I didn't realise he'd been listening from the door. The courtyard was a suntrap, baking hot even under the large parasol that stood over the table. Once again I realised how easy it was to find yourself being slyly interrogated by Valentina Fabbri without knowing. These three were all locals, Venetians born and bred. I was an Englishman, a foreigner, accepted but still an outsider.

'I can't help but think there's more to this than we realise,' she said as Ugo reached for his glass, a spritz, Select as always. A little strong for me at that time of day. 'If you're to deal with the last of the Scacchi clan, Arnold, it's important you know where she comes from. What she must have been through. Ugo?'

Of course. He must have been a serving Carabinieri officer back in the eighties, when Lucia Scacchi disappeared.

'Not a pretty story,' he said, taking one of the patio's barrel seats. 'Or one of which I'm proud.'

Over a slow lunch in the airless midday heat, he took us back to that time, a Venice I never knew, one where Valentina was an infant and Luca a doubtless popular and loquacious boy at school.

Four decades earlier, there was little in the way of mass tourism, few cruise liners, no crocodile lines of day trippers meandering through the city behind a tour guide waving a flag. Venice was quieter, with a larger resident population, though one that was struggling to earn a living and beginning to disperse. But what it had back then, what marked it out for those affected, was a sharp and intense sense of hierarchy and class.

The Scacchi clan had been a part of that as far back as records went, a family that was sufficiently noble to gain an early mention in the Libro d'Oro, the Golden Book, a directory of the republic's favoured aristocrats. Only those listed in its pages could take part in the higher realms of Venetian politics – and gain the favourable financial advantages that came with privilege. Generations of Scacchi had prospered for centuries, but like a good number of patrician families, they stumbled into difficulties after the Second World War. Properties were sold, businesses liquidated.

Then along came an ambitious young man called Enzo Canale.

Ugo took another swig of his drink. 'I will not speak ill of the dead, only facts as I believe I know them. Lucia Scacchi's father was a gullible fool. The man was always desperate for money, willing to cling on to anyone he thought might offer a way out of his dire circumstances. Like an idiot, he continued to live as if he was still wealthy. That little plane. A private boat. Favours Canale offered in return for . . .' He stopped for a moment and his usually genial face fell into a bitter scowl. 'That creature was a punk. Still is. His family owned a run-down dump of a bar on the Lido. Didn't have two cents to rub together. All of a sudden, Enzo comes to own a small hotel on the Lungomare. Not long after, another. Restaurants. Properties in the city. Where does the money come from?'

A long silence so I asked: *where?*

'I never found out for sure. Just heard the rumours, as we all did. Drugs. Smuggling. Laundering money for his criminal pals. To begin with, anyway. Crooks like that are smart. They run the gauntlet of the law just long enough to prime the pumps. When they're up and running, they mostly put that behind them. Buy smart suits from one of those designer places in San Moisè and mingle with the upper class they think they've joined. I was just a lowly foot soldier. Randazzo, the bastard in charge back then – he's dead now, and I *will* speak ill of him – never let us near that kind of question. Different days.' He rubbed his fingers together: *money.* 'Different rules. Enzo

Canale has been spreading his loot around this city for fifty years. If we'd gone for him when he was young, we could have brought him down.' A frown, regretful, ashamed even. 'But we didn't. Soon he wasn't a jumped-up punk any longer. He was a hotelier. Then a property magnate. After that, a benefactor for all the charities that wanted to pick up a few crumbs spilling from his napkin.' Ugo slammed his big fist on the table. 'He's a smart cookie. Doesn't get up to anything they could take him for these days. Doesn't need to. He's rich. Still a crook at heart. If someone looked hard . . .'

Valentina touched his hand. 'We've been through this before. The statute of limitations. It was all a long time ago. Too long for us to take him to court.'

'Once a villain, always a villain,' Ugo grumbled. 'Here's the thing, though. I *know* he and old man Scacchi were up to stuff. I got a tip-off they were bringing in drugs on that little plane of his. He'd started to hang out with that music guy from London. Hawker. It was one long party in that place. Rock stars. Hangers-on. Loose women. Day and night, getting up to who knows what. If someone wound up on the street – human trash – we looked the other way.' He rubbed his fingers again. 'I tried to get a warrant for a raid. Randazzo never even put it in front of a magistrate. Enzo had money, friends, power. Untouchable. He swaggered round like he owned us all. Still had all his hair and no gut back then. Wasn't a bad-looking guy. Got his picture in the society magazines swigging wine at fancy functions. I'm guessing here, but I'm good at that. Old man Scacchi decided part of the deal was handing over his beautiful daughter. I mean, for an old-time aristo, it was OK to use your pretty kid to trade for dope or money or whatever he got in return.' He took another swig. 'All the magazines wanted *her* picture. A real beauty. Sweet, smart, educated, could have married good if she'd wanted. Or so they said. Then, right after her old man and her mother died in the plane crash up in the mountains, she tells Enzo to get lost and runs away with the Englishman. Marries him, just like that. Got a kid on the way soon. Jesus. The way they lived.'

He leaned back in his chair and looked at each of us in

turn. 'The papers went mad for a while. The runaway countess, they called her. An aristocrat who'd dumped a rich Venetian punk for a rich English punk. They set themselves up in that creepy palace, and for the English guy it was party time twice over. You name it, with a kid upstairs too. I thought of trying to get in there with a child protection order. No one dared touch it. Five years or so after all the fuss in the papers . . .' he picked up a slice of sausage and downed it one, 'I get that Englishman at the front desk crying his eyes out and saying she's vanished. He tells me she'd been using bad hard dope for weeks, which was news to me. I thought that was his thing. Now he thinks she might be dead.'

He poured more Pinot Grigio into his glass, so much the Select thinned to the colour of watered-down blood. 'Seems he was right.'

Valentina reached into the briefcase she'd brought with her and placed a thin blue folder on the table. Three pages, all signed off by the late Randazzo.

'Three pages?' I said.

'If he'd had his way, it would have been just one,' Ugo grumbled. 'Simple case of a beautiful young woman who turned to drugs. Went crazy. Lost it. Vanished and killed herself somewhere.'

Luca Volpetti was running his finger over the typed report. 'There must have been more than this.'

The old Carabiniere shook his head. 'Randazzo was adamant he knew what had happened. Chas Hawker did look genuinely despondent, I'll admit. We went through the motions. Took a look at the house, the garden. Never realised there was something underground. Whether Hawker did . . . who's to say? His story was she'd got hooked on heroin some months before, wasn't happy being a mother. Didn't like the girl.' He screwed up his eyes, remembering something. 'The kid wasn't there. The father had a plan for her. Show business. Acting. They'd got her with an agency in London, doing advertising and bit parts in films or something. I never saw her after the mother was gone. Went to the top floor where she lived. It was like a separate world. Now that had a woman's touch.

Didn't look like the home of a kid whose mother didn't want her. Still, it happens. When we found nothing, Randazzo signed her off as a missing person. The papers went wild again for a while. The doomed countess from the accursed palazzo. Another victim of Ca' Scacchi. Society beauty turned suicidal junkie. A chance to use all those photos of her looking like a million dollars. But something else soon came along. There was no note or anything—'

'Wait.' That didn't sound right. 'There was. I saw a page, it's still there in the typewriter.' I'd taken a photo of it with my phone when Lizzie wasn't looking. It seemed curious. I held it up so they could see. *You have my silence now, husband. For the Lady L you know where you must look if you dare.*

Ugo raised an eyebrow. 'Oh, yes. That. We did see it. Doesn't sound like a suicide note, does it?' Valentina waved at him with her fingers. A gesture I recognised. It meant *not now.* 'I asked Hawker, and he wept like a baby. Said she used to write all kinds of nonsense and leave it lying round the place. Especially when she was high. He'd no idea what she was talking about.'

'Did you believe him?'

He leaned over the table. 'Are you listening? I didn't have the opportunity to push it. Randazzo closed us down. Lucia Scacchi was dead somewhere. Killed herself. He was sure there was nothing in the house to suggest there'd been a fight or an argument. She hadn't taken any clothes. Any money we knew of. There was no indication she had travel plans. She hadn't been talking to the few friends she still had of late. To be honest, it had the feel of suicide. Everyone thought her old man had killed himself and taken his poor wife with him in that plane. Stuff like that does run in families sometimes. The offspring feel they've inherited it, like a bad gene or something. God knows there'd been plenty of mysterious goings-on with that blasted place. Hawker looked like a grieving husband too. From what little I saw, it never seemed like anything else. Anyway, Canale was leaning on his tame Capitano. He didn't want us sniffing through all the dope and dirt that went on there, who came and went. Randazzo closed the file as probable suicide, body yet to be found.'

Valentina reached into her briefcase again and pushed a set

of photos across the table. From a magazine shoot in the eighties. Interiors of Ca' Scacchi. It looked quite different from the empty shell of a building I'd seen. There were paintings everywhere, cabinets with ceramics and statuary. The place seemed as rich as a small museum.

'And when you went in . . . it looked like that?'

He frowned. 'Kind of.'

'Ugo . . .'

'I mean . . . I haven't been in many places like Ca' Scacchi. There never was a need. Yes, it was full of stuff. I just don't think there was quite so much . . .'

'Because Chas Hawker had been selling it on the black market,' said Luca.

'Didn't he have the right?' I wondered.

It was Valentina who answered. 'No, he did not. Even if he had ownership of the property – and he didn't. Luca can tell you. We have inventories for some of the objects the Scacchi family owned over the centuries. Paintings by Venetian artists. Classical statuary. A collection of Byzantine jewellery that was supposed to be as fine as anything in the museums. All gone. All, we assume, disposed of. Illegally.'

'One other thing,' Luca added. 'Something else that's vanished. As far as the art police can work out, it's yet to surface anywhere. We'd surely know. Here, Arnold. Read the words of your poet Lord Byron, who swanned and fornicated his way through this city for three years before heading off to die in Greece. Some lines he penned for his friend Thomas Moore, the Irish writer.'

Luca was one of the most adept researchers I'd ever met, able to retrieve obscure material from the flimsiest of traces. It was a printout from an old reference work. The letter was dated 9 January 1817, from Venice, addressed to 'Jolly Tom Moore' in England.

> My flame is still my 'Lucrezia'. By far the prettiest woman
> I have seen here, and the most lovable I have met with
> anywhere – as well as one of the most singular. I believe
> I told you the rise and progress of our liaison in my
> former letter. Lest that should not have reached you, I

will merely repeat that she is a Venetian of the bluest
blood, a family from the Golden Book, two-and-twenty
years old, married to a minor lord who does well to keep
himself with his harlots in Ferrara. She has great black
oriental eyes, and all the qualities which they promise.
Whether being in love with her has ruined me or not, I
do not know; but I have not seen many other women
who seem so pretty. And now the sting that hurts and
pleases. You recall that lock of golden hair I acquired
when I was in Milan? Here, I have met that dead lady
in person and reacquainted her with her locks. Here, she
is as lovely as her namesake and the two of us disport
before her in all our joy.

'Byron was the lover of an earlier Scacchi countess,' Luca
said. 'The one he called "Lucrezia". The lock of golden hair,
the one he refers to, is still stored in the Biblioteca Ambrosiana
in Milan. It belonged to Lucrezia Borgia and was, he said, so
extraordinary he stole some strands. By all accounts, from a
later letter he wrote to Moore, he saw a private and highly
erotic portrait of Lucrezia here in Venice, in the bedroom of
the Scacchi palazzo. Byron says he gave the hair to his lover as
a present. She attached it to the painting in a small glass case.'

I was lost for words. There were too many possibilities
revolving round my head. Uppermost the memory of Lizzie
entering the master bedroom, her parents', and looking at that
hidden panel on the wall facing the bed. A painting had once
lived there for sure, secret except to those who knew.

Valentina took over. 'From what we've learned, Hawker was
selling items illicitly from Ca' Scacchi before his wife died.
Perhaps that was the source of an argument between them.
We'll never know. The body has been recovered. We're having
to bring in specialist pathologists. A corpse from thirty-five
years ago is beyond us. But it does seem that Lucia Scacchi
took pains to hide the most precious item, this secret painting,
before her husband could lay hands on it. But where?'

This seemed incredible. 'How could you possibly know?'

'A dead woman told us. That message in the typewriter.
You have my silence now, husband. For the Lady L you know where

you must look if you dare. What if she took something with her
into that crypt, Arnold? A challenge buried beside her corpse
beneath those chequered flagstones? A riddle that might lead
to this priceless Borgia portrait?'

'You're surely guessing,' I murmured.

Ugo laughed. 'I told you earlier. Guessing is what we do
most of the time. And Valentina here's as good at it as me.'

She didn't much like that. 'It's not all guesswork. As I said,
we recovered the corpse in the crypt this morning after
Ballarin's men cleared the area. It escaped the collapse apart
from some dust and rubble. The ceiling fall was primarily on
you and Signora Hawker. Beneath the body, well . . .' She
waved at Luca to continue.

'There's something you need to read. Something we need
to decipher between us. I'll send you a copy later, after the
forensic people are done with it.'

'Then,' said Valentina, 'we'll see where this may take us.
Where it may take Signora Hawker as well. If this mysterious
painting remains here, it must be found.'

I was fighting to keep my temper. 'This is why you asked
me to help? So I could be your spy?'

That seemed to offend her. 'If criminal acts have occurred,
I need to know about them. You work with the State Archives.
The care of our national heritage is as important to you as it
is to the rest of us, surely?'

A low blow, one that hurt. 'Lizzie told me her father came
back from time to time over the years. She accompanied him
just once. He never let her set foot in the place. Not since her
mother died. I saw her there. I saw her reaction. I believe her.'

'In that case, your friend has nothing to fear. We must get
to the bottom of this. If that's possible. To be honest, I'm not
sure. Besides, if we find this mysterious canvas, it will belong
to her, won't it? Along with Ca' Scacchi. Once her mother's
death is confirmed, she'll be very wealthy indeed – on paper.
Would you care for more wine? Something else to eat?'

No, to both, I said. I had an appointment.

It was a twenty-minute walk from Ugo's to Campo San
Giovanni e Paolo, with the great basilica of the same name

and the beautiful facade of the old Scuola di San Marco, now the elegant entrance to Venice's principal hospital, stretching from the *campo* to the waterfront of Fondamente Nove. Along the way, I stopped for a coffee. I was early. I hadn't needed to leave that little gathering so quickly. But I was angry too, mad that Valentina had an ulterior motive for persuading me to get close to Lizzie Hawker. Concerned, as well, that the problem that faced Lizzie, complex already with Canale's lawyers hovering, now appeared yet thornier.

I'd no idea what they'd found next to Lucia Scacchi's corpse in the old Templar crypt. That would have to wait on Luca Volpetti. All the same, I felt I was being treated as an outsider, not to be trusted, only used. After all the work I'd put in to trying to adapt to the occasionally arcane ways of Venice – efforts I'd made sincerely and thought rewarded – that felt like a betrayal.

A single macchiato and some time to myself. I was calmer by the time I got to the hospital desk.

'You could have come earlier, sir,' the woman said. 'The lady's in a private room. They're a little more liberal with visiting hours.' She smiled. 'Better food, too. Here . . .'

A card with directions. It took me to a lift and then a smart modern section of the hospital, where, with the help of a friendly nurse, I found Lizzie seated upright in bed in sky-blue pyjamas, perky as ever in a room overlooking the lagoon, her first words, 'For pity's sake get me out of here. I hate hospitals. Had enough of that with Dad.'

'One more night,' the nurse said with a shake of her head. 'The doctors insist. We should be able to discharge you tomorrow around three or four.'

'The doctors, the doctors . . .'

I placed the case I'd packed by the window and took a seat next to a large bouquet of flowers.

'Thanks for those.'

'I didn't send them.'

'Then who . . .? Are Italian hospitals always this wonderful?'

'It's a private room. How are you?'

'I'm fine. A bang on the head. A bruised arm. You?'

Nothing much, I said. There were more important matters.

I took her through what I'd just heard at Ugo's – some of it anyway. Along with Valentina's expectation that she would soon be confirming Lucia Scacchi's death, which would surely make Lizzie the legal owner of Ca' Scacchi.

'That's not what you-know-who thinks. More work for lawyers. I don't want the damned place. They can sell it.'

'They think your father was smuggling art, valuable art, out of there for years. Illegally. Perhaps before your mother died. They seem very sure.'

She frowned, unconcerned. 'And . . .?'

'They're bound to call you in for interview. They'll want to know if you were aware of it.'

'You mean if I was his accomplice? No, I wasn't. I thought I said. Dad used to come here on his own, two or three times a year. He never wanted me with him apart from that one time when I was fifteen or so, a couple of days before we went off to Rome on holiday. That apart, I haven't been to Venice since I was a kid.'

'When he came home . . .'

She shuffled upright, folded her arms and looked right at me. I saw her mother then, I thought, the same direct gaze, the same searching eyes.

'When he came home, he'd always bring me a present. Something from here. Then he'd go out on what he said was business. I never asked. Jesus, Arnold, he was getting sued right, left and centre by bands he'd dragged out of the gutter and turned into stars. All complaining he'd ripped them off for royalties or something. All winning mostly too. We went from owning a palace here, an apartment in Miami, a mansion in Surrey, to living back where he began. His mum's old house. A grubby dump in East Ham, so close to the Tube the trains shake the walls day and night. I don't know where what little money he had came from. I do know where most of it went.'

That was a prompt. 'Where?'

'On me. On keeping us going.' She hesitated. 'Trying to find me a stupid career. Dad thought I could make it in acting. He pumped money into films that never got made, or worse, they did, all on condition I got a part. He tried to talk me into TV ads. On to the radio. I was doing it when Mum vanished, in London for a soap commercial or something. Still trying when I was thirty, indulging him in that little fantasy. I never wanted it. Dad used to be good at music contracts, so he thought he could do the same in the movies. They saw him coming. What money he still had went into the pockets of people twice as sharp as he was. And what did I get? A few lines on IMDb for bit parts in shows no one ever watched.'

'They'll still ask—'

'What he did, he did for me. I never wanted to know. When it got too ridiculous, I took him to one side and said enough was enough. I was never going to make it. I didn't have the talent. I didn't have the ambition. Besides, he was getting sick then. The doctors said it was going to be slow and there was nothing they could do to stop it. So instead of him trying to care for me, I took on the job of caring for him.'

'And he still came out here?'

No answer. She was staring furiously at something, someone at the door.

There was a smell I recognised, dark and acrid. Cigar smoke.

'Contessa,' Enzo Canale said, walking in with a wave of his arm. He threw his white panama on the foot of the bed, brushed back the shiny black comb-over and swept his arm around the room. 'You like this place? You like the flowers?' He looked and me and nodded at the door. 'Get out. We need to talk.'

She was up from the bed before I could stop her, marching across the room towards him, balling a fist.

I raced between them.

'Leave,' she yelled at Canale. 'Leave now or I call the staff.'

He stood his ground, laughing. 'Do you think they will throw Enzo Canale out of the room he's paying for? Almost a thousand a night. This is Venice.'

'I think you should go,' I told him. 'Money doesn't buy you everything.'

I got that contemptuous look I'd received outside Ca' Scacchi the day before.

'You are a man so out of your depth you can't even see you're drowning, Signor Clover. I have your number. That is all you need to know.'

I walked to the door and called for a doctor.

'You know she loved me, don't you?' Canale said, sidling round to the bed. Even Lizzie backed off then. He had an air of menace about him.

'Don't be so stupid.'

'You'll soon find out what that fool hid from you all those years.'

'He loved my mother! I could see.'

Canale's face went red with a sudden fury. 'You only saw what he wanted. He was a charlatan. A junkie. An inadequate man. A liar. A failure and a thief. If—'

She grabbed the vase and the flowers, threw them at him. Canale batted them away and stood there, smiling at the roses and lilies scattered across the floor.

A doctor was at the door, a nurse too. They seemed too scared to intervene, so I barged between Canale and Lizzie, and put my face in his.

'You will leave now. You've said enough.'

'Oh, you sorry little Englishman. I have only just begun.' His voice rose to a bellow. 'Lucia Scacchi loved me. She married that idiot on a whim and regretted it from the start. You will know the truth, Lizzie. It was buried in that garden. Why do you think he fought so many years to stop me reclaiming what was mine?'

I grabbed his panama off the bed and pushed him towards the door. He let me. It seemed to amuse him.

'We'll speak again later, when you're feeling better,' he said with a wave of the hat in his hand.

With a brisk greeting to the doctor, in the stale cloud of an old cigar, he was gone.

The nurse raced into the room with a bucket and mop. I helped her scoop up the flowers as Lizzie apologised, half-heartedly it must be said, then clambered back into the bed, pulled up her knees and wrapped her arms around them like a child expecting a deserved scolding.

She waited until we were alone, then muttered, 'Ignorant old bastard. You'd think he'd at least offer a few condolences if he loved her.'

A sound point that hadn't occurred to me.

'There are lots of kinds of love.'

'Very philosophical,' she said in a quiet voice, almost meek, but not quite. 'Thanks for bringing the case. Thanks for being here. I will get round to paying you. Once I have the money.'

'No rush. I had to buy you a new toothbrush. They couldn't find yours.' Just the sort of pointless remark you make at an odd moment like this. 'I wondered . . .'

'Wondered what?'

Whether someone had been in her room. Though that was not the time to say it.

'What do you plan to do? Tomorrow?'

A shrug. 'Go home, of course.'

'To London?'

She turned her head to one side and smiled at me, and I could only smile back.

'Lizzieland, then?'

'You're very observant, aren't you?'

'Observation has been the greater part of my professional life.' It was an instant decision. One I made without thinking. 'Do you have room in Ca' Scacchi for a lodger? I don't think that's a place for you to stay alone.'

Laughing out loud, she threw herself back on the upright pillow. 'Oh my God. I've got myself a knight in shining armour. Well . . .' I was in a cheap checked shirt from OVS and baggy jeans. 'Kind of.'

'There are things happening I don't understand. You neither.'

She folded her arms and said nothing.

'It was just an idea. A stupid one. Doesn't matter.'

She reached down beneath the bed, retrieved her bag and fished out the gigantic ring of keys I'd seen when we first entered Ca' Scacchi. A couple looked centuries old.

'Here. Take my parents' room if you want. It's the most comfortable bed we've got, or so Dad said. Bring your own sheets. The stuff there hasn't been washed since they left. I want peace and quiet, Arnold. No disturbances. I need to catch up on my beauty sleep.'

No, I said to myself. You don't need that at all.

'Could you possibly advance me the money and pick up some bedding for me too? I'll skip the kiddie patterns. No unicorns. Pay you back when I'm rich. When . . .' Her eyes glazed over. 'When I finally get to bury her.'

I needed a drink. A stiff Negroni in the student bar near home, a solitary seat by the window where I could watch the queue for cakes in Tonolo and people skipping in and out of Mamafè down the way.

Ferragosto. The university was mostly closed, so the bar was empty and I could listen to the hard rock from the music system cutting through the confused thoughts in my head. Lizzie Hawker and the fix she was in. Valentina and Luca seemingly plotting to work out whether she was an art criminal like her father.

Finally, feeling tired and idle, I picked up a kebab from the fast-food place in the neighbouring *sotoportego* and wandered home. The sun was setting, casting burnished gold on the stretch of water behind my little flat. This part of the city was rarely busy. Even at the height of the tourist season, the crowds only found their way into my quiet corner if they were lost.

Just after I finished eating, a message from Luca came in, an email saying we should meet for lunch at a place I didn't know on the Riva del Vin, the stretch of Grand Canal in San Polo leading to the Rialto. A popular location for visitors, somewhere my friend usually avoided.

There had to be a reason, but he didn't mention it. Plenty else to occupy me besides. Two attachments, the first a series of newspaper cuttings culled from the British press and a few Italian sources, some as far back as four decades. Flesh on the bones of a story I'd already come to guess. Chas Hawker was a thuggish roadie who'd moved from lugging the amps of budding rock bands to managing them. Three well-known names in particular had joined his roster, become worldwide stars and made a fortune. For their manager, anyway.

At the peak of his career, Hawker was a force to be reckoned with in the global music business, an impresario whose ambitions soon stretched beyond stadium rock concerts into musicals and film. But tastes changed and his acts either began to lose their recording contracts or, if they stayed successful, started to manage their own careers. The theatrical projects stalled, the few movies he invested in – all of them with a young Lizzie in the cast – were so poor most never reached the cinema and went straight to video.

The rot had set in not long after he married the 'runaway countess', Lucia Scacchi. A group of his former artists sued for royalties they'd never been paid and won handsomely in court. The tax authorities started to take a closer look at his offshore bank accounts. Later, widowed with a young child, Hawker tried to break new acts. But none succeeded. Then, as coverage of him dwindled to the occasional tabloid story about his fall from grace, and the failure of his daughter's theatrical career, he was diagnosed with early-onset Parkinson's disease, not long after his fortieth birthday.

One last story, from the previous year, seemed to take great pleasure in depicting him as he struggled to leave an east London supermarket with Lizzie holding his hand. The man looked frail, lost, broken, a shadow of the muscular, confident figure I'd seen in that photograph with his wife and young daughter on the Lido. A little while later, he was dead. There, for the papers, the story ended. But for a grieving Lizzie, as she'd told me in a halting fashion already, it was only beginning. She started opening all the letters he'd left unread for ages. Charges for unpaid taxes, bills, solicitors' correspondence, and finally a summons to Venice from the city council to discuss what was to happen with the last asset the Hawker family might have owned, Ca' Scacchi. A property her father had seemingly ransacked over the years for income, while ignoring Enzo Canale's claim he was owed the freehold at a price agreed thirty-five years before.

It was a depressing tale, but I could appreciate why Luca wanted me to see it. I could understand, too, why Valentina would take an interest in the fate of that strange palace on the Grand Canal and what had taken place behind the fading mosaics of the chess players on its facade. There was something strange here, something that might come to damage Lizzie as it once appeared to have hurt her mother.

The second attachment was a scan of what looked like an old-fashioned book manuscript, double-spaced and carefully typed, with the odd pen correction in an elegant, flowing hand.

We couldn't talk about this when we met earlier, Luca explained in the email. *The forensic people . . . These pages were found beneath the body. They appear to be a story she was composing that she seems to have amended before killing herself. It seems certain it was written on the typewriter in the house. The annotations match the handwriting of Lucia Scacchi, which we have on file from some papers she submitted while a student at Ca' Foscari. They were so exceptional her professor had kept copies. I don't know what to make of it all yet. If anything. Perhaps they're the ramblings of a disordered mind. Perhaps not. I look forward to your opinion. I should warn you there is something dark in this story, something dark about the Scacchi too, I fear. Goodnight, my friend.*

I printed it out, all twelve pages. Three times I read them, finishing around one in the morning just as a private boat, some partygoers on it playing a radio loudly, slipped down the narrow *rio* outside my bedroom. An annoyance usually, but just then I was glad to hear proof there were still people out there, laughing, singing, enjoying their lives in the dark.

All the same, I didn't sleep much at all.

Four

Madame Corneille

From the secret memoir of
Giacomo Girolamo Casanova

Venice 1754. A letter from my adorable nun of Murano.
The one with the beautiful bouncy tits.

> It is more than love I feel for you, it is idolatry;
> and my mouth, longing to meet yours, sends
> forth thousands of kisses which are wasted in
> the air. I pant for your divine presence and the
> taste of your amorous lips. Till then, I trust
> the gift I send will prove equally dear, for it
> seems to me that nature has created us for one
> another. You will find enclosed the key to my
> bureau in our joyful cabin on San Cristoforo.
> Open it and take a parcel on which you will
> see written 'For my darling'. Relish the night
> of bliss ahead, for it will be like none you have
> ever known. San Samuele when the bells toll
> six. Adieu.

The ladies, eh?

I like both promises and mysteries, so I bellowed for
a gondola and set out across the water for that small
island of feverish memories. At the time I was living
in a tiny hovel in Fondamente Nove, one unfit for the
vilest of dogs. The rent was minimal. Since I hadn't
paid it in three months, I refused to feel I was cheating
anyone. As I told the landlord: don't blame me, blame
the cards.

It was a fine June day, two months after I'd turned

twenty-nine. The lagoon didn't stink at all. Along the placid grey water boats large and small raced, oarsmen puffing and grunting as they practised for the coming regatta. All that effort for what? I had other exertions on my mind.

There was a minor altercation with my gondolier concerning the fare as we sought a way through these sweating fools. Then it was across the lagoon to the tiny island of San Cristoforo, where I paid sufficient for him to wait while I found the cabin close to the church that was our private den of pleasure.

Women haunt you. Nuns especially. Only the neighbouring prison island of San Michele stood between me and my holy love at that moment. As I pushed open the door to our little nest of desire, I had a brief memory of our last meeting here. The dark hair. The white skin. A wimple and a black and white habit on the rushes of the floor. Did I mention the tits?

Being so close to her nunnery in Murano I felt myself in some hellish gaol, tempted to swim straight across that brief stretch of crystal water, then dash to her convent, demand entry and throw myself upon those soft and fleshy pillows. If only . . .

The bureau was new, as was the key enclosed with her billet-doux. Tucked inside I found a letter written in a female scrawl and a box wrapped in brown paper and twine.

The single page read as follows.

> That which a lady hopes will render this present dear is the likeness of a woman who will adore you. This box contains two portraits by Longhi, which are to be enjoyed in different ways: if you remove the bottom part, you will see her as a nun; if you press on the corner, the top will open and expose her in a state of nature. You will soon be given the route to a further offering. Should you find this later rare and valuable item to your taste, as I expect,

your lady bids you follow closely the directions
you receive, since its remarkable nature is
unnerving and perhaps even perilous to those
of weaker and less imaginative dispositions.
Herewith but a promise of what is to come.

Anxious, excited, I tore off the brown paper. Inside
was a black veneer and gold casket the length of a man's
hand and three quarters the width. Naturally I followed
the instructions given in the letter. Beneath the lid, I
first saw a masked woman in the costume of a nun,
standing and in half-profile, black feathered wings
sprouting from her back. The secret spring brought her
before my eyes entirely naked save for that same mask,
lying on a mattress of scarlet satin, asleep, fingers only
half over what in another might be called the lady's
'modesty'. A somewhat feminine cherub leered over
her, a quiver, bow and arrows at his feet, a scandalous
glint in his beady eye, a strapping cock in his right
hand.

Such a promise indeed. What fresh treasures might fate
bestow on impoverished, lowly young Casanova in his
hour of need? I must find out.

As the bells of San Samuele tolled six, my mistress skipped
from the gondola, a luscious sight in her golden silk gown,
masked and full of joy, a ridiculously tall gilt wig wobbling
from side to side as she walked. Lord knows which
admiring follower of the Murano congregation paid for
all that. The only offerings I had to delight her were of
a more personal and physical nature.

We went to the opera nearby then, full of anticipation, left halfway through at her suggestion to repair to
the musical masquerade cum gambling house of the
Dandolo palazzo. There she amused herself by looking
at the ladies of the nobility, who alone had the right to
walk about without masks. A hidden swan able to stare
at exposed geese. Though something of her ardour had,
it seemed to me, cooled. I was used to being the master

of ceremonies at our dalliances. On this occasion it appeared she felt the duty was hers, which I found both odd and curiously arousing.

After wandering about for half an hour, we entered the hall where the cards were played. Before I could ask what lay ahead, my mistress abandoned me to chatter to some fool in the mask of the Medico della Peste. While I was considering the purpose of this insult, a lady whose features were hidden by a beautiful black leather *moretta* – I wore a plain *bauta* – approached and enquired whether I wanted to play. As I was about to come out with an excuse – my nun was getting far too friendly with her new companion and I was quite bereft of funds – this lady, tall, of an upright, athletic stature, came near and whispered, 'I did not mean the cards, *monsieur*. You have the gift from your Murano nun?'

Ah, I thought. The two of them together. That must be it. A tempting proposition.

'Indeed.' I noticed then that the edges of her mask were fashioned from the black feathers of a crow. 'But, lady, we have yet to be introduced.'

She laughed, a deep, odd sound, almost masculine in its tone. 'Time for that to come, Casanova. The chest of promising treasures she gave you . . . is where?'

Downstairs, I told her, with my cloak, in the custody of the servants.

'Then,' she whispered, winding her arm through mine, 'we must go.'

The *moretta* was an exquisite piece. New, shiny, tailored to her own features, I didn't doubt. I found myself staring at that beautiful feathered mask, longing to know what might lie beneath. My Murano nun had vanished. The Plague Doctor had found a new woman to accost. I felt as if I was being pushed upon a journey by unseen hands, one that offered arcane pleasures as bait. At some peril, perhaps. Still, the mystery of my new companion, the warmth, the fragrance of her . . . all this was impossible to resist.

'If we leave, where should we go?'

'The kind of destination a man like you will always seek. In search of pleasure. La Donna Nuda. The Naked Lady.'

'As cryptic an answer as I could ask for.'

'Then let us decipher it together.'

No one noticed us stride out of that room, arm in arm. The *ridotto* was in full swing. Cards and drink, scheming and the game of seeing who would leave with whom that night. It was a world of masks in which none of us was truly real.

In the light of a lamp by the palazzo water gate, she took the casket, turned it over, then removed a set of screws in the base. A piece of folded paper was secreted there, spidery writing on it I couldn't make out.

'The most cryptic riddle is the simplest once you learn to join the dots,' she said, holding it aloft. 'One by one. In the order they are perceived. Don't you agree?'

'I'm at a loss to understand you, lady.'

'No matter.' She handed me the page. 'I've no need of this, Casanova. The mystery is for you to pass on as you see fit.'

I squinted at the spidery hand and she punched me lightly in the chest. 'Not now.'

Bemused, intrigued, I tucked the sheet of paper into my jacket, then, as she asked, called for a gondola.

The night was warm, bathed in the darkness beloved of villains. Yet she seemed fearless as she ordered us down narrow, Stygian channels that even I, a native Venetian, barely knew. Finally, in a place I may not name, we pulled into a rickety wooden jetty. She ordered the gondolier to hand us a lantern and wait. He looked reluctant until she threw him a generous coin. It was a gloomy, foul-smelling spot more suited to cut-throats and thieves than two well-dressed fugitives from the *ridotto*.

There was the stink of tar, and I thought I heard the working of wood somewhere. At the end of a cul-de-sac where black water rippled under the moon, she stopped, retrieved a strange key from her cloak, one that, like her mask, was in the shape of the outstretched wings of a bird, and bade me go ahead. I hesitated for a moment. Something odd was in the air.

'This is the place that bears my name. Walk through that door and there is no going back. Your world will be changed for ever. Refuse and you will never learn the delights and mysteries of which your trepidation has deprived you.'

I was Giacomo Casanova, a man who never feared to tread where others did not dare. Without a second thought, I marched inside.

Where and what it was like I will not say. Only that the room was small and short on windows, made for warehousing, nothing else. And full of seeming riches – canvases, glassware, porcelain – stolen, hidden, I wasn't to know, and it seemed to me that if I did, such intelligence might place me in the Doge's dungeons before the night was out.

One piece alone interested her. A rectangular package wrapped in sackcloth, perched on a heavy artist's easel set against the corner of the wall by the water.

'That's for you,' she said. 'To fetch and carry.'

The thing was light, the width of my chest. A painting in a frame by the feel of it.

'And now?'

A rook or some such bird screeched somewhere. A creature I've never liked, one rarely met in the city.

She touched me below, a firm and deliberate hand searching, pinching beneath my cloak, and instantly I responded.

'You know what's next, sir, surely.'

The gondolier took us to the Albergo Cavalletto on the Orseolo Basin. The *cavalletto squarciapalle* is, of course, the Spanish donkey, a device of torture used by merciless gaolers everywhere, the ghouls in the Doge's secret chambers among them. By the time we docked, I was inclined to feel it had been inflicted upon my own person, since this masked lady's manner, mode of speech and deportment, the strange prize I had in my arms, her own feverish and anxious excitement about our new-found discovery . . . all this had brought me to a state of aroused anticipation so delicious I had quite forgotten my little lover from Murano.

Along the way, my companion leaned over and whispered in my ear. She was from Paris, a widow called Corneille. A woman of substance, she had rented an entire apartment on the third floor overlooking the water. The footman on the door barely looked at us as we entered and ascended the winding staircase. We made no small talk. There was no doubting which direction our path would take. Throwing off her wig to reveal a head of shockingly short dark hair, she reached for a bowl in which a sheep gut sheath was softening and with a coy smile handed it over. A woman prepared. I put my mouth to its opening, blew and filled it with my breath like a balloon.

'You are a man of much experience,' she said, toying with my collar. 'Or so I hear.'

'I am an artist, *madame*, and an artist must always practise and hone his craft. Though I do not doubt there are skills a woman like you may teach me.'

With that, she leaned forward, lifted her mask an inch, no more, then with eager, sharp teeth fixed upon my neck so hard I shrieked and felt blood come.

My shaking fingers untied the ribbons that bound her as she returned the favour to me. Gown and jacket, shirt and blouse, corset and trousers all fell gently to the Cavalletto floor. In the wan winter moonlight, as a gondolier sang softly outside the window, she stood there naked save for the feathered mask. Her skin was the colour of alabaster, her body full and soft, ageless, like a statue carved by a master.

'My Naked Lady,' I said, removing my *bauta* and reaching for the full black *moretta* she still wore.

'No, no!' she cried, as if in horror. 'This is my way. In truth, sir, I would rather you had worn your own.'

'You should have commanded me. I will replace it.'

'Too late,' she said sharply. 'Too late. Besides, I am not her.'

She broke away and found the package we'd hunted for that long, dark night, then snatched at the sackcloth, threw the fabric to the carpet and placed the contents on the escritoire by the window. As if to order, the moon appeared from behind clouds. Silver light flooded the room, illuminated the canvas in front of us. The note-perfect tones of the musical gondolier, so high they sounded contralto, faded along with all rational thought I owned.

'This is the Borgia portrait. Do you like her?'

I stared. I gasped. A nervous shock ran through my body so fierce, so full of delightful fright, I let out the faintest high whimper as my companion ran her sly, hard fingernails across my navel, then below.

Golden hair, eyes an icy blue, the face of a young goddess, full of both innocence and carnality. The painting seemed alive, more so than either of us in that room, the naked beauty lying on a divan flesh and blood, so close I longed to hear her speak, so vividly portrayed I felt I saw her bare bosom move slightly with her breathing and wondered if she might step straight from the canvas, stand up to her full height, then join us on the bed. To the right of the gilt frame, attached almost as if it were an afterthought, was a narrow glass case, in it a long lock of golden hair, the same colour as that of the goddess stretched out before me.

The pose I'd seen before, in Giorgione's *Sleeping Venus*, a naked beauty, drowsily awake in a country glade, right arm raised to point up to her breasts, the left daintily over her thighs. This vision lay on the snow-white sheets of a scarlet bed, lounging in a rich boudoir, the tower of a church, rooftops and a campanile in sunlight beyond the window.

I've enjoyed sufficient such enticements over the years, some crude, some clever, some, not many, arousing. This was quite different. It was as if all the heated insanity of the divine act had been distilled into an image that seized the beholder in a savage instant, summoning in the blood an urgent desire for heated consummation.

Those calm, intent eyes bored straight into me. The shape of her, the look on her face, more demand than invitation, sent my mind and body reeling with a paroxysm of such lust I felt like a beast in search of shameless satisfaction.

My companion seemed to sense this, withdrew her fingers, then stepped back. Which was more of an enticement than her touch, and she surely knew it.

'Borgia? You mean . . .?'

Her voice was calm and flat and businesslike, almost that of a high-class Parisian courtesan hired for the evening.

'I mean the infamous Lucrezia. Who else? Cesare commissioned this for his private quarters, to be hidden away for his enjoyment, and that of his lovers, alone. A sensual depiction of his adored sister to remind him of her unique beauty and allure. Not a family portrait, as you may see. But we all know the stories. Brother and sister. Father and daughter. All within the holy precincts. You've seen the *Flora* by Bartolomeo Veneto?'

Only a copy, kept by an aristocratic lady of advanced years I brought pleasure to in her palace in Castello years back in return for money. That a picture was enough to stoke the ardour of the weakest man. One of the few known portraits of the infamous Lucrezia, there the very picture of innocence, with ringlets of golden hair tumbling down to her shoulders, one young breast bared, eyes on the viewer, the lightest of smiles on her pink lips, a face full of promise and invitation behind a show of virtue.

This was the very lady, without a doubt. She wore the same expression; the same gilded locks fell around cheeks flushed from some recent exertion. But here she was naked save for a pearl necklace, a white cap embroidered with jewels and a circlet of silver, a band of enamelled gold around her waist. She lay head back on a pillow, left hand splayed across the nest between her thighs, a few dark tufts there showing, a detail that meant this canvas would never have seen daylight, but lived inside a case, displayed only to the privileged in the secrecy of the bedchamber. The Pope's daughter pictured after coupling, perhaps with her brother, inviting a second bout. In the time of the Borgias, a man might die for hearing of it, nothing more. Cesare murdered one of her husbands and butchered the servant who was her lover. He disposed of his own brother, Giovanni, Duke of Gandía, stabbed to death and dumped in the Tiber. Heaven knows what he might do to anyone who saw this frank and sensual depiction of the sister he coveted for himself.

Another erotic work came to me from a copy in my elderly lover's collection: Titian's *Venus of Urbino*. This must have crossed the painter's path. Though even that great master could not imbue his naked beauty with all the fierce anticipation of the coming act that consumed me here.

'Then this was Bartolomeo Veneto too? A second commission? A private one from Cesare?'

There was that laugh again, a throaty rumble to it that made me wonder if she was ill.

'This is the work of the Devil, sir. Commissioned by his creature Cesare. Gifted by Lucrezia to her secret lover in Venice. But fear not. The Devil offers only delights for now. Payment comes later. But perhaps there will be no shadows in the future if you return the lady whence she came. And keep with you this note that led us to her. For future use by others who seek her gaze when you are in the earth.'

'Why must I return her?'

Those dark eyes gleamed in anger behind the mask. 'Because she belongs to another. You promise?'

'One night is not enough.'

'One night is all we have.'

Not another word and the black mask was upon me, her hands clutching at my neck, those cold, stiff feathers grinding against my skin.

I write these memoirs in old age, feeble mind fighting to distinguish true memory from false. Yet still I see

Lucrezia's heavenly face, imagine her breasts moving with each breath, feel in my old bones the promise of her body. As the English poet said of drink, such memories both provoke and unprovoke; they inflame the desire but take away the capacity, firing a need that may never be met. It is my opinion that some drug or potion had been introduced into my wine. While I dallied at the *ridotto* perhaps. Or in the water I sipped briefly in the Cavalletto before we fell to. Though it's possible that is merely a hope on my part. And that in truth I did witness a canvas painted by the Devil, a lascivious horror that came to life as we slept exhausted, drained.

The woman in the mask, Madame Corneille, though I doubt that was her true name, devoured me that night – I can think of no other word. Like a thirsty vampire, she sucked at my soul with such a savage energy as I have never known, before or since. Watched all the while by the knowing Lucrezia, rousing us to our efforts, we wrestled and whimpered in a clammy bout that seemed pain as much as pleasure, hate as much as love. It was not desire that joined us. No tender thing at all, and that I say with shame, for tenderness is everything, the sweetest, kindest aspect of our nature. Her *moretta* she never removed, though I could not help but notice the dampness – tears, sweat, who knew? – that gathered around the edges of that ebony conceit while we fought and coupled like wild creatures the whole night through.

As dawn broke, spent, broken, I slept. When I woke, we were both naked on the velvet double couch by the window. I could hear the gondoliers calling their trade below. A gentle summer sun hung weakly in a sky the soft blue of a songbird's egg.

My lover lay back, her head set awkwardly against the window ledge. As I gazed at that pale, still body, my heart rose to my mouth. Her chest did not move. Her skin was as cold as the lagoon in January.

Desperate, I snatched off the mask. There could have been no servants within earshot at that hour. If there were, I doubt this memoir would have found its subject, for Giacomo Girolamo Casanova de Seingalt might have been executed as a common murderer with the brisk, blunt cruelty the Venetian Republic displays to those it deplores.

Her face beneath the *moretta* was as black as the ebony leather that had covered it the night before. I cannot say whether she had once been beautiful or not. Her eyes protruded in bleak terror, her lips were dry, cracked and bulbous. Bile and reddish vomit spilled from her open mouth to her chin. The poor woman's body seemed locked in a frozen rigour much as if turned to the same hard marble as the Lapis Niger in the Forum of Rome.

There was a vial in her dead, cold fingers. A dark, sweet-smelling liquid dripped from it onto her pale and bloodless thigh. To this day I do not know if her own hand administered the poison, or whether some villain crept into that room while we slept and murdered her.

I shrieked, I spewed. I ranted and beat my chest. Like a coward I dragged on my breeches and shirt, my jacket and hat. And then my mask and a cloak I stole from her wardrobe and threw around me as if it was the depths of winter. After which I seized Lucrezia's illicit portrait and ran.

Why, I do not know, but it seemed important – no, essential – to return that blasted, demonic canvas to the place she found it. To keep that curious note about me until I found another to whom I might pass its curse.

My nun pleaded ignorance when next I saw her. The casket, she said, came from a stranger who'd paid for the glorious robes and wig she wore that night. Of its contents she was quite unaware. Nor did she know a Madame Corneille who kept an apartment at the Cavalletto. It was her assumption she was part of some humorous prank.

Before long, rumours were spreading around the city, gossip and accusations, never said out loud in my presence but muttered among those who knew me. Whispers that my behaviour was an affront to Christian morality and common decency. That I was on secret terms with spirits and demons and cavorted with them to weave spells that would ensnare innocent women into my bed, where I would inflict all manner of carnal acts upon their person.

Villain, monster, degenerate, criminal. Was there nothing of which I wasn't accused?

Oh Lord, forgive them. It was I who was ensnared that night.

I, Casanova, who must pass on something too, lest it trigger the final malady that will take my life.

The note I keep still, forty years on, secreted in my private papers. A riddle I recognise in parts, one I would never presume to solve.

The writing is spidery, sloping to the left, a learned hand or that of a servant from Hell. Directions to eight places in Venice that, when followed in strict order, will lead to the lady Lucrezia for those who dare face the task.

> By the *condottiero*'s fearsome gaze, Il Gobbo writhes naked in his glassy tomb.
> Red marble where the Virgin holds back plague.
> Eight great dead lie in holy water.
> The hound of the Lord and the lily where water once ran.
> Black marble, saintly, over old bones and the eight-point star.
> In wood the secret fellow sits, by chained and sightless Fury.
> Traitor, not a traitor, nor painter, homeless by the Dolphin and the Anchor. Loc. Col. Bai. The. MCCCX.
> Lady L! You must be left to last. Replace those beautiful eyes that others may look around and truly find you.

I exorcise the demon! I cast it out! Let others make the circle and join the dots! Then go to the lair of

Madame Corneille, find Lucrezia and gaze upon her deadly beauty.

This old fool is headed for the tomb and fears a dark and hideous woman awaits me there.

Five

A Trail of Dots

First thing the following morning, I went to the Chinese shop near Campo Santa Margherita and bought all the items I felt would be necessary to make Ca' Scacchi halfway habitable. Sheets, pillowcases and towels, cleaning materials, bathroom stuff. Then I stopped off at the supermarket for some basics: milk and butter, coffee and tea. It felt odd to be thinking about anyone but myself.

Thanks to Luca Volpetti, I'd found a wonderful cleaner called Chiara, a bubbly woman of thirty or so, sturdy, with arms covered in tattoos and an earthy sense of humour. She'd recently been released from the women's prison on Giudecca, briefly imprisoned for what I'd no idea, and was now living with one of her former wardens in a public housing block in Santa Marta. Every week she breezed through my small home in a couple of hours, leaving it spotless, and managed the laundry. Fortunately, she had some free time that morning, and happily accepted the offer of three hours' work somewhere new.

'Cheeky boy. You never said it was the spooky place,' she said, folding her beefy arms as we met in the narrow street just along from the Guggenheim.

'I didn't want to put you off.'

'Puh.' She waved a hand at me. 'You think I believe all that nonsense? We're the monsters, Arnold. Not ghoulies in the dark. A clever bloke like you surely knows that.'

Ballarin was at work with his team, crawling over the garden. The chequered paving slabs had been lifted all around the steps. Men were taking photographs, others digging into the hard-caked soil. To my relief, they seemed to be taking little interest in the building. The electricity was still on and would remain so for the duration of their stay, along with water, but no gas. No one seemed interested in knowing who might pay.

Chiara stopped on the threshold as I fiddled with Lizzie's set of keys, trying to find the right one.

'You never ask.'

'Ask what?'

'You're about to let me into this fancy palazzo, and you've never wanted to know why I went to jail.'

'Is it any of my business?'

'It might be.'

Finally I got the right one and tried to wave her in.

'I stole stuff. I was broke. I was hungry.'

'Good reason for pinching things, it seems to me. Most of what was worth taking here's gone already, I suspect.'

'I don't steal things any more!'

'That's why I never asked.'

'It's good to be trusting. What's not good is to trust too much.'

I saluted, then waved again until finally she moved.

Ca' Scacchi was still a mystery to me apart from that brief and confusing visit with Lizzie. How that ended had rather obliterated my memories of it.

Priorities.

We went to the top floor and the sign *Lizzieland*, and I asked Chiara to do what she could to make the bedroom habitable, with fresh sheets and a scrub round the adjoining bathroom. Then to do her best with the main bedroom downstairs. She was whistling tunelessly as she set to work – as she always did – while I decided to explore. This was the first time I'd been left to myself in a pocket-sized fifteenth-century palace on the Grand Canal. The last too, probably. An opportunity not to be missed. There were answers here to questions that would soon become apparent, perhaps even clues to the curious riddles in Lucia Scacchi's extraordinary Casanova story.

The layout of Ca' Scacchi was standard for Venetian palaces of the time. The bottom floor with its water gate served as access to the Grand Canal via a small jetty that was now a battered wreck no one in their right mind would trust to set foot on. Behind the iron bars of the entrance was a storage area with bare stone walls, nothing in it but a small fibreglass boat, holed in the bows, next to it an outboard engine in rusty pieces. The place, I imagine, hadn't been used in decades, even before Chas Hawker abandoned Venice to waste away in London, cared for by his daughter.

The front of the next floor up was mostly given over to the *piano nobile*, the large front room I'd visited briefly with Lizzie, with a small chamber on each side, both bare of furniture and anything else. We'd scarcely spent a minute here then; Lizzie, for whatever reason, had seemed anxious to escape and look upstairs. Now, with time to think, I started to get an insight into how Ca' Scacchi must have looked when it was in its prime, one of the finer small palaces in Dorsoduro.

It was the largest room in the house, a reception and dining area, perhaps a modest ballroom when needed. The family name was reflected everywhere, a chessboard pattern in the marble slabs of the floor, etched with the shapes of the various pieces at either end. In the centre at the back was a massive marble fireplace, chimney bricks still stained with soot, the frame chequered once more, life-size statues of a white king and queen on the left and a black pair on the right. When I looked more closely, it seemed someone might have taken a chisel to the hem of the white queen's robe. The damage was clumsy. Perhaps Chas Hawker had wondered if there was some way he could get that piece out of Ca' Scacchi onto the market. A ludicrous notion – the thing would have required a block and tackle to manoeuvre it down to the water gate below, and could hardly be smuggled out of Venice unseen.

Most of the furniture was gone, apart from a few cheap foldable metal chairs stacked clumsily against the wallpaper peeling at the back. From the marks on the worn marble floor, there must have been a number of tables and chairs by the window, perhaps moved for occasions. At the Salute end of the chamber stood a low wooden stage that looked as if it was made for a small group of musicians; next to that, a piano stool with a ripped red velvet seat, and four wooden pads for the feet of what I assumed was a full-size grand. When I opened the stool, I found a Led Zeppelin CD, several packets of Rizla cigarette papers and an Old Holborn tobacco tin I decided to leave untouched. Evidence from the time of Lizzie's parents, I imagined, since compact discs presumably had just emerged when they lived here.

The three dusty and frankly ugly chandeliers must have been a nightmare to keep clean, and were threaded through with dodgy cables, presumably when converted from candles to electricity. The brown curling wires had been snipped, so they now hung from gaps in the plaster like dead worms. The cuts were fresh. Ballarin's men had been at work securing the place. I checked the light switches. A few wall lamps were still working. I did that with every room in the house. It would be so easy to tumble down those long, winding staircases in the dark. For the parts we'd use, I thought we'd be fine.

The kitchen looked like something from a domestic museum, with a battered dining table and chairs at the centre, all dusty and cracked, a massive sink we'd call a Belfast in England, and a large gas hob of no use at all. Still, there was a smaller electric hotplate that worked, though the kettle next to it had recently been home to a colony of mice. Not a sign of plates or cutlery anywhere. Clearly, they'd been sold; everything of any value that was removable seemed to have been. I made a note to get a new kettle and some cheap plates, bowls and cutlery from the Chinese shop. The long windows gave a good view of the courtyard and the giant chessboard, now partly in pieces. Ballarin was talking to six or seven workmen, while Valentina had placed a couple of uniformed Carabinieri alongside him with what looked like a small forensic team. The remains of Lucia Scacchi may have been removed, but from what little I knew of police investigations, the specialists might work on the scene of an unexplained death for days.

Upstairs was the master bedroom I'd seen already. A few clothes, dusty and moth-eaten, were still in the wardrobe: men's jeans, underwear, nothing female that I could see. What was, I presumed, a light fitting had been removed from the Salute end of the room. It occurred to me that perhaps Ca' Scacchi had been looted over the years by more than Chas Hawker. The place was easily entered, as I'd seen already. A bedside lamp still worked and would, I hoped, be enough to read by. As to the mattress itself, the sheets I'd bought in the Chinese shop would just about fit. I didn't plan to be there long, just enough to see Lizzie on a firmer footing than she stood on at the moment, sufficiently confident about her own position to return to London and leave the legal mess surrounding Ca' Scacchi to the lawyers. As she'd said in hospital, the building was surely hers without argument now her mother was about to be certified dead. Even if she wound up selling it to the government at a knockdown price or coming to some agreement with Canale, she wasn't going to be penniless any more.

The adjoining bathroom must once have been sumptuous. A large tub, a shower with the glass door half hanging off, toilet fittings that looked as if they must have passed through several cycles of fashion, in and out. Out now probably, though I was never an expert on ceramics. The water pressure was weak, and when I tried the taps, the pipes sounded like a mechanical beast with bad indigestion.

Along the corridor were two small guest bedrooms and another bathroom, all stripped of furniture, decorations and principal light fittings. On the Salute side lay the study with Lucia Scacchi's portable typewriter and that odd cryptic sentence. Obviously Chas Hawker had thought he wouldn't get much for an old Olivetti. Or perhaps there was something there that scared him, a hidden meaning in the message quite beyond me.

At the other end was the tiny library I'd glimpsed earlier, the shelves full of Italian and English paperbacks mostly, some literary, some popular, all a good forty years old or more. Of junk value, or so Lizzie's father must have thought. There was one shelf of hardbacks. They looked like the kind of tourist guides a host would provide for visitors new to the city, with faded coloured photographs, references to restaurants priced in lire, and a picture of Marco Polo when it was a tiny regional aerodrome where, the book said, you could walk straight from the plane to a water taxi in a minute or two. Very different to now.

One title caught my eye, since it lay on the small desk beneath the window. It was called *The Secrets of Serenissima*, a thick tome, published in London in 1948 by one Arturo Machiavelli, a pseudonym surely. Tiny type, no photographs, only the odd line drawing here and there, quite amateurish, the work of the author probably. I've always enjoyed obscure books. You never know what you might find. This one would go by the bed.

'Arnold?' Chiara's loud voice by the door made me jump. 'I'm done with those two rooms. Come and take a look.'

There was no arguing. Lizzie's bedroom was as spotless as anyone could make it, the en suite too. It was the same downstairs.

Enough. The rest I could manage myself.

Back on the ground floor, by the side door, I paid up and Chiara complained, 'But I only did two and a half hours . . .'

'You did three hours' work. You get three hours' pay.'

'Are you really moving in here?'

'Just for a little while. I've a friend. She needs . . . She shouldn't be on her own.'

'I was wrong.' Chiara scowled, wrinkling her nose as if smelling something bad, perhaps the mustiness that hung around the place most of the time. 'It feels dead. Like someone stripped the flesh and the life off everything.' She glanced at the men working in the garden. 'I read they found that poor woman buried down there. Rather you than me.'

She shook her head then set off down the alley. I went back inside and walked round, room by room again, checking the lights, the wiring, making sure I knew what was where and that everything was as safe as it might be. On Lizzie's floor at the back, I found a skylight open near a long tracery window. It was here, I felt sure, I'd seen the intruder, that face. One I would not forget. I pulled the clasp shut and sealed it as best I could from the inside. The truth was, anyone could get into the place if they tried hard enough. The windows were rotten, the locks ancient and easily broken.

After that, I popped back to the Chinese shop, bought a kettle, plates and cutlery, left them in a bag in the kitchen and went to the master bedroom – mine, for a few nights anyway. The odd book I'd found was where I'd left it by the bed. When I flipped through, I saw someone had ripped out pages here and there.

Ca' Scacchi was a palace of mysteries for sure.

Time to go and see Luca, for what I felt might be an interesting conversation.

My phone rang, too loud in that echoing room, and I jumped again. Maybe I was going to be doing that a lot in the days to come.

'Arnold?'

'Have they let you out?'

'No. Damned paperwork or something. And they're waiting for Enzo Canale to agree to the bill. He'll have to. I can't.'

'I'm sure he will.'

'I'm sure too. He booked it, didn't he? Anyway, I should be free by four o'clock.'

'Ca' Scacchi is ready for your return, Contessa.'

'Don't call me that!'

'Sorry. Lizzieland is fit for occupation. And I've bought a kettle and a few things. Also—'

'Your policewoman's been on the phone. I'm supposed to turn up for an interrogation at five. Some place called San Zaccaria.'

Odd. 'She used that word? "Interrogation"?'

'Not exactly.'

'In that case, don't be overly dramatic. It's only to be expected she'll want to talk to you.'

'Drama is what I do, love. Or tried to.'

A thought struck me. 'Did she tell you anything about what they found in the crypt?'

'It's my mum. What else is there to say?'

Nothing about the pages, then. Valentina would never be liberal with information unless she had a reason. Not that I had to play that game.

'There was something else in there. A story. A very strange one. I'll send you a copy.'

A pause, then she said, 'You're being enigmatic. It sounds out of character.'

'You don't know me.' I mailed her the Casanova pages. 'I'll come and meet you. We can see Valentina together.'

A pause. 'Valentina. First-name terms, I see.'

'She's a friend.' Even if Venetian friendships might have limits. 'Has my email come through?'

'On my phone now, sir.'

'Good. Keep it to yourself.'

Time for my meeting near the Rialto. I locked up the palazzo as I left, again struggling for the right key. It was only then that I noticed one seemed older than the rest, black, iron, uncomplicated, the kind someone might use for an ancient outbuilding little visited or used.

The head was in the shape of a bird, wings outstretched, beak open, tiny holes for eyes.

I usually looked forward to lunch with Luca. Without his kindness and his ability to open doors that would usually be firmly shut to outsiders, I would never have settled in so quickly when I moved here – fled almost – after Eleanor died.

Now, for the first time, we were ill at ease with each other.

The Riva del Vin was the bank of the Grand Canal where once wine barges unloaded their wares. Everything around here was to do with daily commerce. On the other side of the Rialto bridge were the famous markets, fish and meat and vegetables, struggling against modern commercial competition but still alive. Venetians never give up easily. Across the canal was the Riva del Carbon, where coal had once been delivered. Next to our table by the water was the Dogana da Terra, the customs house for goods from the mainland where shipments were weighed, wine barrels measured, taxes paid and, some thought, crooks and fraudsters hanged outside from a rope on an open beam. Justice in the republic was often swift and summary, at least for those whose names did not grace the Golden Book.

Luca was a fine archivist, a man as familiar with the vast records of the Archivio di Stato as it was possible to be, both in the headquarters next to the Frari and across the water in its satellite building in Giudecca. Bureaucracy and organisation were important to Venetians from the earliest days, so the material to which he had access went back to the beginning of the republic, through its battles with the Ottoman Empire, covering intelligence, military assessments, diplomatic gossip, lawsuits, murder and treason along with the everyday paperwork of bills and debts and legislation. If anyone could extract from those miles of shelves some scraps of information about a noble family, a legendary painting and an infamous crooked palazzo in Dorsoduro, it was him.

We'd both read the strange story left beneath the body in the Templars' crypt. Lizzie, I imagine, was going through it now. I didn't like the idea she'd be walking into a meeting with Valentina Fabbri ignorant of the mystery her dead mother appeared to have left us, whatever our friend in the Carabinieri felt.

It was soon apparent Luca and I had come to the same conclusion about this odd stab at fantastic fiction: the work was, to begin with, an attempt on the part of Lucia Scacchi to concoct what she'd once promised, a historical tale about Venice, tapped out on that Olivetti portable in her little study. In this instance, a Gothic story set during the decadent days of the eighteenth century when the republic was approaching its end and characters like Casanova, charlatans and crooks, played the casino tables hunting for women to seduce and the gullible to mug.

The clues to its fictional origins were there in the language, too modern to be the voice of Casanova. And in a simple chronological error, which both of us spotted immediately. The painting described in the tale bore the added detail of a small glass case attached to the side containing a hank of golden hair, supposedly Lucrezia Borgia's. Yet as Luca had already ascertained, the hair story came from Lord Byron around 1818, when he was enjoying an affair with a member of the Scacchi family and boasting he'd stolen the locks in Milan. Casanova died twenty years before Byron appeared in Venice. He could never have written such a detail. The painting Lucia had placed in the story was the one she knew, the one, I assumed, that had once sat hidden on the wall opposite the bed she shared with her husband. A treasure of Ca' Scacchi that had been a coveted secret for generations.

That much we got out of the way early on. It was hot already, the air swimming above the canal the way it did in such weather, while sweating tourists idled along the Riva del Vin, mopping their brows.

Then Luca pulled up on his iPad *Flora,* the portrait of Lucrezia mentioned in the story, the work of Bartolomeo Veneto, a Venetian as his name suggested, supposedly painted around 1510, when his subject was turning thirty. Court artists were always expected to flatter their patrons. Here, she looked a decade younger, with her golden hair, a flower in her right hand, a garland of leaves and a jewelled medallion around her forehead. It was a work of open and deliberate erotic power, and that wasn't just the bared breast, so frankly presented. It was there in her gaze, a steely and direct intent, a challenge to the prurient, as if saying: you may stare in lustful hunger, but have you the courage to go further?

A remarkable portrait undoubtedly of a remarkable woman. I was ashamed to admit that when it came to the famous family, I was largely an ignoramus. The Medici in Florence I'd found fascinating, in part for their colourful history but also for the role they played in fostering the Renaissance that came to change Europe. The infamous stories about Rodrigo Borgia and his family during the three decades they controlled and manipulated the Vatican and beyond – through power, through violence, through their sexual appetites – I'd always found a touch tawdry. The stuff of tabloid histories and scandalous TV dramas. As far as I understood it, they bequeathed little in the way of art and culture. Patronage was necessary for power, nothing else. Theirs was a showy, bloody performance at the pinnacle of Roman society for the briefest of periods. Then they were gone.

'For some reason,' I said, 'I always imagined her differently. She was Spanish, wasn't she? I thought . . . dark hair, dark skin, seductive eyes, the allure of the Mediterranean beauty. Yet here I could almost think she was English.'

Luca harrumphed and muttered something about prejudiced opinions based on nothing more than gossip and ignorance. 'Rodrigo, the father, was Spanish. And yes, Cesare was dark-haired. But Lucrezia took after her mother, a Roman woman, one of the Pope's many mistresses. Here . . .' He reached into his case and pulled out a hefty paperback. 'I rather suspected you'd have the usual misconceptions in your head. Most people do. Just as they have the wrong idea of Casanova. A romantic, my foot.'

A modern biography of Lucrezia, with the same portrait on the cover. More reading. I thanked him.

'Most of the stories about their wickedness come from their enemies, as usual. You know what they're worth, Arnold.'

'You can't mean they were innocents?'

He found that amusing. 'It was Rome. The beginning of the sixteenth century. No one got to wear the papal crown through righteous piety. For what it's worth, I believe the evidence Rodrigo slept with his own daughter is flimsy and unconvincing. On the other hand, I tend to think she and Cesare were closer than one expected of brother and sister. What we do know for sure is that she was a woman who took three husbands – one of them murdered by Cesare, perhaps out of jealousy – and a good number of lovers, a few of whom may have met the same fate. Private bedroom portraits – some tasteful, as this missing item seems to be, some quite pornographic – were not unknown. Especially among cardinals who were wont to father bastard offspring everywhere they went. It is . . . plausible. No.' He corrected himself. 'It's quite likely such a painting was commissioned by Cesare. That it may still exist here in Venice. And that the dead Lucia Scacchi is, in her own obscure way, pointing us in its direction, as she once did for her English husband, only for him to fail to read the clues.'

'Ah, yes,' I said. 'The clues. One, I presume, is the fact you've invited me here, somewhere that's almost a tourist trap, to eat overpriced pasta that's not a patch on our usual lunch in the Pugni.'

He looked briefly guilty. He enjoyed this slight awkwardness between us no more than I. 'Forgive me. There's a lot to think about. Let's see if we can, as Lucia Scacchi says, begin to join the dots.'

The place to start, it seemed, was across the canal, a large palazzo, Venetian Gothic, burnt-umber facade, one grand building among so many.

'You know this?' Luca asked.

What a question. 'It's the Grand Canal. There are palaces everywhere.'

'The name of that one is the Palazzo Bembo.' He pushed to one side his half-eaten plate of pasta with a dismissive wave of the hand. 'Ancestral home to one of the twelve original noble families of Venice. There was a Bembo doge, endless politicians and clergymen, and, most interesting of all, a fellow who was born in that very place five and a half centuries ago. Who offers, I suspect, the explanation of how an erotic portrait of the daughter of a pope found its way to Dorsoduro.'

'Pietro,' I said, gazing at the grand balcony of the palace across the water. It was so easy to become inured to the extravagance of this city. 'Of course.'

He smiled. 'At least you've heard of him.'

No one who'd read Venetian history could have missed the chap. Pietro Bembo was both an intellectual and a player in the complex politics of sixteenth-century Italy. A poet. A historian of the city, whose work was still recorded on the shelves of the Archivio di Stato. Along with Petrarch, whom he adored, one of the early architects of the Italian language. And, Luca swiftly added, a famous lover of Lucrezia Borgia.

He took out a single sheet of paper with dates and references to material he'd found, in Venice and online in the archives of Modena and Rome, which appeared to offer a timeline for the journey of the mysterious picture from Cesare Borgia's private apartment in the Vatican to a bedroom in Ca' Scacchi.

It began with the death of a pope, Alexander VI, the infamous Rodrigo Borgia. In the sweltering August of 1503, Rome riddled with disease and plagues of mosquitoes, Alexander had noted the sudden passing of his corpulent nephew Cardinal Juan Borgia, and muttered as the funeral cortège passed through the Vatican, 'This month is deadly for fat men.' A chubby fellow himself, days later he fell sick with a fever and vomiting. Within the week he was gone, his corpse quickly rotting and bloating in the heat, shocking those who witnessed it. Some thought he was being reclaimed by the Devil, to whom he'd sold his soul in return for the papal throne. The loss of their father as pope and protector left both Cesare and Lucrezia in peril as the many enemies of the Borgias began to circle.

Cesare, sick with malaria and the continuing effects of syphilis, would soon fall under the thumb of a new pope, Julius II, the former Giuliano della Rovere, his father's deadliest enemy and a hater of the Borgia clan. While her brother fought to maintain his position in Rome, Lucrezia, just twenty-three yet married to her third husband, the Duke of Ferrara, Alfonso d'Este, was pursuing a passionate affair with the Venetian Pietro Bembo, one recorded in a series of florid and suggestive letters between the two as they sought to avoid detection. Mostly these were transmitted in secret by the poet Ercole Strozzi, who would be savagely murdered shortly afterwards – on the orders of Alfonso, many believed.

On hearing of his father's death, Cesare had scoured the papal apartments and seized 300,000 ducats' worth of silver, gold and coin. This, with 'tender personal belongings', he dispatched by covert messengers to his sister. Most of the baggage fell into the hands of the Florentines on its way to Ferrara through Tuscany. But not all.

Luca's research through an online database held by the Ambrosiana library in Milan had uncovered a diary entry of Bembo's from a visit to Lucrezia not long after her father's death. In it he'd referred to her as 'f.f.', seemingly a code they'd agreed in order to disguise her identity in case the correspondence fell into the hands of her husband. Bembo recorded how 'f.f.' was quite inconsolable, petrified for her future, unwilling to allow him close, unsure whether she even dare continue to see him on the sly.

> Further to my dear heart's distress, her brother has sent a private talisman of theirs so shocking in its depiction of her I both dare not look at it and dare not refuse. It is either the work of an angel or a demon, I know not. But I will keep it private to myself in my quarters in the palazzo in Venice since she must not have the scandalous canvas about her in Ferrara lest Alfonso see. A necklace of fine pearls, golden hair down to her shoulders, a jewelled cap, a band of gold at her slender young waist. Naught else.

'The painting,' I said. 'Cesare's. The one from the story.'

'It seems to fit the description. She was certainly playing a perilous game.'

Danger, I was to learn, was something the Borgias invited, almost craved, all their adventurous lives.

Luca nodded at the palace across the canal. 'Pietro must have secreted it away there for years. He was no stranger to women, you know. I imagine it had the desired effect. And then . . .' A dismissive wave of his hand. 'He rose to become a cardinal of the Catholic Church. Here, in his native city. There's a portrait of him by Titian. It's in America now.'

He passed over the iPad and there was a severe elderly man in the full regalia of a Catholic cardinal. Red cape and red hat, stern gaze, grey beard, a churchman through and through, or so it seemed. It was hard to believe that forty years earlier, he'd been engaged in a steamy affair with none other than the Pope's captivating daughter. As if he read my mind, Luca then pulled up a quote from a letter Bembo had written to her as the doomed romance was petering out and she was falling into the arms of a very different fellow, her brother-in-law, Francesco Gonzaga, Marquess of Mantua, a womanising warrior to whom she seemed more physically drawn, tiring of the intellectual comfort Bembo offered.

Her rejected lover told Lucrezia he was either 'communing with all those dark things and horrors and tears of yours, or else writing pages about you that will still be read a century after we are gone'.

'There he was right, up to a point anyway,' Luca added.

Lucrezia would die in agony after a difficult pregnancy at the age of thirty-nine, mother to at least seven children, though the rumours were she'd borne more, several stillborn, out of secret affairs, one with the servant Cesare had brutally murdered.

'And after Pietro Bembo,' Luca went on, showing me the family line, 'came that Bembo doge. Politicians. Churchmen. All, I believe, party to the secret they kept in that palace. There are references in some of the diaries we have on file in the Archives, cryptic ones I've never understood. References to the "private beauty f.f.", often couched in lewd terms. Then, finally, in 1732 . . . this.'

I should, I imagine, have expected it. A marriage certificate between one Giovanna Bembo, of the palace across the way, and Count Ludovico Scacchi. With a mention of a dowry that had caused much excitement among those privileged enough to witness it. Among the items included 'a private portrait to be confined to the bedchamber'.

'You see? Our lady f.f. crossed the Grand Canal to Ca' Scacchi. Where Lord Byron would meet her eighty years later. And where she would remain until . . . whenever.'

'It still doesn't explain why Lucia Scacchi wrote that strange story and took it with her into the hidden Templar crypt beneath her garden.'

'She's dead. Who's to know? But I agree. All we have are theories. Many holes in them. Mostly I set out to establish if we were chasing a real masterpiece here, or just a piece of fiction. Another fable hanging around that odd palazzo of theirs.'

He went back to the pages of Lucia's story and pointed out the first of the puzzles. '"By the *condottiero*'s fearsome gaze, Il Gobbo writhes naked in his glassy tomb." What does it mean? Do you have any idea?'

I had to admit I'd pored over each of those eight riddles. Without much luck.

'Not really. You?'

'As I said. I've been chasing a strange painting.' He gave me a look I couldn't quite read. 'As has Valentina. The steps to follow the trail . . . I don't know.'

'Perhaps Lucia never meant Chas Hawker or anyone else to get to it.' This was my first thought. My preferred one, if I'm honest. Something told me the search for Lucrezia Borgia's private portrait was not one that would uncover much in the way of contentment, for the contessa's daughter most of all. 'Perhaps it no longer exists.'

That look again, and he said in a low, dark voice quite unlike him, 'You'd better hope for the sake of your girlfriend that isn't so.'

I felt the dimmest spark of anger at that. Something else new between us. 'She's not my girlfriend. Don't be so ridiculous. I'm old enough to be her father.'

'Exactly,' he said, then got up, threw some money on the

table for the bill and said he had to be off. Another appointment. 'I can't be there when you two meet Valentina later. I'm sorry. There's a lot happening back at the office. I hope it goes well.'

'Why shouldn't it?'

He hesitated on the pavement as I finished my coffee. 'I'm not sure you understand, Arnold. This concerns our heritage. Its theft. Its disappearance for good. Half this country's treasures are elsewhere or lost for ever. It's been happening for far too long.'

That was a bit rich coming from a Venetian. The city was full of treasures the old republic had looted over the centuries, from the great horses of San Marco to the stone lions at the gates of the Arsenale. But I kept that to myself. There was something going on here I didn't understand. It seemed to me my friend was in much the same position. All the same, we spoke briefly about how the task ahead might be approached and then, on awkward terms, we parted.

A couple of hours later, I was back in Valentina Fabbri's office, remembering how I'd felt the first time I was summoned to her presence, during the Godolphin affair the previous February. There, over endless cups of coffee and meandering conversations, she'd unpicked the complexities of the strange death of a famous British historian piece by awkward piece. One thing I'd learned she hated: dangling threads. Pieces of a story that didn't fit or failed to link to the rest of the narrative in front of her. Godolphin presented a few; the strange events at Ca' Scacchi more than I could begin to number.

Lizzie was straight from the hospital, feeling fine she said very briskly when Valentina enquired, impatient to move into the old palazzo regardless of Ballarin's workmen. She'd begun the interview by interrogating Valentina. What had they found? When would she be able to arrange a funeral for her mother and pass on the paperwork necessary for what she hoped would be a swift and simple probate? She was the last surviving member of the Scacchi line, and of her father's too. The property, its debts and problems, would, she believed, soon be hers to deal with and dispose of. Once she was confident that could happen, she'd leave for London and wrap up the continuing issues with her late father's affairs there.

It was clear Valentina thought there was more to the matter than this. She listened and told us what I'd gathered already. The body in the crypt had been removed by a forensic team and was now undergoing medical examination. It might be days before they could come to any conclusions.

'How many conclusions do you need?' Lizzie asked. 'I told you what my dad said. She was suicidal.'

'As soon as I know something, rest assured you will hear of it. It's not the only matter of interest for me. Will you please look at these?'

They were the photographs I'd seen already. The interior of Ca' Scacchi from decades before, when the place was occupied. Paintings on the walls, cabinets of pottery, gold plates, silverware. All the riches that had now vanished.

'What, exactly, are you asking me?'

'None of this remains. Everything of value that can be removed has been. Including a valuable painting your mother referred to in a story we found with the body.' Valentina retrieved some pages from her desk. The same scan Luca had sent me. 'I would be grateful if you would take the time to study it and tell me what you think.'

'Read it already,' Lizzie said, pushing the pages back. 'Arnold sent me a copy this morning.'

I got a fierce stare for that.

'The pages were found on Signora Hawker's property,' I pointed out. 'They belong to her. She had every right to read them.'

'This is a police investigation, Signor Clover. I would be grateful if you didn't interfere.'

'You asked me to help.'

'I did not ask you to intervene. This story—'

'This *fantasy*, you mean.' Valentina wasn't the only one fighting to keep her temper. 'I told you. My mother was a junkie. She made things up.'

'You were five when she vanished. How would you know?'

'My . . . my father told me.'

There was a brief expression of triumph on Valentina's face.

'Precisely. Your father. Who, it seems, stripped Ca' Scacchi bare and sold what he could on the black market.'

Lizzie was not about to deny that. 'He was her husband. It belonged to him.'

'Your mother is not yet declared dead. It was not his property in law. Therefore, he had no right to remove those items and place them on the market. In addition, we have export rules. You cannot simply take valuable parts of our national heritage and sell them as contraband. That is a criminal offence.'

'He's dead.'

'You're not. Are you telling me you didn't know?'

'Know what?'

'That your father was smuggling historic material out of Italy.'

She leaned back in her chair. 'Dad came here a couple of times a year until he couldn't travel any more. He only took me once, when I was a teenager, and never let me through the door. He said that place, the palazzo, was bad news. I wasn't to go near. One day he'd sell it. Once the lawyers let him.'

Valentina flicked through some pages on her desk. 'He could have applied to have his wife declared dead.'

'Maybe he hoped she wasn't. I don't know. I didn't ask. He was sick. We had lawyers coming at us from all sides. Chasing royalties. Trying to bankrupt him. We were living in the grotty dump he'd inherited from his mother. I never asked where what little money we had came from. And if I had . . .'

She stopped. I got in first. 'If you had?'

'Dad wouldn't have told me. He was very old-fashioned. I was there to offer comfort and support, to cook and care for him. Especially towards the end. And work in bars and restaurants to earn a little money myself too. That was how we lived. I'm afraid your picture of him as some international art thief doesn't really stack up.'

'All the same, you can't prove you never knew.'

'This is outrageous.' It was my turn to get cross. 'How can one prove a negative like that? What's the point of this interrogation? Lizzie's been frank and cooperative with you throughout. She's just out of hospital and—'

'Is this Enzo Canale's doing?' Lizzie interrupted. 'Is he pulling your strings as well?'

Of all the things she could have said . . .

Valentina leaned forward and glared at her. 'No one pulls my strings. Your father was a criminal. I've spoken with the Metropolitan Police in London. They were investigating him for smuggling at the behest of our own art theft division. They'd detected illicit sales of items in Russia and the Middle East, works that belonged in Venice. From the dates we have, I believe he was doing this before your mother died. I believe she knew. I believe . . .' she waved the pages of the story, 'she hid the most precious item the Scacchi owned before she died and left this . . . conundrum as a taunt to him to find it.'

Lizzie shook her head. 'I never saw that painting . . . What was in their bedroom. I don't know what it was. What it looked like.'

It was as if Valentina Fabbri had been waiting for that prompt. She got up and walked to the corner of the office. There was something there, wrapped in dark cloth, about two feet wide, one deep.

She came and unwrapped it in front of us.

'It looked a little like this.'

To my inexperienced eyes, it was a poor piece of work. An elongated nude on white sheets in a scarlet room. The face was indistinct, the brushwork haphazard. Bright yellow paint for hair. A white cap. Jewels. A belt around a waist so narrow it seemed ridiculous. Her face was almost blank, little more than a crude smear in which eyes melded into brows, lips into teeth. A hank of blonde hair seemed suspended in bright blue air in the right-hand corner.

'And what,' Lizzie asked, 'is this?'

Valentina pointed to the scrawl of a signature in the right-hand corner. Just legible. It seemed to say, *Annibale Scacchi, MCMX.*

'A tribute, it seems. By a relative of yours. Great-great-uncle, perhaps. You tell me.'

As usual, she'd known where to look. That morning she'd called round acquaintances in the city's galleries, asking if any had heard of a legendary painting that was once in Ca' Scacchi. An official at the Correr Museum had managed to find mention of some precious, scandalous canvas in a notebook kept by an official in the 1920s. That was all. But at the modern art museum, Ca' Pesaro, there was a nude listed under Scacchi. The one Valentina had placed before us, clearly some kind of modern tribute to the vanished original.

It was the work, she said, of a rebel member of the Scacchi family. Annibale was twenty-one when he painted it – in 1910, according to the Roman numerals. He'd been a student at the old Istituto di Belle Arti when it was based at the Accademia. There, he'd fallen in with a scandalous set, among them a fellow pupil, Amedeo Modigliani. This rang a bell for me – near the Chinese café close to San Basilio I used on the way to the supermarket, there was a plaque saying Modigliani once lived there.

Annibale Scacchi, it seemed, was an admirer, and followed the finer artist to France, where he sought to emulate both Modigliani's extraordinary life of drugs, drink and countless brothels. This, Valentina said, was one of his few extant canvases, seemingly his amateurish attempt to match the style of Modigliani's erotic nudes that had so scandalised Parisian society.

'He died two years before Modigliani, in the 1918 flu pandemic. The family were scandalised by the company he kept. They didn't want this in the palace, so they donated it to Ca' Pesaro, where it went immediately into a storeroom. They have Rodin, Miró and Kandinsky, to name but a few. No room on their walls for third-raters. But . . .' she moved the canvas closer so we could get a better look, 'it must be based on the missing Veneto work. Just as your mother described, even down to the hank of golden hair. There's no way she could have seen Annibale's version. It's sat in the storeroom of Ca' Pesaro for a century, never put on display. This original she described existed. I'm sure of it. When you were a child, it was there on the wall of their bedroom. Where we can see the hidden panel now.'

'You've been all over my house, then?'

'Of course.' She waved her varnished fingernails at the

painting. 'This is poor stuff. But the original. You have these eight bizarre clues.'

'I know nothing of this. Nothing of where this painting might be.'

A smile, a shrug. 'You have Arnold, who is more of a detective than he lets on. Between the two of you, I feel sure you can begin to unravel the puzzle your mother appears to have left you.'

'Isn't that your job?' Lizzie asked.

Valentina laughed, in a way that was rarely a good sign. 'My job is detecting crime and apprehending the people who commit it. Not finding missing art treasures. However, should those treasures vanish from the country without permission, then I will pay attention. In instances where it may have happened in the past as well. I may reactivate the interest the police in London took in your father's transactions. They have the authority to examine bank accounts, to investigate travel plans. To do whatever they like. International fraud. There's too much of it. We've been lax in the past. No more.'

Lizzie stayed silent, so I asked on her behalf, 'Is that a threat?'

'Does it sound like one?'

'Yes.'

Valentina wrapped the cloth around the Annibale Scacchi painting, then glanced at her watch. A sign the interview was over.

'Find the Lucrezia Borgia portrait, the two of you, and Signora Hawker will be acclaimed as a wondrous benefactress of art. The only problem she'll face will be what to do with the work, since it can never leave Italy.'

'And if I don't?' asked Lizzie.

Valentina slammed her notebook shut. 'Let's hope it doesn't come to that. You must excuse me. I have to return this to Ca' Pesaro. I find it rather disconcerting, if I'm honest.'

There seemed little point in trying to explain that Valentina Fabbri was a good and fair officer of the law. Someone who, as I knew from the conclusion of the Godolphin affair, was willing to turn a blind eye when she thought it warranted.

Lizzie was simply outraged that, on top of everything else, she now found herself under suspicion of being party to her late father's art smuggling. Though not, I have to say, surprised to find he was involved in it. The complexities of the Hawkers' home life in London seemed manifold: no money, just the two of them struggling to live, constant legal battles over Ca' Scacchi and his failed music business, unpaid royalties, the never-ending threat of bankruptcy and lawsuits. The last decade of her life, after she finally persuaded him to give up any hope he had of a theatrical career for her, seemed to be spent caring for him during his decline, managing his fall from the heights of wealth and influence.

That photograph Luca had come across still troubled me: Chas Hawker, once a fit and burly player in the international world of show business, reduced to a broken, sick man as he struggled down a grimy London street, leaning on his daughter for support. He had, it seemed from other cuttings I'd read, a reputation with the London media, being a source of scandal and rumour at his peak, and of ridicule in his decline. If there was one thing sections of the British press fell upon more avidly than success, it was, it seemed, failure. Hawker had given them acres of copy on both fronts over the decades.

Now, just a few months after his death, his daughter was walking through Dorsoduro with a stranger, grumbling every step of the way. Starving, too, since she'd missed lunch in the hospital due to the paperwork. Food and a glass or two of wine often change moods in this city, so I managed to divert her from going straight to Ca' Scacchi – in part because Ballarin's men and the Carabinieri team would still be working – and into a small restaurant, Ai Cugnai, between the Accademia and the Guggenheim, one of the few still open during the holiday.

A shady table in the street beckoned where we could amuse ourselves watching tourists sweating as they slogged along the way. As usual, a couple of local gondoliers were having a noisy meal inside. They seemed to love the place, and on occasion I'd find a group of ten or so cackling over the tables. Just two could make enough noise to fill the room, and Lizzie was mightily impressed when one came out and greeted me by name.

'Who is he?' she asked when we were alone again.

'Someone who works the traghetto from time to time. The ferry between Salute and San Marco. A friend of Valentina's.'

'Does she know everyone here, then?'

'It seems that way on occasion.'

The waiter, someone else I recognised, rushed out with a gigantic wild bass in his arms. 'Arnold! Arnold! You and your beautiful friend deserve this, surely? We cook it however you wish. Local price. I promise.'

The woman at the next table was making delighted noises as she tucked into an oily plate of squid ink spaghetti, big chunks of rings and tentacles coated in the sauce.

'I want that,' Lizzie said. 'It matches my mood.'

'Me too. And a half carafe of white.'

He shrugged, then frowned. Nice try, I thought.

The weather was close, still scorching though it was early evening. I was coming to recognise the city's many meteorological moods. This was one that hovered on the edge of a storm, rapid, short and violent, often with downpours so intense there was nothing to do but hide in a café until the tempest subsided and that delicious smell of fresh rain perfumed every cobblestone and corner.

'I'm sure with Luca's help we can crack your mother's riddle. Find that painting. If it's still here. Valentina may be a friend of mine, but she's still an officer of the law. She has to do her job.'

'Fair enough.'

The wine came, the bread, some free *cicchetti*. The gondoliers were telling ribald jokes to one another inside.

'Lizzie—'

'I haven't told you everything. I didn't think it was necessary.'

I caught sight of someone down the street. A thin man, scruffy, staring into the window of one of the art galleries, not that he looked as if he had the kind of money to buy anything there. For a second, he turned and glanced our way. Then saw I was watching and quickly walked off.

'If it's not necessary, you don't need to tell me at all.'

The food came out. I ran a fork through the black sauce and tried a chunk of squid. It was strong, salty, perfect.

'That painting. I did see it. Once.'

The man was gone. Maybe it was my overzealous imagination.

'What was it like?'

'I was four or five. You don't understand things then. All I remember is . . . a naked woman. She was very beautiful. Her eyes kind of held you the moment you saw her. It wasn't a big painting. It wasn't . . . flashy or anything. There was just something magnetic about it.'

'And normally they kept it covered up?'

She put down her fork for a moment, and I thought again there was the slightest sheen of tears in her eyes.

'You don't need to talk about it. It doesn't matter.'

'But it does. And I don't know how. Look. I was a kid. In the bedroom above them. I heard noises. You know what I mean. We don't understand what's going on at that age. Is it someone in pain? Or laughing? Or crying? Or all that and more?'

I shrugged. 'It happens.'

'Not like this. One time I couldn't help myself. I was too curious. It was the afternoon. Sunday, I think. Normally I only heard it in the evening, but . . .' She threw back half a glass of wine. 'I waited until I thought they'd gone. Then I sneaked downstairs. Their door was open. So was the cabinet for the painting. I just walked in and looked at that. Then I heard them. They were still there.'

'Oh dear . . .'

'Oh dear's not enough. It wasn't Mum and Dad. She was there with someone else. I don't know who. He stayed hidden underneath the sheets. She got out, nothing on, all tears. Shame. I don't know what. She looked upset and I don't think it was just me. She said I had to keep it a secret. They played games. Dad as well. Sometimes with each other. Sometimes with someone else.'

'Your father too?'

'Haven't I painted you the picture yet? When we lived there, it was a kind of bacchanalia. He had his rock star friends in all the time. Doing dope. Doing whatever they wanted.

Sometimes when I heard those noises it wasn't even Mum and Dad or one of them with someone else. It was a guy from one of his bands and a groupie, I don't know. It was as if it was some kind of ritual. Sex in front of that painting. As if they wanted the woman – Lucrezia, I guess – to watch them. To cheer them on.' She reached across the table and touched my hand. 'That's it, isn't it? That's what it's there for. I mean . . . centuries of them. Byron and all my ancestors. Screwing away in front of that thing. As if that's all that mattered in the world.'

'Perhaps that's what they needed. To get out of it. To be somewhere nothing counted but the two of them.'

My words trailed off. She doubtless thought it was embarrassment. Not me looking down the street.

'How long were you married? You don't mind me asking?'

'I don't mind.'

'How long then?'

I thought for a moment. 'I think it began around the time of the Black Death. I remember there was a lot of wailing.'

She rolled her eyes. 'Very funny.'

'I've never liked wailing. Thirty-four years, since you ask.'

'I was lucky if any of them lasted thirty-four days.'

'You're still young . . .'

Wrong thing to say. I knew that instantly from the scowl it got in response.

'If we're to find this painting . . . Do you have any ideas? I know my mum could be a bit odd. But all that stuff, her weird story. The riddles. Who on earth is "Il Gobbo", for starters?'

I told her. *Gobbo* is the Italian for hunchback. In *The Merchant of Venice*, Shylock's treacherous comic servant, Launcelot Gobbo, is a jester, though Shakespeare never makes him out to be suffering from any infirmity.

'Are we looking for a clown or a hunchback? Or both?'

'Ultimately, we're looking for the painting, wherever your mother hid it. We'll talk about it with Luca in the morning. He'll have ideas. One way or another, you'll find a way out of this.' I had to ask. 'You're sure you want to stay in Ca' Scacchi?'

'Very. You're sure you want to be there with me?'

'Why not?'

'Just the usual.' She waved a hunk of squid around. We were almost done. 'The headless spectre who wanders round sometimes. Harmless, but a bit of a shock. Stay away from the gateway to Hell. It's next to the guest toilet, same floor as you. But it only opens if someone flushes.'

I raised my glass. 'Thanks for the tip.'

She could laugh in so many different ways. Sometimes it was ironic. On occasion self-deprecating. Just then it was genuine, plain, simple amusement from the company. I felt the same way.

We finished with a couple of coffees, and I insisted she try the tiramisu.

Home was two minutes along the way. We got to the corner of the alley that led to the side of Ca' Scacchi. Ballarin's men and the Carabinieri were surely gone by now. The most we'd meet would be the barriers and equipment.

Then, as we turned into the shadows, I saw him. Coming straight from the canal side, from the palazzo, there was nowhere else he could have been. The same man. The face I'd seen in the window. And in the street outside. The intruder I'd come to suspect had entered Lizzie's room in the hotel too, taking things that seemed to make little sense.

I passed my phone to her, stepped forward, held out my arms to block the way.

'Speed-dial number three. It's Valentina Fabbri. Tell her I've caught—'

A punch. A kick. I wasn't sure. Before I knew it, I was on the ground and Lizzie was screaming blue murder right above me.

I'd never been in a real fight before. Nothing more than the odd tussle – as victim, not perpetrator – all those years before at school in Yorkshire.

Lizzie, it seemed, had more experience in the field. While I rolled on the grubby cobbles struggling to get upright, she was on the fellow like a banshee. Shrieking foul abuse, flailing at him with her fists. One moment I was pressed hard against the wall wondering how on earth we could restrain him until the Carabinieri might appear – which was bound to take ages. Then he was gone, fleeing back to the main street, Lizzie's imprecations in his ears.

She helped me back to Ca' Scacchi. I was shocked more than hurt. A couple of blows, a hard fall to the ground. One of the things you learn when you get older is gravity gets more painful with the years. Where once I'd have picked myself up in an instant after an accidental trip, now I ached and creaked and groaned. As little as possible. I didn't want to worry her.

The house and the grounds were empty. There were barriers around the end of the giant chessboard where they'd found the steps, and a timber hut to block the entrance.

Inside, I sat at the kitchen table while she looked me all over, asked how I felt, more than once. A routine, I imagined. The same she must have used with Chas Hawker when his strength began to fail.

'I was punched in the guts and kicked in the shins. I'll live.'

'Good.' She poured some wine I'd bought from my favourite local wine shop, Danilo in San Barnaba, the Pinot Grigio from their vineyard. 'I need you to.'

The memory of her going for the man was quite distinct. When he'd turned on me, she'd flown at him, so quickly and with such vehemence he'd fled.

'Where did you learn to do all that?'

'London. Where else?' she said, looking at the grazes on her knuckles. 'Had worse. Much. You seem to have led a sheltered life. The rule is immediate response, maximum force. Lots of noise. Usually works.'

'I'll try to remember.'

She smiled. 'Don't bother. You're not a scrapper. Stands out a mile.'

'Do we have any idea who he is?'

'I don't. You?'

'He was here yesterday. In the house, I think. He's been following you.' I didn't know whether to say it or not. 'I have a feeling he may have got into your hotel room as well. The missing things. It's just a guess.'

She closed her eyes and groaned. 'God. You know, I could

have stayed home serving warm beer to drunks and bad pizza to anyone who'd buy it. Why the hell did I let Ballarin talk me into coming here?'

'It was him?'

'It was him. He said the future of this place needed sorting one way or another. I am, as you said, Contessa Scacchi.' She glanced out of the window at the courtyard. 'The last of my line, it seems.'

An hour later, I was glad to be between the sheets, even the thin new ones in the master bedroom where countless lovers must have entertained one another in front of the infamous secret portrait of a pope's scandalous daughter. I had the biography Luca had given me. The strange old guidebook with the ripped-out pages, too. I managed a little of the first, but I was too tired, too confused, my head full of conflicting thoughts. It wasn't a night to read. It wasn't a night to sleep, either. I kept thinking of what must have been hidden behind that panel on the wall opposite for centuries, since a relative of Pietro Bembo passed the canvas to the Scacchi family. The chances of our finding it – even if the thing still existed – seemed slim to say the least. My best bet might be to persuade Valentina of Lizzie's innocence, in the event of our failure. Assuming she was unaware of her father's dealings. She certainly seemed to understand he'd been up to something.

The noise on the Grand Canal was constant: vaporetti and smaller boats, voices, the occasional snatch of music. It was hard to picture myself as I was now, in a grand bed beneath cheap Chinese sheets, trying to sleep behind those faint mosaics of chess players so tall they passed from the *piano nobile* below to the top floor, Lizzieland itself.

I was just about to nod off when the door opened, the light came on and Lizzie tiptoed across the room in her bright blue pyjamas.

She threw herself on the bed next to me, something in her hands. 'You all achy?'

'I'm old, not ancient.'

'Don't be touchy. I wasn't calling you decrepit. You're clearly not. Here. A prezzie.' She threw a tiny plastic camera on the sheets, square, with a large lens and a miniature screen on the back. 'I didn't tell you. I thought I heard him drop something when we were scrapping. Decided I'd go back and take a look.'

I let slip a mild curse. 'He might have come looking for it himself.'

'But he didn't. Maybe he hasn't noticed yet. I didn't want to bother you.'

It was something called an action camera, a kind of selfie device on steroids. It could shoot stills and video and was so small you could pin it to your jacket.

'What's it for?'

'I was going to show you in the morning. Decided it couldn't wait.'

A click on the back and then she placed the screen between us. The first pictures were videos of the inside of Ca' Scacchi, dated a week before. The next ones the same, the day I'd seen him.

'He was looking for something and couldn't find it,' Lizzie said, not that it was needed. 'Then . . .'

A narrow corridor, cheap red carpet. The hotel. I recognised the colour. The door was open, a bucket along the way seeming to indicate a cleaner was nearby. He went in quickly, rummaged around, then went into the tiny bathroom and seemed to be looking through things there.

'He stole your toothbrush. I had to buy you a new one.'

The obvious question was: why? Neither of us wanted to ask it.

'OK,' she said. 'I'm going to skip what he's got from earlier today and show you the last bit.'

It was the two of us seen from afar, outside at the Cugnai table. Looking happy, relaxed, just one more couple out for the night.

'We need to give this to Valentina. If someone's following you, there has to be a reason.'

'The reason?' She tapped the back button. It took me a moment to recognise the place. Then it came. Campo della Bragora in Castello, just behind the waterfront, a small square, one I'd sought out early on with Eleanor. Vivaldi had been baptised there and you could still see the font the priest had used and a copy of his birth certificate.

There was a café opposite, only one customer, a big man wearing a panama hat, seated at a table smoking a cigar.

The camera lurched up and down as its bearer approached, his breathing heavy and laboured, the picture seared at times by the strength of the August sun.

'*Signore*,' said a low, rough voice.

A large tanned hand tipped back the hat and Enzo Canale glared up at us.

'That damned camera's not on, is it?'

'No, sir. Of course not.'

A finger popped in front of the lens and the screen went black.

'Ah . . .' I said.

'One for your friend from the Carabinieri, don't you think?'

'Definitely.'

She wriggled closer. 'Now . . . I would like something in return.'

I waited, a little disconcerted by her nearness and the edge in her voice.

'Eight clues, eight dots. I know the story says we have to follow them in strict order . . .'

It was clear what was coming. Luca and I had discussed this point at the end of our awkward lunch.

'It does indeed.'

'But why? We only need to track down this painting, not jump through all her crazy hoops. Let's go straight to the last one. Find the blasted thing. Then I'm done here.'

I kept a notebook and pen by the bed, standard practice for when I woke up in the night with thoughts that always seemed so important, only to reveal themselves the following morning as gibberish. I asked her to pass them over, then drew eight dots in a circle.

'I talked to Luca about this . . .'

'Really?'

'If the story says the dots must be approached one by one, there has to be a reason. What it is we won't know until we uncover them. But it seemed to us that what your mother was offering was a puzzle in which the answers are places in the city. A riddle where the solution is somehow Venice itself. Mark each one with a dot. Join them and you get a circle.'

She leaned on one elbow. 'I had got that far myself, thank you. But why can't we just cut the corners and go for the last one?'

'Probably because the painting isn't there. It's a marker to point to Madame Corneille's lair, wherever, whatever that may be.' I connected the dots and made the circle. 'If the shape she describes is small, then perhaps it's like a target and what we're looking for lies in the middle.'

'You're guessing.'

I laughed. 'What else can I do?'

'And if it's a big circle?'

That, Luca and I had agreed, was more likely. 'Then the probability is that we're being asked to look in the gap that emerges between the last dot and the first. Here . . .' I pointed to the final segment.

'Then let's start by looking for those two.'

If only . . .

'Do you think your mother would have gone to all this trouble if it was that easy? Also . . .' This had been nagging me for a while. 'That last clue is odd. Different to the others. It almost sounds as if it's not about a place at all. It's a person. Maybe we need to connect all the dots beforehand to get an idea who that might be.'

She grabbed the page, looked at it, then threw it back at me. 'You're probably right, I suppose.'

'We can't risk shortcuts. Whatever state Lucia was in when she wrote that story, she wasn't confused. She seemed extremely organised, and I suspect very knowledgeable.'

'I told you. She was clever. Knew history. Knew languages. English. French. German. Knew lots of things. Just not how to be a mother.'

There was nothing I could say.

'And all this you've discussed already with your friend? With Valentina too?'

'No. Just Luca.'

She prodded me in the chest. 'Let me make one thing very

clear, Arnold Clover. I may be in some distress, but I am not a pitiful damsel waiting to be rescued.'

'I believe I got that message loud and clear this evening, thank you very much.'

Lizzie lightened a little at that, prodded me once again, more gently this time.

'Good. In future, keep me in the loop.'

Six

A Glassy Tomb

In the morning, I woke to find an uncharacteristically curt message from Luca saying we were to join him at a café in the Rialto the following day. Urgent work in the Archives meant that he couldn't meet us before then. But he had made a start and hoped to unravel that first riddle in Lucia Scacchi's story by the time we met. From the location he'd chosen for our meeting, I suspected I knew what he meant. I'd travelled down that path already and believed it led nowhere. I was right as well.

Since the day was now free, Lizzie decided she wanted to do her best to tidy up the parts of the palazzo we were occupying. I left her to it. Perhaps she didn't want to face Valentina when I went to hand over the incriminating camera. The right decision in all probability. My Carabinieri friend took one look at the pictures and video and demanded an explanation of how we'd come to acquire it. I gave her a concise version of the scuffle and told her I thought it clear evidence Enzo Canale had arranged for someone to stalk Lizzie as she went around the city, and to investigate inside Ca' Scacchi, presumably in search of the missing painting.

She folded her arms, then stared at me with the kind of expression she might have reserved for her chef husband had he served one of his customers rancid fish. There were, it seemed, more important matters in the San Zaccaria Carabinieri office at the moment than an unknown lout who'd broken into an abandoned building and seemed to be obsessed with a visiting Englishwoman. Not that she was minded to explain what they might be. Canale would be interviewed *a tempo debito*. Which would usually be translated as 'in due course', though a more accurate rendition in this case might be 'if ever Capitano Fabbri felt like it'.

When I returned and told Lizzie, she saw it as yet more evidence of Canale's sway over Venetian institutions, from city hall to law enforcement. I didn't accept this for one moment. Those days, it seemed to me, were for the most part past. Foreigners all too often assign malign and criminal influences to everyday events and mishaps in Italy. The English in particular still seem to live under the illusion that graft and corrupt practices have never travelled beyond the Mediterranean to the streets of the City of London and elsewhere. I always groan when I hear a tired 'well, that's what *they* are like' remark. It seemed to me to be uttered by people who never read their own newspapers.

The work outside had subsided to people taking photographs and vanishing into the crypt for an hour or two. Within, we were left in peace to clean, to sort and sift through what remained inside the extraordinary palazzo that now, it appeared, belonged to a woman from a terraced house in the East End of London.

By the end of the day, the place was quite habitable. We even found an electric immersion heater in the main bathroom that provided a trickle of hot water, just about enough for a shower. That evening we set up a table on the *altana* behind Lizzie's quarters on the top floor. I walked out and bought a couple of takeaway pizzas and salad from San Trovaso, not so far from my real home. Then, as a glorious sunset fell over the rooftops of Dorsoduro, listening to the distant hoots of traffic on both Grand and Giudecca canals and the squawks of raucous gulls, we sat down to dine. More Danilo wine as we chatted idly about all manner of things except a painting of Lucrezia Borgia and a man called Enzo Canale. Valentina Fabbri had, I knew, a point. The camera we'd found was hardly proof of criminal activity. It was more use to us than her.

'That was a day wasted then,' Lizzie said, picking at the last pieces of semi-burnt crust on the plate.

She'd spent a long time in the shower, then emerged in a fresh red shirt and a pair of cut-off denim shorts, dark hair wet and clinging to her neck. More at ease despite the strange events around her; almost younger too. It was just over a week since Valentina had asked me to give a helping hand to a stranger from England, lost in the city, faced with bureaucracy and a language she couldn't understand. There was, I now knew, an ulterior motive to that request. But I had no complaints. Lizzie was excellent company, unpredictable, different. Mostly I'd spent my time around interesting if rather dry academics these last few months, delving into documents in the Archives, showing visitors around various collections. On occasion translating for Valentina in the Carabinieri office when she needed help. Lizzie Hawker was a breath of fresh air, much needed.

'Doesn't feel that way to me.'

'Really? Cleaning and being a dogsbody? How *does* it feel?'

'As if a little normality has emerged from somewhere. I like normality. The predictable. The boring sometimes. Just as I sometimes prefer ignorance over knowledge.'

She wrinkled her nose and stared at me as if I were mad. 'What on earth are you going on about?'

'Acquiring knowledge. Not thinking you have it already. You watch. You learn. Not easy when you're encountering skeletons in ancient crypts. The Carabinieri. City surveyors. Lawyers.'

'Lawyers!' She'd picked up her emails on the phone that morning. They'd been pestering her from London, wondering when probate for the property might go through. In other words, when they might be paid for the hefty bills her father had run up. 'Bloodsuckers every one.'

'A day without Enzo Canale too,' I added. 'That can't be wasted. And . . .' I raised my glass, 'we had dinner up here. What else might we have done?'

I'm not sure she was listening. She seemed lost in her own memories at that moment. There must have been so many, and they were those of a child. Always confused and confusing. Often, I guessed, pictures, voices, people she wasn't sure were real at all.

Finally she turned to me, very serious, and asked, 'Be honest. Does Ca' Scacchi feel wrong to you? Bad? I hate to say it, but . . . cursed? Evil somehow?'

'Not at all.' I meant it too. Even with the grim discovery out back. 'It's beautiful old stone and mortar. Just . . .

neglected. That's all. Houses need people to breathe life into them. Palaces too. Without that they're like a book without a reader. Pointless. Invisible. Lost. Did it feel that way when you lived here?'

'Maybe. Maybe not. Like I told you, I was a child. A child accepts what it finds as normality. All the people coming and going. The parties. The . . .' Her eyes fell to the floor. 'The noises I heard from below. The things I glimpsed. It seemed . . . not happy. That's the wrong word. Active. Busy. Engaged in something I was too young to understand.' She tapped the table with her fork. 'It should be like that again. Not with me. Whoever I sell it to. They can make it theirs. Breathe life into it like you say. If . . .' she sighed, 'I'm allowed. If your Carabinieri friend doesn't throw me in jail as a thief.'

Fine. My aim of avoiding the hunt for Lucrezia Borgia's portrait was never going to work. I went inside and returned with that odd old guidebook I'd found.

'Here,' I said, passing it over. 'This was in your little library. Seen it before?'

She flicked through the yellowed pages. 'No. I didn't read much when I was young. Dad didn't bother. Mum did. She always had her head in a book or was at that typewriter tapping away at something. It's a guidebook to Venice. She didn't need it. She knew this place inside out. So Dad said.' A recollection seemed to come back. 'They used to argue about that. He wasn't interested in the least. She nagged him into getting out more. Not just sticking to all the tourist places. Or taking his shotguns out shooting ducks somewhere with his mates. There was something special here on our doorstep. It wasn't Disneyland. I remember her saying that more than once. I don't think he listened. Rather be out there blowing ducks out of the sky.'

I told her about the pages that had been ripped out. 'There are eight sections here that have been removed. Eight deletions. Eight clues. What I think happened is your mother left those pointers in her story. Then realised anyone who picked up this book might find them straight away and tore them out. It wasn't meant to be that easy.'

'Can't we find another copy and see what's missing?'

I'd thought of that. Even the most obscure second-hand booksellers had no copies of the work. If we went back to London and the British Library, they ought to have one on record. But there was nothing online we could read.

'There,' she said when I told her. 'You are good at this.'

'Not good enough.'

'We'll see. Funny.' Something seemed to amuse her. 'Mum egging him on with that message in the typewriter. Then making sure it was going to be so hard for him to follow everything through.'

'Do you think he tried? When he came back?'

Lizzie smiled right at me. I hadn't been close to a woman since Eleanor died, not like this. 'As I told your Carabinieri friend, I never knew what he did here. I didn't ask. All I saw was that he was a bit happier when he came home. And we had a little money. I'd never have got answers anyway. He wasn't that kind of man. He never shared much with anyone. Never delegated. He always thought he could do the job better himself. It was enough to see him happy once in a while.'

'And he never once talked about trying to sell this place?'

'He didn't own it.'

'If your mother was declared dead—'

She shrieked and balled her fists. 'How many times? Then he'd be putting up with all the crap that's hitting me now. The council. Lawyers. Enzo Canale. He was sick, Arnold. He was dying.'

It was a reasonable point. The palazzo did seem to be wreathed in a web of legal issues and trouble with the authorities. All the same, that body buried in the garden might supply a convincing reason why Lizzie's father would allow no one near the place. Lizzie understood that too, I felt sure. One more doubt to trouble her, not helped by Valentina Fabbri's cagey and inquisitive approach to their past.

She picked up the last page of Lucia Scacchi's story with the list of riddles. '"By the *condottiero*'s fearsome gaze, Il Gobbo writhes naked in his glassy tomb." If she's ripped out the pages in that guidebook, I guess there's nothing in there about a hunchback?'

That was one more mystery bothering me.

There was.

It was clear the following morning that Luca Volpetti – who hadn't needed an old book to guide him – had pounced upon the same discovery. That was why we were drinking coffee in plastic cups and eating *cornetti* in the small *campo* in front of the Gothic portico of what was thought to be Venice's first church. San Giacomo di Rialto was a modest-sized place of worship close to the San Polo end of the Rialto bridge, mostly eleventh century, though legend suggested its predecessor was consecrated six centuries before. The Rialto and the Piazza San Marco are Venice's tourist magnets, places I never linger. Streams of visitors were trudging through that August morning, dithering over the T-shirts and souvenirs on the stalls that lined the bridge approach. After that, they'd usually take their phones and cameras around the corner to snap the ever-busy Rialto market – fruit and vegetable stalls outside, fish merchants working undercover from Tuesday to the weekend – rarely buying a thing. Of an evening the area was transformed by nightlife, bars and restaurants, people wandering the squares, drinks in hand.

Venice will always be a city of details for me, a treasure trove of objects, signs, marks of the past, often cryptic. Luca and I knew already what we were looking for that morning. Il Gobbo di Rialto, the local hunchback, a marble statue of a crouching man struggling to support a small set of steps and a platform above his bowed head. It stood on the far side, opposite the church, in the shadow of the colonnades.

When we showed her, Lizzie stared at the thing with an expression close to horror. There was something decidedly cruel in the depiction of the figure's sorry pose. Perhaps familiarity meant we simply didn't notice.

'What does that mean?' she asked, pointing to a Latin inscription on the front.

'"This is the rock where the republic's laws were declared",' Luca explained. 'Though since that was added in the nineteenth century, when it was restored . . .'

There was a darker side to this sorry figure, not that I was going to let it cast a shadow on what might already prove to be a difficult day. While the statue of Il Gobbo was a place for public declarations, during the days of the republic it also served as the finishing post for a bloody and heartless punishment imposed upon minor criminals. They had to race naked from the Piazza San Marco all the way to the bridge and across, running the gauntlet of the mob in the streets, only safe when they kissed the crouching man's head. Venice abounded in such stories, some true, a good few perhaps apocryphal. I'd no idea whether this one was genuine or not. It didn't matter.

'We're in the wrong place,' I told the pair of them. '"By the *condottiero*'s fearsome gaze, Il Gobbo writhes naked in his glassy tomb." He's not writhing. Where's the glassy tomb? The fearsome gaze?'

'Where,' Lizzie added, 'is Lucrezia Borgia? I hate puzzles. Always have.'

'Well,' said Luca brightly, 'I *love* them.' He clapped his hands and crumbs fell everywhere. 'Let's get on with it.'

She harrumphed and finished off her *cornetto*. I wasn't sure she knew what to make of Luca. While I was in my usual worn shirt and jeans, he'd dressed for the occasion, smart navy slacks, blue and white shirt, navy neckerchief, sunglasses up over his forehead. Paul & Shark must have made a fortune from that one outfit alone. His face had the tan of summer; his smile was quick and always convincing.

'Let me get this straight, gentlemen,' said Lizzie. 'We have eight clues. We need to crack them all to find the painting. And you're both convinced we need to solve them in the order my mad, dead mother dictated. Do I read that right?'

Perhaps. Or perhaps the whole escapade was a wild goose chase leading nowhere.

'For the life of me,' I said, 'I can't see how we can approach this in any other way.'

Luca agreed, then added, 'I'm sorry. This is the only hunchback in Venice I know.'

'Being picky,' Lizzie noted, 'he's more of a hunched back than an actual hunchback.'

'Il Gobbo is what he's called,' Luca replied, a little tartly.

'And since the clue begins with "Il Gobbo", that is what I put my mind to.'

I was never much of a crossword addict. But it did strike me that one trick used by those who set them was economy. Every part of a clue mattered. It was a mistake to focus on the most obvious element alone.

'Let's put him to one side for now,' I suggested. 'The rest of the sentence. The *condottiero*—'

'What in God's name is one of them?'

I let Luca explain.

'They were the captains of companies of mercenaries, soldiers for hire back when we were a succession of warring city states.'

'How very Italian.'

'Not really.' My turn to intervene. 'They fought elsewhere in Europe as well. Nor were they all Italian. One of the most famous was a brute from Essex called Sir John Hawkwood, who's now buried beneath a rather splendid funerary monument in the Duomo in Florence.'

'We're a long way from Florence, aren't we?'

Luca was staring at me.

I knew straight away what he was thinking. While we'd been fixating on the hunchback, we'd missed the most obvious sign in Lucia Scacchi's curious riddle: the *condottiero* with the fearsome gaze.

There was, perhaps, one chap she might mean.

He was ten minutes away by foot. We went a slightly crooked route, by Campo Santa Maria Nuova, at my suggestion. I wanted Lizzie to see the charming church of Santa Maria dei Miracoli there, an ornate confection of coloured marble by the side of its own narrow *rio*.

'Looks like a very fancy Battenberg cake,' she said as we stood and admired the pink and white exterior.

'Familiar?' I asked.

'What do you mean?'

'The architect,' Luca pointed out before me, 'was one Pietro Lombardo. Who, if the records are to be believed, also designed Ca' Scacchi.'

She walked round the ornate exterior. We followed in silence. The similarities in the coloured marble and the circular windows were obvious. Parts of the palazzo on the Grand Canal might have come from the same initial sketch.

'Interesting,' Lizzie said. 'Where's our fearsome captain?'

'Onwards!' I declared, and Luca snapped down his sunglasses like the visor on a warrior's helmet.

The moment we crossed the bridge into Campo San Giovanni e Paolo, with its vast basilica and, to the left, the elaborate entrance to the civil hospital, Lizzie started muttering about how she didn't intend going back to see the doctors in there again.

Then she saw the statue, a strutting horse, an armoured knight on the saddle, baton in hand, staring defiantly across the piazza.

'Bartolomeo Colleoni,' I said. 'Is that fearsome enough for you?'

She shuddered. 'What an ugly, horrible-looking man. Who was he?'

No arguing there. A cruel, downturned mouth set in a snarl, Roman nose, bulging eyes beneath a heavy helmet. An extraordinary monument to an extraordinary warrior, the work of Verrocchio, a teacher of Leonardo da Vinci.

'A mercenary who fought both for and against Venice over the years,' Luca explained. 'And perhaps was poisoned by us when we were worried he might change sides again.'

'You poison people then raise a statue to them?'

Luca shrugged. 'He paid for it. This is all well and good, Arnold, but where do we find our hunchback now? And what about a glassy tomb?'

Good questions.

We went into the basilica and left Lizzie wandering round admiring the grand tombs of doges and warriors. No sign of a hunchback. Not much in the way of glass tombs either, unless we were to count the mummified foot, supposedly of St Catherine of Siena, in a small case in the nave. Luca and I stood in front of it, lost at that moment.

'I'm sorry,' he said. 'I'm not being much help, am I?'

'You don't need to trouble yourself. Unless Valentina demands it.'

An unnecessarily provocative thing to say. I regretted it immediately and apologised.

'I don't believe your friend has been up to no good,' he said in half a whisper. 'I do believe she may have to prove it.'

'But how?'

'That I don't know. Any more than I understand these strange riddles.'

I was barely listening. Instead, I was trying to think like Lucia Scacchi when she put together her strange story of Casanova, Madame Corneille and a painting with a fearful power. Did she see her husband as the famed Venetian rake reborn? A man intent on using women for his own pleasure, nothing else? Was she the mysterious woman behind the mask? Fated to die, poisoned by whatever fate had delivered?

More prosaically, it seemed to me, how had she come to concoct these clues? From what we knew, she'd grown up with her parents in Venice, studying history at Ca' Foscari until she eloped to marry Hawker. That old guidebook with its ripped-out pages was something for visitors, not locals. University would have provided her with academic sources. Yet many locals took their history just as much from rumour and legend, passed on by word of mouth. The way to disentangle Lucia Scacchi's puzzle was to unpick it element by element after the fashion she had surely assembled it.

I wandered over to the booth at the entrance to the church where we'd bought our tickets. The woman there was as friendly as when we'd entered, if a little bored. I bought a couple of postcards, which caught her attention, then said, 'This is going to sound a very strange question. But I'm on a kind of treasure hunt with my friends. We're looking for something curious, perhaps something physical. A hunchback enclosed in a glass case. We thought perhaps Giovanni e Paolo . . .'

She nodded towards the door. 'If it was me, I'd try San Marco.'

'That's not the way to San Marco.'

A chuckle. 'Foreigners. You're as bad as that old fool on his horse out there. We've more than one San Marco. The place next door. If you want dead things in glass cases . . .'

Luca had sidled up to eavesdrop.

'I don't think it would be in a hospital,' I said.

'I didn't mean the hospital.'

'Oh,' Luca said. 'Then where?'

She stared right at us and smiled. 'Are you squeamish?'

'A bit,' I admitted.

'That's a shame,' she said, then rubbed her hands together and grimaced.

'This is fun,' Lizzie said with a grin as we blinked against the scorching sun outside. 'Getting a tour of Venice with a couple of blokes I thought knew the place like the back of their hands. Turns out they're as lost as me.'

'No one can know every last cobblestone,' Luca objected. 'Not even those of us born here.'

'I heard what that woman said. Why's the chap on a horse an old fool then?'

That I did know. 'Bartolomeo Colleoni thought he was so important he ought to be commemorated outside San Marco, meaning the piazza. The city agreed. But they chose a different San Marco. That one.' I pointed to what was once the entrance to one of the city's many *scuole*, religious brotherhoods, now the way into the hospital. 'Why did she ask if we were squeamish, Luca?'

He didn't answer, just walked on. I'd never taken much notice of the grand staircase in the hospital lobby. There'd always been a more practical reason to come here. But Luca was striding up it without a word, so we followed, and by the time we got to the top, he was talking our way in at the ticket desk. The old Scuola Grande di San Marco, it seemed, still existed, one floor above the hospital.

'My friends and I,' he was saying as we arrived breathless from the many steps, 'are embarked upon an investigation.' He flashed his ID card from the Archivio di Stato. 'An official one. I have the authority, should you care to check. Now, if you would be kind enough to—'

'We're looking for a hunchback writhing in a glass box or something,' Lizzie interrupted. 'Anything like that here?'

The fellow at the desk nodded sagely, then said, 'Here? No.'

'Bugger,' Lizzie muttered.

He reached for the phone and called for someone to take over. 'The Rialto dwarf is downstairs. Closed today, but . . .' He looked Luca up and down. 'For a gentleman from the Archivio di Stato, Anna may, if she sees fit, oblige.'

I was wandering around already and beginning to understand the comment about being squeamish. What had once surely been a meeting hall for the members of the *scuola* was now a museum of medical instruments, creepy anatomy diagrams, sharp implements for sawing and carving the human body, and a wealth of old books depicting every last sinew and organ along with all the deformities and maladies that might afflict them.

My stomach began to feel delicate. Lizzie, on the other hand, evidently found the place fascinating, in particular some of the terrifying medical instruments invented over the centuries to tackle everything from a tumour to an amputation.

I was glad when the official finally came back in the company of a diminutive woman with long grey hair, a medical coat and heavy glasses. Anna, it seemed, the guardian of something known as the Museum of Pathological Anatomy 'Andrea Vesalio'. Somewhere even Luca had never heard of.

She led us back outside and along to a door next to the church, unlocked it and let us in, all the while treating us to a lecture on what we were about to see. Vesalio turned out to be a sixteenth-century physician who had pioneered techniques in the dissection of the human body that formed the basis of modern anatomy, correcting centuries of misconceptions about the skeleton, the muscular, vascular and nervous systems, as well as the principal organs. A hero of medical science, as our guide, clearly an ardent fan, was keen to explain.

The first room was an old apothecary, full of jars of cures, herbal and chemical, unremarkable, no preparation for what was to come.

'If you don't mind, I'll stay here, thanks,' I said, trying to look interested in all the many jars.

'No you won't,' Lizzie insisted, and grabbed my arm.

I held my breath and tried not to faint as we passed into

the anatomy room, case after case of sliced organs in liquid, hearts and guts and brains, skulls and limbs, shapes both alien and familiar alongside gory illustrations of how they'd been surgically removed, all neatly arranged and labelled for this tiny temple of severed remains. The creature we sought was the star turn, surely the very object Lucia Scacchi had challenged us to uncover. Luca had turned pale. Lizzie was silent, fascinated. Only our guide was overflowing with words and enthusiasm.

It was the body of a dwarf, twisted, deformed, preserved in a glass case, that much was clear. Sixty-seven centimetres tall, the label said, skin brown as leather, eyes still discernible, hair too, that cruelly distorted body bent into an awkward pose that seemed like nothing more than a painful attempt at dance. A cut across the skull indicated where the brain had been removed.

'What you see,' our guide said, 'is unique. This poor soul was afflicted by what is now called osteogenesis imperfecta. Brittle bone disease. He was a familiar figure around the Rialto, it seems. Almost fifty when he died. This was some time in the early nineteenth century, we believe. He wasn't mummified, like the Egyptians. This is taxidermy. Like the preservation of birds or animals. He was X-rayed a while ago and it was clear there is nothing left except the deformed skeleton and the skin, which was tanned probably with mercury and arsenic. You see before you the only known example of a human being who was subject to the process of . . .'

I walked straight out of the little room into the bright day, breathing quickly, hoping I wouldn't throw up. Then I sat down at the café opposite and ordered a bottle of sparkling water. How long it was before they emerged, I've no idea.

Finally, they bounced across, looking quite jolly.

'Well, that was fascinating,' Luca said.

'Very,' Lizzie agreed. 'Are you all right?'

'I am now.' I downed the last of the bottle. 'Did you learn anything other than they used to stuff people here?'

Luca looked a touch taken aback. 'We ticked off the first riddle on our list, didn't we? I asked the woman if she knew of anything hereabouts to do with a Madame Corneille. She stared at me as if I was mad.'

'Perhaps we are.'

'I wondered if she knew anything about red marble or plague,' added Lizzie. 'That's the next one, isn't it? Nope. Her thing was dead bodies and organs. Tip-top on all that. Not much else.'

She turned and stared at the facade of the *scuola*, more animated than at any time since we'd first met. Lucia Scacchi had given us something to aim at, a target, a reason for getting away from that strange palazzo. I knew we ought to feel grateful. But somehow . . .

'This looks a bit like the last place. The miracles church. A bit like Ca' Scacchi too.'

'Ah!' Luca brightened the way he always did when he had the chance to offer up a morsel of history. 'Well observed. You're getting an eye for my beautiful city. One of the architects was none other than that same Pietro Lombardo who designed Miracoli and perhaps your own home. Should you go to Ravenna and visit Dante's tomb – the real one, not the empty memorial in Florence – you can see the lovely marble bas-relief of the poet reading, sculpted by Lombardo. And . . .' he prodded a finger into the steamy air, 'that was commissioned by none other than Bernardo Bembo, father to Lucrezia's lover Pietro. You see how things connect here. Most things do in the end.'

'We make the circle, we join the dots,' she whispered.

I pointed out that Luca had yet to tell Lizzie about Bembo and Lucrezia and how the painting had arrived in Venice.

'Later,' she said, still fixated on the *scuola*. 'All those colours. It's very . . . intricate.'

Luca was in full flow. 'You should also see the monument Lombardo designed for the tomb of one of our greatest doges, the warrior Pietro Mocenigo. That's quite something.'

'Is that in Ravenna too? Wherever Ravenna is . . .'

He pointed at the door of Giovanni e Paolo. 'We strolled right past it in the basilica earlier. Would you like a closer look?'

She was cheering up. That was good to see. 'I'm starting

to like it here. There's more to this place than stupid masks and hordes of aimless tourists, isn't there?'

Much more, I thought, than I'd realised. It was going to take a while to get the image of that poor creature in his glass case out of my head.

'Quick look around, Luca,' she added. 'Then you can tell me about Bembo and all the rest. Also, I'd like to know where you boys are taking me for lunch. Can't live on one croissant alone.'

I stayed in the shade of my table outside the café. It was good to see the two of them start to get on. Lucia Scacchi's riddles were getting to me. Along with Lizzie's pertinent observation – why offer up cryptic clues, then remove the means to follow them from the old guidebook I'd brought along in my jacket pocket? Did she want the Borgia portrait to be found at all? A woman who would soon kill herself . . . would she even know her own mind, come to that?

One other thing occurred to me about her desecration of that book. After a general introduction, the work was divided logically, into chapters based on the city's *sestieri,* its six neighbourhoods. We were in Castello. Three pages from the chapter covering this area had been ripped out, one, presumably, relating to the *scuola* and the disturbing exhibit we'd just visited. Dorsoduro was missing one page, San Polo two, Cannaregio just a single entry. San Marco, to my surprise since it was the focus of so much activity in the centre, had no omissions. Nor Santa Croce.

Make the circle.

It seemed a reasonable bet that the next line in Casanova's strange riddle, the one about red marble and the plague, referred to somewhere else in Castello, a huge chunk of the city stretching from the *rio* by the Doge's Palace, north to the Fondamente Nove, then past the Arsenale to the old working-class neighbourhoods around via Garibaldi, the distant island of San Pietro, and the easternmost stretch of Venice proper, Sant'Elena.

Luca and I couldn't possibly rely upon our customary skills – academic research, documents and databases – to throw up the answers we needed. We'd have to abandon our usual organised way of working and tread the streets, asking questions, following leads, testing the veracity of what we found. Like detectives, I suppose.

But where to start?

That, it occurred to me, was obvious. Where Valentina Fabbri did so often.

With a man called Ugo Abate.

Cicchetti for three booked on the phone – I wanted to make sure he really was open and hadn't provided that earlier lunch for Valentina alone – I followed the happy couple as we strolled there, Luca giving a flowery account of Lucrezia Borgia's affair with Pietro Bembo, talking of Lord Byron's adventures in the city, a place for lovers always, and a hank of golden hair.

Seven

The Sotoportego

'A piece of marble to hold back plague.' Ugo poured us glasses of his best Pinot Grigio from the carafe. 'Which plague do they mean? The old ones or the new?'

We sat in his tiny courtyard, shaded by the surrounding buildings, the only customers. He greeted Lizzie with great courtesy and made no mention of his knowledge of her family. It seemed Valentina hadn't shared with him Lucia Scacchi's strange piece of fiction. If he'd read it, he'd surely understand why we were scouring Castello for a slab of miraculous stone.

'The old,' I said. 'We just wondered . . .'

He scratched his head. 'I'm the wrong person to ask. I grew up in Burano. The people round here know this place better than I ever will. My wife's uncle owned this bar. I promised I'd buy it from him when I retired and run it when he was gone. Now she's left us too, but I keep my word.'

'Sorry we bothered you, Ugo,' I said. 'I just assumed . . .'

'No bother. Enjoy your food. I must make some calls.'

The *cicchetti* were wonderful as usual, and Luca took great delight in introducing Lizzie to all the local specialities Ugo had brought for us – *baccalà,* tuna salad, aubergine *polpette.* After a few minutes, I left them chatting and went inside. Ugo was off the phone, seated in front of an ancient computer behind the bar.

'Ah, Arnold. You couldn't wait.'

'Did Valentina fill you in?'

He beamed at that. 'See. It's like she always says. You have the makings of a detective. No, you are one already.'

'I don't need to be a detective to understand Ugo Abate knows every inch of this part of Castello, and most of the people who live here.'

'Not the latter so much any more. Half the houses are damned tourist rentals these days. Venice has changed.'

I pulled up a seat next to him. 'She told you about the story, then?'

'When I pressed her. She wished to keep it close, I gather. She was less than impressed you shared it with your friend.'

'I felt Lizzie had the right to know. Her mother wrote it. The thing was found on her property.'

He frowned and rolled his head from side to side. 'She doesn't look like a crook.'

'She isn't one, I'm sure.'

'The best crooks don't. There's something I should have made clearer when we spoke of this. Perhaps more than one thing. I'm old. It was years ago. I had that bent bastard Randazzo on my back. A poor excuse, but it's all I have.'

'What?'

'Your friend's father claimed Lucia was a junkie.'

'Seems so.'

'I really don't remember her like that at all. The Englishman . . . he was usually out of his head on drink or dope, wide-eyed, grinning like a loon, when we went round there to tell them to cut the party noise. Pretty much that way when he thought she was dead too, just without the grin. But the woman was quite different. She seemed more level-headed. Serious. As if she tolerated his crowd. Not a part of it. There was a divorce on the horizon there. Not far off if you ask me.'

He went back to the computer and started printing off a page. 'Do you really want to find this painting? Are you sure it's a wise move?'

'Valentina will let Lizzie off the hook if we do.'

That seemed to shake him. 'Does she really think she's got the evidence to put your friend in front of a magistrate?'

'I don't know. I'd rather not find out.'

The printer started churning out pages.

'A woman hides something priceless, something very rare and special. She leaves a set of cryptic clues for someone to find it. Then she kills herself. You're kicking at her grave, Arnold. Tread carefully.'

I reached for my wallet.

'Don't be ridiculous,' he said, patting my hand. 'This one's on me.'

I followed him out. Luca and Lizzie were laughing and joking over what little food was left.

'The place you're looking for is a *sotoportego*,' Ugo said, placing the pages on the table.

'A what?' Lizzie wondered.

'A passageway beneath a building. Here.' He handed over a cutting. 'It's two minutes away. The next bridge up from Carpaccio's charming dragons. The Sotoportego di Corte Nova, they call it. You'll need the map, because it's not easy to find, even when you think you're there. Go into Corte Nova, then look for an opening into a little street called Calle Zorzi on the left. You can read all about it.'

One of the printouts was from the Save Venice website and talked about the *sotoportego*'s restoration in 2016, the interior and four votive paintings brought back to life by students and professors from the Istituto Veneto per i Beni Culturali. The history of this hidden place was fascinating, and news even to Luca Volpetti. Which was hardly surprising, Ugo pointed out, since Luca came from the Lido, a few minutes away across the water, which he scarcely regarded as Venice at all.

'I used to feed those students while they were working on it,' he added. 'Lovely bunch. Off you go.'

We struggled even with a map. The warren of alleys and dead ends defeated us until Lizzie stopped, folded her arms, looked theatrically cross and declared, 'How on earth do you find your way around this place?'

'Easy,' said Luca. 'You keep walking until you come across somewhere you recognise.'

'And if you don't?'

He shook his head, puzzled. 'Then you're lost, aren't you?'

'Like now?'

His eyes narrowed. She wasn't the only one who could put on an act. 'Luca Volpetti is never lost for long.'

There was no direct way from Ugo's, he said, because the massive priory and garden of the Knights of Malta stood between us and our goal. Finally, we edged back in the wrong direction, then crossed the *rio* by a solitary bridge. And there it was. One more dead-end alley like so many others in the more modest parts of Venice, plain two- and three-storey terraced houses, washing lines crossing from side to side, colourful sheets, shirts and underwear drying in the faint August breeze.

The *sotoportego* was on the left beneath an arch. Quite unre-markable at first glance. Then we walked into the shady interior, just a few metres long, and saw what had made the rich foreigners of Save Venice take so much interest in this tiny out-of-the-way detail in an unremarkable section of Castello. Ugo's printout told the story. During the plague of 1630, which killed a third of the city's population of 140,000 and hastened the republic's economic downfall, a resident named Giovanna painted a portrait of the Virgin on the wall of the passageway. The locals in Corte Nova prayed to her for salva-tion against the sickness ravaging the city. No one in the little street fell ill. More votive images, of the guardian saints Rocco and Sebastiano, were painted on the shadowy walls over the years, fine wood-panel walls built to house them. Twice during the nineteenth century cholera outbreaks devastated parts of Venice but never reached Corte Nova, any more than the bombs of Austrian aircraft did during the First World War.

All this was in Ugo's pages and repeated in a marble plaque set into the arch at one end of the passageway. And there, in the middle of the *sotoportego*, was a red marble flagstone to mark the sanctity of the place, one locals still avoided stepping on out of respect.

Luca walked out into the light and asked a woman cleaning her front windows the inevitable question: was there anything hereabouts that concerned a Madame Corneille? And received what I imagined was an answer we'd hear a lot until we unpicked each of Lucia Scacchi's eight riddles: no.

We strolled on, and soon I was back where I'd been when I first moved to Venice the year before, entirely lost inside a tangle of twisting, narrow alleys, no signs to offer a clue where we might be headed. Luca, I suspect, felt much the same way, though perhaps he possessed a Venetian sense of direction. Lizzie was silent, lost to some reflection I'd no wish to disturb.

Eventually, as if to prove Luca's earlier point, we emerged in a street with a sight I half recognised: La Beppa, the extraordinary hardware shop that seemed to sell everything from birthday cards to cooking utensils, artists' easels and everything for *fai da te*, do-it-yourself. As ever, the front window was full of boxes of dry paint, its interior an Aladdin's cave of wood and plastic and metal spewing onto the pavement. Finally I knew where we were.

Luca marched ahead, and then we were outside the grand grey Palladian frontage of the church of San Francesco della Vigna, the sun beating down on us, free of the dark and claustrophobic alleys we'd scurried through, still seeking answers.

'I need a coffee,' Lizzie said, and neither of us was moved to argue.

Even that wasn't easy. After two more bridges and a good ten minutes' walking, we settled on the outside chairs of a place in Barbaria de le Tole, the long, straight street that would soon take us back to Giovanni e Paolo.

'I hate riddles,' Luca grumbled, stirring his macchiato.

'A couple of hours ago you said you loved them,' Lizzie pointed out.

'That was then. I don't know if I'm helping here or not.'

'You are.' She raised her cup. 'Cheers.'

'But how? What did we learn? Two riddles ticked off. Interesting places. Bizarre. Quite unknown to me, and it's my job to know things. Are we any further forward?'

'The circle,' I said, and pulled out the pages from Lucia's story, along with a fresh tourist map of Venice. 'Here.' I scrawled a mark on the Scuola di San Marco, then another on Corte Nova, and drew a curving line between the two. 'We have the start of it.' I pushed the map in front of them. 'It must run south now, because if it went the other way, we'd end up in the lagoon. So logically, the next dot must lie somewhere—'

'Where's the last one?' Lizzie demanded.

'Will you please stop asking that? We've been through this.'

'You two have.'

Luca waited for a little of the heat to subside. 'If we're correct in thinking we have to make this circle, then that's just the start. You've seen what Venice is like. All alleys and dead ends and hidden little squares. We don't even have proper street addresses like other places. I've checked gazetteers, property and business titles, everything I can think of. I haven't come across a mention of Corneille or anything like it anywhere.'

Lizzie muttered something under her breath, then said, 'I was making a point. I know Mum liked cryptic things. She used to buy a puzzle magazine from the newsstand every week. Crosswords, too.' She nudged me with her elbow. 'And yes, I agree. We find the dots. We join them. Then in the end we meet Madame Corneille. And Lucrezia Borgia. With one bound I am free. Well, quite a few bounds really.'

Luca was looking at my map. 'Would your father have managed all this?'

'If he'd had you two on his side, maybe. Anyway, he never got the chance. Mum took that story thing with her right to her grave.' She finished her coffee and slapped the cup on the table. 'God she must have been out of it. Worse than I ever appreciated.'

I remembered what Ugo had said and kept quiet.

Luca was still engrossed in the tiny portion of a circle I'd drawn on the map, clearly trying to work out where Lucia Scacchi might lead us next. He was about to speak when my phone rang. Valentina Fabbri.

'I don't have a number for your English friend,' she said.

'I'm with her now.'

'Does she not want me to keep in touch?'

I'd had this conversation with Lizzie already. 'She only switches on her phone occasionally, mostly when she wants to pick up any messages. Seems the only people who call her are ones she doesn't want to talk to.'

'I need her here. Immediately. I have Enzo Canale in my office. There's a conversation that needs to take place.' She hesitated, sounding uncertain of herself for a moment. 'I think it's better you come along too. This matter gets stranger by the minute.'

Luca looked puzzled when I said we'd have to give up the treasure hunt for the day. I could live with that. We left him outside Giovanni e Paolo, then I led Lizzie south through Campo Santa Maria Formosa to the Carabinieri office. She was silent most of the way after I told her I'd no idea what Valentina Fabbri wanted. Only that she was with Canale.

'I doubt your friend's going to arrest him,' she said finally as we walked past the church of San Zaccaria. 'Canale owns half this city, doesn't he?'

'No. He doesn't. A few hotels and restaurants. He's part of the past. This place has changed over the last forty years. Italy has. The old ways . . .'

No answer.

A uniformed officer ushered us straight into Valentina Fabbri's office. I still couldn't take a seat there without recalling the first time I'd encountered her, that day she pulled me in to face questions about the death of Marmaduke Godolphin. It was a lesson in teasing details and admissions out of her suspects, me among them, as delicately as a surgeon might untangle the malignities of a wounded heart. In many ways that was just what she'd achieved, and perhaps she was surreptitiously attempting the same now. Valentina didn't simply seek answers; she also sought to heal invisible wounds.

Canale was there, sweating in a cream linen suit, hat on the desk, black hair sticking to his shiny scalp. No cigar, but I could still smell it on him. He looked, for once, ill at ease. Valentina could do that to people.

'Signor Canale has an apology to make,' she said.

Not willingly, I thought. He didn't look directly at Lizzie for a moment. Then, with a shrug of his broad shoulders, he said, 'I was concerned for you. For your well-being. Your safety. I had someone keep an eye on you.'

Before Lizzie could explode, I intervened. 'You had a man follow her. Break into her home. Her hotel.'

'He punched Arnold,' she added.

Canale chuckled. 'Your friend described it as a "scuffle". Anyway, nothing to do with me.'

I couldn't believe he was trying to pretend this was all to protect Lizzie. 'You did this for yourself. To pursue a ridiculous legal claim—'

'Keep out of this affair if you know what's good for you,

Clover. As to the ownership of Ca' Scacchi, that remains in dispute. Hawker never once sought to have it assigned to him. I still have a contract sealed with a down payment—'

'And never concluded,' Lizzie interrupted.

'Not for want of trying.'

'Who was he? This man you set on me.'

A shrug. 'Some guy from Naples who likes to take photographs of abandoned buildings. He was hanging round Ca' Scacchi already. I merely extended his remit.'

Lizzie looked at Valentina Fabbri. 'Isn't that burglary?'

'What was stolen?'

'I don't know.'

'Then . . .' She gave Canale a cold look. 'I don't like this any more than you. I do not approve of any of it. Nevertheless, it's such a minor misdemeanour, I fail to see—'

'Does he own you all then?'

'He hasn't finished. Have you?'

Canale reached into his jacket, took out an envelope and threw it on the desk. 'You should read this.'

I had a horrible feeling about what was coming. It had been bothering me ever since I'd begun to wonder why Canale's man had been scouring Lizzie's hotel.

'It tells you who you truly are.'

I snatched the envelope off the table. 'She doesn't need to. You broke into her room. You stole her personal things. A toothbrush. For pity's sake, what kind of man does that?'

He waved his hands in a gesture of despair. 'A man who wishes to know what legacy he's left in this world. Lizzie has the right to know who her father truly is—'

'What?' She was on her feet, getting red in the face.

'Read the report. It's from a reliable laboratory. I sent them a sample. Mine too. Your mother and I never really broke up. Hawker knew this all along—'

Tears, curses, and Lizzie flew out of the room, slamming the door behind her.

Canale grunted something inaudible under his breath, then added, 'She'll be back. She'll see sense. She has no choice.' He wagged a finger at me. 'Hawker was a criminal. Stealing things from that place. We both know Lucia had to hide the most precious item she owned. She left those riddles, too. Help me, Clover. We can find it. We can save my daughter from her present misery. Bring that poor place back to life. Find that painting . . .'

'What the hell is the painting to you?'

His face fell. 'You haven't seen it. You haven't lain beneath it with the one you love. I have. Ca' Scacchi is mine. I'll pay Lizzie well for it. But Lucrezia belongs on the wall there, nowhere else. It goes with the property. Part of the fabric.'

Valentina's eyes were on me. 'Your friend needs you, Arnold. Go to her.'

'She needs her father,' Canale roared. 'Her real father.' A stab at his chest. 'Me.'

'That,' I said, getting to my feet, 'will never happen. Capitano, you must make it clear to this man he cannot come near her.'

'I agree. You will not approach her, Canale,' she replied, in a tone that brooked no argument. 'I will not turn a blind eye a second time. Unless Signora Hawker allows it . . .'

He was laughing. Not the thing to do at that moment.

My phone buzzed with a message. It was Lizzie. She was making her own way back to Ca' Scacchi.

'You think this is funny?' Valentina asked.

He waved a dismissive hand in her direction. 'I think, Capitano, you, like your Englishman here, have no idea who you're dealing with.'

'If you approach the lady without her permission, you will encourage my displeasure.'

He looked round the little office. 'And you are who, exactly? A minor bureaucrat in an organisation that should have better things to do than meddle in family affairs.'

I got up and opened the door for him. Canale made sure to barge me in the shoulder as he left, and turned to wink, an expression on his face that said: *I am big and you are small and need to know it.*

'It seems I've made an enemy,' I said, taking a seat.

'I told you already. You need to see your friend. She looked very upset.'

She did. But Lizzie was on her way home, and I already knew she was tougher than Valentina Fabbri appreciated.

'That's understandable, isn't it? She's been threatened with prosecution. Got Canale's lawyers chasing her. Plus some hood he hired on the street. And now that thug telling her he's her real father.'

Valentina pushed her chair back and ordered more coffee. Not for me, I said. Lord knows how many she got through in a day. When the tame officer had delivered, she stirred a whole pack of brown sugar into it and said, 'I won't be prosecuting her, Arnold. Not unless there's something in all this I've yet to discover. But we would like to recover that painting. The city museum is interested. It's part of our heritage, after all. God knows, it seems her father . . . Hawker stole enough of that out of the country already.'

Which was fair enough, not that I was going to let on. 'What's happening with the medical examiner? Lizzie wants to know what she's expected to do. A funeral. She's got no money, of course.'

'It's complicated. I can't say more.'

'Can't or won't?'

A tap of the pen on the desk. I knew all her gestures and what they signified. That was the mark of a question she didn't want to hear.

'This grows more problematic by the day. A dead body. A historic property in jeopardy. Lawsuits.' She nodded her head from side to side. 'Family issues now, which appear devilishly convoluted and barely understood by those they concern. We are on the same side in this, you know.'

I said nothing.

'So how did your day go? You and Luca trying to solve this riddle she was left?'

'It's complicated. I can't say more.'

She laughed. We were still friends, just a little at odds at that moment. 'Very good.'

'You shared it with Enzo Canale. Lucia's story.'

Valentina scowled and shook her head. 'I did not! Someone else passed it on. Canale is a man with a lot of money. He has friends, or contacts, everywhere. Never forget that. I won't.'

I told her anyway. About the taxidermy skeleton of a crippled man of middle age in an anatomy museum hidden away in what was now the Ospedale Civile. And a red marble flagstone in the back alleys of Castello that once supposedly saved a short street from the plague. She looked fascinated, astounded too.

'Did you not know any of this?' I asked. 'You're local.'

'I've said this many times. Venice isn't a city. It's a world. A universe even. Who gets to know all that? No. I've never heard of these things. Sometimes outsiders like you see more than those of us who've grown up here. I've no need to find taxidermy specimens of little fellows in jars. How did the woman come up with this kind of thing?'

I retrieved the guidebook with the ancient pages and showed her the sections that had been torn out. She flipped through it, fascinated. 'These omissions in themselves are a hint, surely?'

'I believe so.'

'And now you have the first three parts of the riddle solved.'

I blinked. 'No. Two. The anatomy museum. The red marble—'

'"Eight great dead lie in holy water." Please. You're almost sitting on top of them.' She closed the book. 'Tomorrow, I think. Now I want you to go and find Signora Hawker. On the way, you will stop by Il Pagliaccio . . .'

That made no sense. 'It's closed. You said Franco's on holiday with the kids in Sardinia.'

'He is. But when we shut for Ferragosto, we let one of the local catering colleges use the kitchen to learn what a real restaurant is like. They invent things. Good things sometimes.' She grimaced. 'Sometimes . . . not so great. I will call them. You take your pick, a bottle of wine as well. Tell Lizzie Hawker she needn't worry about Enzo Canale, funerals, or what's going to happen to that palazzo her mother inherited.' She threw the book across the desk. 'We will, I trust, find solutions. *Buon appetito*, Arnold. Tomorrow is another day.'

Franco's smart restaurant was a three-minute walk from Ca' Scacchi. I found the kitchen full of enthusiastic students chopping and frying and talking in excited tones about the meals they were preparing for a select group of guests that evening. So much choice, so many dishes being foisted on me. I left with more food than we could possibly eat: a salad of tiny octopuses and baby artichokes, squid ink ravioli stuffed with wild bass, mantis shrimp in citrus oil, *vitello tonnato*, that odd mix of veal with a tuna sauce, a box of pastries filled with pistachios and figs, *gianduja* and *zabaglione*. And a bottle of chilled white from a small vineyard in Conegliano run by one of Valentina's many cousins.

There was a flower shop by the next canal. I picked up some roses and lugged everything down the alley to Ca' Scacchi. The barriers were still up in the courtyard, but there was no sign of anyone from Ballarin's team or Valentina's. A quiet meal on the *altana*, flowers, fine food, cheap plates and cutlery. On another day it would have made a pretty picture, all those dishes created so lovingly by the happy young people in Franco's kitchen. Just then it was the best I could offer.

Lizzie was in her room. I knocked and she came to the door, pink-eyed, cheeks flushed.

'Food,' I said. 'And drink.'

'Not really hungry, thanks.'

'You haven't seen what I've got.'

She did, at least, appear curious. Impressed too when she saw what waited for us on those rickety timbers jutting out from Ca' Scacchi's walls.

A line of puffy white clouds was bubbling up to the south beyond Giudecca. Sometimes, on days like this, they'd rise into anvils of cumulonimbus, turn black and crash thunder and sudden downpours on the city. But not this time, I felt sure. They were too distant and too feeble for that.

Lizzie sipped a glass of Verduzzo and picked at the seafood. 'Where on earth . . .?'

'A gift from Valentina Fabbri. Her husband's restaurant is round the corner.'

'Oh.'

'She says not to worry. Canale's been warned. She doesn't think you're a crook.'

'Ha! That's a relief.'

I said nothing and served myself a plateful. It was almost as good as anything Franco himself might have made.

'We still have to find that painting, don't we, Arnold?'

'We do. We will. Tomorrow. I know where to start.'

'Where?'

'Not now. Don't waste this food. A lot of young kids worked hard to prepare it.'

She snorted. 'Bloody hell. You sound just like him.'

'Your father?' It was a clumsy thing to say. I regretted it immediately. 'Sorry. That was thoughtless.'

'Not really. And I'm wrong. You're not like him at all. He *was* my father, too. I don't care what that old bastard's piece of paper says. Not that I know much about all this, but I imagine you get to be a parent by what you do. How much you care. How hard you try to keep someone safe and happy. He did that. When he got sick, I tried to do the same for him. Where was Enzo Canale all that time? Trying to set lawyers on us to steal this place. Chas Hawker was my dad. I loved him. He loved me. That's all that matters.'

Half the takeaway was gone already. I must have been looking.

'Sorry. I was hungry after all. I suppose your friend's not as scary as she seems.'

'Depends on the context. A lot does around here.'

The plates were cleared. The wine just a couple of glasses left. She insisted on washing up in the kitchen, staring out at the stones of the chessboard in the garden. I couldn't get out of my head a mental image of the games they'd once played out there, real people as pieces, half in white, half in black. Winners and losers back in a time when Ca' Scacchi was alive. The late Lucia Scacchi, it seemed, was doing much the same with us.

When Lizzie was done, she said, 'You're a kind man. I'm lucky you're around. When I get some money, I promise I'll pay—'

'You don't need to worry about money. I'm retired here. I have a pension. Nothing much to do.'

Her eyes were on me in a way that felt uncomfortable. 'You must have something to aim for. A reason. A goal.'

'My goal is to be happy and to learn a little more each day. I have to say you're helping with both.'

Her cheeks flushed again, and she said goodnight.

I crawled downstairs to bed and started to read under the weak light of a battered table lamp that once must have been quite grand. Luca's book on Lucrezia Borgia was gripping now I'd got past the preliminaries of the Borgia tribe. As usual, my Venetian friend was right. Like many, I'd misread the woman, believing myth over what was real and known. I'd imagined Rodrigo Borgia's daughter to be made in her father's mould: manipulative, wicked, heartless. There *was* that side to her character, though as Luca had said, the times she lived in weren't made for the frail and feeble. But she was also both victim of her family's constant bargaining with her hand for political advantage, and a woman who was loved for her kindness and, later in life, her piety. The affairs with Pietro Bembo and her very different, martial brother-in-law appeared genuine and deep. At the same time, her third husband, an adulterer himself, continued to love and admire her.

I could only wonder about the picture of Lucia Scacchi we'd had painted for us, primarily by the circumstances of her strange death and the word of a man who might have made a good father but a terrible husband. Ugo Abate, a shrewd judge of character, didn't think her a feckless junkie, part of the hedonistic dream world Hawker had established in those few years they'd occupied Ca' Scacchi. There was also the academic side to her nature, evidenced in the strange Casanova story itself. A complex woman who'd led a complex life and, it seemed, come to regret it deeply.

The doors were open to the space the Borgia portrait had once occupied on the wall at the end of the bed. The look on Canale's face when he'd talked of the canvas was quite memorable.

You haven't seen it. You haven't lain beneath it with the one you love.

What a formidable spell Bartolomeo Veneto's masterpiece must have cast over men across the centuries, from Pietro Bembo to Byron, the unfortunate Annibale Scacchi to Chas

Hawker and his wife's secret paramour. I couldn't help but wonder what stories the women who'd seen that painting might tell too.

There was a knock on the door, and before I could answer, Lizzie was in. Blue pyjamas, and two glasses of wine in her hands.

'This plonk is far too good to leave,' she said, and placed one by the bedside before climbing onto the thin sheet, sitting upright, hands around her knees.

I took a sip. I'd had enough to drink, however excellent it was. 'Please don't ever describe it as "plonk" in Valentina's presence. Or Franco's.'

A scowl. 'I don't plan on being round long enough to get to know them. I meant it, you know. When I said Canale's not my father.'

'I know.'

'What does he want? To get me to pretend he is?'

That, I pointed out, was a question only Enzo Canale could answer. And in the circumstances . . .

'He never married,' she said. 'Lots of girlfriends. Luca told me. Maybe he thinks my dead mum's the only real love he ever had.'

The empty space on the opposite wall seemed to be staring at me. I wasn't going to tell her what Canale had said after she'd stormed out of Valentina's office.

'You're very quiet, Arnold.'

I held up the book. 'I was reading. About a young woman who led a very difficult life. Who was used by men, her father among them. It made me realise that sometimes we never quite know what's true about someone and what's made up. Sometimes those questions never get any answers. Perhaps that's for the best.'

She nodded. 'Why didn't you have kids?'

'It never happened. There wasn't a conscious decision.'

'You could have adopted. They'd have liked you. The adoption people.'

We'd talked about that. Eleanor had never felt ready. What I didn't say was that I didn't think she'd wanted children at all. Too much trouble. Too much of an interruption.

Lizzie had finished her wine. 'I always thought I'd be a mum one day. A boy. A girl. Just two. I thought I'd find someone and we'd be . . . ordinary. Normal. No idiotic ambitions. Just a family, happy, getting by. Instead, I became the failed actress daughter of a bankrupt showbiz mogul getting sicker year after year. Too late now.'

'Is it?'

'I'm nearly forty. Too old to change.' She snorted, a short, wry explosion. A little drunk, I guessed. 'And anyway . . . you need a man, or so I'm told. Only a fool would hang around a mess like me.'

Quite gingerly, I reached out and touched her arm. 'This will get sorted, Lizzie. We'll find your picture. You'll bury your mother. Then you can deal with the future of this place, in your own time, in your own way. It will happen.'

With that, she rolled over, lay full length on the bed, looked at the empty space on the wall, then right at me.

'Why should you care?'

'Very good question.'

'How about a very good answer?'

'Because,' I said, 'until this affair's settled, I'll never get you out of my hair and return to my bachelor flat, my books, and find some peace and quiet and time to myself.'

Another laugh, then she rolled off the bed.

'Soon enough,' she said. 'I hope.'

Eight

The Hound of the Lord

At eight, just before we left for breakfast with Luca, there was a hammering on the door. I went down to answer. Ballarin, the surveyor, was there with a smartly dressed woman in a black pinstripe suit, 'lawyer' written all over her. She was bearing papers.

'We need to see the lady,' he said. He looked downcast, even ashamed.

'Why?'

'I don't think that's any of your business.'

I sent Luca a quick message: he would have to wait.

'Trust me, Ballarin. It is. Why? She's busy. She's got a lot on her plate.'

The woman introduced herself as Elena Esposito, an advocate with the council. 'She'll have a lot more on her plate if she doesn't talk to us.'

'Arnold.' A voice from behind. Lizzie had come downstairs barefoot, quiet as a mouse. 'It's all right. They can come in.' She was back in her jeans and a fresh cotton shirt, hair tidy, face fresh, no make-up, unlike the Esposito woman, who looked ready to audition for a cocktail ad.

We went upstairs to the *altana*. They turned down my offer of instant coffee. Ballarin seemed more than a little nervous about walking onto the ancient wooden platform.

Lizzie sat down and took the envelope out of the woman's hands.

'I assume this is for me.' One glance, then she threw it on the table. 'I don't speak Italian. And I'm not asking Arnold to translate either. You tell me what it says.'

Ballarin cleared his throat and looked at Elena Esposito. She took up the challenge. After surveying the palazzo, the technical report indicated Ca' Scacchi needed urgent repair.

Lizzie raised a finger. 'I thought you said it wasn't so bad.'

'Not as bad as I expected,' he replied.

'So . . .?'

Esposito took over. 'What he means is it's not about to tumble into the Grand Canal.' She glanced back at the corridor behind us. 'That's not the same as saying it's safe.'

I jumped in. '*Signora*, you're not the only one with access to legal advice. I've checked. You only have the authority to seize this place if it's uninhabitable or in danger of collapse. Not without going through a lengthy legal process. Cut the pretence, please.'

I'd made that up, of course.

Ballarin's eyes were on me when he said, 'If you wish to stay here, that's your choice. As your friend says, it's your prerogative.'

The lawyer glared at him. 'A foolish one. You wouldn't stay here yourself, surely?'

'That is a hypothetical question. There's no point in my addressing it. Signora Hawker is, I believe, somewhat short of funds. After confirmation of her mother's death, it seems to me she has every right to use this place as she sees fit. For now.'

'For now,' the woman agreed, then reached for the envelope and took out a couple of pages. 'It's the considered opinion of the authority that a building as historic and potentially as beautiful as this needs to be put on a secure footing. With established ownership, a plan for its future, proper maintenance and care.' She leaned forward. 'You're not in a position to offer any of those things, are you?'

This was too much.

'Lizzie stands to inherit,' I said. 'She hasn't done so yet. In the tragic circumstances, this is understandable. I'm appalled you should be putting pressure on her at such a moment. She won't be in a position to make any kind of decision on Ca' Scacchi until the issue of probate and her mother's death has been dealt with. Currently, it seems to me, you are pitching your approach at a woman who until the other day lay dead and invisible beneath the giant chessboard out there. You can't expect an answer.'

'That,' Ballarin said with a grimace, 'is not entirely accurate. The law gives us certain rights and duties.'

I stomped my feet hard on the altana timbers. They shook and he winced. 'This place has stood leaning like this for centuries. You know it's not about to fall down. When probate is through, when Lizzie knows she's the lawful owner on paper, then I'm sure she'll want to speak.'

'If I decide to sell.' Lizzie waved a hand at the rooftops of Dorsoduro. 'I'm starting to like it here. May just keep it for myself and—'

'It needs five million spending on it,' Esposito said, looking her up and down. 'Minimum. Do you have that kind of money?'

'I could always take out a mortgage.'

'This is not a laughing matter.'

'Believe me, I am well aware of that.'

The lawyer tapped her fingers on the papers. 'If the ownership of a historic property is in doubt, and that has been the case here for more than three decades, we may apply for a compulsory purchase to protect our national heritage. Especially when there's an interested third party who's willing to undertake much of the necessary cost of repair.'

There, I thought, we have the real purpose of this visit. 'Do you have a particular third party in mind?'

Ballarin kept looking at me.

'We're not at liberty to say,' the lawyer continued. 'But if Signora Hawker is willing to sign away her claim to the property now, she can save herself much uncertainty and possible ruin in the future. Nor will she go unrewarded. If—'

'How much?' Lizzie demanded.

The question threw the woman for a moment. 'I believe you could expect a substantial sum as a show of good faith. Paid within a matter of weeks out of the generosity of the party concerned. A handsome gift given you don't as yet have any legal right to be here.'

'Tell Enzo Canale he can shove it up his arse.'

Silence. I broke it by getting to my feet and announcing we had an appointment. 'We're late already.'

'You forgot this,' Lizzie added, handing Elena Esposito her envelope.

The lawyer shrugged and dropped it back on the table.

We trooped in silence downstairs to the side gate. There, Ballarin announced he needed to take another look at the emergency work on the steps down to the Templar crypt.

'I'll see you back in the office,' he added, and walked off towards the wooden hut his workmen had built over the entrance.

Lizzie went inside to get her bag.

Ballarin didn't seem a bad man. Just someone sent on a mission he didn't like. Once the lawyer was gone, he was swiftly back.

'I have to say,' I told him, 'the timing of this offer, if it is an offer, seems unfortunate and ill-judged to say the least. Don't you think the woman in there has enough on her mind?'

He wasn't looking at the barriers and the earthworks around the crypt at all.

'The timing was not mine. Nor anything else. I should warn you both. Enzo Canale is not a man who takes losing lightly. He's been badgering the administration over this place for decades. For some reason, it's an obsession. Before, with Lucia Scacchi just missing rather than dead, we were able to send him packing on the grounds there was nothing we could do in the face of such a legal morass.' He raised a finger. 'Never a good idea with someone like him. I'm likely to pay the price for that. If you or your friend try the same . . .'

'He's just a man,' I said. 'Bound by the same laws as the rest of us.'

Ballarin glanced back at the palazzo. 'This is a beautiful building, for all its grim past. But it's not a hill I'd choose to die on. Tell her. Your friend should sign away her interest, take Canale's money and make herself scarce.'

I said nothing.

'Still,' he added, 'I see my words count for little. In which case I advise you to tread carefully and be wary who you trust.'

Luca Volpetti had invited us for the usual breakfast of coffee and pastries, this time in the museum café of the Palazzo Ducale, a quiet prelude before the serious work ahead. The sounds of Venice echoed all around. The plaintive wails of hungry gulls, vaporetti horns on the Bacino San Marco, distant cries and laughter from the people filling the Riva degli Schiavoni by the lagoon. Just audible from time to time the strains of vibrant strings, Vivaldi naturally, bait for tourists from a nearby restaurant patio or hotel.

Lizzie was entranced when he led us past the hordes outside the palazzo using his city pass into that great courtyard with the Giants' Staircase, its statues of Mars and Neptune, the searing bleached white of marble everywhere. The café was on the ground floor. He would, he promised, take her on a personal tour of the entire complex, including the hidden secret quarters, one day when she was ready. It was good they were getting on. She needed more than me on her side.

To my relief, she hadn't so much as mentioned Enzo Canale's devious shadowing of her, and the shocking declaration he was her real father. I assumed from our conversation the night before that this meant she accepted it was true, and decided to ignore the fact altogether.

I listened to them chatting as we watched the grey waters of the *rio* stir lazily beneath the *fórcola* of a gondola vanishing towards the Bridge of Sighs, a young couple arm in arm on the leather seats. He had a single red rose in his hand, she wore a smile that seemed for him alone. Lost to the dream of the enclosed and extraordinary city that had briefly consumed them. Still, there was the faintest fragrance of decay, chemical and mortal, rising from the *rio* as it made its way to the lagoon beyond the bridge. If they noticed, they didn't mind.

'So . . .' Luca clapped his hands, '"Eight great dead lie in holy water." Where do we go now?'

The last torn-out section of the Castello chapter in the old guidebook lay between articles on the Doge's Palace and the Arsenale. It was a sure sign our destination lay somewhere there. Not that I needed it. Valentina Fabbri had solved the riddle for us the night before.

'Around the corner,' I said, then went and paid.

San Zaccaria. The name of one of the vaporetto stops close to the Doge's Palace, Valentina Fabbri's Carabinieri office, and the small campo on which it sat. But it all came from the church of that name in the square at the very edge of Castello, polychrome marble and pure white Istrian stone, the style spanning from Gothic to Renaissance.

Hiding the clue to a riddle in a Venetian place of worship was always going to pose a challenge. There were something like a hundred and eighteen of them throughout the city still open, including the Anglican St George's not far from Ca' Scacchi in Dorsoduro where I sometimes went for the concerts. A good hundred more had been lost to development, other uses or fire over the centuries. But Valentina knew the neighbourhood near her office, every inch of it. The Carabinieri building had once been part of the same complex. The church shared one unusual feature with Ca' Scacchi: a crypt.

There wasn't a ticket desk at the door, just a friendly chap at a table halfway down the nave accepting donations and selling postcards. It was the modest-sized interior, a rich wonder of curving stones and frescoes and canvases, that always drew me, both for the quiet and for the richness of its art: the gilded altarpieces, *The Flight into Egypt* by Tintoretto's son, Domenico, and most of all, Bellini's *Virgin and Child*, painted for the church when he was seventy-four, stolen by Napoleon's soldiers, then recovered from Paris and returned to its original home twenty years later. You put a coin into a machine and a light brought to life the enthroned Madonna and child, surrounded by four saints, an angelic musician playing what I took to be a viol at her feet.

Before anything else, I walked up to it and stuffed a coin into the box. Lizzie, who was I think more in the mood for being a visitor than a hunter of treasure that day, came and stood next to me.

'It's beautiful. So . . . peaceful. It looks as if they might break into a stately dance or something.'

'Bellini,' Luca said as he joined us. 'Funny to think he painted something so peaceful when the whole of Italy was racked by war.'

'Against who?' she asked.

Luca threw up his hands. 'What do they teach at school in England? Against each other! Oh, Lizzie. You have so much to learn.'

She took that well. 'Perhaps peace and beauty are what you need in times like that.'

I'd noticed the signs for the crypt before. But I was a recent widower when I came to live in this city, and hidden underground chambers seemed to speak of dust and decay. I had never wanted to look.

'Eight great dead,' I said. 'They were early doges. Three of them murdered in the street not far from here.'

Tickets bought, it was a short walk through a small museum and a quiet chapel, then down some steps worn away by centuries. A minute, no more, in which we seemed to travel from the Italy of the Renaissance to the simpler Venice of the tenth century. At the foot of the stairs was a dimly lit chamber, a high line of stone only just keeping us from the shallow pool of clear water that ran from the steps to an altar, or perhaps a tomb, flecked with algae, a statue above it, a woman in a winding robe, the Madonna perhaps. It was hard in the low light to tell. The place had the dank, close smell of somewhere the lagoon penetrated regularly, half land, half the muddy swamp from which Venice had emerged fifteen hundred years before.

The reflections of the columns and arches in the still water made it feel as if we'd walked inside a painting or a strange dream. There wasn't a sound, not a voice, nor the shriek of a gull.

We stayed silent, waiting on Lizzie to say something. She had to be thinking about that other crypt, the one in the courtyard of Ca' Scacchi where we'd stumbled upon the corpse of her mother. That, surely, was the reason Lucia had put this place in her riddles. Finally she bowed her head and murmured, 'I don't like it here. Can we go?'

Outside, the air was hot and sticky, that sense of a coming storm in the pressure and the way the breeze billowed from time to time.

We stood in the sunshine close to the Carabinieri building as I held the map. The third dot was now there, forming the curve of a circle from the Scuola Grande di San Marco to the *sotoportego* of Corte Nova then south to San Zaccaria. From here it was obvious it could only go in one direction, across the Bacino San Marco and the mouth of the Grand Canal towards Salute.

The hound of the Lord and the lily where water once ran.

Luca's phone rang and he walked off to take the call. I'd never heard him angry except when dealing with people he loathed, and they were rare. Now I heard him speaking the name of his department boss at the State Archives, a charming former academic from Bologna, the two of them good friends. Though not, it seemed, at that moment. His voice was raised, and that seemed to surprise Lizzie as much as it did me. When the call was done, he came over, face like thunder, and said he was being recalled to base.

'Is everything all right?' Lizzie asked.

'It appears someone has been complaining about my absence. I'm sorry. Call or email if you need more help. Here . . .' He scribbled a name on his notepad and passed it over. 'This priest only deals with outsiders by request. I'll phone him and make sure you're welcome.'

The Library of the Venice Seminary. Monsignor Fabrizio Ricci.

'I've never heard of this place, Luca. What is it? Where?'

'No surprise.' He was about to make a call. 'We don't open the doors to everything.'

'But—'

'As the name says, it's a library. A small but rather special one run by the Church.'

'Where?'

'Ah.' He smiled. 'Like many of the best things, hidden in plain sight. Between Salute and the Punta della Dogana. The door next to the Pinacoteca Manfrediniana. I imagine you've walked past many times and never looked twice.'

He whispered a low, sharp curse and glanced at Lizzie. 'I'm sorry. You're on your own. They've made it very clear. I can't play truant any more.' He took her hands. 'If anyone can help, it's Fabrizio Ricci. Take the traghetto. Show Lizzie our side of Venice.' He was upset, genuinely so. 'Try and forget all this worry, clear your heads and explore. Find yourselves lost. No idea what's up or down, north or south. Sometimes serendipity is the best way to discover what you're really looking for.'

Then, with that piece of advice and a quick frown, he was gone, back towards the Piazza San Marco.

'What's a traghetto again?'

I told her. The ferry like a large gondola. There were several, my favourite being the one Valentina had introduced me to. It ran between the Vallaresso vaporetto stop on the other side of the square and Salute.

'You mean where those noisy men we saw in the restaurant work?'

She didn't miss a thing.

Ten minutes later, Lizzie was standing entranced as we rocked on the wake of the traffic at the mouth of the Grand Canal, while I, forever the tourist, took a seat and listened to the gentle teasing banter of the oarsman, who now realised I was never going to make this journey on foot like the locals.

It was hotter than ever, with a heavier beat to the breeze. There were signs the holiday mood was slowly coming to an end. More people, locals by the looks of it, more life to the city as the cafés and shops started to reopen. Lizzie remained upright and smiling in the bows, facing into the faint gusts of wind rolling across the Basin, gazing at a scene I was beginning to take for granted: the spike of the Punta della Dogana jutting out into the gleaming waters, the grey dome of Salute, the vaporetti and gondolas and commercial traffic on the Grand Canal, the great palazzi on both sides. Ca' Scacchi too, visible as Dorsoduro curved gently towards the Guggenheim and the Accademia. From this distance the decay wasn't obvious. It appeared a crooked little gem set amidst an array of larger jewels in the glorious necklace winding through the heart of the city.

Not that Lizzie was looking that way. As we approached the jetty, she was mesmerised by the great dome of Salute, happier than I'd seen her at any time since we'd met. Luca Volpetti was right. It was time to give ourselves over to the game. To treat it as an escapade, however dark the journey, however elusive the prize.

Fabrizio Ricci – a monsignor, no ordinary priest – turned out to be a man of around seventy. Short and stout, he seemed almost doll-like, dressed in clerical black, with the inquisitive round face and half-moon glasses of an academic and a gaze so penetrating it might cut glass. He was waiting for us at the door of the Patriarchal Seminary, leaning on an elegant cane, a smiling fellow who seemed intrigued to be receiving visitors at such short notice. We were to be treated as welcome guests in the building that sat between Salute and what was now the modern art collection of the Pinault Foundation, based in the old customs building at the tip of Dorsoduro.

'Luca says you're the lady who now owns the notorious Ca' Scacchi,' he said straight out in excellent English.

Lizzie blushed, I'd no idea why. 'My mother's dead. My father too. I guess so, yes.'

'A burden, I imagine. I read in the paper about the terrible find in the garden. This city throws up so many surprises on occasion. Did you know they recently found a Roman road out there in the lagoon, submerged for two millennia?'

'History isn't my thing.'

'History's all our thing, my dear. We forget that at our peril. And you, sir?'

I kept it brief because I felt sure Luca had told the man all about me.

'Friends,' he said, watching us both.

Lizzie agreed and briefly brushed my arm. 'Arnold is my guide here.'

'A good and honest one, I'm sure. In this strange and damaged world, Lord knows how much fine friends are needed. Come!' He rapped his stick on the marble floor. 'First, I must show you round our home. No arguments. It helps me think. With a little luck, it may do the same for you.'

We listened to the tapping of his cane on the way to the small library on the first floor, a place full of obscure religious works from what I could see, leather-bound with gilt lettering, titles in Italian, authors I'd never heard of. Shelf upon shelf, mostly of interest to the academic clergy and researchers of arcana, he said. The place spoke to me, as it would to anyone who'd spent their time in academic archives. It had the pleasant, slightly musty smell of old paper and the quiet that only a true library knows. Two globes sat by a glass table in the centre,

images of the world as the old republic envisaged it. Close by
there was a strange geometric model in a glass case, a dodeca-
hedron patterned with stars that was, according to the
monsignor, a mark of Venice's links with the goddess Venus.

'You see the connection?'

'Not at all,' I admitted as Lizzie shook her head.

'Venice and Venus. The goddess of love and beauty, desire,
victory, prosperity. There's a similarity to start with, or so our
forebears always hoped. Etymologically, through various twists
and turns, both come from the same source, over a period of
a couple of millennia naturally. This city, you see, is a nexus,
a place of origin for some, a destination, a final one for others.
And for Venetians like me – I was born within the sound of
Salute's bells – both.'

Lizzie was rolling her eyes in a way that said, *What is he
talking about?*

I nudged her discreetly. 'As Luca may have told you,
Monsignor, my friend and are I embarked upon a kind of
quest.'

'Aren't we all?' Fabrizio Ricci beamed. 'You two, I gather,
are in pursuit of a scandalous portrait of Lucrezia Borgia that
once belonged to our poet and cardinal Pietro Bembo. How
exciting!'

'You've heard of it?' Lizzie wondered.

He performed that mix of frown and shrug so common I
wondered if they taught it in every Italian school. 'Not in
detail. Luca dangled the prospect in front of me like a lure for
one of those grey mullet we have in abundance in our waters.
He knows full well I'm a sight easier to hook than they are.' He
took a long, old-fashioned notebook out of the pocket of his
jacket. 'I did sift through a few references we have here about
the great Pietro. There was mention of the fact he owned a
few works of art that were never available to general view.
With a hint that at least one might have been of dubious taste.
There's always been an abundance of gossip about the Scacchi,
of course. That palazzo of theirs. The clan themselves, well . . .'
He grimaced. 'A man of the Church only hears confessions
of which we shall not speak and whispers that may best be
ignored.'

'I'm a Scacchi,' Lizzie reminded him. 'Half one anyway. I must admit, till now, it's not been the most exciting or scandalous of lives.'

He chuckled. 'You're still young. I can see that sparkle in your eyes. There's always time. I meant no disrespect.' He slammed the pages shut with a grin. 'Do you think you can find this strange masterpiece?'

'We have eight clues,' I told him. 'One of them, or all of them in concert, will perhaps lead us there. Together with a reference to a character named Madame Corneille.'

His eyes narrowed. 'Who's she?'

'The truth is,' said Lizzie, 'we haven't the faintest idea.'

He put a finger to his cheek. 'And the riddle you think refers to your next stop along the way?'

I showed him, and he ran a stubby finger across the words. '"The hound of the Lord and the lily where water once ran."' He nodded and put his finger to his lips. Then said, with a perplexed expression, 'Very well. I think best while walking. Follow me, please.' He tapped his way towards the door. 'I trust you both have a head for heights.'

Down a long corridor in the labyrinth of the building stood a winding spiral staircase, black iron, steep, vertiginous. I took a look up when we reached the foot. It seemed to stretch to the sky, with windows set into the wall at intervals.

'Let me lead,' Fabrizio Ricci announced, and started off up the steps, cane now under his arm as he gripped the circling balustrade with the speed and agility of a man half his age.

It was a dizzying climb. At the summit – I'd no idea how high we were, and a touch of vertigo was already setting in – we entered a room full of strange contraptions: astrolabes and other ancient devices for navigation. A large telescope was perched on a stand by the window, aimed at a slit in the domed roof.

The priest beckoned us to take two chairs by the desk. 'Excuse me while I ramble. I think while I speak as well.'

Lizzie had my arm. 'Are you all right?'

'Never a fan of heights,' I admitted.

'Ah,' said Ricci, 'but if you could be here on a clear night, no moon, only stars and the endless heavens above you, then you'd forget your fears. This is where we used to come and wonder at the firmament. Little used now. Out of date. The Church may have had an argument with Galileo once upon a time, but after that was settled, we became rather fond of astronomy.'

Never would I have guessed that there was an observatory in Venice, let alone one run by the Catholic Church. Lizzie Hawker seemed to be introducing me to aspects of my home that were quite new. Among them a compact circular room high above the rooftops of Dorsoduro next to Salute, dedicated to stargazing.

'Apologies,' Ricci added. 'I omitted to show you the quotation at the foot of the steps. "Look toward the heavens and count the stars." Good advice. At Castel Gandolfo, the Holy Father's summer palace in Lazio, we have a proper observatory, a serious one. An interest in another in Arizona, too. Faith, you see, inspires science. Galileo demonstrated his first telescope from the campanile of San Marco, you know. The Doge was mightily impressed, though more by its trick of spying on enemy ships than its ability to spot the moons of Jupiter. Outside, please. Tread only where I say. There is a point to all this. I shall come to it shortly.'

I took a deep breath and followed them, Lizzie almost skipping through the door into the fresh breeze. In front of the observatory dome, a flat roof twice the size of Ca' Scacchi's *altana* projected out into thin air, parts of it taped off for safety. The view from Ca' Scacchi was spectacular; this was of an entirely different order. We were so high we stood far above the triangle of terracotta that formed the roof of the Punta della Dogana as it jutted into the lagoon. The panorama was astonishing, all the way across to San Marco on one side and San Giorgio Maggiore on the other. The Grand Canal was visible behind the vast Salute dome, the palazzi there like gorgeous miniatures from the model of a talented architect. In the opposite direction, on the Giudecca Canal, the churches of Zitelle and Redentore stood bright white in the August sun, the view of the island opposite clear all the way to its end at Sacca Fisola. On Dorsoduro itself, I was surprised to see courtyards I'd never known existed, some of a considerable size, and a bright green sports pitch marked out for play. It was like being given a different and entirely fresh perspective on a vista I'd been coming to take for granted.

'I mention astronomy not idly,' Ricci went on. 'For Galileo, the distant heavens might have seemed uncharted territory, infinite, unknown and unknowable. But not for us. We mostly know where to look, and when, provided we understand the movement of the constellations, the rules that guide them.' He waved his notebook. 'Rules. It seems to me the woman who posed your riddle was aware of this. Perhaps she did crosswords. Or other puzzles.'

Lizzie came back from the railing. She'd been leaning over, much braver than I felt at that moment. 'Mum loved those things.'

Mum.

For the first time, I thought I detected a note of affection in her voice.

'As the heavens have maps, so puzzles must have logic,' said the priest. 'For example, "where water once ran".'

Lizzie sighed. 'There's water running everywhere, isn't there?'

I was beginning to see Fabrizio Ricci's point. 'It's not as simple as that. Nothing ever is here. Some of the old waterways have been filled in over the years.'

The best known, for me at least, was Via Garibaldi, now a busy shopping and restaurant street at the eastern end of Castello. Once, until Napoleon decided otherwise, a broad canal, a section remaining on the approach to San Pietro.

'We have a name for a closed waterway . . .' Ricci waited, smiling at me.

'*Rio terà*,' I said.

'Luca said you were a knowledgeable fellow.' He pointed along the length of Dorsoduro, past the green sports field, towards the line of the Zattere promenade. 'I was born in a dead-end alley off the Fondamenta Fornace, down there behind the stores where the Bucintoro society keep their racing skiffs. The American poet Ezra Pound lived with his mistress a couple of doors away when I was growing up. An interesting man with some strange ideas. I believe he said something about how the days aren't full enough, the nights neither. While life slips by like a field mouse, never troubling the grass. All true. A lover of that devil Mussolini, but a poet nonetheless.' He seemed to be remembering something.

'Then we're looking for a *rio terà*, Monsignor?'

'I would imagine so, though I did not set these riddles. My life is very much embedded in this part of the city, you see. Cannaregio is another world. As is the other half of Dorsoduro. I deal with the books here, the lives of the people in our flock as much as they desire it. Local details, and even after all these years I remain an ignoramus at best. Still. The *rio terà* of the Foscarini. You know it?'

Of course. It was one of the main thoroughfares of central Dorsoduro. A broad street that ran from the side of the Accademia on the Grand Canal across to Zattere and the Giudecca Canal.

'There, I think, you should start to look. After that, the rest of your riddles, I'm afraid they mean nothing to me. Black marble, old bones, an eight-point star. No . . .' He held a finger upright in the air. 'Here I am lecturing you about puzzles and leaving out the most important detail. The hound of the Lord and the lily.' He gestured for us to return inside. 'Back the way we came, please.'

That spiral staircase was worse on the way down. I was glad to be on the ground again. Fabrizio Ricci was already out in the street, blinking at the fierce sun, when I got there.

'Now,' he said, 'if this were a crossword puzzle set by a knowledgeable person – and it seems to me it most certainly is – I would ask myself about the Latin. The hound of the Lord. *Domini canis.* Which is quite close, you see, to Dominicani. The order of the Dominicans. Known in some quarters as just that – the Hounds of the Lord – which is why you will sometimes see a dog of some sort in their iconography, though I believe there may be other fables behind that too. You have a map?'

I took it out. The line I'd drawn joining our three dots seemed to be pointing to this part of Dorsoduro even more firmly now.

'Here,' he said, placing a wrinkled finger on the church at

the foot of Foscarini, 'is the church most people know as the Gesuati, though strictly speaking it's Santa Maria del Rosario. The home of the Dominicans for four centuries or so, a rich place for art, the walls full of their saints, though there was a time when it was richer still, before the thieves came along. I suggest you start there. Then, if you strike gold as it were, turn your telescope further afield. I'm afraid I can think of nothing else in Venice that might aid your quest.'

He hesitated as we thanked him. Finished, I thought, but not quite done.

'It was my pleasure. A mental problem to keep me agile in my dotage,' he said with a shrug. A small man physically, but with the presence of one much larger. 'I hope that what you seek, if indeed you find it, turns out to be worthwhile. I'm too old to go looking for hidden treasure.' He held out his hand. 'Though as a Scottish writer I like to read once said, "Little do ye know your own blessedness; for to travel hopefully is a better thing than to arrive".' He took both our hands and held them together. 'You should know your own blessedness, the pair of you. I see it, even if you can't.'

Nine

All the Saints

Fabrizio Ricci was right, though it took us some time to realise. We wasted half an hour wandering round inside the Gesuati trying to find something that might tell us this was the place Lucia Scacchi meant. Lizzie was enthralled by the rococo Giambattista Tiepolo works, standing for a good five minutes to admire three female saints, one holding the baby Jesus in front of a haughty-looking Madonna. But as to dogs and lilies . . . no luck.

A couple of gelati from Nico's by the vaporetto stop were in order to fend off the scorching day. Perhaps it was the pistachio and the cassata, but only after that, almost in unison, did we realise we'd been chasing the wrong quarry.

The line in the story was clear: *where water once ran*.

That surely referred to something outside, since water couldn't run through a church. Except when we finally found the spot, we realised that wasn't quite right. The proof was there in that broad street leading from the waterfront back to the Accademia. In the side wall of the Gesuati stood the vault of an arch that must once have been a bridge over a channel running beneath the building, now filled in and bricked over. There at the top of the remaining portion was what we sought: a stone shield, a rather comical dog grinning at the top, paws over the edge, beneath lilies and a crown. A sign the Dominicans owned this part of Dorsoduro.

Lizzie beamed and punched my arm, and I said *ouch*. We were, of course, regarded with polite if blank expressions when we asked around about the mysterious Madame Corneille.

'This is hopeless,' she moaned as we stood in the searing midday sun.

'Nothing, in my experience, is ever hopeless.' I took out the map and filled in the fourth dot, drawing a line from San

Zaccaria to the Gesuati, the longest we had, across the Grand Canal. 'We do have more of the circle.'

'It's rather misshapen.'

'It would be hard for your mother to describe a perfect one. Perhaps she was in a hurry.'

'Makes sense. Next up . . . black marble and old bones.' She shuddered. 'I don't like suggesting this, but it could be Ca' Scacchi. There's black marble on the giant chessboard out back. We've seen the bones for ourselves. Down there in that awful place we found her.'

Like most newcomers to the city, her understanding of Venetian geography was limited. I knew that couldn't be right. I drew an imaginary line on the map from where we stood directly back to Ca' Scacchi on the other side of Dorsoduro, close to Salute.

'That wouldn't be a circle, misshapen or otherwise. And what about the eight–point star?'

She folded her arms, then tossed back her head, an attempt I thought to show me the rotten actor she once was. I applauded.

'Fine then, genius,' she said, mock sharply. 'What do *you* suggest?'

It seemed obvious that the next dot on the map would lie to the west, along the remaining length of Dorsoduro. The missing pages in the old guidebook suggested the same. 'A church, I think. Or a convent or monastery. Where else would have an ossuary?'

'You do like your big words.'

'Sorry. Would you prefer bone dump?'

She was looking at her watch. 'Seen one of those already, thanks. Actually, it's gone one o'clock. What I'd prefer is lunch.'

'You just had gelato!'

'Thinking requires sustenance.' She pulled a twenty-euro note out of her jeans. I didn't imagine there were many in there. 'Now let us feast.'

An outside table by the San Barnaba Canal at the Osteria ai Pugni, the place Luca had introduced me to when I first arrived as a raw newcomer, unfamiliar with the busy community of locals half hidden in the shadows away from the tourist trade.

I gave Lizzie her twenty back and asked her to go to the counter and pick whatever she wanted from the display. I was going to pay.

Then, when she was out of earshot, I called Luca. He was still in the office – alone, thankfully, which meant he could talk.

'I gather Fabrizio had some ideas,' he said.

'One. Very accurate. We have another dot, another line on the map. No idea where we go next.'

'Ah . . .'

'I need a list of every church in Dorsoduro. Every convent and monastery. Open or shut.'

I heard the clacking of a keyboard. 'That will be a long one. I'll send you what I can find. Anything else?'

The way he'd made an excuse that morning and vanished was suspect. 'You tell me.'

'I sometimes wish you weren't so very quick. Truth is, I can't be seen with you. Not till this is over. Canale is causing havoc everywhere. Complaining over Valentina's head to men who'll listen to him more than her. Whining to the council. To people who wield power over the likes of little me. Pulling strings. Making offers.'

'What kind of offers?'

'How would I know? He's not making them to me.'

'Does he really have that much influence any more?'

'He's got money. Lots. Sometimes that's enough. The fellow's set his heart on that palazzo. He wants the Borgia portrait too. He's accustomed to getting what he desires. Any way he can.'

'The bastard was having Lizzie followed. By some little thug I came to blows with.'

Luca positively squealed in shock.

'Valentina never said?'

'Good God. Are you hurt?'

If only he could have seen Lizzie in action. 'No, largely thanks to the formidable Miss Hawker. She's quite something when roused.'

'That I can imagine.'

Not a word of Canale's claim to be her father. Valentina would never have mentioned that outside her office, not without good reason. It seemed the man himself was keeping quiet about it too.

'Our mutual friend in the Carabinieri has warned the fellow off. If he keeps on harassing Lizzie, there'll be trouble.'

Silence.

'Luca . . .'

'Valentina's a clever woman, but even she has her limits. There's something bad here. Something I don't understand, but I can sense it. You want my advice?'

'Always.'

'Make an excuse. Step back. Tell your friend to return to London and leave this to the lawyers. Forget about Ca' Scacchi and Venice. That painting most of all. Whichever way this ends, she'll surely wind up in the money. Isn't that enough?'

I could see Lizzie at the counter. Chatting with one of the staff over the *cicchetti*. She was starting to look at home in Venice.

'No. It isn't.'

'Then what does she want?'

'The truth, I suspect.'

He grunted a low curse. 'People always say they want the truth. Then they hear it and—'

'She's owed. I think she wants to find out what it's like to be happy. I'm not sure she's known that in a long while. Perhaps ever.'

There was a buzz on my phone. An email. He never took long.

'I wish you well. Both of you. The list should be with you. From my personal email. Please don't use my work one for now. *Ciao.*'

Lizzie was back with two glasses of Piedicero red perched on a large plate of *polpette*, *baccalà* and prosciutto *crudo*.

'I like this spot,' she said, and took the seat opposite, by the canal. A white egret stood on the stern of a boat tied up on the other side, looking at us with a cranky expression as it stood on one long, skinny leg.

Luca's list must have come from an internal database. Some

of the churches I knew. One, San Barnaba, was just across the nearby square, now a tourist 'museum' full of wooden models of Leonardo da Vinci's creations. The Carmini was the other side of Campo Santa Margherita. San Pantalon, with its extraordinary ceiling, stood round the corner from the flat I called home and hadn't seen for a while. But a good half I'd never heard of, nor had any idea where to find them. Even what some – Le Eremite, the Pio Loco dei Catecumeni – actually were.

'You look worried,' Lizzie said, exploring an aubergine *polpetta*.

'More puzzled.' I showed her my phone.

'They did like their churches, didn't they? Why so many?'

'Different communities, different orders. There was a rivalry too. A need for one neighbourhood to show it was more devout – and more willing to display its wealth – than others.'

'We never went to church,' she said, mouth now half full of salt cod. 'Except for weddings and funerals, and he hated them. The churches here are different. All the paintings. It's like walking into the past. A museum with saints and a bit of God.' She ran her finger across the names of a few. Salute. Santa Maria della Carita. Spirito Santo. 'I know that last one's a vaporetto stop in the wrong direction. Salute too. And it says the other one's now the Accademia. We rule out what seems pointless, then I expect a personal guided tour of the rest.'

Fair enough.

'*Don't Look Now*.'

'At what?'

'The film. Donald Sutherland. Julie Christie. Have you never seen it?'

'Ah. Yes. Dad had the DVD and used to hide it. I sneaked a look when he was out. Must have been fifteen or so. Wow. The one with the scary red dwarf running round waving a knife. Also, you catch a glimpse of Ca' Scacchi in a couple of scenes when they're on a boat, which is probably why he kept it.' She seemed lost in some recollection.

'This place . . .' I pointed to an entry on Luca's list, San Nicolò dei Mendicoli, 'is probably where we should start. That was where a lot of it took place.'

She bit into some raw ham. 'It was a story, Arnold. It never took place at all.'

'A story . . .'

'Quite racy, if I recall correctly. Well, very, actually. Wasn't it?'

'Rings a faint bell,' I agreed.

With two glasses of good red wine and a decent offering of *cicchetti* to fuel us, we set off to investigate every last church this half of Dorsoduro was meant to possess. My plan to start at the furthest, San Nicolò, soon vanished when I realised how many stood along the way. Over the years I'd visited plenty of places of worship in Venice, mostly for specific works of art. This was different. We weren't looking at frescoes and canvases above the altars, on the ceilings, on the walls. We were seeking a slab of black marble, that eight-point star, and some dark history of bones.

With so many places to hunt them.

First, San Trovaso, next to one of the few remaining gondola yards, on the way to the Zattere. There I had to drag Lizzie away from a lurid Tintoretto, *The Temptation of St Anthony*, where a voluptuous horned demon, flames issuing from her thighs, loomed over her stricken victim as he reached out to Christ for salvation. Just her kind of thing, it appeared.

The nearby Le Eremite was firmly closed, with no sign it welcomed visitors at all.

The nave of the Carmini was filled with a service; a wedding, it turned out, something that again fascinated Lizzie, though our enquiries were politely rebuffed with puzzlement.

Then it was across the Ponte San Sebastiano, the border of a part of the city few tourists ever seemed to navigate. On the other side lay the furthest reach of Dorsoduro, unassuming, even ugly in parts, home to university colleges in former industrial buildings, a popular local market and what was once the ferry terminal. A place where one saw cars too, parked along the waterfront of San Basilio. But it was one of the oldest quarters of the city, so it was as full of ancient churches as any other: the abandoned shell of Santa Marta, now home to Biennale events; Santa Teresa, once a convent, now part of the architecture university campus; Angelo Raffaele, with its famous depiction of an angel appearing to Tobias; San Sebastiano, the parish church of Veronese, which he transformed into a gallery of his own work, canvases and frescoes everywhere, so many they overwhelmed me whenever I returned.

Finally, the place where, in my hopeful innocence, I'd suggested we might start: San Nicolò, no longer the dusty shell of Donald Sutherland's art restorer, now a gloomy, quiet church in a part of the city foreign voices were rarely heard.

We found no black marble, no bones, no star anywhere.

Not a word from Luca or Valentina Fabbri. At that moment we weren't just at the very edge of Venice. We were outside the maelstrom of emotions Ca' Scacchi and its hidden history had revealed, adventurous tourists exploring territory that was largely unknown.

'Is there even a café round here?' Lizzie asked inside San Nicolò's echoing nave. 'I could use a drink and a loo stop.'

'Modigliani,' I said.

She nudged me with her elbow and said not to be so cryptic. We'd had enough of that for one day.

'True,' I agreed.

We walked out into the late-afternoon sun, retraced our steps and returned to the Ponte San Sebastiano and the little Chinese café next to the plaque to the artist who'd once known Lizzie's distant relative, Annibale Scacchi. A man who'd seen that missing painting in the palazzo and made a humble attempt to re-create its sensual power.

Campari spritz for two and seats by the *rio* with a view over to the grey marble facade of San Sebastiano, Palladian after a fashion with its columns, triangular pediment and statues.

'At the risk of repeating myself, this really is hopeless.'

'If I hear that one more time, it will be.'

I was going through Luca's list again.

'Have we visited every last one?' Lizzie asked.

No, we hadn't. But some were closed, some I still struggled to think of as churches at all. Besides, as I pointed out, she was the one demanding a stop.

'Ideas then, please,' she said, which wasn't helpful, since I was somewhat distracted by the woman behind the bar humming an Oriental tune very loudly.

'Black marble,' I murmured. 'Old bones and an eight-point star. Not a clue.'

She tapped my arm. 'Saintly. You forgot saintly. It said—'

'Idiot.'

I pulled out the map and began to run my finger over it.

'I beg your pardon.'

'Me. Not you.'

Saintly.

Missing fine detail wasn't my style. But then I wasn't quite myself around Lizzie Hawker at all.

'Come,' I said, and took her arm.

It was a narrow passageway I'd never even noticed, though I often walked past on the way to the supermarket. Another side to the city lurking in the shadows.

'An explanation would be nice.'

'Saints.' A narrow canal opened ahead of us. 'This is the *rio* Ognissanti. All Saints. I knew that at the back of my head. Never connected it with a church. Stupid.'

The back street began to broaden. Before I knew it, we were in a wider lane next to the canal hidden away between the Zattere waterfront and the busy alley between San Sebastiano and San Barnaba. I was starting to wonder if I'd ever really know this odd city.

The place was up ahead, old ochre walls, two half-moon windows. It was only when we edged towards the canal that we could make out there was a campanile too. Another Dorsoduro place of worship, ten minutes from home, that I'd been unaware of.

Ognissanti was gloomy inside, most of the light coming from a small side room where a monk in a brown habit sat at a wooden desk, head bent over what looked like an ancient book, surrounded by small ornaments and leather-bound volumes. The sight of him gave me a shock. For a moment he looked just like the studious Augustine in Carpaccio's glorious painting of the saint in the Schiavoni *scuola* in Castello.

He looked up, peered at us with eyes that seemed to struggle with the sunlight, then said, 'Visitors? Please come in. I won't bite. No one does here.' We thanked him and stepped through. 'Two of you. A man and a woman. From your voices, English. I speak a little. There's a pamphlet by the door. Italian only, I'm afraid. A donation box too.'

The room was small, seemingly made entirely of carved wood and exotic veneers. Before we could say a word, the monk had launched into an explanation in a voice that was slow, precise and learned. We were in Ognissanti's most precious chamber, a sacristy filled with a detailed sermon on the nature of life, one told not in words but in the carvings and strange veneers around us. Wind and rain, monks, Christ's burial and resurrection and much else were all half hidden in the mysterious patterns. Lizzie, ever curious, set off to find them.

'We don't get many people here,' he said, still squinting my way. It occurred to me the man could barely see beyond his own hands. 'It's not the Frari. Or San Marco.'

'I think it's very beautiful,' Lizzie said, peering at one of the veneers. '*Molto bella.* Is that right?'

Walnut and fir, the man said, ten thousand pieces of wood in all. He laughed. 'What's happening to this place? More visitors in a day than we usually get in a week. Will you wish to know about the dead here too?'

Lizzie glanced at me. I said, 'We're not the first?'

'Did I not say? Quite why . . .'

'There's a kind of treasure hunt. A quest. A riddle, if you like. We were searching for a black marble stone and bones. An eight-pointed star. A . . .' She looked at me again. 'An ossuary I believe it's called in English.'

'Ah. That explains it.' He waved a bony hand at the nave. 'You can see it on your way out. A slab of marble decorated with those stars, as you say. Heaven knows how many of my brethren lie beneath it. As I've explained once today already, the monastery used to bury us here. That flagstone marks the spot. Napoleon put a stop to it when he said the dead had to be laid to rest on San Michele. Though why anyone should be interested when you can admire our wooden sacristy is beyond me. Read the pamphlet. It's all there.'

'Who was he?'

He pointed to his eyes. 'Who was who? Books I can still hope to read with a little luck. People . . . you're all shadows to me, I'm afraid.'

'Your earlier visitor. Foreign?' I asked. 'Italian? Local? If you had any kind of detail . . .'

'This sounds a strange hunt you're on.' It was only his sight that was defective. 'Why is it so important that you interrupt an old friar in a chapel only those of us who live nearby ever use?'

Lizzie took that question. 'We're looking for something. Something that was lost a long time ago. My mother . . . my late mother . . . she left directions of a kind. But they're not easy to understand. To be honest, I'm not sure my friend and I will find it at all.'

He rested his elbows on the desk, leaned back, closed his eyes, almost seemed to go to sleep for a moment. 'There were two of them. Only one spoke. He had a calm voice, a fellow sure of himself, I thought. The other kept quiet. All I heard was Italian. Local, I'd say. He asked much the same questions as you. Then the two of them left. One walked slowly. The other was younger, I suspect. What either of them looked like, who they really were . . . I do not know. I cannot. I've been visiting this place so long I can walk around it blind, which is just as well these days. Two rough shapes were all I saw. The hospital are doing their best for my poor eyesight, but it's a losing battle. I pray to the good saint from Siracusa for relief, of course. As one would. But in this bleak world of ours, she must have so many begging for her help.'

Lizzie came to join us. 'Did they say nothing else? Who they were? Why they were here?'

'Just a couple of friends out looking for curious aspects of churches few ever visit. Mysteries to solve. I remember he used those words.'

'He was looking for a black marble stone?'

'I'm half blind, not soft in the head. A black marble stone. An eight-pointed star. And something to do with bones. Which is special to this small place of worship, at least as far as I know. Nowhere else in Venice has it, surely.' He hesitated. 'I told him what I've told you, not that I heard a rattle in the donations box on the way out. Perhaps I left him disappointed.'

'Because?' I asked.

'Because he wanted to know if I'd seen anything here to do with a lady . . . I forget the name.'

'Madame Corneille?' Lizzie said before I had the chance.

He laughed, coughed, then laughed again and looked up with his milky eyes. 'You too! I thought it the oddest question. I've lived here all my life. I've never heard anyone of that name.' He pointed to his face. 'Besides, asking the likes of me if I've seen anything is rather pointless, don't you think? If the hospital or that nice lady saint of ours ever make these better, perhaps I'll take another look, but I doubt there's much out there.'

'No,' I agreed. 'I doubt it too.'

On the way out, after we paused for a moment by the black marble slab with its ornate stars, I dropped a couple of coins in the collection box. When we were back in bright sunlight, I took out the map, drew another dot, then a line joining Ognissanti to the Gesuati.

'It was stupid of me to say it was hopeless, wasn't it?' Lizzie said with a shrug. 'Sorry. I'm a bit of a downer sometimes.'

We had more than half of Lucia Scacchi's circle now. From this point in Dorsoduro, it had to describe a curve upwards to the two points in San Polo that matched the missing pages in that *sestiere*'s chapter. Then on to the final location, somewhere that would surely be in the direction of the starting point by Giovanni e Paolo. Then . . . empty space, the gap where, I hoped, our prize lay. It was impossible to judge where that might be from here.

'It was stupid of *me* to think Enzo Canale wouldn't get his hands on Lucia's riddle,' I retorted.

'Who passed it on? Valentina?'

'No. She wouldn't. The council. That lawyer. Someone in Ballarin's team. It could be anyone. If it was Canale here—'

'Then he's one step ahead of us.'

'Only if he's doing things in order, the way we are. I don't know. Neither do you. Best we focus on what we can control and change and fix. Not the unknowns.'

That made her smile. 'You are so very sensible. And logical. Everything I'm not.'

She always ran herself down. It must have come from the life she had before, little to do except look after an ailing father, never think of herself.

It felt like a long day. We'd started it in that halfway state, not strangers, not yet close. Thrown together, without Luca along for the ride, entertained by the intriguing Fabrizio Ricci, we'd walked miles trying to delve into the puzzles her mother had left us, talking constantly. Scoring if not a conclusive victory, then some kind of progress. Even if we now knew we weren't alone in seeking an answer to the riddle of Madame Corneille.

Lizzie wound her arm through mine as we began to walk back to San Sebastiano.

'I don't care what Canale thinks,' she said. 'We are going to find her like you said. We're going to join all those dots. I'll sort out that weird palazzo Mum left me. Tell that wicked old sod to bugger right off. Get things sorted.'

There was a noise, distant, low, the growl of thunder. Anvil clouds were building on the mainland again, bigger, closer than before, dark shades among the swollen balls of white.

'That was the loveliest day I can remember in a long time.' She squeezed my arm. 'I keep thinking about what that nice priest said.'

Robert Louis Stevenson. It had taken me a while to remember the source of the quotation. '"To travel hopefully is a better thing than to arrive"?'

She looked at me and shook her head. 'The other bit. About knowing your own blessedness. Whatever that means.'

Soon we were back in known territory, by the bridge. There was a restaurant I'd heard about, the Anzolo Raffaele, Venetian for the church our list called by its Italian name, after the angel Rafael. It had tables outside in fine weather, local food, the look of a place that hadn't changed much in years.

I was never much for eating out. Dining on your own seems a sad exercise, food and drink, nothing else, no company, no diversions, no discoveries.

But this was different. There was that rumble of thunder again. Still some way off. There was time.

A plate of fish and seafood antipasti shared across a table on the old cobblestones of Campo Anzolo Raffaele. A couple of glasses of Pinot Grigio. Only a small, quiet, happy family alongside us that balmy evening. A chorus of church bells from all directions – there seemed so many campanili within earshot – marked the hour: eight. Scarcely any other sound except for the footsteps of locals headed home across the square, the shriek of gulls chasing over the rooftops and the distant, breathy sound of singing from the convent by the bridge. A day quite unlike any I'd known in Venice was coming to a close.

Lizzie chose ravioli with ricotta, orange peel and saffron. I stuck to the classic *fegato*, twists of tender calves' liver over a swirl of soft, fresh polenta, white, the way it was meant to be in the Veneto. Bright August daylight was fading to a wash of rose, broken to the west by those towering clouds that spoke of storm. Every few minutes the waiter came and hovered around outside, not for us but to scan the sky. I knew this ritual. People like him could interpret the Venetian weather the way a ship's captain might read the ocean. If he thought the downpour was imminent, and with it not just rain but sudden violent squalls, he'd be ushering us inside and folding the umbrellas before they were blasted across the square. When the tempest was over – and usually it was a matter of minutes – he'd be back seeing if the way looked clear to bring us back to the tables.

But not yet. In the growing twilight of a temperate late-summer evening, an unpredictable breeze gusting round us, we ate, we drank and most of all we talked. Enzo Canale I avoided. Instead, at length, we discussed Lucia Scacchi's strange story. How it might have come about. What it really meant.

It seemed obvious to both of us that the tale must have been building inside her for a while, even if there was a roughness to it that suggested she'd finished it in a rush. And what was it really? A first-person account by a fictional Casanova in which he revealed himself for the man he truly was: a selfish, obsessive brute, interested primarily in sex and money and power. A beast seduced by a mysterious woman, Madame Corneille, whose identity was never revealed, even when he removed the mask from her corpse.

What was Lucia Scacchi trying to say? That she was Corneille herself, a fated instrument of justice, vengeance even? But for what? And who was the venal, bed-hopping Casanova? Chas Hawker? Enzo Canale? Another man altogether? Or just men in general?

Lizzie scraped the last pasta onto her fork and said, 'Men in general, I think.'

'Why?'

'Because . . .' She hesitated, and it was so obvious now that the note of resentment and hatred towards her mother had diminished during the day. 'Because she felt miserable. And alone. So miserable she'd take her own life. I don't recall much in detail. But in general – and I don't think this is from what Dad told me – I remember she never seemed comfortable. It wasn't the place. I think she liked that palazzo.' The last of the ravioli vanished. 'I always used to think it was me.'

'You know it wasn't really.'

She sipped at her wine and thought about that. 'Logically, I do. But families aren't built on logic. Not mine anyway. They're made of memories. False ones sometimes. Whispers. Suspicions. I don't really know what's true any more. That bastard Canale telling me he's my real father. Your friend in the Carabinieri saying Dad was a crook. A real crook. Not just a bit dodgy, which I'm sure he would have admitted to.'

The wind caught the umbrella over the table and started it flapping. The waiter was there in an instant telling us we needed to get inside. I hadn't noticed, but the sky had darkened in just a minute or two. Across the square, fat, reluctant raindrops were starting to fall as if uncertain of the pull of gravity.

The restaurant was dark and cramped and delightfully unadorned by modern trends, music, cool decor, the desperate search for some kind of artificial ambience. This was old Venice, a place the characters from that movie I'd mentioned might have visited in the 1970s. They found us a small table next to a piano that had been turned into a wine rack, and I ordered a couple of *dolci* to share: a semifreddo with lavender, rum baba and hazelnuts. Then coffee.

Outside, the rain arrived for real, beating against the windows with force. When it abated a little, I said, 'I feel your mother left us more than a riddle. A come-on to try to find that painting. There's a broader message as well. For whoever found it. You, perhaps. It was her way of saying: don't believe everything you hear. This is all more complicated than it appears. Unwind it and perhaps you'll see.'

Lizzie reached across the table and touched my hand. A gesture she seemed to like, and I wasn't complaining. 'You always want to say something kind and reassuring.'

'I mean it.'

'I'm sure you do.'

She held her napkin in front of my face and squinted at me. 'I have to ask what on earth you're doing.'

'Just checking.'

'For what?'

'Smiley eyes, of course. Don't you?'

'I've no idea what you're talking about.'

'Remember how we all had to wear those masks? The pandemic?'

'Who'd forget that?'

'I'd quite like to really. But . . . how do you tell what someone's like? When there's a mask in front of most of their face?'

All that was in the past. Or so I hoped.

'You can't.'

'You need to learn the trick. I did. While Dad was getting sicker, and I was having to go out and earn what I could. Doesn't work with everyone. Just some people. They have smiley eyes. You can tell over the mask. I still look. I only want to be near people with smiley eyes. You can trust them with your life.'

People were going to the door and peering outside. It seemed the storm was like so many in the lagoon, fierce and brief. And now vanishing as quickly as it came.

Lizzie held her napkin up to her own face. Just her eyes there, bright, smart, watching me.

'Well?'

'I think . . . I think they're learning to smile.'

She dropped the napkin on the table and grinned. 'A clever and diplomatic answer.'

But an honest one. I paid the bill, and we stood on the patio for a moment. Night had fallen with the suddenness it always did at the height of summer. The sparse street lights in this out-of-the-way corner looked like stars on the sheen of the black cobbles. The smell of petrichor, the unique perfume that rain leaches out of stone, was everywhere, an invisible cloud, fresh and delightful after the heat of the day.

Twenty-five minutes it took us to get back to Ca' Scacchi, walking along the Zattere waterfront, expecting the heavens to open any minute. But they didn't and still we barely spoke. I was exhausted, Lizzie too probably, but she was taking in the view I knew so well: the night traffic on the Giudecca Canal, the lights of the bars and restaurants on the other side, the basilicas of Redentore and Zitelle, then the campanile of San Giorgio Maggiore, a mirror image of the tower across the water out of sight in San Marco.

If we were followed, it was done well. I kept looking, trying not to let her see, which was probably pointless. Lizzie Hawker didn't miss much at all.

By the time we got home, the rain was starting again. Drops began falling through the flimsy glass roof over the kitchen. We got buckets and saucepans and put them where the water was pouring in.

'I never wanted to be domesticated,' she said with a yawn when it was done. 'I never thought anything would ever domesticate me.'

'I doubt it will. Now . . . may I return to my book?'

She put a hand out to stop me. 'Lucrezia Borgia?'

'Not halfway through.'

'Do you feel like reading?'

An awkward question. I pulled out the old guidebook from my bag. 'There's this as well.'

She stepped closer. We were pretty much the same height. I couldn't avoid her eyes.

'Not the question I asked, Arnold.'

'Yes. I think there's more to learn.'

Silence. I didn't know if it was the right answer. For me. For both of us.

'Sleep well,' she said, and headed off up the stairs.

I tried to get into the biography of Lucrezia first. Then Arturo Machiavelli's curious guidebook. Neither worked. I was tired, confused, by what we'd learned, by my fears for Lizzie and the mysterious presence of someone seemingly on the same treasure hunt, equipped with the same puzzles, chasing the same goal.

Enzo Canale? He seemed to have his tentacles in everything, from the police to the local state and its employees. Or perhaps we had more than one rival in the field.

That wasn't all that worried me. There was Lizzie herself, the way we'd changed in that long, strange, deeply enjoyable day. The words of Fabrizio Ricci echoing in her mind, in mine too.

You should know your own blessedness, the pair of you. I see it, even if you can't.

I gave up on Lucrezia Borgia and the torn pages of the guide-book, lay back on the double bed and looked at the empty panel on the opposite wall, just visible in the lights from the Grand Canal.

What had really happened here? In this palazzo? In this room, when the naked figure of the daughter of a pope was revealed from her hiding place on that wall opposite?

Were Luca and his friend Monsignor Fabrizio Ricci right in hinting that sometimes it was better to travel than to reach your destination? That the truth might destroy as much as it would reveal?

I didn't know. I couldn't. All I was sure of was that the woman who lay in bed above me in the room she'd occupied as a damaged child was not going to give up on the chase. If Lizzie wouldn't, nor could I.

I reached for the biography again and gazed at that beautiful face on the cover: a woman younger than Lizzie, hair golden not chestnut, left breast bared, serious dark eyes darting sideways at the beholder as if daring them to imagine what she might be like in the flesh.

Only a man could have painted that image, only a man must have commissioned it.

What would she really look like in that lost painting we sought? And that glass case with her hair: how much gold would be left in those tantalising locks stolen by a famed English poet and aristocrat after five centuries?

I ached to know. Sometimes it's not the things you seek that hurt you. It's the idea of them. Their tantalising absence from your life.

Ten

A Winged Fury and a Wooden Spy

Just after seven the next morning, I was out of the bathroom, hearing Lizzie on the move upstairs, when my phone buzzed. Not Valentina or Luca as I might have expected. It was a message from that blasted reporter who'd tried to attract our attention when we first went into Ca' Scacchi.

Alf, the name he preferred, was an affectation of commonness that convinced none who knew him at all. Because in reality he was, and always would be, the Right Honourable Gervaise Alfonso Lascelles.

A figure of both fun and notoriety among the expat community, he was a foppish man of fifty or so, portly, usually in an old-fashioned suit that looked like a cast-off bought by a late uncle in Savile Row in the 1970s. The expression on his largely featureless face was as blank as his smile, that of an upper-class buffoon bemused by the world, a trick he used to good effect, since it meant the unwary failed to take him seriously. An offshoot of an ancient and now impoverished Hampshire family, Lascelles was an old Etonian who, on his own proud admission, had abandoned Oxford after two years of rampant dissipation, then, through the inevitable connections, crawled his way onto one of the rabid tabloids. There, he worked as a diary reporter, mainly covering the London 'social scene' – mostly debutantes and Z-list media folk – sliding around the capital from one glitzy shindig to the next. Somewhere along the way, one of his colleagues taught him the trick of hacking voicemail, only for Lascelles to be found out during what he termed 'the great media witch hunt', prosecuted and sent to jail.

The loyalty of rabid tabloids proved absent when, after a mere five months, he emerged blinking into the sunlight from the relative luxury of open prison. But Lascelles' grandmother had been born in Rome before moving to London at the age of five. This gave the man the Italian passport he so craved and an excuse to escape a vengeful England and move to a rented flat in Cannaregio.

He tried his hand at writing the inevitable thriller, with no luck, before falling back on the equally perilous career of freelance journalism. A few decent foreign reporters were making an honest if precarious living doing the same thing. I'd met several and had no problem with them. Alf Lascelles, in spite of his fey appearance, was quite different, the sort of hack who decided what kind of story would sell then set out to try to find some facts to support it. I'd encountered him in the messy aftermath of Duke Godolphin's death, when he was desperate to turn what was already a nasty tragedy into a sordid tale of sex and deception. Which in part it was, though that was no business of a prurient public, let alone him.

There'd also been an outcry when he kept selling the English papers stories about Venice continuing to flood in spite of the MOSE barrier, which was meant to keep the city safe, always with pictures of the Piazza San Marco under water. What he never mentioned in any of his coverage was the plain fact, which everyone understood, that San Marco would still flood, even with MOSE, since it was one of the lowest areas of the city and beyond absolute protection. Bad as that was, MOSE had still saved most of Venice from the disastrous inundations of previous years, not that Lascelles ever mentioned this.

Lascelles knew his market among the Europe-hating English tabloids. He fed them a steady stream of tales about bans on wheeled suitcases, restaurant rip-offs, ticket barriers and entry fees, strikes and scandals among the stars visiting for the annual film festival, all read with astonishment by locals, who knew they were either gross exaggerations or, on occasion, plain invention, never corrected.

When cornered, he would always put on that amiable, guilty smile of his and say simply, 'A fellow's got to earn his gin, dear boy.'

The last thing the players in the Godolphin drama had needed was Lascelles, with his weasel smile and persistent, intrusive manner, digging up more dirt. The idea he might get his teeth into Lizzie was deeply alarming. I'd also learned that the biggest mistake in dealing with the man was to ignore him. That only made the hack in him more persistent and obstinate than ever.

'Arnold,' he said with a cheery laugh when I called. 'How *are* you doing, old cock?'

'Fine but busy. What do you want?'

'Buffing up all those dusty records in the Archives, eh? I still think there's more to tell about old Duke Godolphin and his lady friends. Why won't you talk? The man's long in the ground, and his wife, I gather, has, as they say, moved on. More than once if the stories I read are right. A merry widow indeed.'

'Old hat, Alf. No one cares any more.'

'I'll be the judge of that. Perhaps something new, then . . .'

'I'm really strapped for time. Honestly.'

A pause. 'Ah. It's going to be like that. Shame. I'd hoped for a little cooperation.'

'About?'

'The dead woman in the fancy palazzo, of course. Lucia Scacchi. Quite the beauty from what I've seen. An aristocrat too. Perfect. London weren't that interested in more than a para or two, not to begin with. I told them, there's mileage in this yet. What with her being married to Chas Hawker. Impresario my foot. He was a crooked bloodsucker ripping off people with genuine talent. A failed movie mogul. A deadbeat who wound up back where he came from, scraping a living in glorious East Ham. Ugh . . .'

I could imagine his theatrical shudder. Lascelles had been doing his homework.

'You think?'

'I do. Then he finally shuffles off his mortal coil, and a few months later his wife shows up as a pile of bones in their old back yard. I understand you're not an imaginative kind of chap. All the same . . .'

'Wait—'

'And now you're chaperoning their lovely daughter round town, dodging lawyers, popping into the Carabinieri office in San Zaccaria.' He chuckled. 'Falling out with Enzo Canale.

That's not a smart thing to do, is it? Enzo's a sound fellow mostly. Kind of royalty round here in some circles. A decent, kindly, generous man when he feels like it. When I was a little short of resources a while back, he put me on a retainer doing public relations for his hotels. Press releases. Glad-handing visitors of a certain status.'

'Not the hoi polloi then? Do you look down on the likes of us?'

His voice fell a tone or two and lost what little charm it possessed. 'Don't try and get clever with me, mate. You ought to know better.'

'Last chance. What do you want?'

'Can't believe you keep asking. What I always want. The story. A belter. One I can flog everywhere. Or if it's big enough – and I think it's going to be – pitch as an exclusive to one of my old tabloid chums back home. Then sell it all again to everyone else when the bomb goes off.'

'There is no bomb.'

He laughed out loud. 'Oh, but there is. A big one. How big I don't quite know. But from what I've heard, it's going to be a cracker. A priceless painting missing for thirty-odd years. Clues left by a dead woman in some strange story she wrote about Casanova. And – here's the luscious thought – the exquisite Lucrezia Borgia in the altogether. No wonder you're all chasing her.'

Damn, I thought. Was there anything he – and by implication Canale – didn't know?

'Where did you get all this?'

'A reporter never reveals his sources, does he? Like I told you, this story's going to break whether you like it or not. When that happens, it's mine. I'll see your lady friend comes out of it well. There may even be a bit of money if she's willing to play. But I get her all to myself. I want pictures, proper ones, done in a studio, not the tasteless glam stuff she did for her old man back when she was young. Oh yes, I found that too. We'll get her some decent clothes this time round. Can't have a future contessa looking like a Page Three tart.'

Still I said nothing.

'A response would be appreciated, Arnold.'

'I'm struggling to formulate one that doesn't include the phrase "fuck off". No. Can't manage it.'

He paused for a second. 'I'll forget I heard that. The question people in your situation need to consider is this. What do you reckon will work out best in the end? A story with me on your side? Or me on your back?'

Lizzie was at the door, waiting. Blue shirt, blue jeans, hair wet. She looked bewildered.

I cut the call without another word.

'What was that?'

'Nothing you need worry about.'

'I distinctly heard you swear.'

'It happens.'

'First time for me.'

She came and picked up the biography of Lucrezia lying on the crumpled sheets, looked at the cover, the fetching portrait of a woman long dead. 'I did a little reading on my phone last night. Lucrezia wasn't the monster they painted at all, was she?'

'No. Her father. Her brother. But not her. She was no shrinking violet, but I think she was a victim too. Twice over. Once in life. Once when she was dead and the focal point for the imaginations of her family's enemies and a good few dubiously creative authors over the years.'

'Maybe we should let her be. Let old bones lie.'

I'd wondered if she was thinking about her mother. Not that I wanted to intrude on the very private grief there.

'Don't think Enzo Canale feels that way, does he? He's not going to let anything lie.'

'True.'

'Don't give up, Lizzie. Not now. When we're finally getting somewhere.'

'I wasn't planning to give up. Just checking you're still in the game. So where next?'

My phone buzzed again, and just then I was glad of the interruption.

This time it was Valentina Fabbri. A message from her was odd. She usually preferred to call.

There are developments. I want her in my office immediately. It's essential. You may come if she wishes.

'Later.' I showed her the phone. 'Valentina wants to see you.'

That didn't go down well. 'Oh. Your friend. Why?'

I shrugged. 'You know as much as I do. But it sounds important.'

'To her? Or to me?'

'Lizzie—'

'I want a day off from the Carabinieri. I want breakfast. A good cup of coffee. After that, I want to find . . . What is it?' She checked her phone. 'Some chained and sightless Fury. Any ideas?'

'It's not a good idea to ignore Valentina Fabbri.'

'Oh dear. Shall we go?'

'Out of interest, what exactly is the nothing I needn't worry about?' Lizzie asked as we walked past the Accademia. I should have known she wouldn't let my throwaway comment about Lascelles go unremarked. 'You're a terrible liar. I admire that in a man. On the rare occasion I get the opportunity.'

The weather was hot, gusty, with clouds flitting across a light blue sky that looked as if it had set itself to complement the darker tone of the lagoon.

'Very good.'

'I thought so too. Where are we going?'

I told her we needed two things: excellent coffee and some fancy pastries. We were headed for a little place I knew, another find of Luca Volpetti's, the Pasticceria Toletta, a tiny bakery and coffee shop in the passageway between San Trovaso and San Barnaba.

'No arguing there,' she agreed. 'Except it's four things. Our sightless Fury and you telling me who you were swearing at.'

There was no avoiding it, so I gave her an abbreviated biography of the Right Honourable Gervaise Alfonso Lascelles, the aristocratic hack who was now, it seemed, on her case. Or, perhaps, ours. Very likely at the behest of Canale.

'What a bunch of names. He's a toff?'

'He's a chameleon. Whatever he thinks people want him to

be. I gather he comes out with the most awful rubbish about history and art when he gets the chance to spout off to a bunch of tourists he can fool into thinking he's an expert. But people get taken in. He prefers to be called Alf these days, which is, I think, a way of appearing a commoner without actually being common.'

She sniffed as we crossed the San Trovaso bridge. 'Reporters. My dad had plenty of them on his books.'

'I'm sorry?'

'On his books. Paid for. Money sometimes. Girls. Dope. Trips to Miami to see their favourite band. I was dealing with them back when I was a teenager and he was trying to get me parts. Did photo shoots.'

I grimaced. 'Lascelles said. It seems he's been doing some research.'

She slapped my arm. 'It was all tasteful. Dad sat in on them.'

'I can't see you acting. Can't see you being anyone but yourself.'

'The point about acting is you don't see it, silly. Or so I was told. Toffs or scumbags, Dad taught me how to deal with hacks. You get pally with them when they're useful, and ignore them when they've nothing to offer but trouble. Oh . . .' she waved a finger in my face, 'and never, ever think they're your friends.'

That, I felt, wasn't going to be an issue with Lascelles.

'I'm not afraid of Enzo Canale. Why would I be bothered about some two-bit reporter he's set on my tail? More importantly, where the hell is my breakfast?'

Just around the corner. The place was empty, the counter stacked with so many different kinds of pastry Lizzie's eyes lit up with delight. I stood back and let her ask what they all were, translating as needed. In the end, it was something with almonds and marzipan for her, and a chocolate *cornetto* for me, two macchiatos to complete the order. Then we went outside and grabbed a small table and two seats by the door.

'"In wood the secret fellow sits, by chained and sightless Fury",' she recited as she pulled apart her pastry. 'Was your Carabinieri friend maybe calling us in to offer help on that?'

Probably not, I told her.

'That's a shame.'

I brought out the map. The circle I'd drawn around our five confirmed locations was a malformed one, more an oval, and now ran a good one hundred and eighty degrees from Giovanni e Paolo, through Castello, across the Grand Canal to the Gesuati then Ognissanti. After that, it ought to curve upwards to two points in San Polo yet to be determined, then on to the final destination, the one site in Cannaregio with a missing page. Or so the guidebook suggested. Then – and this was beginning to worry me more than anything – the gap.

The next stop might be quite close to my home near San Pantalon and the great Frari church itself. But where?

It was still early. I imagined Luca Volpetti would probably be having breakfast in Adagio, one of his favourite cafés near the Archives. The women there joshed with him constantly, the coffee was good, the pastries and, for lunch, the *cicchetti* too.

I was thinking of calling him when there was a tap on my shoulder. Luca was going to be late for work, which was quite unlike him. Just as it was unusual to see the way he stayed hidden in the shadows of the café awning, a floppy straw hat and a pair of black sunglasses obscuring his face as he glanced around, looking to see if we were being watched.

Lizzie caught the unspoken exchange between the two of us and said she was going inside. Moments later, she was back with a coffee and a *cornetto* for Luca.

'I'll be at the counter when you need me,' she said.

'I wondered if we might be followed. Hope it was only you.'

He looked out of sorts, guilty. 'I'm sorry. None of this is of my choosing.'

'You don't need to apologise. I know you're doing what you can.'

He shook his head. 'There are things happening I don't begin to understand. It's not my boss. Everything's coming from the top. How's the quest going?'

'The fifth place, the one with the black marble, was a church I'd never heard of, let alone seen, called Ognissanti.'

He was silent.

'Enzo Canale has Lucia Scacchi's story,' I went on. 'Everything. The riddles. So has that hack Lascelles.'

'Oh my God. Not him as well.'

'He works for Canale, it seems. I think the two of them may have been in Ognissanti already. Someone got there before us. Looking for the same thing. Asking about Corneille.' It was so unlike Luca to stay quiet when interesting questions were raised. I thought about the friar at the desk, looking like the learned Augustine. What he'd said, the vague but intriguing details he'd given. 'Unless that was Fabrizio Ricci and you.'

He grunted something, then screwed up his eyes. It was just a guess, a stab in the dark. I felt guilty, not that it was merited. Luca remained a good friend. Still, it was clear already that this whole affair had placed him in an awkward position. Siding with Valentina Fabbri when it came to relocating a priceless piece of Italy's heritage. And then, from quarters I could only guess at, finding himself under intense pressure to steer clear of Ca' Scacchi and the search for the Borgia portrait altogether. To leave that to us and, in all probability, whoever Canale had working for him.

'Fabrizio came up with it after you left,' he said, tearing at the *cornetto*. 'He was worried about the two of you. He called and asked what we ought to do. I didn't dare tell you from the office. They'd have known.' He shrugged. 'We took a look during my lunch break. I went round to your place to tell you last night, but there didn't seem to be anyone in. So . . .' He blushed. 'I wondered if perhaps you were staying elsewhere. If you two were walking out together. And here we are.'

This was good news anyway. It perhaps meant Canale was one step behind us.

'Thanks. I understand.'

'Do you? That wicked bastard's got everyone by the balls. He says if the future of Ca' Scacchi remains unresolved, the city should step in, force its purchase, sell the place to him and then he'll lease it back to us. For a museum. For whatever we want. All at a peppercorn rent.'

'A bribe, then.'

He muttered a low curse. 'On paper, a generous and charitable offer. Ballarin's against it. There'd be precious little to stop Canale reneging on the deal and keeping the place for himself. Everyone knows that. But . . .' he rubbed his fingers together, 'money talks. A free mansion for the city on the Grand Canal? No real cost to us? Perhaps even a modest profit? All above board. No question of corruption. No problem with the paperwork. A gift.'

Lizzie was watching us from inside. Luca glanced in her direction.

'Your friend could get a lot of money if she accepts she's lost and takes what's on offer. All she needs to do is get her mother's death certificate and sort the probate. Even on a compulsory purchase from the public purse, you've got to be talking . . . I don't know, a good few million.'

'I thought I'd made this clear. It's not about the money. She needs to know what happened. She needs to get things clear in her head about her family.' It came out of the blue, a sudden epiphany. 'Also, we have to find that painting. If we do . . . if we recover a precious piece of Italian art everyone assumed was lost, there's no way the council and Canale can come for her, is there? How would that look? An impoverished young woman puts her dead parents behind her and finds the masterpiece one of them tried to hide. I'd even offer that to Alf Lascelles. He'd make a story of it. Money's one thing in this city, I'm sure. But so are politics. So is prestige. So is something that might make people look like graceless, churlish jerks.'

Luca Volpetti patted my back, then looked at his watch. 'You are getting to know us.'

'After Ognissanti,' I added, 'we're lost. I haven't a clue about this sightless Fury. Not a one.'

Luca looked astonished. 'Are you sure?'

'Very.'

'One problem of ours is that on occasion there's just too much to look at. As a result, we tend to focus on the obvious and let the subtle and the arcane pass us by. Especially when the object we seek is on our very doorstep. A pity, since the subtle and the arcane are often far more interesting.'

I usually told him off when he started being pompous, but not now.

'Please don't be so obscure. My head hurts quite enough already.'

Luca pointed up the alley towards San Barnaba. 'Ten minutes that way. Spitting distance from your home. Good Lord, Arnold. That was the only clue I got straight off. Well, after a bit.'

He passed me a pamphlet. 'As to the traitor, the Dolphin, the beautiful eyes . . .' He tipped the brim of his straw hat and smiled at Lizzie inside the pasticceria. 'There, I'm afraid you're truly on your own, along with Madame Corneille.'

'Tell me the story then,' Lizzie said as we stood outside the Scuola Grande di San Rocco, midway between my San Pantalon flat and the Frari. There was another half-hour to kill before the place opened. I had time. 'And also tell me why it's called a squalor.'

'*Scuola* means "school".'

'Doesn't look like a school.'

'That's because it isn't one.'

A sharp look. 'Venice could drive me nuts. And the people.'

I did my best to explain, as concisely as possible, that in this very local context, a *scuola* was the home of a historic lay brotherhood that carried out devotional and charitable acts, offered commissions for artists, and food and medicine for the poor. San Rocco — St Roch in his native France — was particularly popular because he was traditionally invoked for protection against the plague, a scourge Venice knew only too well.

'There were five or so six grand *scuole*, if I recall correctly. The Carità, which is now the Accademia gallery. San Marco, which is part of the hospital we've visited quite enough already. Carmini and San Giovanni Evangelista are a few minutes away. The others I forget. Along with a few hundred minor *scuole* run by the less well-off.'

She sniffed. 'You're never going to make a tour guide, you know.'

'I've no wish to be one, thank you very much. That's a job for a local.'

'A story, Arnold. All these places Mum mentioned seem to

have a story. Maybe that's important. I don't know.' People were turning up, visitors with cameras and guidebooks in their hands. Like us, waiting for the *scuola* to open. 'That's what they've come for too.'

Always best to show as well as tell in my experience. Especially with someone like Lizzie Hawker.

'Come on,' I said, and we walked to the church of San Rocco opposite the *scuola*. That was empty – almost everyone came for the place across the way. I led her to the painting I had in mind and said, 'Tintoretto. You've heard of him.' She couldn't stop looking at the huge, long canvas on the side wall. 'Although really he's called Jacopo Robusti – Tintoretto comes from the fact his father was a dyer of fabric. So "Tintoretto" means "little dyer". This was one of his early works when he joined the *scuola*.'

San Rocco healing the sick, an extraordinary scene, light and shade, the saint, complete with golden halo, administering to plague victims, their blisters, their wounds, their pain, in an almost too realistic medieval hospital. Lizzie seemed drawn to images of death and suffering. Many people are, I imagine, which is why artists choose those subjects so often.

'The story . . .' I began.

The young Tintoretto painted the work in 1549, a tribute to the saint interred in the high altar, attracting a growing number of pilgrims who saw their journey as a votive ritual against the plague. The result was so admired, he entered a competition with three other artists for a rich commission, the painting of the walls and ceilings of the great *scuola* across the way. Desperate for the work, on decision day Tintoretto secretly produced not the sketch that was asked for, but a finished canvas, and somehow managed to instal it in secret in the room where the organisation's leaders met.

'This fait accompli won him the commission as the principal artist for the entire *scuola*.'

'Sneaky,' she said.

'His rivals certainly thought so.' I checked my watch. 'Time for you to see.'

The small queue of visitors waiting for the place to open

was gone. We went inside, lingered briefly on the gloomy ground floor, then ascended the broad and grandiose staircase. She was wide-eyed by the time we stepped into the vast Chapter Room, but no stopping there. I marched her straight through to the Sala dell'Albergo. Tintoretto's *St Roch in Glory*, the work that won him the commission, above us in the ceiling. But she didn't look at that when I mentioned it. All she could manage was what most of us did when we walked into that room: stare at the vast, dramatic *Crucifixion* on the opposite wall, Christ high on the cross, soldiers raising the two thieves who were to die with him, the grieving Mary, spectators, some horrified, some entertained, a landscape full of activity and life amidst death.

'It could be a movie,' Lizzie whispered.

'I suppose back then it was. But where's the sightless Fury?'

'So many paintings . . .'

As Luca Volpetti said, sometimes there was too much to see. One missed the important details.

'Wood,' I said, and walked back into the main hall. True, there were paintings everywhere, the walls, the ceiling; thirty-three in all, Luca's leaflet said, all Tintoretto, with assistants, among them the son, Domenico, we'd met already. But the room was also lined with panels in dark walnut, only one of which I'd given much attention to in all this magnificence. I took Lizzie to see it: an old man with a beard, a tortured expression on his face, paintbrushes in a pot in front of him.

'Tintoretto,' I explained. 'From life. An allegory of painting. Perhaps he was so exhausted . . .'

She was gone, marching a few yards along. And there it was. Another figure in agony, a winged angel, blindfolded, fury on his face. Next to him the shelves of an exquisitely carved bookcase, the volumes so real you felt you could reach out and take one to read or annotate with the quill in an inkpot set in the middle. On the other side, a figure hiding himself inside a billowing cloak and beneath a floppy hat, a spy with natty black boots.

'The secret fellow is a bit overdramatic,' Lizzie said. 'The most obvious spy I've ever seen. I can't believe you never noticed all this before.'

I turned and did a three-sixty on my heels, looking at the ceiling, the walls, the entrance to the Sala dell'Albergo with its cinematic *Crucifixion*.

'Fine,' she conceded. 'But we have riddle six cracked, don't we? The map . . .'

I took it out and showed her where to draw the dot for San Rocco. The rough circle was now around three quarters complete. One more stop in San Polo, then a last one across the Grand Canal, which would reveal the loop back to the Scuola Grande di San Marco.

'Arnold. Let's face it. There's no point in keeping asking about this Corneille thing, is there?'

'I don't think so. Your mother did make it clear there were no shortcuts. Quite why . . .'

'Thank goodness I've got you.'

And Luca, I thought. Fabrizio Ricci, too. We weren't alone in this, even if it felt that way at times. The trouble was, it seemed they were genuinely lost about where we might go after San Rocco. As was I.

'Ideas?' Lizzie asked.

'We could always call Valentina Fabbri and find out why she wanted to see you. She's not a woman to turn down.'

'And I'm not a woman to be ordered around either. The cops can wait.'

There had to be some kind of logic to Lucia Scacchi's thinking. This wasn't a random list of obscure places in Venice. A taxidermy dwarf in an anatomy museum even Luca hadn't heard of. A hidden passageway supposed to protect against the plague. Dead statesmen in a crypt. The Dominican hounds of the Lord and an ossuary named after all the saints. Now a blindfolded Fury and a spy who would not show his face.

What was she trying to say? Something about heartless cruelty and a blatant disregard for life. But also, I thought, a need for salvation, a redemptive act. A countervailing balance of kindness to set a crooked world right. Truth against lies. Compassion against callousness.

Perhaps. First we faced another mystery.

Traitor, not a traitor, nor painter, homeless by the Dolphin and the Anchor. Loc. Col. Bai. The. MCCCX.

Somewhere between here and the Grand Canal lay the penultimate discovery. I needed books, faster broadband, my laptop. More than anything, I craved a fresh eye on all the material I'd been struggling with, trying to decode the next stop along the way.

Eleven

The Column of Infamy

Lizzie was the second woman to walk through the door of my one-bedroom home near San Pantalon, the first being my ex-con cleaner, Chiara. Thanks to her, when we arrived, it was far too organised and spotless to be classed as a bachelor flat. Eleanor had found the place, Eleanor had negotiated the sale. Weeks before we were due to leave for Italy, my ever-active wife had ordered the furnishings, arranged for the power and gas to be turned on, and dealt with a welter of local bureaucracy that would have been quite beyond me.

Then, very suddenly, she collapsed and died, with a heart ailment she'd hidden from me entirely. Confused, racked by grief and entirely lacking any sense of direction, I'd simply followed the path she'd set, moving into a home she'd created but would never set foot in when it was ours.

The place was modest, a former shop worker's flat, on the ground floor of a cul-de-sac that rose just enough to keep the floor an inch or two above the worst *acqua alta* the city had known in recent years. Thanks to MOSE, that threat now seemed gone. The neighbours were local, only one rented tourist property in the entire street, novel for the city these days. From time to time I'd hear a little noise from revellers exiting the nearby bars and barging their way across the bridge. But it never lasted long. The narrow *rio* at the back was used by canal traffic night and day, even by a delivery boat at three in the morning on occasion. The previous owner had installed a floor-length glass door by the water side, meaning I could step out and sit on a tiny jetty if I was so minded (which I never was, too worried about tripping and falling in). Overcautious, Eleanor would have said, since she'd have lugged a deckchair out there and chattered with the pensioners who occasionally rowed past with bottles of wine and lunch boxes amidships.

And now I had Lizzie Hawker wandering around, checking out the bedroom, the bathroom, the tiny kitchen and the front room I used mostly as a study.

'If I'd known you were coming, I'd have bought flowers,' I said, for want of anything better.

'Bit of a waste given you're round my place for the duration.' She picked up an ancient photo I kept on my desk. Eleanor and me outside the old Historical Manuscripts Commission building in Chancery Lane, before we were merged into the National Archives and moved to Kew. It was the day of our registry office marriage, a return to work for a small reception, a logical step since most of our friends were fellow employees too. There was confetti all over our shoulders. She wore a smart two-piece suit; I was in what I thought of as a green tweed sports coat and rather creased navy slacks that even with the faded colour of an old picture very obviously clashed.

'You look very happy,' said Lizzie.

'We were.'

She pointed at the photo. 'I like her smile. She looks a handful.'

'My wife was never in need of assertiveness training, that's for sure.'

'Thirty-four and a bit years . . .'

'A long time.'

'You don't look *that* much older.'

'Well, I am.' I gestured at the bookshelf dedicated to my reference works on Venice. Norwich, Morris, Ruskin, Lane, and an excellent translation into English of Tiziano Scarpa's *Venezia è un pesce – Venice is a Fish*. 'Can we get to work?'

She pulled up a stool and gestured for me to take the office chair at the desk. 'You've read all these, time and time again, haven't you?'

'True.'

'And?'

'Nothing stands out, to be honest.'

'You don't really expect me to go through them all now, do you? That one alone . . .' she pointed to the Norwich, 'is absolutely huge.'

'True again. But—'

She grabbed my laptop. 'It's the third decade of the twenty-first century. If we seek answers, we seek them here.'

The browser was open already. She typed 'Corneille Venice' into the search bar.

'Luca's been through all that, Lizzie. A lot more sources than Google. Nothing.'

She pushed the laptop away. 'I give up. Is anything in this city simple? Straightforward?'

Yes, I thought. Most things, in truth. Provided you were able to see them correctly, through the distorted prism the city demanded. We were coming at Lucia Scacchi's riddles from the wrong direction. As outsiders, trapped in the logic of foreigners. It was no coincidence that the solutions only appeared courtesy of Venetians – an attendant at Giovanni e Paolo, Ugo Abate, Valentina herself, Fabrizio Ricci . . . and Luca Volpetti by stealth.

'When in doubt,' I suggested, 'coffee never goes amiss. There's a place round the corner.'

'Do they do ideas?'

'No. But the pastries are excellent. Lots of them. And some savoury things too.'

'Later.' Lizzie tapped at the laptop again. 'What about the Dolphin and Anchor? It sounds like a pub. Did you look it up?'

'There's no pub in Venice called the Dolphin and Anchor. Believe me.'

More taps. 'But you didn't look it up? Great name for a boozer.'

'No. I—'

'Can't even pronounce this, Arnold. You?'

She turned the laptop round and showed me the page she'd somehow arrived at. It was the last thing I'd expected to see. The front cover of a very old book.

'Oh. The *Hypnerotomachia Poliphili*.'

'That's a mouthful for Waterstones.'

I'd heard of the work. Luca had mentioned it once, wondering if he could find a copy for an exhibition he was working on. It was a bizarre and complex love story from the very end of the fifteenth century, set in a dream world and illustrated by woodcuts that would later inspire the likes of Aubrey Beardsley. Full of arcane references written in a mix of Latin and Italian, it was not my cup of tea and never would be.

'Look,' said Lizzie. 'It says the dolphin and anchor was a graphical device used to represent the saying "*Festina lente*", meaning "make haste slowly". Not sure how that works, but . . .'

'The anchor represents the slow and steadfast. The dolphin speed. Obvious, isn't it?'

'If you say so. What do you make of it?'

'Look up Aldus Manutius.'

She asked me to spell it, then rattled the keyboard again and there it was. Not an answer, but the start of one. The *Hypnerotomachia Poliphili* was one of the first works produced, elegantly and to great acclaim, by Manutius, a Venetian publisher. He would later adopt the dolphin and anchor as the printer's mark for his imprint, the Aldine Press.

'Uh-oh,' Lizzie muttered, scanning the article quickly, in a way an old archivist like me never would. 'Here we go.'

Manutius, the article said, was a friend of Lucrezia Borgia, who greatly admired his publication of 'enchiridia', handy-sized works of popular classics, like modern paperbacks. They were beautifully produced, using newly designed typefaces and designs – it was Manutius who invented italics – and brought reading to a wider audience beyond the upper classes. The dolphin and anchor device came from a coin from Vespasian's reign given to Manutius by none other than Pietro Bembo, Lucrezia's lover, the man who had brought her missing erotic portrait to Venice in the first place.

'But who on earth is the traitor who's not a traitor? And not a painter either? Mum, I hate you.' She slapped her own hand. 'Just kidding. Must stop saying things like that.'

My head was starting to spin. 'When in doubt . . . coffee.'

She was heading for the door already, making nice noises about what a lovely little home I had. Not a palazzo on the Grand Canal, I replied. But enough for me.

The temperature seemed to have gone up a good five degrees while we'd been inside. There was that pressure in the air too that sometimes brought on a migraine. More puffy clouds wondering whether to form an anvil shape, grey bases threatening thunder.

We walked through Campo San Pantalon, past the stall that sold tourist tat and newspapers. I couldn't help looking round to see if someone was watching. I'd never noticed Luca Volpetti following us that morning. This kind of thing was not my forte.

If there was, they were better at subterfuge than me. And they wouldn't be wearing that obvious cloak and floppy hat of the wooden spy in San Rocco.

As always, a billboard with the local news headlines was parked outside the stand.

I came to a halt, heart pumping, staring at the words there. Aware immediately why Valentina Fabbri had summoned Lizzie to her office, and how rash we'd been to ignore the call.

'Arnold?' Lizzie said, and touched my arm. 'What's wrong?'

The billboard said simply: *Ca' Scacchi Mystery – Now It's Murder.*

'I don't ask twice.'

We were back in the San Zaccaria Carabinieri office, Valentina Fabbri looking troubled across the desk. No coffee. No offer of it.

'You shouldn't have to,' I said quickly, before Lizzie could explode. 'We were wrapped up in the story. It tends to consume you.'

That interested her. 'You've made progress?'

'Just two left. The traitor who's not a painter—'

'You have no ideas?'

I shook my head. 'Nothing.'

Lizzie looked ready to scream. 'Could you please stop talking about riddles and tell me about my mother?'

'I wanted to. First thing.'

'Instead, you told the newspapers.'

'No.' Valentina hesitated, wondering whether to go on. 'I did not. For that, I suspect you can thank Enzo Canale. He has friends everywhere. Here. In the city. In Rome.'

'Dad didn't kill her. I don't care what you say.'

'I don't think Valentina is suggesting such a thing.'

The Capitano's face remained impassive. 'I'm suggesting nothing at all. I wanted you to come here so I could explain what we've learned as a result of a very problematic post mortem.' There was a blue folder on the desk. She flipped it open. A printed report with photographs. 'You don't need to look unless you want to. It's in Italian, of course.'

'Just tell me.'

The autopsy was complicated because of the state of the remains. It wasn't just that the body in front of the altar had lain there for thirty-five years. The ceiling collapse had made the work more difficult and protracted. Specialists had had to be brought in from Milan and Rome to try to separate old injuries from new. Expert advice sought from medical examiners with experience of buried remains from war zones, the graves of conflict victims.

'You said my mum killed herself.'

'I said that was how it appeared. What you told us. What your father told you.' There was a moment's hesitation again, so unlike the usually confident Valentina Fabbri I'd come to know. 'Canale believes your father had been violent towards her on more than one occasion. That he was aware the two of them were still having an on–off affair. While she knew he was removing items from the palazzo and selling them on the black market. If this is true—'

'I don't believe a word that bastard says. Dad loved her. Sometimes he'd tell me he didn't think she was dead at all. One day she'd walk right back into our lives. I lived with him. I know he couldn't have hurt her. He never even raised a hand to me. God knows I gave him cause sometimes. I . . .'

Then came the tears, the fragile woman beneath the steely facade.

'I'm sorry,' Valentina said. 'Truly.' She pulled out the last page of the autopsy report and pushed it across the desk. No photos, thank goodness. Just a summary in Italian I read with a sinking heart. 'It might be easier if it came from you, Arnold.'

'How?' I wondered. 'Do tell.'

That hurt my Venetian friend, and I never meant to.

I picked up the page, read it again, carefully. 'They say she died from several blows to the head. It was a prolonged and violent attack. A broken arm. Two broken ribs. They say—'

Lizzie snatched the page from my hands and tore it in two. 'I don't believe it. The ceiling fell on us, Arnold. Remember? That must be the explanation.'

'But it's not,' Valentina insisted. 'It took some time, but they were able to separate the roof collapse from the blows that took her life.'

'You can't be sure.'

'We can.' She leaned across the desk and tried to peer into Lizzie's glassy eyes. 'We are. They're still checking a few other things. Things we would normally have dealt with earlier, but this death is so strange, so unusual. The normal way does not seem appropriate, or so I'm told. The principal thing I'm ignorant about is what actually occurred beforehand. Your father's not here to tell us. The only people from that time I can talk to are Enzo Canale and you.'

'I wasn't there.'

'You never saw your father act violently towards your mother?'

Lizzie hesitated, and I think we both knew. Something must have happened.

'People argue,' she said. 'It's only natural.'

There was a commotion beyond the door. An officer in a plain dark suit came in and announced the team was in place.

'The team?' Lizzie asked when he'd left.

'This is now a murder investigation. I've asked for a forensic unit to take another look at the crypt. They will also need to examine the palazzo more closely. If you could let us in . . .'

'Here.' Lizzie pulled out that massive iron ring, tore off two keys and threw them across the desk. 'The gate. The house. They're spares. Keep them. Keep the whole damned place if you want.'

Valentina folded her arms, sat back and looked at us. The meeting was, I knew, coming to an end. 'I will keep you informed of developments, of course.'

'Whatever happened, it was thirty-five years ago. My dad's dead. I was a child. You think I care?'

'I believe you do. I've posted two officers outside your gate. The media have latched on to this story. August. What else do they have to write about? If they become a nuisance, let me know.'

Tears of fury, tears of impotence. Or both.

'What exactly am I supposed to do?' Lizzie wondered. 'Go and watch your people try to make my dead father a murderer?'

'I don't rush to conclusions. Nor should you. Arnold . . .'

'Capitano.'

'Your traitor who is not a traitor. Nor a painter. Does the name Tiepolo mean nothing at all?'

The question baffled me. Lizzie and I had seen the work of one Tiepolo already in the Gesuati. Giambattista had had two sons who were artists too. I'd never read a thing to suggest they were anything but painters.

'I'm sorry. There's so much been running through my head – *our* heads – these last few days. And now . . .'

'I don't know the answer to your riddle,' she said, scribbling something on a piece of paper. 'But the Tiepolo you're looking for is surely much earlier than the painters and went by the name of Bajamonte. If you read the darker corners of Venetian history, I believe you'll find it's thanks to him we came to create the notorious Council of Ten. And . . .' a sudden memory that made her smile, 'there's a reminder of the man across the piazza. Find an archway in the Merceria.' More scribbles, a map. 'Go take a look. Learn about Bajamonte. Forget about the Carabinieri and bodies in the ground as much as possible. There's nothing you can do now. When I have news, you'll be the first to know.' A wave of her admonitory finger. 'Provided you answer my call.'

It was almost three by the time we found ourselves outside the white facade of San Zaccaria. Lizzie's tears had stopped, replaced by bemusement and a nagging form of anger. It had never occurred to me to wonder what someone did when they discovered a close relative had been murdered.

Disbelief, rejection, fury, a sense of helplessness. All and more combined.

'You don't need to say anything, honestly.'

'I do.' She squinted against the sun, eyeing the pigeons on the parapets. 'Dad could be mean. Never with me. Just other people. I remember once, in the palazzo, he got out his shotgun. The one he used for hunting. He was waving it around at some jerk musician who was demanding more money. Threatening to shoot him and dump him in the canal.'

'Lizzie . . .'

'I want to say it. Never have. I just walked into the room. Little me. That stopped him. He looked ashamed. I think he was quite a lot. Imposter syndrome. That's what they call it, don't they? When someone achieves something but a little voice nags at them saying they don't deserve it. He had that when he was up. He had it in some funny way when he was down.' A quick smile. 'I never achieved anything, so there was never that problem with me.'

'No one knows what happened. Perhaps we never will.'

She smiled. 'I know you're trying to make me feel better. It's kind of you. You're always kind.'

It was the only thing I could think of to say.

I waved Valentina's piece of paper in front of her. The quest for the penultimate link in the hunt for Lucrezia Borgia's portrait. 'May we . . .?'

Another smile, and she nodded.

The sight Valentina had guided us to was something I would never have noticed without her help. Venice is littered with cryptic external details: statues and shields, dragons, monsters, masks both terrifying and comical. There are solitary Madonnas left over from minor *scuole* and religious buildings, family crests, figures that represent old folk tales, eccentric door knockers, window ledges, drainpipes even, a plethora of architectural follies placed there for the ancient hell of it and nothing else. Plain and unadorned was never the Venetian way.

At first, I didn't even spot this one until Lizzie reminded me of something I'd told her earlier on our walks: this was a city where you must always look up. There, in stone, above an arch set in the street behind the San Marco clock tower: the head and shoulders of an old woman, posed at a window, gazing down at the stream of people below, a heavy mortar in her hands, seemingly about to tip it onto our heads.

'Got to be a story, hasn't there?' Lizzie murmured, looking up at it.

'If you'd rather have some time to yourself . . .'

'I would have said. She's right. There's nothing I can do. About Mum. Or Dad. Just this. Let's keep looking, shall we? You won't be happy till we've finished this game. Me neither. The story, please . . .'

This time round, I hadn't the foggiest. But I was certain I knew a man who would.

I had the good fortune to spend a few happy minutes with John Julius Norwich at a Christmas book event at Waterstones in Piccadilly a few years before he died. He was from an aristocratic background, a learned fellow who'd led the kind of life I could only envy. He'd been introduced to Venice when he was just sixteen, and his world seemed to revolve around the lagoon in so many ways, even to the extent of living in Little Venice in London. Coming as I did from a lowly Yorkshire background – we were never poor, my mother insisted, we just didn't have any money – I expected to feel uncomfortable in his presence. But in truth he was such easy, genial company, and so open to talking at length about his writing, I almost wondered if we might not knock off for a drink around the corner somewhere later.

Not that it happened, but I got my two volumes of his Venice history signed. Then, later, when Eleanor and I decided Venice was the place we wanted to live, I bought the electronic edition too. That was easy enough to carry on a phone and a tablet, and after some initial misgivings, I grew to love the ability to search and bookmark and annotate the work as I saw fit.

There it was in its entirety on my phone in the Merceria on that airless, sultry August afternoon. We strolled away from the tourist honeypot of the piazza and found a café off the beaten track halfway to the Rialto – not that I could stop myself glancing round to see if anyone was watching.

I typed *Bajamonte* into the search box for my digital copy of *A History of Venice*.

Viscount Norwich, I felt sure, wouldn't let us down.

The old woman was called Giustina Rossi – or perhaps Lucia; Norwich felt unsure, and he was never one to hide his doubts or, like some of his peers, portray rumour and speculation as fact. She became the heroine of Venice – or at least the part that held the reins – on the Feast of St Vitus, Monday 15 June 1310, a day much like ours, with storm clouds gathering and the threat of violent sudden downpours.

Revolution was in the air. Bajamonte Tiepolo had been chosen to lead an uprising bent on overthrowing – and doubtless executing – the Doge of the time, Pietro Gradenigo, and his supporters. For some, Tiepolo was a hero, a figure of honesty and justice fighting against the tyrannical rule of Gradenigo and his crew. Hence, I imagine, Lucia's depiction of him in the riddle as a traitor who perhaps wasn't, with a hint that he had the same name as the later family of painters. Truly the clue of a lover of puzzles.

Gradenigo had word of the plot through an insider who defected to his side. Three groups of armed rebels had assembled to attack the Doge's Palace, one on the mainland, the second under the command of Marco Querini – another famous surname in Venetian history – and the third headed by Tiepolo.

The city groups met at Querini's palace in San Polo, then set off over the Rialto bridge, dividing their forces with the aim of reuniting in a two-pronged attack in the piazza. Querini rode alongside his son, shouting, 'Liberty and death to Doge Gradenigo!' Careering on horseback into the square, he was met by a large military force assembled by the fore-warned Doge. Father and son were killed almost instantly, while the rest of the rebels retreated to Campo San Luca – around the corner from where we were enjoying our spritz – only to be slaughtered there.

Bajamonte Tiepolo, meanwhile, rode at the head of his

troops down the Merceria towards the basilica. It was there, in the narrow street now given over to expensive shops and cafés, that they met the wrath of Signora Rossi, though whether she was outraged by the threat of political mayhem or simply annoyed by the racket they were making remains a matter of speculation. The old lady launched her heavy mortar from her window, missing Tiepolo but killing outright his standard-bearer.

The sight of Tiepolo's banner reading *Liberty* lying in the Merceria mud – the street was unpaved in those days – coupled with rain and the number of opponents waiting in the square, swords raised, brought the rebellion to a swift end. Most of the insurgents were quickly beheaded without trial. Bajamonte Tiepolo proved too popular in some quarters to kill and was allowed to go into exile. The city, meanwhile, decided it needed a firmer grip on security and the threat of insurrection, and created the Council of Ten, a much-feared committee of patricians with the power to fund informers and spies and punish anyone they deemed a threat to the state. An arm of the republic that would have a busy time in the centuries to come, as the vast array of its papers I'd seen in the Archivio di Stato attested.

As for Signora Rossi, she was hailed as the saviour of Venice and asked what she wanted in return. Two things only, she said: the right to fly the republic's banner of a winged lion from her window on feast days, and a promise that her landlord, the Procurators of St Mark, who owned the square, would never raise the rent. Both were granted, for a little while anyway. As Norwich rightly points out, it was never likely that prime property at the heart of the city was going to be available for fifteen ducats a year for long.

The statue in the window, unseen by so many who pass, remains her legacy, along with a flagpole raised in Campo San Luca marking the bloody defeat of Querini's cornered soldiers.

We walked round to take a look after we'd finished our drinks. Seven centuries on, the scarlet and gold banner of Venice still fluttered there in the uncertain afternoon breeze.

'Hell of a story,' Lizzie said. 'Thanks.'

Thank John Julius Norwich, I told her. Not me.

'Where does it leave us?'

It was all there in the book.

'Where your mother says. "Homeless by the Dolphin and the Anchor. Loc. Col. Bai. The. MCCCX." Tiepolo may have escaped with his life, but he was in disgrace, his family name and crest, and that of the Querini, removed from all public monuments. Their houses pulled down and reduced to rubble, in Tiepolo's case replaced by what the city called "the column of infamy".'

'And the Dolphin and Anchor? This publisher and friend of Lucrezia's . . . what was he called again?'

'Aldus Manutius. His printing house was in San Polo. Tiepolo's house must have been close by, I think.'

She groaned. 'And they pulled it down all those years ago?'

I shrugged. We didn't have an answer. Just the start of one.

'Is it far? My feet are killing me. I haven't walked so much in years.'

The grim interview with Valentina Fabbri hadn't vanished. But the tale of Bajamonte Tiepolo had, I felt, at least pushed it towards the back of her head.

'We can walk. A leisurely stroll.'

An exaggeration. But by then Lizzie had fallen into the habit of the Venetian regular, understanding that it was often more rewarding to make your way on foot than take the slower route by vaporetto.

We'd just turned on to the Riva del Carbon and had almost reached the Palazzo Bembo – everything was starting to link in my head thanks to Lucia Scacchi – when my phone rang.

I don't know why my heart leapt. Just the mood. The plain fact I couldn't stop scanning round to see if someone was following us, while trying to make sure Lizzie never caught me.

It was Luca. He'd gone outside to make the call. I could tell from the noise of tourists in the background, and the sense of something uncharacteristically furtive in his voice.

'How is she?' he asked. 'Can you talk?'

Lizzie was watching me like a hawk. She must have read

something in my face. Without a word, she walked off and started looking at the hats and loose dresses in a cheap clothes shop on the canal-side terrace.

'I can.'

'God,' Luca sighed, 'this is awful. I can't imagine. Murder now. We never have murder in Venice.'

That was a frequent refrain of Valentina Fabbri's, too. Although the word 'rarely' might have been more accurate.

'There's nothing we can do except keep looking for the elusive Lucrezia.'

I told him about Bajamonte Tiepolo and how we were close to unravelling the penultimate piece of the puzzle Lucia Scacchi had left us.

'The Manutius house is marked,' he said. 'A plaque on the wall. I've walked past it many a time. Modest place by our standards. Funny to think the idea that books were for everyone, not just the clergy and the aristocracy, began there.'

'Then this column of infamy's nearby?'

'Definitely not. It's somewhere in the Doge's Palace, I think. I vaguely remember them bringing it out for an exhibition years back. Tiepolo's palace they pulled down like you said. Then the column was demolished, centuries ago. Perhaps we were wrong. Do you need an exact location? Doesn't it matter that you have a rough idea?'

That had occurred to me too. The truth was we simply didn't know. Something was missing, and I was beginning to suspect it was more than just two dots on a map.

'I understand completely,' Luca said when I explained this. 'If only I could help.'

'You have.'

'Not so much. Fabrizio and I are struggling for ideas about this last place of yours. The beautiful eyes. That could mean anything. But it's not why I called. There's something happening with the palazzo. Canale seems to have persuaded the council to act.'

'Meaning what?'

'Meaning this evening there's a meeting of heritage people and the ones who hold the purse strings. I know someone who's been invited along. She warned me. They seem intent on forcing through a compulsory purchase on heritage grounds. Immediately, even before Lizzie can have her mother declared officially dead.'

That made no sense.

'Why the rush? Ballarin said the building was in reasonable order considering the circumstances. Surely—'

'Arnold! I know no more than I'm telling you. Canale is making his move. Everyone's being very secretive. Even Valentina. There's something going on. Something she won't talk about. I've no idea what. But I wanted you to know.'

'There's just two of us. Lizzie is broke. Friendless. We can't fight everyone.'

'She isn't friendless. She's got you, and you may be the only friend she needs. Find that painting. Quickly. Steal his thunder. Do that, and the city will be looking at Lizzie Hawker, not him. They won't dare try to steal that place from the woman who found our lost Lucrezia.'

I thanked him.

'It's nothing. No more than you both deserve. I'll take another look at our friend Bajamonte when I return to the office. If someone notices, then to hell with it. Things are moving one way or another. This will be done in days, I suspect. I hope to your friend's benefit, and the city's. No one else. I have to go.'

Lizzie was back, smiling, a new floppy straw hat on her head. The price tag still dangled from the brim. Ten euros. I pulled it off.

'I was just trying it on,' she cried. 'Haven't bought the thing.'

'It suits you,' I said, 'and this is hat weather.' I looked up at the darkening sky. 'Umbrella weather soon, I guess.'

'I loathe umbrellas. Annoying things.'

We had that in common. For people who live on the water, Venetians seem to hate the rain more than anyone I know. Dodging the spikes of their brollies is often as dangerous as evading the bikes of Amsterdam.

I went and paid for the hat.

She was still there by the water when I came back, gazing up and down the Grand Canal, caught by the moment, trapped by the still, sudden beauty of the place.

She looked just as lovely. Perhaps it was her mother's genes. That hint of Italian in her face, her hair. For a second or two she seemed to belong here, among the canals and the alleys, the tourist tat stores and the mask shops, the strange mix of old and new, elegant and decrepit.

We crossed the Rialto, and on the other side, close to the market, I bought us a couple of cups of orange juice straight from the press. The day was getting hotter, more humid, the barometer rising.

Then I led her into the warren of lanes that spread out from the market area, wondering where we were headed.

There are parts of Venice I doubt I'll ever really know. Much of the more obscure parts of Cannaregio. The same with Castello around Celestia. Then there's the section of San Polo that lies behind the bend of the Grand Canal from the Rialto up towards the transport hub of Piazzale Roma. This is an ancient part of the city, home to some of its greatest museums and palazzi. Yet it seems the neighbourhood was constructed on the basis that a straight line is an offence to creation, while curves and dead ends and snaking dark alleys that promise to open out into an interesting *campo* only to end in a sluggish stretch of grey water make life so much more interesting.

'We're lost again, aren't we?' Lizzie said as I stopped to work out where to try next.

'Not at all,' I said, striding off ahead. 'We're merely temporarily uncertain of our position.'

Luca's dictum – keep walking until you end up somewhere you recognise – usually worked. After a minute or two, I turned a familiar corner past the largely vegetarian restaurant of La Zucca, a place beloved of foreign visitors, then, finally, out into an open space, San Giacomo dall'Orio, a local spot with a fetching church, a neighbourhood Coop, a few restaurants with outside tables, and plenty of red wooden benches where elderly couples snoozed in the afternoon sun.

Lizzie plonked herself down on one of the seats, folded her arms and announced she wasn't walking a step further without knowing exactly where we were headed.

The church was somewhere I'd always thought intriguing.

There was a painting in there I was sure Lizzie, with her fascination for the grim, would admire. It was the funeral of the Virgin Mary and depicted a pagan priest running up to her coffin to try to overturn it, only for his hands to be chopped off by some miracle. They remained stuck to the wooden bier while he rolled on the ground in pain and astonishment.

'If you wanted to see a weird painting . . .'

'The only weird painting I'm interested in is Lucrezia.'

We were in Santa Croce anyway, on the border of San Polo. It would have been a distraction, nothing more.

'Also, we haven't eaten since breakfast.'

'It's the afternoon, Lizzie. No restaurant worth patronising is going to be open right now. And . . .'

The message tone buzzed on my phone. Lizzie looked at me, hope in her eyes.

'Luca,' I said with a grin, and let her read what he had to say.

MCCCX means 1310, the date of the rebellion. I should have spotted this. There's a record in the Archives for a memorial slab in the pavement somewhere near Campo Sant'Agostin. I don't have the exact location. But it seems the message stands for 'Locus Columnae Baiamonti Theopuli'. In other words, this is the place the Tiepolo column of infamy once stood. I'm sorry I never spotted this. Contessa Scacchi was a good puzzle setter. As always with the best riddles, you kick yourself the moment you know the answer, wondering why you were so stupid you never saw it in the first place.

'On your feet, Arnold Clover,' she said, and off we went.

The home of the publishing house of Aldus Manutius, friend to Lucrezia Borgia and Pietro Bembo, and the man who in many ways helped fan the fire of the Renaissance, turned out to be at the foot of the narrow street that led from San Giacomo back into San Polo. An unremarkable house opposite a busy takeaway pizza place, a Latin plaque on the wall talking about typography – *tipographica*, a word I doubt existed in Roman times.

Campo Sant'Agostin was to our right, a small square, one restaurant, mostly private homes. A single gift shop stood on the corner. While I was still trying to work out my bearings and thinking of Luca's message, the words we sought, Bajamonte Tiepolo's palace reduced to rubble, a column, now vanished, in its place, Lizzie, more practical than I could ever be, spotted something in the cobbles. It was a change in colour just outside the gift shop. Off-white marble against the more common grey stone.

The centuries had taken their toll. A crack, filled with dirt and dust, ran down the middle of the slab where it abutted the shop wall, separating the letters. But they were still readable: *Loc. Col. Bai. The. MCCCX.*

'Drink! Map!' She kissed me quickly on the cheek. 'Just one last mystery to solve, love. Then we're done.'

If only the portrait of Lucrezia Borgia was the solitary outstanding riddle surrounding her. Bravado. Lizzie Hawker was never short of it.

We had to walk to Campo San Stin to find a café with seats outside. Spritz – Campari, of course – two bowls of crisps that the pigeons and the gulls kept eyeing. I took out the map and drew in the last dot for San Polo. It was clear where the last leg would lead. Across the Grand Canal, through the busy midst of Cannaregio, then looping back to Castello and the Scuola Grande di San Marco. That final element in Lucia Scacchi's puzzle surely lay in a part of the city teeming with tourists, history, churches, palazzi, most of them quite foreign to me. I tried to hide my despair, which was probably pointless.

Lizzie was slumped back in her chair, eyes closed, looking ready to doze. Ever since we saw that dreadful newspaper billboard, I'd been wondering how the news her mother had been murdered might affect her once the shock had worn off. Perhaps the reaction was delayed. Perhaps, after Canale's intervention, and the revelation he was her father, she'd been expecting something like this all along. If so, she wasn't going to say.

Still, I needed more.

'Your mother must have worked really hard to come up with this puzzle. How? Where did it all come from?'

Her eyes didn't open. 'I said. She was a history student at the university here. Gave up her studies on a whim to get married. A sudden decision I guess she regretted.'

'Hardly fits with the picture of her being a junkie, does it?'

'Hardly fits with her marrying a man like Dad. People make strange decisions. I listened to his stories. I took them as gospel. The way kids do.'

I hesitated to ask. But it came out anyway. 'And now?'

'I haven't the faintest clue what to think. What to believe.' She reached across the table and briefly touched my hand. 'Except when it comes from my one true friend in Venice. How much do I owe you by now?'

'Nothing. I'd have paid for the privilege. This has been a fascinating escapade. I'm only sorry it's brought you so much pain.'

'Not as much as you think. I loved him. My dad. But I never quite believed all his stories. I just didn't let myself admit it. One last piece of the puzzle. I don't need to ask, do I? Whether you've any ideas. I can see the answer in your face. You're an open book, Arnold Clover. A dangerous thing to be in this world.'

It didn't matter. We'd been clueless every step of the way. Then work, imagination, luck and the assistance of Luca, Fabrizio Ricci and, in the end, Valentina had lifted us when we stumbled.

I pulled out the map and looked again at the gap in the circle that remained. A curve that ran across the Grand Canal some way above the Rialto markets then continued through the alleys of Cannaregio. That *sestiere* stretched all the way to the canal by Giovanni e Paolo and the anatomical museum where we'd begun our quest. It was a vast area, much of it given over to tiny streets, a maze through which I only knew a few routes.

All the same, something nagged at me. The previous seven riddles we'd unpicked had something to say about Lucia Scacchi and her predicament. A wounded figure imprisoned in a glass cabinet. Bones deep in the Venetian mud, just as they were, unknown to most, in the courtyard of her ancient family home. Chained and sightless Fury divided from a furtive spy by a library of books. And now the destroyed palace of a man some thought wronged by history, a traitor who might have been a beacon of light and justice given the chance. How much of that reflected her thinking, her assessment of herself and the two men – Chas Hawker and Enzo Canale – who seemed to feel they owned her?

More importantly, why in that last line in the Casanova story did she finally use a name?

'"Lady L! You must be left to last. Replace those beautiful eyes that others may look around and truly find you",' I read out from my phone.

'We will,' said Lizzie. 'I've no idea how. But you told me . . . we'll do it. We'll find that painting. I'll deal with Ca' Scacchi. On my terms. No one else's. Then I'll bury my mother and weep over her grave. Whatever happened, it was thirty-five years ago. Your friend in the Carabinieri may be very clever, but she doesn't have a time machine. We're never going to know what happened. Maybe it's best that way.'

A fat drop of rain landed on the table, staining the paper cloth. Then another. When I looked up, the sky, eggshell blue a few minutes before, was black with swirling clouds so low they seemed about to touch the rooftops. There was a rumble of thunder close enough to feel it through the cobbles. Then the downpour began, and the tardy waiter was out apologising for the fact he'd failed to spot its arrival, shooing us to shelter under the awning at the front door. A rerun of our flight from the storm outside Anzolo Raffaele, though something had changed between us in the meantime.

This was a storm to remember, short and noisy and violent, the two of us close together, laughing at the way the rain fell with such force it rebounded from the paving stones, formed quick puddles, small lakes, sending a swollen rivulet dashing down towards the ancient drain cut in the middle of the square.

'We will find it,' I said when the thunder took a pause for breath and the lightning that followed cracked loud and fierce from somewhere to the north. I could read these summer tempests almost as well as the locals now. This one would run along the Giudecca Canal and deliver the worst of its anger somewhere around Campo Santa Margherita, not here, not now. Though later its successors would be back and there'd be no telling where they might land.

'Good,' Lizzie said. 'Of more immediate importance, I'm famished, for a change.'

We nabbed an outside table at Birreria la Corte in Campo San Polo. A spot I'd found without Luca's help. Being reluctant to dine in a restaurant on my own, I'd only ever used the place for takeaway pizza, which was always excellent. I'd have happily done the same that night, but Lizzie was adamant: we'd scored if not a victory, at least the penultimate lap before the chequered flag. I'd given up counting the pennies. She – and this, I suspect, was a habit inherited from her father – hadn't even started. Still, there was no arguing. This time she'd pay, on the one credit card she felt sure was not yet maxed out. One course only, though. For her, tagliatelle with herb pesto, scallops, lemon and liquorice powder. I stuck with the much cheaper Diavola pizza, only nine euros for San Marzano tomato, mozzarella from Agerola on the Amalfi coast, and spicy Calabrian sausage.

The house wine was enough, I insisted, not that I'd ever tried it. I got a minor scolding for being parsimonious.

Then, to take her mind off Ca' Scacchi, her mother and Valentina Fabbri, I told her the story of Lorenzino de' Medici, the fugitive aristocrat from Florence who'd once lived in a mansion a few doors along the way. How he'd murdered his cousin, Alessandro, then the Duke of Florence, and fled across Europe, finally settling in obscurity – or so he hoped – in Venice, conducting a love affair with a married woman who lived around the corner.

'I've a feeling you're going to tell me these violent delights have violent ends,' Lizzie said, raising her glass.

I chinked mine against it. 'You're quoting Shakespeare at me.'

'Auditioned for *Romeo and Juliet* when I was a teenager and Dad was putting me about. The outdoor theatre, Regent's Park. Spent ages learning Juliet's best speeches. Got offered a walk-on, no lines. The crowd at the banquet. Didn't even get a spear. Just a plastic bouquet. They had some bloke in his thirties playing Romeo and a very pretty model type not much younger as Juliet. Which kind of missed the point of the whole story if you ask me. They're kids. Mixed-up kids trying to find out what love is and only learning the cost of their mistakes too late.' Another touch of the wine glass. 'My acting may not have been up to much, but by God I had the backstory to do it. What happened to your Lorenzino?'

I told her the lurid tale in brief. How he was stalked by two assassins one February in 1548, followed from his home across the square and slaughtered on the Ponte San Tomà. And the way that story had come to obsess the late TV historian Marmaduke Godolphin, who thought he could revive his flagging broadcasting career by throwing a sensational new light on the killing.

'I remember reading about him,' Lizzie said. 'Didn't he get murdered here himself?'

'Accidental death. The circumstances were somewhat strange, not least that Duke died in the very place Lorenzino did. The racier stories you read doubtless came via the pernicious imagination of Alf Lascelles, that hack I mentioned. Sordid is his speciality. Shame really. On the rare occasions I've talked to the man seriously, I felt he could do much better if he tried.'

'There's money in sordid. Not so much in truth.'

The food arrived. She looked delighted. It was a very pretty plate, and my pizza appeared perfect too.

'You were involved in all that. Valentina told me when she said she'd ask you to help out with Ca' Scacchi. She said you'd proved yourself as honest as they come and that was just what I needed.'

If only it was so simple. There were aspects to the Godolphin story I'd shared with no one but Valentina Fabbri, and I was content for matters to stay that way.

'Godolphin hired me to try to prove his strange theory about Lorenzino. Luca too.'

'And instead, you disproved it?'

'Valentina said?'

She laughed. 'No. It was written all over your face. I told you already. You'd make a rotten liar.'

I tore off a piece of pizza, the crunchy, burnt edge along with a smear of San Marzano, and handed it over.

'Wow,' she said, taking a bite. 'That's not like you get back home.'

'This isn't England. Nowhere near. And yes, we told Godolphin he'd got it all wrong. His arrogance and his craving to get back into the limelight had obscured his vision. He was a decent historian once. A professor when I was at Cambridge – not mine, I hasten to add. I wasn't that bright. Or ambitious.'

'What's the point of ambition? It only leads to disappointment. One reason I never got those acting jobs. I wasn't bothered. All that mattered was Dad. Trying to stop him going off the rails. Later, trying to look after him. That was all I wanted. Failed there too, it seems. He was never totally honest with me. When he got really sick, I never found out until the doctors took me to one side.'

That rang a shrill bell. 'I never knew my Eleanor was seriously ill. It was only after she died . . .'

A bunch of kids had turned up in the square, playing with a small dog, throwing a ball across the cobbles. An everyday scene in a place where so many extraordinary events had occurred, so many figures of both note and notoriety had passed through over the centuries. Their ghosts still lingered, at least for me.

'I couldn't work out with Dad whether he wanted to hide it. Or thought I'd just magically work it out by telepathy or something. When you love someone, there's so much goes on that's unspoken. Sometimes the closer you are, the harder it is to talk. Talk frankly, that is. Too many bruises you can step on. Too many potholes in the road.'

She forked up the last of the scallops and purred as she finished them.

'I think you're right,' I said.

Her keen eyes flashed at me. 'I know I am. And maybe your friend is too. Maybe Dad did kill Mum. Maybe there were two of him. Dad before. Dad after. I don't know. He was a sight better at acting than I ever was if that's the case. Not that it'd be hard. Sometimes, when he wasn't so lucid, he really did seem to think she might come back.' A recollection, an unwanted one. 'Those were bad days. I struggled. I hated them.'

'Eleanor always led me to believe we'd be living here. As a couple. She must have known it was probably not going to happen.'

'Like I said. The ones you love . . .'

I had to point it out. 'Valentina never came out and said your father was a murderer. Not in so many words.'

'As good as. But who else?'

I struggled with that. 'Canale? Someone you never knew about? You were in London.'

'Yes. And more to the point, I was five years old.'

The sky rumbled again, low black clouds scudding over the ancient rooftops. Once again, a waiter had come to lurk by the door, watching the fluttering of the table canopies, wondering whether to shoo us in.

Lizzie put on the floppy hat I'd bought her. 'Where's your titfer?'

'Sorry?'

'Hat. Rhyming slang. How long have you spent out here?'

'I don't have a hat.'

'Then you're going to get drenched.'

'I'm from Yorkshire. It's only water.'

The thunder was closer then, and the lightning.

'It's going to be raining cats and dogs.'

'A touch of drizzle, we call that up north.'

'*Il conto*,' she said to the waiter, waving her card.

'You're getting the hang of things.'

'He went to jail. Dad. When he was a teenager. I should have told you, but I wondered if it might have got back to Valentina. Guess she already knew. Thieving things. Handling stolen goods, as they say. Everyone did it where he came from. The papers never found out. Or if they did, he stopped them printing it. Soon enough he had the money to rub out all that stuff. But he told me. He said the oddest thing was when he came out. A year he'd done, before he was even twenty. Then they let him loose and he said the world looked different. New. Full of things he had to explore, things he'd never noticed before.' She leaned forward. 'That's what it feels like for me now. Like being let out of prison. Except I served thirty-four years.'

'Thirty-four,' I whispered.

Her hand went to her mouth. 'Oh my God. I never realised. That must have happened the year you and . . . Eleanor?'

'Eleanor.'

'The year you got married. I was five. There you were getting hitched.'

I raised my glass. 'Thanks for the reminder.'

'You don't seem old to me. Not at all. I've met kids who wear the world on their shoulders. You don't.' She looked round the square. 'Is that what this place does for you?'

Before I could answer, the waiter was back with his machine. Lizzie put her card in the slot. She looked nervous and couldn't hide it.

We waited and I knew what was about to happen.

'I'm sorry,' the man said, embarrassed. 'It won't go through.'

'There must be some mistake . . .'

'Doesn't matter,' I said, and pulled out some notes then threw them on the table. 'We need to go. The weather . . .'

'Arnold!' She was livid. 'I've got the money.'

'It's fine.'

'It's not bloody fine. I'm not paying you. I'm not doing anything except taking up your time and getting you punched in the street.'

I walked out into the *campo*. At this point in an impending storm, the weather was quite unpredictable. Maybe we'd escape the rain altogether. Or have one of those sudden tropical downpours that caught you unawares and left you soaking.

'I will find you the money,' she said. She took my arm, then delivered a light punch to my chest.

'All in good time. Where now?'

'Home. My home. I'm not being chased off by a bunch of reporters and coppers.'

'Carabinieri.'

'You're very pedantic sometimes.'

'It's in my nature. Walk or the vaporetto?'

One glance at the sky, and out of nothing more than sheer bloody-mindedness she said, 'Walk.'

We went by the Ponte San Tomà so I could show her where Lorenzino de' Medici had been assassinated, and where, five centuries later, Duke Godolphin had died in circumstances that seemed similar on the surface, though very different when they were picked apart by Valentina Fabbri with a little help from me.

Then past the Frari, through Campo Santa Margherita, over to the Accademia and finally that long stretch of Dorsoduro towards the Guggenheim and Salute.

The rain held off, though the sky stayed dark. We were approaching the Corner pub, a popular bar near Il Pagliaccio. There, to my astonishment, was Valentina on her own at an outside table, civilian clothes for once: pressed white shirt, black jeans, umbrella coupled with sunglasses – pointless in the circumstances, but that never stops some people – pushed back over her dark hair.

When she came and greeted us, there was something unusual in her voice. It almost sounded like trepidation.

'I do wish you'd keep your phone on, Lizzie.'

'You could have called Arnold.'

A glance in my direction, then she said, 'May we talk? Let me buy you a drink.'

I thought of Luca's last call, the tone of his voice too. His warning that something was happening, something new.

'I'll be going then,' I said.

'I want you with me,' Lizzie insisted. 'And a spritz.'

Another.

I went to the bar. Prosecco for Valentina, a small beer for me. Then the three of us perched on the hard stools at a little table by the bridge over the narrow canal. Staff were locking up the Guggenheim. Ca' Scacchi was a minute or two away.

The police guard had gone from the palazzo, Valentina said. The media too. They'd got bored waiting when no one was around. 'They will be back. I will do what I can.'

'I can deal with reporters.'

'No doubt.'

She sipped her wine and closed her eyes for a moment. It was obvious this was one of those rare occasions she was struggling for the right words. 'I haven't been entirely candid with you these last few days.'

Lizzie laughed, just a little. 'You don't say?'

'This is the most unusual problem I've ever encountered. Quite unique. It presented me with a dilemma. There are few things I dislike more than uncertainty. Than making a statement only to find it was quite wrong. That I've misled people, accidentally, through laziness or a slipshod decision. Whatever.' She sniffed at the Prosecco and pushed it to one side. 'I may not have been entirely successful in this over the past few days, but I've tried, as much as I could, to refer to the corpse we found in your crypt—'

'*We* found,' Lizzie interrupted, and patted my arm.

'Tried as much as I could to refer to it without a name. As a woman; a suicide, it seemed at first. But now, as you know, the victim of a vicious assault. Of that we are absolutely certain.'

A group of happy tourists marched past, half drunk already, singing loudly in English. Valentina waited, then said, 'The one thing I stupidly assumed I didn't need to focus on was her identity. It seemed obvious. This was my mistake and I apologise for it.'

'What?'

'I had to wait until I was certain. Now I am. It's not your mother you found down there. The forensic people couldn't find a match with the dental records they located. In the end, they asked for a blood sample from the hospital, from when you were admitted.'

Lizzie shrieked with fury. 'Christ! First that bastard Canale, then you.'

'I could have asked,' Valentina added, 'but I didn't want to raise your hopes. If that, indeed, is what this news means. The woman was around your mother's age. As you know, she died in a violent attack. That's as far as I can go. We can find no medical records, nothing to indicate who she might be.'

'The dress!' Lizzie shook her arm. 'I saw the dress. I know the dress. That was hers.'

'A dress is rarely unique.'

'That one was. It was from a designer or something.'

'Then . . . I don't know. Who else might have worn it?'

'No one.'

'The woman is not Lucia Scacchi.'

Lizzie looked lost. 'Then what happened to her? Where is she?'

Valentina picked up her glass and raised it. 'A question I'd like answered too.' She finished the Prosecco and looked ready to go. 'I wanted you to be informed. Accurately. Not from guesswork. We have an unidentified corpse from the depths of your courtyard. A murder victim. Killed by whom, for what reason, I cannot begin to guess. Any more than I should speculate about what happened to your mother. Except . . .'

I knew what was coming. I half suspected what Lizzie's response would be as well.

'Except what?'

'The last line in this strange story we assume your mother left by the woman's side for some reason.' She checked her phone. '"Lady L! You must be left to last. Replace those beautiful eyes that others may look around and truly find you." I imagine you assumed, like me, that referred to Lucrezia Borgia. But perhaps . . .'

Lizzie glared at her. 'You think it's my mother? She's dead somewhere else?'

'I really have no idea.' Valentina picked up her bag. 'Nothing but a series of dangling threads, as Arnold once put it. No rational way to link them. May I ask if you're close to solving that final riddle? Finding wherever . . . whatever it seems to hint at?'

'Struggling,' Lizzie told her before I could speak.

Valentina gazed at me.

'It's . . . difficult,' I said, trying my best to look and sound convincing. 'Very. I can't help but wonder if whoever set that puzzle – Lucia Scacchi, we presume, but now who knows? – whether they expected it to be solved at all.'

'And yet they set it. When I have more information, I'll let you know. I trust you'll do the same with me.'

With that, she was gone.

'*Un altro.*' Lizzie waved her index finger round and round in a circle, just like a local. 'There. Did I say it right?'

'You don't need another drink.'

'Fine. I'll get my own.'

She was soon back with a second spritz, chucking the green olive in the bin straight away, eyes as liquid as the canal glistening by the bridge.

'I don't wish to take this out on the innocent, Arnold. Perhaps it would be best if you went back to your bachelor flat. Stayed there. Left me to this mess. It's mine. Not yours.'

I folded my arms and tried as best I could to look like a parent dealing with an irksome child. 'I've not invested all this time and effort to give up now. On our quest. Or you.'

That seemed to amuse her. 'I'm a disaster zone. Haven't you got the message yet?'

'Never met one before, so I wouldn't realise. I do know this, though. Giving up on things halfway through is not my way. I don't believe it's yours either.'

'Oh for God's sake! I've no idea who this other woman is. But Mum . . . she's dead. She must be. No one can go missing for thirty-five years and keep quiet.'

'You don't know that. You can't.'

'Really? Why would she vanish for all that time? When there's a palace worth a fortune waiting for her to claim it here? Explain that, because I can't. Maybe your copper friend's going to tell me Dad killed them both.'

'She didn't accuse him of—'

'That woman never says a thing till she wants.'

There, I thought, Lizzie had Valentina Fabbri in a nutshell. Doubts were something she kept to herself unless there was some good reason to voice them. All the same, I felt I knew her well enough to understand our conversation had been candid. She was telling us all she knew. There were no sudden surprises on the horizon on her part. The identity of the body in the crypt had been in question for some time. That she'd withheld for fear of misleading Lizzie.

'Canale was in on this, wasn't he? He knew it wasn't Mum down there.'

It was obvious from Valentina's not infrequent moans that the man had ways of finding out what was going on within the council and the Carabinieri.

'I got the impression from that fiery encounter we had in the hospital he definitely thought she was dead back then.'

Lizzie was thinking this through. 'There's nothing I can do. I'd have to jump through all those legal hoops Dad talked about. Trying to prove she's really dead. Lots of money. Lots of time.'

I nodded. 'Which is why Canale's pushing the council to move swiftly. A compulsory purchase. I imagine it's easier in those circumstances. If there really is no prospect of finding the legal owner . . .'

'Don't give a damn. Let them have it.'

She surely didn't mean that. 'If we can find that painting . . .'

'What difference would it make?'

'I just have a hunch it might.'

I got a cold look for that. 'You're not a man for hunches.'

'I'm not. All the more reason we should be listening to this one. Your mother left those directions for a reason. Maybe we can still find it.'

'Don't give a damn about that either. Don't you understand? I want to know what happened. Who I am.' She gulped at her drink. 'Enzo Canale's bastard, it seems. Stuck in a place I'll always be a foreigner.' The briefest of smiles. 'Alone if it wasn't for you.'

The thunder resumed, deep and close enough to send a tremor through the air and make us wait a second or two for the lightning to follow. Bright blue-white forks speared the clouds somewhere near Salute. I thought of Fabrizio Ricci's hidden observatory and wondered what this dark, disturbed night might look like from there.

Lizzie screwed her eyes tight shut, rubbed them with the back of her hands like a child, then pushed the drink to one side. 'You're right. I don't need it. You're always right. I never listen.'

I couldn't suppress a brief sigh. 'You listen to me a sight more than Eleanor ever did.'

'I don't believe that.'

'Why?' It seemed an odd thing to say. 'You never met her.'

'Because I don't think you'd stay with someone all that time if they were horrible to you.'

That needed putting right. 'She was never horrible to me.

We just did things differently. Came to problems from opposite directions. Head-on in her case. Whereas I tend to a sideways path.'

'And you still miss her.'

It was a statement, not a question.

'She's gone. There'd be no point. She'd have been the first to tell me that. In a way . . . a strange way, she did.'

Lizzie stared right at me. 'What way?'

'That's a story for another time. It's late.'

She got to her feet and walked to the bridge. I followed.

The thunder bellowed again, so near I felt its breath.

'What the hell's going on, Arnold? I don't know where I am. What to do. What's the point?'

Another bellowing crash and the rain came, sheets of it, thick and powerful, icy cold and close to hail. A sudden gust of wind had risen by the Accademia and decided to sweep Dorsoduro, all the way to the tip then out into the Bacino San Marco.

'The point . . .' There was a flash of lightning so close I thought I saw a jagged fork of electric blue dash down to the rooftops over the Zattere. 'The point right now is you don't stand outside in a storm.'

She pulled down the floppy hat. Another bolt crashed nearby. She pointed back towards the Accademia.

'You're that way.'

'I'm not leaving. Not when you're in this mood.'

'This is my usual mood. I was pretending to be someone else. For you. Pretending's what I do.'

The sky replied with a shower of sharp, freezing rain. I shivered in my summer shirt and jeans, all soaked. She was trembling too.

'I don't know where to turn. What to do. I'm pathetic, and there's nothing I hate more in someone than that. Shit . . .'

Maybe they were tears. Or rain dripping through the floppy hat.

I took her by the shoulders, moved closer than I'd ever dared. Her mouth was half open. Her eyes wide too.

'Please . . .' she whispered.

'We'll finish this, Lizzie. Find out what happened. To your

mother. To whoever was in that crypt. She left us the key. You can't ignore it. We have to find where it is. What it unlocks.'

'Arnold. You're not getting it . . .'

'Just this once, will you kindly listen to me?'

She closed her eyes and laughed. 'Oh God. What a pair we make. You've been out of the world as much as me, haven't you?' She edged close and grazed my lips with her slender finger. 'I wasn't thinking about Mum. Or Lucrezia. I was thinking about . . .'

There was a long moment in which I doubt I even breathed. Then I kissed her. Or she kissed me. I don't remember. Didn't matter. It wasn't the booze, the emotions, the storm raging all around us. It was need, that urge to drown yourself in someone else. To make everything bad and unwanted go away if only for a little while.

As the sky opened all round us and rain bounced hard on the cobbles, we clutched one another tightly, lost to the night, the raging wind, the figures dashing through the diagonal lines of rain pelting down from the lowering sky.

'Time,' she said, her clammy hand taking mine. We walked slowly through the downpour, not minding the rain, the sudden cold, the way our clothes clung to us as if we'd just stepped out of the canal. A sudden gust of wind took her hat and blew it into the water. If she noticed, she didn't care. Soaked to the skin, mind reeling, wondering where all this was going, and whether it was right, I watched as she fumbled with the keys to the palazzo. Then upstairs, one place only.

Lizzie walked to the windows, threw one open. Night air, cool and fresh, came into the stuffy interior, and with it the voices of the Grand Canal: water, wind, distant music from somewhere, strings and a woman's singing, accompanied by the ceaseless traffic along the black water.

Then she went and unlatched the panel in the wall. I came and stood next to her, and we stared at that empty space, just fading silk wallpaper, dirty cream now.

'I wonder what it felt like,' she said. 'When it was there. All those people, all that time. It must have been a kind of ritual. Like something holy. The way it's meant to be and isn't.'

Pietro Bembo, Byron. Annibale Scacchi too. Perhaps even his friend and mentor, Amedeo Modigliani. They'd all seen Lucrezia's private portrait for her amorous brother. Then, finally, Lucia Scacchi, sometimes with her husband. Sometimes with Enzo Canale. Perhaps another. Who was to know? Who *deserved* to? Everyone had their secrets. Even me.

'And so to bed,' she said.

Twelve

The Circle, Closing

I dreamt, and it was as bright and lucid as a summer's day by the beach on the Lido. The two of us were back in the Ognissanti church watching the friendly old friar bent over his books. Nothing new. Just a replay of the same conversation we'd had there. One part in particular standing out.

Then I was sitting bolt upright in bed, wondering whether I was awake or still in that midway place between sleep and consciousness. The curtains were half open. The first signs of soft dawn light were starting to peek through the windows. This was real.

It took me a moment to remember I wasn't alone.

As gently as I could, I shook her shoulder. Lizzie stirred beneath the single sheet.

'I think I've got it. Lady L.'

A couple of blinks, then bleary-eyed she said, 'Do you always wake someone up with an inconsequential remark after sex?'

'Doesn't everyone?'

'Not if I remember right.' She scrabbled by the sheets for her pile of clothes, then came back with a watch. 'It's four in the morning. I'm shagged out. Twice over. Can I sleep now, please? We can talk about this later.'

'I'd rather talk about it now, if that's all right.'

'Not really.'

Pictures were flashing through my head. That strange, word-less act that makes two into one, takes you out of yourself, puts the external world, the real one, in its place, makes you believe for one fleeting moment there just might be something eternal out there.

'Been a while,' I said. 'You know.'

'Me too.'

'I'm sorry if . . .'

'There's nothing to be sorry about, Arnold!' Then, more softly, 'You know you're lost now? Welcome to the club.' She yawned, and I watched every moment, every changing aspect of her face. 'Can we please discuss this later?'

'Lady L. The friar in Ognissanti. You remember what he said?'

She pulled herself up in the bed and leaned against the wall, hands behind her head. 'Can't say I do.'

'When he pointed at his eyes. "If the hospital or that nice lady saint of ours ever make these better . . ." We keep thinking Lucia was referring to Lucrezia. But what if—'

'What if we talk about this in the morning?'

'Who's the patron saint of the blind?'

A shake of her head. 'The woman who runs Specsavers?'

'It's . . .' I needed my books. A connection to the web. My phone. 'This is important. I guarantee it. Give me a little time.'

'Arnold. Did you hear me? It's *four in the morning*.' A groan and she pulled a pillow over her head. 'Goodnight. Sleep tight.'

Eleanor and I spent a couple of weeks exploring Sicily when we were mulling over where in Italy to move to. Venice won in the end, in part because we adored the idea of a place where you never saw a car. But Ortigia came a close second, though much of the time it was choked with traffic along its ancient snaking lanes and alleys. It's a small island connected to the larger Siracusa by two narrow bridges. The oldest part of a very ancient city that was once home to the Greeks who'd emigrated to form the colonies of Magna Graecia. Its story embraced Athenians and Phoenicians, Carthage across the sea in Africa, and brutal conquest by the Romans. It was here, somewhere in those narrow streets, that the famed philosopher and inventor Archimedes was murdered by a Roman soldier during a bloody invasion.

History was everywhere, in the columns of the Greek temple that formed the handsome Christian cathedral, in the hills outside where classical dramas were still performed in the semicircular theatre the Greeks had built more than two millennia before. We dined on fish and fruit and vegetables from the busy market. And we absorbed the tale of one local saint in particular.

Many of the more lurid stories of Christian martyrs were at best dubious or, in the case of a few, such as the Ursula depicted in Carpaccio's cycle of paintings in the Accademia, creations of the lively imaginations of later writers. No one had heard much of St Ursula, a legendary British princess, until the tenth century or so, a good four or five hundred years after she was supposedly murdered by marauding Huns. Not that this made Carpaccio's paintings any the less moving. Most martyr stories are fairy tales of a kind.

Ortigia's local saint was different. Her name was Lucia, Lucy in English, and her story was being recorded by the late 400s AD, perhaps a hundred and fifty years after she died. It was as colourful, as cruel and as miraculous as any of those invented by later fabulists. She came from a wealthy Ortigia family and converted to Christianity as a child. When she wanted to donate the family wealth to the poor, the young pagan who hoped to marry her betrayed her to the Roman authorities. This was during the reign of the vile emperor Diocletian, one of the harshest tyrants when it came to seeking out and punishing anyone who followed Christ. Lucia was dragged before the Roman governor and ordered to make an offering to the pagan gods or be sent to a local brothel and raped.

She refused, naturally, and here the miracles begin. No soldiers could move her to the brothel, even when they brought in oxen to pull her out of her cell. Wooden pyres were built around her, but they refused to light. And then, the inevitable gory detail no martyr legend can do without, we come to the eyes. Some stories claim the furious governor ordered them to be plucked out. Others suggest Lucia gouged them out herself and gave them to her former suitor, since he'd told her they were the most beautiful in the world.

In the end, the story says, a soldier ran a sword through her throat. But when they came to bury her, they found her eyes had been miraculously restored, as they were when her tomb was uncovered a century later.

That detail came to define her, not least because the name Lucia comes from *lux*, the Latin for 'light'. During the Middle

Ages, when she became one of the most popular Catholic saints, she was commonly depicted holding a plate on which her eyes rested. Her name was invoked to aid the blind and those suffering from ailments of the eyes. In Siracusa, she was the local hero, celebrated by a gloriously spooky depiction of her burial by Caravaggio, painted while he was on the run for murder. It was just two years before his own death, and there was something prophetic in that dark, strange canvas that brought us back to see it twice in the church just along from the cathedral where, legend had it, the brothel to which she was condemned once stood. I can still remember . . .

'This is all quite fascinating. But we're not in Sicily. This is Venice. Which I'm pretty sure is quite a long way from there.'

We were in Mamafè for what was either a late breakfast or an early lunch. Lizzie had slept till gone ten and I'd no intention of rousing her. There'd been plenty of work to do anyway, reading and checking my memories against what I could find online and in the old books of Ca' Scacchi's little library.

'I was getting to that.'

'Good.'

She'd chosen one of the sweet pies, full of pale green pistachio cream. A tiny smear was dripping down the side of her mouth. Without a second thought, I picked up a paper napkin and dabbed at it. The kind of automatic intimate gesture I'd have made with Eleanor, who was just as messy an eater. It never occurred to me this was someone I'd only known for little more than a week. Someone who was still in some ways a stranger.

'Thanks.' She took the napkin and did the rest herself. 'Do we not talk about last night?'

'If you want.'

'Was it a mistake?'

'It didn't feel that way to me. Anything but.'

She finished her coffee. 'Me neither. I will leave you, though. You do understand? Whatever way this works out. I don't stick with people. I don't have the patience. Or the temperament.' She raised the empty cup in a toast. 'It's not you.' She looked around the charming little café. 'It's not this place. It's me. Sooner or later, I'm going to want to be on my own. Stories . . .'

'What about them?'

'I feel as if I've lived my entire life stuck inside one written by someone else. That it's time I tried to write my own.'

I thought of her mother, and that strange tale of Casanova she'd left us. 'Stories are ways we have of talking to one another. Of saying we feel the same things. Terrified at times. Elated at others. We need them.'

'We do. But after all these years, I want one that belongs to me.'

'Perhaps your mother felt that way too. She invented all these riddles.'

Lizzie sighed. 'I don't know what to think any more. Whether to believe the picture Dad painted. What to trust. What's . . . true.'

'I know you'll leave,' I said, and it wasn't a lie. 'I don't expect anything. I'm just glad we met. Glad you brought something bright and young and sunny into my life when I least expected it.'

That was it. The only real conversation we'd ever have on the subject, or so I thought. Brief, circular, evading anything that might edge too close to the emotional. I must have sensed that too, because I did something quite unlike me. I held both her hands across the table, then leaned over and kissed her quickly, fondly on the lips. She tasted of pistachio and deep, dark Italian coffee. In my memory, she always will.

'Back to St Lucy,' she said.

It was complex in the way the remains of saints so often are. Holy martyrs were, it seemed to me, the celebrities of the Catholic hierarchy, stars to be lauded, worshipped, remembered on their name day each year. Icons served up to flocks around the world as proof that God was real, along with deliverance for the pious and damnation for the wicked. Lucia belonged to Siracusa and always would. But her earthly relics were the property of the Catholic Church and would come to be scattered across Europe like sacred confetti made of flesh and bone. She would lie undisturbed in Siracusa for four centuries, only to be disinterred and moved to Abruzzo when Sicily fell to a Lombard warlord. From there an arm would be dispatched to a monastery in Germany, and the rest of her to Constantinople. In 1204, when the Venetians and their fellow Crusaders sacked the city – still a holy Christian site – Lucia's relics fell into the hands of the then Doge, Enrico Dandolo. They would be shipped back to the lagoon along with priceless works of stolen art, among them the famous four bronze horses that adorned the loggia of the basilica of San Marco until weather and good sense saw them replaced with copies and moved to the museum inside.

Two centuries later, another Doge gave Lucia's head as a present to the king of France, a bribe in the savage and complex politics of the day. The rest of her would remain in Venice, in her eponymous church in Cannaregio. Even then, her journey was not at an end. In 1860, the Austrians who then occupied the Veneto demolished the church, despite its connections with Palladio, to make way for a railway station that would be reached by the first ever bridge from *terraferma*. Not that many of those who pass through Santa Lucia station today know the origins of its name.

Fourteen hundred years on, the saint's remains would be transferred to another church in Cannaregio, San Geremia, where they would remain in a glass case, partially 'incorrupt', clothed and with a silver mask placed on her in the 1960s to hide the empty sockets of her skull.

'Cripes,' Lizzie said after I related the narrative I'd built that morning while she slept upstairs. 'Old Lucy did get about, didn't she?'

'Haven't finished. In 1981, two men wielding guns broke into San Geremia, dragged her mummified remains out of the glass coffin and left in such a rush her head and mask broke off and got left behind as they made off with the rest.'

'I thought you said the head was in France.'

Lizzie Hawker never missed a thing. 'Perhaps it was a fake head. I don't know. Saintly parts tend to multiply over the years. There's one chap from Spain I read about who has thirty-seven recorded penises.'

'I imagine that's a curse rather than a blessing.'

'Definitely.'

'Why on earth would someone pinch an old corpse?'

A question that had struck me too. There was a suggestion that the ransom note demanded a passage of a book by Primo Levi about his experience in Auschwitz during the war be read out in all schools in the Venice area. But the details seemed hazy.

'In any case,' I added, 'the relics were found five weeks later. Intact. On her saint's day, December the thirteenth.'

'A happy and fortuitous ending then.'

'Very saintly, I suppose.'

'You're good at this. Finding stuff out.'

'It's what I do. What I've always done. It's the only thing I know.'

'Not the only thing, love. You've found it then? This St Jeremy place?'

'San Geremia.' I hesitated, wishing I hadn't sounded quite so certain of all this. 'Possibly.'

We walked outside and went round to stand in front of San Pantalon. Lizzie put her sunglasses on immediately. The day was so bright it hurt the eyes. The newsstand by the bridge had a new billboard for the morning paper. The shout line on it now: *Scacchi Mystery Deepens, Dead Woman Unknown.*

I was still blinking when a hand touched my arm and a too-familiar English voice, half public school, half rogue, said, 'Mr Clover and Miss Hawker. What a lovely couple you make. A word in your shell-likes, if I may.'

Once again, I felt it would be impossible to meet Alf Lascelles – or Gervaise, as he introduced himself now – without the phrase 'bugger off' leaping instantly to my lips. But before I could utter it, Lizzie was smiling at the fellow, acting as if she was perfectly fine with having a lowlife tabloid hack on her case.

Our case, in fact. I didn't like the way Lascelles was looking at the pair of us. Wondering, perhaps, if he had another twist to tell in whatever sordid tale he had in mind.

'Rum do this, love,' he said as he pulled out his phone. 'Mind if I take a photo of the two of you?'

'We do actually,' I told him. 'So put that thing away.'

He did, with a shrug. 'You made a canny decision getting Arnold on your side. Hasn't been here long, but he's made some good friends. Got to know the ropes.'

'Did Enzo Canale send you?'

He didn't like me asking that at all.

'I'm not here on anyone's behalf but my own, thank you. Canale and I aren't exactly the best of chums at the moment.'

Lizzie's ears pricked up. 'May I ask why?'

Lascelles looked briefly embarrassed. A new one for me, and rare perhaps for him. 'Is it true he's your dad?'

'Is that really any of your business?' I asked.

'No. Not really. I do have my standards, Arnold. I know there's a damned good story here. A messy one, if I'm honest. Dead woman in the ground behind that palazzo. Turns out it's not Lucia Scacchi either. So where is she? What happened?'

'We don't know,' Lizzie told him. 'Maybe we never will.'

'That's what I gather. Doesn't stop Canale telling me I've got to write some cock-and-bull piece saying Chas Hawker murdered them both. That he's your real dad. That he's going to get his hands on Ca' Scacchi and turn it into something the city will be proud of.' He leaned forward and jabbed a finger first at me, then Lizzie. 'I don't like being used. Even if I do believe that bit about him being your dad. He showed me the papers. The rest . . .'

Lizzie asked, 'What do you want?'

He nodded at me. 'Like I told Arnold, I want the story. The real one when it comes out. I want it all to myself. I'll tell it straight. No twists and tweaks, I promise. There could be a bit of money if you need it.'

'How much?' she said.

He smiled, and I said to myself: you think you have her now. How wrong you are.

'Depends on the tale you've got to tell, love, doesn't it?' He glanced at me. 'How much you're willing to say.' He flipped out a business card. 'Mostly I've written opportunistic rubbish round here, as Arnold's doubtless told you. But I would like to have something proper in my portfolio. Something of substance. If you promise me you won't talk to anyone else, I'll stay shtum until the time's right. You have my word.'

'And if not?' I asked.

A shrug. 'Then I guess it's back to flogging crap to the tabloids. Like I said . . . best having me on your side, not your back.'

Lizzie held out her hand. He looked surprised, but he shook it.

'One other thing I should warn you,' he added. 'Canale's getting more than a little obsessive. He was trying to pay me to spy on you until I told him to get lost. I doubt he's given up.' He tapped his nose. 'Be wary. And good luck. I await your call.'

It was a twenty-minute walk to San Geremia, across the Scalzi bridge then along Lista di Spagna, the busy street that led from Santa Lucia, the station named after our distant saint. I kept looking round, Lizzie ticking me off at regular intervals for being so nervous. I didn't trust Lascelles and I doubted I ever would. The man was a chameleon, changing his appearance according to the company and the need. All the same, he had warned us in a manner that seemed quite genuine. It would be foolish not to listen.

She came to a sudden halt outside a shop window I'd noticed in the past, not with great interest.

'Isn't that lovely?'

Pastries, sweets, chocolates. All very fancy, not my thing at all.

'Pasticceria Dal Mas,' I said reading the sign. 'Rings a bell. Think it's quite famous.' She couldn't take her eyes off the window. 'You just ate a pistachio pie.'

'I know, I know, but it was tiny . . .'

No, it wasn't.

'You need to take care around Alf Lascelles.'

'Gervaise, please. It seems to be his preference now.'

'I don't care what he's called . . . Can you stop staring at the pastries?'

She nudged me with her elbow. 'Not easily.'

'Lascelles is a hack.'

'You said.'

'Untrustworthy.'

'Of course.'

'Then . . .' I was lost trying to understand whatever point she was trying to make.

'Told you already. I dealt with journos for Dad. Lots. You heard him going on about Canale telling him what to write?'

'Yes.'

'It's what they hate most. The good ones anyway.'

'Alf . . . Gervaise Lascelles is not a good hack. He writes for the most awful rags.'

She groaned. 'You're letting your prejudices get the better of you. The man has ambitions. Something better than his tabloid rubbish, he claimed.'

'They all say that.'

I checked up and down the busy street.

'Spotted anyone?'

'Well, no . . .'

'Then,' she went on with a triumphant smile, 'let's find Lucy.' She headed for the shop door. 'After I've picked up a snack.'

The rear wall of the church backed onto the Grand Canal. I'd seen it often enough from the vaporetto, and the lettering there that spoke of Lucia, Siracusa, a martyr in Christ now reposing inside, and a call for light and peace for Italy and the world. The front of the basilica seemed unremarkable, at least in a city so full of extraordinary sights. Except for the painting that featured above the entrance: a young woman in a pale red dress, extending a plate in her right hand, on it a pair of eyes.

'What does that say?' Lizzie asked in a quiet voice, pointing to the words above.

'"In this temple we worship the body of St Lucia."'

She stood on the steps, finishing the last of her pastry, and didn't move.

'Out with it. Something's not right here.'

I didn't rise to the bait. Inside, San Geremia was dark and vast and empty. The moment we were through the door, an elderly church helper sidled up and told us we had to be out in ten minutes; the place was about to close. The research I'd done that morning suggested there were interesting paintings tucked away somewhere. But there was no time. The man led us to the chapel where what was left of Lucia rested. I was glad of the silver mask, though her feet, as dark and gnarled as ancient oak, were still visible protruding from a gold and scarlet gown.

Our guide crossed himself, realised we were prurient visitors, not the faithful, and retreated to the door.

'OK,' said Lizzie. 'I've seen enough. Are we going to try the Corneille question?'

No luck there yet again. I dropped a couple of coins in the collection box and we left. Not that the man seemed to notice. He was on the phone.

It was good to be back outside in the sunshine.

Even better to find a café where I could enjoy a beer.

'You still haven't answered my question,' Lizzie said. 'What's wrong?'

'This.' I took out the map and ringed San Geremia in its small *campo* along from the station. We were looking for somewhere to complete Lucia Scacchi's circle. The church behind us might be the resting place of the Siracusa saint, but the location didn't fit at all. San Geremia was too far north and west. I'd spotted the problem that morning, but all the same, the clue was surely about Lucia, and this seemed the logical place to find her.

Lizzie got it immediately. She ran her finger from the slab marking the site of Tiepolo's column of infamy in San Polo across the Grand Canal to Giovanni e Paolo and the anatomy museum. Then she described a circle around the area where we were surely meant to look, north of the Rialto, all the teeming streets and alleys around the church of Miracoli where we'd walked with Luca that first day looking for our dead hunchback in his glassy tomb.

'Got to be around there, hasn't it? You said it was Cannaregio. The missing page. Where does that end? What comes next?'

'San Marco.' I took out a pen and drew a line along the canal north of the Rialto, left and right until it met the broad Rio del Mendicanti, which ran all the way to Giovanni e Paolo and out to the lagoon opposite the cemetery island of San Michele. 'You're right.'

'One last riddle. Thanks, Mum. You had to make it the hardest.'

'Hello,' said a voice from a neighbouring table. It took me a moment to recognise him: the chap we'd seen in San Geremia.

His English was perfect and punctilious. A retired academic was my first guess. I was right too. When we began to chat, he revealed himself as a former lecturer in town planning at the headquarters of the architectural university near Piazzale Roma.

'What exactly are you looking for?'

'A missing painting. A place that belonged to someone called Madame Corneille,' Lizzie said. 'My mother, or what happened to her. All kinds of things. It's quite complicated actually.'

He took a sip of his coffee and looked at me as if to say: *This does not help.*

'We have a set of riddles,' I told him. 'The last one was to do with Bajamonte Tiepolo and his former house in San Polo.'

'Ah. Tiepolo. Villain or hero. Depends on your point of view. The column of infamy. It's in the storeroom of the Palazzo Ducale now, I believe.'

'The next was to do with Santa Lucia. Or so I thought. Which is why we came to San Geremia.'

'To no avail? And this Corneille lady?'

I had to admit it. 'We really have no idea.'

Lizzie showed him the map and the circle we wanted to close. 'We think the place we're looking for should be some-where here.' She traced a ring around the edge of Cannaregio again. 'Not . . .' her finger jabbed at San Geremia, 'there. It can't be.'

'Not if it's a circle,' he agreed. 'And this last riddle came after the one about Tiepolo?'

I couldn't work out what he was getting at. 'I'm sorry, I . . .'

'Sometimes, with puzzles, one clue leads to another. The Tiepolos were quite a family. Two doges, if I recall correctly. The notorious Bajamonte. Then a few centuries later Giambattista, the painter, and his artist sons. Have you asked yourself if any of them ever painted Lucia? She was a very popular subject.'

'Caravaggio,' I said. 'Ortigia.'

He smiled. 'A dark and moving depiction of a burial. There are lighter portrayals, though she was a martyr, so the grief and the sacrifice will always be there.'

'Are you often in San Geremia, sir?' I asked.

'Only when I'm summoned.'

'We met an interesting churchman earlier on this odd adventure. Monsignor Fabrizio Ricci. Of the Seminary. Perhaps you know him.'

He looked at his watch, finished his coffee and said, 'I must be going. My wife gets cross if I'm late for lunch.' Then he stabbed a finger at the map. 'I suggest you take a look at Santi Apostoli. An interesting church. Who knows? You may find what you seek there. Though as to a lady called Corneille . . .'

'You haven't the foggiest,' Lizzie said.

'What a charming English expression. Quite. Good day.'

Santi Apostoli. A church I'd never entered, along the way from the station to the Rialto. Right in the middle of the area where we ought to be looking for the final dot in Lucia's story.

'Wait a minute,' Lizzie said as we walked at a healthy pace along the hectic shopping street of Strada Nova. 'You think our friend from the Seminary set that up?'

'I rather hope so. He and Luca were checking us out when it came to Ognissanti. Fabrizio would surely guess that last clue was about Lucia. A saint. Wouldn't he?'

'The man could have told us inside.'

That had occurred to me too. 'He was on the phone when we left. Probably checking with someone we were the ones he was supposed to tell.'

I got a nudge in the side and a grin. 'You said we had to complete the circle, not try and rush to the end. We'd never have found it, would we? One Tiepolo leads to another. She did like her puzzles.'

'She did indeed.'

There was a reason I'd never set foot in Santi Apostoli. This was a part of the city where it was impossible to escape the masses. A bustling square at the end of Strada Nova with cafés, benches beneath the shade of trees, the ever-hectic bridge to the former home of Marin Falier, the Doge beheaded for treason. Now a hotel with a restaurant on the ground floor.

The side of the church faced the *campo*, a brick campanile looming over the milling visitors below. A souvenir shop occupied the ground floor. The entrance was around the corner. To my eyes, there was nothing elegant or inviting about this overcrowded square, which was why I always walked quickly past.

Another dark and empty nave. No inquisitive attendant to meet us there. No need of one. We found her in a chapel to the side, one euro in the box to turn on the light. The last communion of Lucia, the saintly martyr painted by Giambattista Tiepolo sometime around the middle of the eighteenth century. Her face was pale and gaunt as a priest held out the wafer. She seemed on the very verge of death. In the corner at the front was a sharp and bloodied stiletto, next to it a silver platter bearing two ragged, severed eyes.

Lizzie wound her arm through mine, kissed my cheek and whispered, 'We did it.'

I passed her the map and my pen and let her draw the final dot and finish the circle. There it was, in the dim light of Santi Apostoli, not perfect but surely complete, the way Lucia Scacchi had intended. A line running from Giovanni e Paolo, out to the *sotoportego* in Castello, south to San Zaccaria, to Dorsoduro, San Polo, here, then back across to the tortured creature in his glassy tomb.

'I shouldn't swear in a church, should I?' she whispered.

'Best not.'

'But I want to. I thought there'd be some big moment of revelation when we got here. There isn't, though. Madame Corneille's lair.' She looked round for a priest or an attendant. A young man had just appeared from somewhere and taken a chair at a desk close to the door. 'Where the hell is it?'

I asked the question anyway and drew the usual blank expression. Then we wasted the best part of an hour wandering the streets between Santi Apostoli and the bridge across to Giovanni e Paolo, around Miracoli, to the north behind Fondamente Nove, lost as to how we might put this last piece of Lucia Scacchi's jigsaw in place.

After a while, even I was hungry. On one random tour through the back streets, we came across a tiny restaurant with outside tables beneath a canopy of wisteria. It looked delightful, and the name I recognised from Luca Volpetti's must-eat list. Lizzie was never going to turn down a meal, and the Osteria Alla Frasca looked too good to miss. We sat at a plain wooden table underneath a parasol and ordered a *misto bollito* of lagoon squid, mantis shrimp, prawns, monkfish, *sarde in saor* and *baccalà*, a plate of grilled octopus and prawns, a half carafe of Pinot Grigio and some water. I tried not to think about how much I'd spent on meals and wine over the last week. More than in a couple of months on my own. But it was good to watch Lizzie's eyes grow wide when something local turned up on the table. I imagined she'd be living off junk food back in London.

The meal almost took our minds off the fact we felt as if we were on the brink of giving up. Of outright, irreversible failure.

The waiter, a cheery chap of fifty or so, came to clear away the plates. Lizzie smiled back at him and, just for luck, I guess, asked if he knew anywhere nearby to do with Corneille.

The chap's eyes lit up. 'Ah. I have you now.'

We looked at one another, and she murmured, 'Excuse me?'

He winked. 'I'm not really a waiter, you see. In truth, I'm a detective. Working under cover.' One of his colleagues taking away the cutlery from the adjoining table overheard and said, 'Under cover talking crap for twenty-five years!'

'Twenty-three, if you please! Anyway. It is my role to judge the foreign guests we have here and, from what I see with these . . .' he pointed to his eyes, 'prise from them their secrets.'

Lizzie waved at him to continue.

'You are clearly a happy couple. Anyone could spot that. Only Detective Roberto can peer beneath the surface and declare . . .' He placed the plates back on the table and opened his arms. 'You are French birdwatchers!' For a moment he hesitated. 'Though your English seems very good.'

Lizzie blinked. I had a sinking feeling deep in my very full stomach.

'We're not French,' she said. 'Or birdwatchers.'

'You're looking for *corneilles*! Crows, as the English would say.'

'And in Italian?'

'*Corvo, signora.*' He winked again. 'You're welcome. Coffee? On me.'

Lizzie pulled out her set of keys.

'First,' she wagged a finger at me, 'you're supposed to be the clever one. You're supposed to know words like—'

'I've a smattering of French only, and much as I love birds, my ornithological knowledge is limited.'

'Second.' She waved the oldest, strangest key at me. The wings, the head, the beak . . . now that we knew, it was obvious. There was the mention in the Casanova story too: *the edges of her mask were fashioned from the black feathers of a crow.*

She raised an eyebrow. 'I don't suppose you mentioned this thing to Luca?'

'It's a key.'

'Which means that all this time, we should have been looking for the word "crow"? Or "*corvo*"?'

I sent off a short message to Luca asking him to check the city property and address records for any that contained a reference to either.

'Not your fault, I suppose,' Lizzie said with a marked lack of conviction.

By the time I looked up from my phone, she'd typed *Crow Venice* into her phone and got nothing but the details of a restaurant in Florida. Then, as I watched, it was *Corvo Venice*, and my head started to spin.

The results were all to do with a strange individual whose story I half knew, Frederick William Serafino August Lewis Mary Rolfe. An eccentric writer, educated con artist, briefly a turbulent priest, Rolfe was the self-styled 'Baron Corvo', who leeched off the gullible wealthy in the city at the start of the twentieth century, only to expire destitute after living in an open gondola in winter while conducting a string of affairs with male lovers, mostly city boatmen. He might well have moved in the same bohemian circles as Modigliani and Annibale Scacchi. They were all here at the same time.

Lizzie scanned one of the many articles about the man online and exclaimed, 'Bloody hell. This is some bloke. I thought Mum and Dad got up to odd stuff, but . . .'

'For the life of me I can't see how he fits in.'

My phone buzzed. Luca coming back with a very short message.

All I get is some very odd material about a very odd Englishman who used this name? Is this really of any use?

Then the waiter returned with our free coffee and a couple of limoncellos on the house.

'By the way,' he said, 'there are no crows round here.'

We were quiet for a good five minutes, then Lizzie gathered herself together in a rather schoolmistressy sort of way, folded her arms and plonked them on the table.

'For someone famed for their logic, Clover, you're not being very rational. We've been wandering round thinking something's going to jump out at us. And it isn't. Forget the conundrum at the end. Let's go back to the story. Didn't Casanova describe where they went? Where this Madame Corneille – or Crow or Corvo – took him?'

A good point. We squinted at the scan Valentina had sent us at the start of this strange game.

> Finally, in a place I may not name, we pulled into a rickety wooden jetty. She ordered the gondolier to hand us a lantern and wait. He looked reluctant until she threw him a generous coin. It was a gloomy, foul-smelling spot more suited for cut-throats and thieves than two well-dressed fugitives from the *ridotto*.
>
> There was the stink of tar, and I thought I heard the working of wood somewhere.

'Rickety wooden jetty,' Lizzie said.

'Doesn't tell us much. They're everywhere.'

She gave my wrist a light slap. 'It tells us there's an entrance from the canal.'

True. I was being slow. 'Then we know it's somewhere that must have a street entrance and a water gate.'

'Sounds like it. Gloomy, foul-smelling spot?'

'They emptied everything into the water in those days, so . . .'

'He says there was the stink of tar and he thought he heard someone working wood. A carpenter?'

'Carpenters don't use tar, do they?'

'I don't know.'

'A *squero*.'

'Come again?'

Osteria Alla Frasca was behind the Fondamente Nove waterfront, not far from the cove of the Misericordia marina. Lots of pleasure boats there, and I'd seen marine repair yards too.

'A boatyard,' I said. 'We must be looking for one of them.'

She grinned, and I could barely stop looking at her. The miserable, troubled woman I'd first met, confused, lost in a strange city, had vanished. Even the bizarre news about her mother, the mysterious corpse in Ca' Scacchi and the unwanted attentions of Enzo Canale seemed to have faded into the background. I wondered about what she'd said the night before. How she was determined she'd leave once she could. What I'd do or want if she changed her mind.

One last paragraph from the Casanova story. She read it on my phone.

> Only that the room was small and short on windows, made for warehousing, nothing else. And full of seeming riches – canvases, glassware, porcelain – stolen, hidden, I wasn't to know, and it seemed to me that if I did, such intelligence might place me in the Doge's dungeons before the night was out.

'Do boatyards have windows?' Lizzie asked.

I thought of the only one I really knew. The Squero San Trovaso, which I passed regularly walking to the Zattere vaporetto stops. One of the most photographed locations in Dorsoduro, with a *cicchetti* bar opposite that seemed packed with visitors most of the time.

'They have big doors, a ramp to the water, and no windows at all from what I recall.'

'Then . . .'

We finished the coffee and the limoncello. For some reason, this close to a solution, neither of us wanted to rush to the climax.

When the waiter came with the bill, I asked the obvious question: was there a *squero* nearby with a name like 'crow' or, more likely, '*corvo*'?

For once, we weren't greeted with an instant puzzled look. Detective Roberto scratched his cheek. 'You mean you weren't looking for the birds?'

'No,' said Lizzie. 'But really, you helped us all the same. A *squero* . . .?'

'I don't know. But if there is, I can find you someone who will.' He looked at the table. 'You'll need more wine.'

I ordered another half-carafe, and he went to the bar to make a call.

Lizzie's foot found its way to my leg beneath the table and her toes ran up and down my calf. 'I think we're about to hear a story, don't you? Our last. Hope so, anyway.'

'Our last,' I echoed.

The kitchen was about to close. We were the only customers left. No one else in the little square. Just a few people walking through, and none of them lingered. Enzo Canale had surely given up following us. He thought he had Ca' Scacchi in the bag.

Ten minutes later, a crooked figure shambled into the square on two sticks. A woman of perhaps ninety, bent, in a long dark skirt, navy jacket and black headscarf. She took the chair the waiter rushed over for her, then watched as he poured a careful glass, half wine, half sparkling mineral water, and placed it on the table along with a small plate of *essi* biscuits.

'My name is Claudia Zanin,' she announced in deep, heavy Italian, a voice that sounded as if it had been shaped by clouds of tobacco over the years.

Her hair was pure white beneath the scarf and pulled back to make the most of a face that might have come from a painting in the Accademia: lined, but proud and beautiful still.

'We've been trying to find somewhere we think is in this area,' I began.

She ignored me completely, took a long swig of her wine. 'I was born around the corner ninety-two years ago. My grandfather fought the Austrians. My great-great-grandfather was a courtier to Ludovico Manin, the last Doge, who surrendered the republic to Napoleon.' She leaned forward. 'I have a fund of stories about that sorry individual. Along with many others. They call me the walking history book round here. Since my husband died, I've taken great care to preserve my memories, writing them down in my notebooks. So many. So many . . .'

Lizzie was rolling her eyes as I translated. I hoped Claudia Zanin wouldn't notice.

'For example, the story of the poor lady who fell into the lagoon along there . . .' She pointed somewhere north. 'When they dragged her out five days later, her skin was slimy, almost translucent, and entirely bloodless. Furthermore, she had the eyes of a squid. I can vouch for it. My late husband's father saw her for himself.' She tapped the table. 'The skin of a squid. The eyes of one . . . Venice is unlike anywhere else in the world. Things happen here that others would find fantastic.'

'We're not looking for someone with the eyes of a squid,' I said, and decided to cut the translations after that.

'What then?'

Half her glass was gone, and it was just wine that replaced it.

I told her what we'd read in the Casanova story. Of a place without windows, perhaps a boatyard, an entrance on the water, one from the street. The smell of tar.

'What you describe, sir, is any *squero* there might ever be. Not that we have so many now. These modern boats are made of plastic and don't require the skills of old. As to how many build gondolas with the traditional craft . . . Few, I think. Around here, one only that I know of.' She pointed back in the direction of Giovanni e Paolo. 'Opposite the church of San Lazzaro and the hospital on the Mendicanti.'

'What's it called?'

'The Vecio.'

'Nothing to do with crows?'

She scowled. 'You never mentioned crows.'

'I was getting there.'

'How am I to help if you don't tell me everything from the start?'

'The name . . . we thought it had something to do with crows. The word *corvo*. But I can't find anywhere that fits.'

'*Corvo*. That's Italian. If it was old here, we'd use the Venetian. *Còrf*.' She laughed. 'That's what you're looking for. And it's not the name of the *squero* either. It's to do with a man. He called himself Corvo. We knew him as Còrf. A lord or something, not that he was. He dallied with gondoliers and men of a similar persuasion.' She punched my arm. 'He came from England too.'

I was torn between wanting to kiss her and curse myself for being so stupid. 'Baron Corvo. Whose real name was Frederick Rolfe.'

'Was it? The fellow was notorious back in my father's time. Forever scrounging off gullible visitors. Taking his boyfriends there after dark. It was no longer a *squero*, you understand. The place had long been abandoned. They used it as a warehouse or something. None of us would go near. Còrf died very suddenly, a pauper in a flophouse in Santa Croce, if I recall correctly. As did some of those close to him, or so I was told. Only to be expected.'

Lizzie was watching me intently. She knew there was something here.

'Why was it to be expected?'

The old woman looked at me as if I was an idiot. 'Because the entire property, the *squero*, the warehouse, the landing, was in the hands of the Scacchi family, of course. Nothing that cursed bunch ever touched came to any good. Just look at that palazzo of theirs. I still read the papers. Nothing wrong with my eyes.'

'Scacchi,' Lizzie said, recognising the word.

Claudia Zanin's gaze was shrewd and unforgiving. 'That's why you're here, isn't it? This isn't a game. A treasure hunt for tourists. You really want to find that place.'

'We have to,' I said. 'I can't tell you why. But we need to see it.' A thought. 'Are we the first to ask?'

'The first I've heard of.'

She finished the glass of wine and pushed it away. I placed my map on the table with the circle now complete in black ink.

'I won't take you there. My father said never to go near when I was a child. I can still hear his voice. There were so many stories about that accursed tribe. Their loose nature. Plenty behaved that way, but none, as far as I'm aware, made such a show of it. Someone put up a sign, hand-painted, by the entrance: "Corte Còrf", by way of warning. The man was in their circle for a while, you see. I've never been inside, never wanted to. I don't know anyone round here who would. We're a superstitious bunch at heart. Lord knows why the Scacchi were marked down by fate, but only a fool would want to share their troubles. That place was abandoned for a reason. Some things are best left that way. They're dead. They're gone. No good comes from digging up old bones.'

I pushed the map towards her, and my pen.

'You're sure?'

'Very.'

She circled a space behind the *rio* along from Mendicanti. 'Go to the waterfront and find Corte Berlendis. It's next to a small joinery. Then the *calle* of the same name behind it. The building you seek lies in a dead-end alley off there. Just that sign I talked about on the iron gates. Probably something saying entrance is forbidden. I don't know if that's there any more. For those of us who live here, it's needless. We know where not to go.'

Her razor stare turned on Lizzie. 'This is the woman in the papers. The daughter of the dead Scacchi *contessa*. One of that miserable, sorry tribe. And you?'

I hesitated, then mumbled, 'A friend.'

Claudia Zanin struggled to her feet, waved to the waiter, then looked round, blinking at the searing summer sun, and picked up her two black canes.

'I rather wish we'd stuck with my story of the woman with the eyes of a squid. Don't you?'

'That was a long conversation. Not that I understood a word.'

We were on the broad waterfront of Fondamente Nove.

San Michele stood behind its castellated walls across the water, Murano, with its glass furnaces, beyond that. Then the northern lagoon, stretching all the way to Marco Polo airport, Burano and Torcello and the wild, deserted marshland at its fringe. The air, the horizon, the water shimmered in the stifling summer heat. The sun always seemed brighter on this side of the city somehow. Though perhaps it was just because we'd walked out of the shade of the restaurant into the searing late afternoon, dodging beneath dark *sotoporteghi* and sheltered streets before emerging on that busy stretch of open water.

'Arnold? What was she saying?'

From the map and my phone, it was clear the place we were looking for was well hidden in the dense web of alleys behind the promenade as it ran towards the hospital.

'She said the place is cursed and no local would ever go near it.'

'She said a lot more than that.'

'It belonged to your family. The Scacchi. Once a boatyard, it seems. Long abandoned. With a colourful history.'

'No surprise if it was ours. How colourful?'

There was the joinery, a carpenter working on what looked like timber window frames outside. After that, an arch, part wood, leading into a passageway. The Corte Berlendis.

We stopped outside.

'She didn't think it was a good idea. Going in there.'

Lizzie took out her set of keys, found the one in the shape of a crow, with wings and those holes for eyes. 'You're in a talkative mood, I must say. It's not up to her, is it? If we owned the place, Mum must have known. Must have used it, I guess. To hide things. From Dad. If you don't want to come . . .'

I was looking up and down the broad waterfront pavement, back to the vaporetto stops, the other way towards the hospital. There were people around, walking, taking no notice of us.

She followed as I dodged beneath the arch.

It wasn't easy, even with Claudia Zanin's directions. Behind the waterfront lay a labyrinth of lanes, small, enclosed courtyards, alleys that led to nothing but the still grey waters of a *rio*. There was the smell of broken drains, and after a while, the houses gave way to empty shells of buildings, long dead, shattered windows, boarded-up doors. Dangerous wrecks, notices of repair long out of date. Signs that said *Keep Out*.

A lone mongrel, skinny, scruffy, with matted black and white fur, began to trail behind us, perhaps surprised it had found company.

We must have wandered down four or five dead ends and found nothing. Then the dog edged past and turned a corner up ahead. When we got there, it was standing close to another *sotoportego*, a small opening in the wall of what looked like the side of a derelict church. There was a stone virgin above the entrance, face broken, eyes blind, framed by pale, rotting wood. Our canine companion was whining. Hungry or just plain scared. Down the short cul-de-sac was a familiar sight, the *rio* again. It seemed to twist and turn here. And an iron gate to the left, black and rusty.

The painted sign Claudia Zanin had spoken of was on a wooden board held to the railing by wire. Decades back, it seemed, someone had scrawled obscene graffiti on it and a crude picture of two men locked together.

'This little chap doesn't want to come,' Lizzie said, looking at the dog still framed in the arch.

Beyond the iron gate was a small courtyard, nothing there except some roof tiles and what looked like rubble, either from ancient building work or a collapse in the fabric of the structure. To the right, just visible, was a weed-covered jetty running down to the canal. Exactly what I'd expect of an abandoned yard for gondolas and local boats.

Lizzie was trying the old crow key in the gate lock. Something that hadn't been opened in decades, perhaps not for thirty-five years. To my surprise, the key turned. She looked at me and smiled, a little anxious, I thought.

The gate wouldn't open. She pushed and pushed, and then I grabbed the iron railings and kicked at the thing as hard as I could. On the fourth attempt, it moved a touch. On the fifth, it broke free of its rusty hinges and crashed to the floor in a cloud of dust and shattered black paint.

'I was about to do that,' Lizzie said.

My foot hurt quite a lot. 'A simple thank you will suffice.'
I hobbled inside.

Across the courtyard sat a low black timber building, planked
sides, no windows, a sloping timber roof, a little like a decrepit
version of the *squero* I knew from San Trovaso. No one lived
in a place like this. From what we'd seen of the area, I suspected
there wasn't a residential block for a street or two. This was a
pocket of neglect and decay tucked away in a part of the city
few ever found.

Another lock on a green timber door. The third key Lizzie
tried from her ring worked. To my relief, this time we
sauntered through. Up three concrete steps we found ourselves
inside the dark and airy workshop of boatbuilders long dead.
A bird, a pigeon by the feathery sound of it, was scuttling
around the rafters. From sounds lower down, there might
have been a few rats. The place had the stale and dusty smell
of somewhere that hadn't been open to the elements for
years. The skeleton of a rotting gondola hull, unpainted, half
finished, festooned with spiderwebs, stood on wooden slats
in the centre.

Lizzie shrieked, hand to mouth, eyes wide open. She was
past the bows of the gondola, and I saw now a bundle on the
floor, not so far off the shape of the body we'd encountered
in the Templars' crypt.

While she cowered back, I crept forward, bending down,
and unravelling a pile of grubby sheets. Nothing inside except
more bedding, an old cotton nightgown, a few women's clothes
and a couple of pillows.

'She slept here,' Lizzie murmured.

'Looks that way.'

The only light came from the afternoon sun bleeding through
the cracks in the wooden doors that led to the canal.

'Wait here,' I said, and fumbled my way through the shadows
until I reached the water gate. There was a heavy iron latch
there, nothing else. I threw it to one side and rolled back the
sliding door. It was right above the *rio*, reached by the remains
of a sloping timber jetty that ran down into the grey water,
all splinters and broken planks. Whoever created this place was

determined it would always stay dry. Those stairs up meant the floor must have been raised. Someone wanted to work here, live here unseen perhaps, somewhere the *acqua alta* never reached. Tucked away in a hidden cul-de-sac at the edge of Cannaregio, it was as good a place to hide a secret as any. I could well believe Frederick Rolfe, the self-styled Baron Corvo, a man addicted to the arcane and the Gothic, might have appreciated its privacy. Perhaps led there by Annibale Scacchi himself.

Strong August sun flooded the room. Lizzie was holding her hand up to shield her eyes as she turned round, taking in what was there. Behind the shell of the half-built gondola, a long line of sackcloth ran up the wall. We walked over, kicking up ancient sawdust from the floor. There was so much timber here, dry too. Someone had thought about floods. I couldn't help but wonder if they'd asked themselves about the possibility of fire.

'Be my guest,' I said, waving at the sacking in front of us.

Lizzie lifted the nearest edge. Beneath, stacked on ancient dusty shelves, stood rows of packages wrapped very neatly in newspaper. All pages from *Corriere della Sera* from the 1980s.

'Mum used to read that,' she said in a quiet voice. 'Every day. Dad got a copy of the *Daily Mail*.'

'Very different papers.'

'They were very different people.'

Inside the first was a porcelain cup, very fine, gold-rimmed, decorated with a pastoral painting. Old, I guessed. Probably valuable.

'Does it look familiar?'

'I'm not sure. Maybe. We had cabinets. In the big room. Lots of bits and pieces there. Bric-a-brac, Dad called it.'

I bent down and helped her unwrap some of the other packages. More crockery. Then porcelain characters, Harlequin and Columbine, religious figures, bucolic scenes.

'Capo . . . Capo something,' Lizzie murmured.

'Capodimonte.'

'I'd forgotten all about that. Mum said we'd inherited a collection. I thought . . . I thought that was what Dad might be selling.'

To my inexpert eyes, it all looked genuine, old, not a modern reproduction.

'Is it worth much?' she asked.

I took the crumpled pages off another item. It was unpainted, an obvious classical scene, Achilles being taught to play the lyre by a bearded centaur.

'Could be.'

We walked along the wall removing the sacking. There must have been a hundred pieces or more, each wrapped in newspaper, stacked against the timber planking.

Nothing the size of a painting.

A boat went past outside, the engine echoing against the wooden walls.

'She's not here,' Lizzie said with a shiver. 'My mum.'

I kept quiet.

'Or Lucrezia and that stupid painting. Sorry, love. I've wasted all your time on a silly goose chase.' There was a distant yelp from the mongrel we'd met, one that turned into a long falsetto howl. 'Let's go.'

I walked back towards the water, thinking, for no good reason, I ought to leave things as we found them. Almost hidden in the corner was a door so small I'd missed it in the gloom. Just a latch to hold it shut, and we had to crouch down to go through. The chamber beyond was pitch dark and bore the musty chemical stink of tar and paint. When I went to the *rio* side and threw open the wooden panel there, filling the place with light and thin summer air, we saw why. Rusty pots of varnish and paint were everywhere, on shelves, on the floor. Splashes, black and green and red, on the planked walls. An ancient sprayer, some brushes and a collection of old carpentry tools sat on a wooden workbench.

In the angle by the water side stood an artist's easel, large and old, sackcloth draped over something that sat on its stand.

The dog barked again. Nearer this time. The sound made Lizzie jump, and somehow her foot must have found a can of something from the days when this was the boatbuilder's workshop. There was the clatter of metal on timber, then a smell like turpentine or white spirit rose over the dry timber planks, rank and choking as the contents spilled onto the wooden floor.

'Oopsy,' she muttered.

'Let's make this quick. If . . .'

I stopped, and so did the mutt. There was something new, something behind us, and it took me a moment to realise, to curse myself for leaving the way open to anyone who might follow.

It was the unmistakable stink of a cigar, dark and acrid, close and getting closer.

'Move,' growled Enzo Canale, barging me out of the way. Before I knew it, he was between us and the easel, a grunting, sweating figure, excited.

Lizzie didn't budge an inch. It seemed outrage more than anything. After all the work, all the challenges we'd been through to get here, Canale, it seemed, had somehow managed to follow us right to the door.

'Leave now,' I told him. 'There's nothing for you here.'

He laughed and nodded at the easel. 'You found her for me. The Borgia portrait. It's what I'm owed for all the years—'

'You're owed nothing,' Lizzie snapped. 'You—'

'I'm your father! I tell you what to do.'

'Just go,' I said. The smell of the spilled chemical was making my throat ache. 'We can talk about this later. With lawyers. With the police.'

'*My* lawyers. *My* police.' He pointed a finger in my face. 'I told you at the start. You're out of your depth and always will be. This . . .' he pointed to the sackcloth behind him, 'this masterpiece is mine too. God . . .' He leered at Lizzie. 'I made her, my child, watched by this beauty. Can you not understand? Or imagine—'

She flew at him, fists beating, eyes wild. He held her back with a burly arm. I came and pushed myself between them, stood there as close as I could manage.

One punch, hard, for me, more a push for Lizzie, and he sent us both reeling.

'Don't you want to look?' Silence except for the squawk of a gull outside. 'Surely you do. No man, no woman alive could refuse. I couldn't.' A nod at Lizzie. 'Any more than her sweet mother.'

'Filthy bastard,' Lizzie cried as I held her back. 'Just piss off . . .'

He had his hands on the sackcloth, grinning like a magician about to perform a trick. Then he lifted the cover.

For the first time in nearly four decades, the private portrait of Lucrezia Borgia, painted by Bartolomeo Veneto on the orders of her infamous brother, saw the light of day.

The question I'll be asked as long as I live is the obvious one: what was she like? What did we see in that derelict Venetian boatbuilder's paint shop, through an airy cloud of dust and mosquitoes hovering like dandelion seeds caught on a breeze? How wonderful, how alarming, how sensual was this depiction of the legend that was Lucrezia Borgia?

That's not something I can answer with any certainty. I recall an image much like the one Lucia Scacchi described in her strange story. A young, alluring woman, naked except for a pearl necklace, a delicate white cap embroidered with jewels and silver, a band of enamelled gold around her waist. Her hair was the colour of a ripe wheat field, her eyes a vivid blue. Just like the fictional Casanova, I wondered whether her breasts moved slightly with each breath, if she might step out of the painting and join us on the dry, splintered planks of the Scacchis' long-lost *squero*. Sure enough, glistening in the bright sunlight, there was a small rectangular glass case attached to the right-hand corner of the frame, in it a lock of hair that seemed to gleam a burnished yellow.

It was an image of intense and extraordinary power, even in those strange circumstances. All the same, it was her face I remember most of all, that disturbing combination of fey innocence and promise, allure and abrupt rejection. There was a Gothic power to her beauty, as there was a distinct and deliberate Venetian Gothicism to the story that had lured us there. Lucrezia Borgia was posed quite deliberately, as if she wished to spend the future centuries gazing back at the men who beheld her, greeting them with eyes so wide, so frank, so piercing, it seemed she judged us just as much as we were drawn to her.

I was lost for words. Lizzie couldn't stop muttering them, dark imprecations under her breath.

'Now do you understand?' demanded Enzo Canale, his triumphant voice the only coarse note in that dingy place. He reached out towards the precious canvas.

Had there been time, I suspect I would have answered: no, I didn't understand at all. There was something about her past comprehension. A glimpse into another world beyond the reach of most of us. A reason we'd been lured there we'd yet to discern.

Before I could speak, he'd taken hold of the frame and was wrenching the painting from its easel.

Lizzie put out a hand to stop him. 'There's something behind . . .'

I spotted it then, though Canale, so absorbed in his desire for the canvas, saw nothing but the woman lounging on the divan, as if he believed she had eyes for no one but him.

The trap should have been obvious from the moment we entered that place. The position of the painting was odd, awkward, and quite deliberate. The easel wasn't set against the wall as one might expect, but diagonally across the corner, leaving space behind. Something lurked there. When I craned my head to look, I saw a shape I began to recognise . . . a weapon.

I think I told him to stop as well. But now those last few moments are mostly a blur.

First there came a deafening roar. Then a storm of flame burst through canvas, frame and pigment, flew into Canale's face, sent him staggering back, mouth open, a bloody picture of pain and terror.

I watched what came next feeling like a helpless child witnessing an accident in slow motion, caught by the expectation of an inevitable outcome, incapable of doing anything but stare.

The blast had torn Bartolomeo Veneto's masterpiece into a flying cloud of shredded pieces, each a tiny candle in a host of sparking yellow flames dancing down to the floor, down to the dry timbers and the spilled spirit misting there after Lizzie's accident. So powerful did that deadly, invisible fog prove, it caught before the burning shards of Lucrezia Borgia could reach the timber planks. There was the softest of sounds, a gasp, no more, as the fumes ignited. Then everything around seemed to light up with sheets of glassy blue fire.

After that came the explosion proper. It was swift, it was violent, it was too much for what was little more than an ancient tumbledown shack. Before we knew it, the walls, the ceiling, the timbers were ablaze, shaking, cracking, falling amidst the stink and crackle of the heat.

'Lizzie . . .'

The dog was barking somewhere. Beyond the window, a passing boat, alerted by the noise, steered towards the *squero*, then held off, the man at the stern peering in at us, horrified.

'*Lizzie!*'

No answer. My eyes smarted from the acrid smoke. Then I heard her screaming. She was on the dusty floor, flames all around her, trapped by a blackened beam, wide-eyed, dazed.

Coughing, choking on the fumes of old wood and burning chemicals, I managed to lift the smouldering timber, throw my arms round her and drag her to the door. We stumbled from the paint shop into the boathouse proper; then, flames starting to lick and race all round us, smoke swirling in a foul and oily cloud, we staggered into the courtyard, and finally the alley.

The mongrel was outside, leaping up and down, yelping crazily. The boat had come to a halt by the end of the cul-de-sac, the man there on the phone.

There was the loudest explosion yet, one that dispatched a shower of sparks, blazing wood and rubble out beyond the *squero*, shattering the arch of the *sotoportego*, sending a rain of brick and stone to the ground. The way we'd arrived was blocked, with no safe route back to the street that I could see.

'Come! Come!' The boatman was yelling at us as he edged towards the ruined jetty. 'You jump. You must . . .'

'Not yet.' Lizzie chased the whining mongrel until she caught the terrified creature and lifted it into her arms.

The roof of the building we'd just escaped twisted, buckled and fell in on itself. The noise was deafening: the roar of flames, the crack of falling timber, and all the while the howls of the terrified animal.

I took her hand. We ran the length of the blind alley, leapt into the boat as the man clung to the wall, keeping it tight to the stonework.

A blast on his outboard, then we reversed into the *rio*.

It was only from a distance that I appreciated how lucky we'd been. Flames were racing through the boatyard, smoke rising in a swirling black plume up to a perfect blue sky. Claudia Zanin was right. We shouldn't have come.

Enzo Canale, the man who'd dogged us for days, was in there somewhere. Dead already. He had to be. Blasted by a hidden firearm, incinerated by the blaze he brought down on the little *squero*, alongside him the painting he prized more than anything. Far more than Lucia Scacchi, her palace and the lost daughter he'd known only in bitter enmity. I'd seen as much in his face.

An extraordinary image of a legendary woman from history had lured us all there. Never truly copied, never photographed. Now nothing more than a memory, too faint, too fleeting to be distinct.

A siren sounded in the distance. Then a second. The Vigili del Fuoco, Venice's fire service, would be on the way. I could almost see them racing through the canals.

Lizzie sat in the back of the boat, weeping; the smoke perhaps, I wasn't to know. The dog was in her arms.

When she looked up, I felt like a stranger. The riddles Lucia Scacchi had set for us were settled, the quest now over. It wasn't just Enzo Canale and the portrait of Lucrezia Borgia that died in those furious, racing flames.

Thirteen

The Unforeseen

The next few hours remain a blur. I dimly remember the fire service racing us to hospital, where we were checked for burns and smoke inhalation then made to wait hours for a discharge when they realised we were mostly unharmed. Physically, that is. We'd had a close brush with death in the *squero* that once bore the sign of Corte Còrf outside. That wouldn't heal quickly.

Valentina Fabbri was soon there, not asking questions, not yet. More concerned about our welfare than anything. Canale's corpse was recovered during the night. The next day was given over to forensic investigations of the charred remains of the boatyard. What both of us had seen that afternoon was soon confirmed. An expensive shotgun, made in London, one of Chas Hawker's hunting weapons, it seemed, had been rigged behind the Borgia painting, pointed directly at its back. Lifting the canvas from the easel made a simple mechanism pull the trigger. Even after three and a half decades, the cartridge inside still worked. The place was a fire trap, made yet more perilous by the spilled chemicals rising from the floor.

There was a reason Lucia Scacchi – Valentina felt sure it was her work, and it did seem obvious – had chosen that place, dry and safe from *acqua alta*. Why? Who was this aimed at? Her husband? Her former lover, Canale? Or just any man who wanted to follow the tracks in that odd story left beside a stranger's corpse hidden beneath Ca' Scacchi's giant chessboard?

Speculation was never Valentina's game, nor mine. If Lizzie was interested in trying to second-guess her vanished mother, she showed no sign of it. Once we were out of the hospital, being ferried back to the Grand Canal in a Carabinieri launch, she hooked her arm through mine, smiled a wan smile and whispered she needed some time alone.

I didn't argue. In truth, I felt much the same. The whirlwind of the past week had exhausted us both, physically and emotion-ally. We'd spent our time obsessed with the hunt for the Borgia portrait, never thinking about how it might end. Success, simple defeat or a win for Enzo Canale seemed the only options. Not death and flames and the loss of the precious object we'd sought so desperately.

The following day, Luca Volpetti called and asked if I wanted a coffee. We walked round to Adagio in the shadow of the Frari and sat outside, watching the tourists and the locals come and go. He was needlessly apologetic about how little he'd managed to help; how if only he'd been smarter, the outcome might have been different. But in what way? If Canale hadn't picked that painting off the easel, it would have been Lizzie. Or me.

Luca confirmed what I'd suspected: he and Fabrizio Ricci had worked in secret trying to penetrate the hidden mysteries of Lucia's story. The gentleman we'd met in San Geremia was an old friend of Fabrizio's, dispatched there by the pair, who'd worked out that the final clue was to do with the Syracusan saint. They felt sure we'd realise too, and that we'd head off to the church thinking it had to be the last piece of the puzzle. Then, checking the map and the circle themselves, Fabrizio Ricci had declared this impossible and set out to find another connection that might fit. We were to be guided to Santi Apostoli by their friend once he'd ascertained who we were.

I finished my macchiato and ordered another. It was a day for strong coffee.

'And the old lady at the restaurant? Claudia Zanin?' I asked.

Luca shrugged. 'I'm sorry. I don't know what you're talking about.'

I told him.

He smiled. 'Well, you were owed a stroke of luck. The two of us were utterly lost when it came to your final destination.'

'I should have told you about the key. Someone . . . you or Fabrizio, would have known *corneille* was "crow" in French.'

'My French is limited. His too. It would have meant nothing.'

I'm still not sure whether I believe that.

'We all make mistakes, Arnold. Don't blame yourself. I

should have searched the property records to see if there was anywhere else owned by the Scacchi. The idea never occurred to me. If I have an excuse, it's that I had a number of people breathing down my neck, desperate to see Canale's plan go through. Once he knew the body in the crypt wasn't Lucia Scacchi, he had the perfect justification to demand action. A historic property, legal owner unknown. The city buys the place, he forks out to restore it. Doubtless with a few gifts handed round in return. He'd have got away with it, too.'

'I rather hoped those days were gone.'

He toyed with the last of his *cornetto*. 'Me too. They seemed to disappear for a while. But the world's gone backwards these last few years. I try not to notice. Canale had so much money. Money always counts. We should never forget that. I like my job. I like living in this city. I'm sorry I couldn't help more.'

'Without you, without that pointer in San Geremia, we'd truly have been lost.' Lizzie apart, one thought more than any other had been nagging at me. 'What happens to the palazzo now?'

He looked round to make sure no one was listening. 'I really don't know. The city won't intervene without the promise of Canale's money. From what little I hear from Valentina, there's no easy way to declare Lucia Scacchi dead quickly. Lizzie is back where she began. In limbo. She doesn't own the place. I doubt she'll find it easy to hire a lawyer to help her overcome that obstacle as things stand. A notorious painting worth many millions lies in ashes. Even if it didn't, it wouldn't be hers.'

'Did nothing survive? We saw some ceramics.'

There were photos on his phone. I recognised the storeroom of Valentina's Carabinieri office in San Zaccaria. Some of the valuable Capodimonte ceramics seemed intact, though damaged by smoke. The remains of the gold frame of the painting were there, little more than twisted, blackened pieces of wood. A plastic bag of charred canvas lay next to them.

'There's no hope of bringing it back somehow?'

'We have some of the finest art restoration experts in the world. It seems one of the professors who teaches the subject came to give an opinion. She burst into tears.' He found another shot. A case, that lock of hair. It was a poor photo, infuriatingly blurry and indistinct. 'This must have been thrown out of the way by something exploding. It's a miracle it survived. A few strands of hair inside a smoke-stained piece of glass. All that's left.' He nudged my arm. 'You and Lizzie are the last two people alive to have seen her. What was she really like?'

A good question, to which there was no easy answer.

'Defiant,' I said. 'Not that many men might have seen it that way, which was possibly what the artist and subject intended. A private conspiracy between them, if you like.'

An inadequate response, I felt, but it was the best I had.

He seemed disappointed. 'Then the rest of us will have nothing more to enjoy than Annibale Scacchi's rather obscure attempt at a copy. I'm sorry things worked out this way.'

But they hadn't.

When I got back to my little *corte*, she was waiting outside the flat. Hair back, face pale, more serious now somehow. Older too, I thought. Or perhaps her real age. The Lizzie I'd known before was still the young woman trying to find a place in a world she barely seemed to understand. That particular quest, it seemed, was gone.

'I'm sorry I haven't been in touch. What an ungrateful cow.'

'Don't be ridiculous. You owe me nothing.'

'Now who's ridiculous? Something's going on.'

'What?'

'I don't know. Valentina Fabbri says she's coming round at eleven. I've got to be there. It's important.' A pause then. 'They can't charge me with anything, can they?'

'Can't think what. They'd have to charge me too.'

It did sound odd. A summons to Valentina's desk in San Zaccaria was the way she'd always worked. I'd been there so often, that small office had come to seem like the waiting room for my life. The place I went to find what happened next. Or at least the pointer to some stop along the way.

'She's coming to Ca' Scacchi?'

'Yes. I was to wait for her. Stuff that.' She took a step closer. 'Look. I know I've been horrible. I know I've ignored you. I couldn't help it. That's me. I need you now. I can't imagine being there alone. I'm . . .' She laughed, closed her eyes, and there was the hint of tears. 'It's stupid and I don't know why. But there was something in the way she spoke. It didn't sound right. For the first time ever, I think I might be scared.'

There were workmen in the narrow alley. Luigi Ballarin had brought his team back to the palazzo. A group of them were labouring in the courtyard, lifting the black and white slabs of the giant chessboard, opening up the entrance to the crypt. The city man watched, hand on chin, lost in his thoughts. Then he saw us, came over and said the warmest hello Lizzie had ever received from the man.

'Here,' he said, handing her a manila envelope.

'What is it?'

'Nothing you need worry about. Just bureaucracy. We have to register the crypt as a historical monument. The culture people in Rome have insisted and there's no arguing with them. They want photographs. Plans. They may send in their own excavation team. This is for information only.'

I wanted to know for sure. 'And the council? Their efforts to purchase the place . . .?'

He frowned. 'That was on the basis of support from Canale. Now he's gone, the plan will be buried with him.' He looked right at me. 'It would never have worked. He was trying his luck.' A nod at the palazzo. 'Hoping to get it for himself on the cheap and strip some value from it, I imagine. Canale was like that. It was what he did.'

'What do you want of me?' Lizzie asked.

Ballarin glanced at the house. I could see Valentina there, in the kitchen, watching us alongside two men in uniform.

'I feel your problems will soon be resolved, *signora*. But it's not for me to say. The Capitano can explain.'

Valentina was coming down the steps, uniform immaculate and pressed as usual. Something new in her face. She greeted the city man. And me. Then, finally, with the briefest of nervous smiles, my companion.

'Lizzie,' she said. 'It's time you met your mother.'

The ballroom had a few chairs set by the tracery windows. Sunlight was streaming through, the dust of decades rising on

the hot, sparse air. Silence once more, an awkward one; not
pregnant like the cliché says, but quite devoid of anything.
Emotion. Surprise. Wonder.

There she was, opposite us, a little way apart from Valentina.
Lucia Scacchi looked younger than her years, and so did her
clothes. Smart jeans, fresh white shirt, a silver necklace around
a long, slender tanned neck, no rings on her delicate fingers,
the hands of a pianist or an artist. She sat there, head up, gazing
at her daughter, not getting much in return. Lizzie was paler,
fuller of face. Perhaps those looks came from her father. But
I could still see the shared resemblance in their intense, sad
eyes, the chestnut hair, straight, pulled back to make the most
of looks that would always attract attention. I could imagine
Lucia as a model still, one of those smiling older women with
a mature beauty the magazines and ad people loved. Except
there was fear and trepidation there too.

It was left to Valentina to break the awkward emptiness. Her
voice echoed round the bare room. The explanation she had
to give was as precise and succinct as I'd come to expect. The
day before, as news of Enzo Canale's death was hitting the
headlines, along with the loss of a precious, legendary painting
in a blaze in a forgotten corner of Cannaregio, she'd taken a
call. It was from the fugitive Lucia Scacchi announcing she was
on a train from Naples and would give herself up to the
Carabinieri the following morning.

'Here we are,' Valentina added. 'Brought together in the
aftermath of an unfortunate death. A tragedy, though I
imagine few think of Enzo Canale in those terms. All the
same, I would like to know, Signora Scacchi—'

'I'm Maria Baldan now. Why did we have to meet here?'

Valentina thought for a moment, then said, 'You flee all
the way to Campania and still choose a surname from the
Veneto to hide beneath. We're here because I deemed it
appropriate. This is where the answers are. At least that's what
I assume. You tell me.'

'If I'm to be regarded as a criminal, should you not be
warning me about my rights?'

A shrug. 'Perhaps that comes later. Enzo Canale is dead.
You are here. You didn't need to be. No one had any idea

you were still alive. I would like an explanation for that as well.'

The woman I would always think of as Lucia Scacchi looked across at her daughter. 'Are you a mother?'

Valentina nodded. 'I am.'

'Then why do you ask? I needed to see my child.'

'Took you long enough,' said Lizzie. 'And a dead man.'

Lucia winced. There was an aristocratic delicacy there that Lizzie lacked. A touch of the *contessa* still.

'Do you imagine I wanted that?'

'Yes. I do.'

'Then it's time I disabuse you of that illusion. Time I told you a story I've never shared with anyone. Not the man who was the greater part of my life until he died. Not my sons, who I love as much as you.'

Lizzie's cheeks flushed. 'You don't know me. Any more than I know you.'

Her mother screwed her eyes tight shut. 'I understand you must detest me. But please. Do you honestly believe a mother is incapable of loving a child she lost? All the more when she was responsible for that hurt?'

'You were dead as far as I knew.'

'And now that I'm not, have I made you any happier?'

Valentina pulled a digital recorder out of the pocket of her dark blue uniform and pressed a button. 'Do begin. Spare us nothing.'

Nothing was spared. Lucia Scacchi saw to that.

Growing up, life at home had been uncertain. Money issues, constant worries about the future, how they might continue their lavish lives, when next a man demanding payment might hammer on the door. Her father always tried to make out these were concerns for little people: taxes and debts, duties and responsibilities. Ties that bound others, never them. The mores of the unwashed mob, he called them. The Scacchi were an ancient clan, with too much historic blue blood flowing through their veins to let mundane details drag them down to the level of others.

As they dodged creditors and sought favours from men who

would one day want their pound of flesh, her mother stayed silent, resigned, obedient, sometimes barely leaving that grand bedroom beneath Lucia's childhood quarters on the top floor of Ca' Scacchi. The room with the Borgia portrait was a place Lucia only got to know when she was older. When it was her turn.

The life they had was theirs, not her own. Study, girlfriends of her own age, the odd innocent boy occupied her time. Then she turned twenty-one, happily absorbed in a history degree at Ca' Foscari, and her father came pleading for help. For once he looked worried. He wanted her to come to the aid of the family by befriending a few of his business contacts, smiling at them, making them welcome.

One was Enzo Canale, a hotelier and restaurateur on the up. Another was Chas Hawker, a brash, loud Englishman quite unlike anyone she'd ever met.

Keep them happy, her father said, then turned his back and took to flying his light plane out of the Lido airfield, mostly across to what was then Yugoslavia, returning with what he never said. Except, for a while, he looked happier than usual and the unopened bills that sat on the desk in his little office seemed less numerous than before.

Canale was good-looking and possessed of a certain charm. Chas Hawker could summon up a private jet and fly her to concerts in London and New York, in the early days anyway. They were in competition for her attention, her beauty, and so her young head was turned. When they offered her something to smoke, she didn't say no. But that was all. She'd seen what other drugs did to people around Chas Hawker. Made them think they were immortal, all-powerful, attractive to everyone.

The first man she slept with was Canale. It happened in her parents' room when they were away across the Adriatic. Nothing planned on her part, a rite of passage, a way of keeping him happy, all beneath the eyes of the woman in the painting on the wall. Before she knew it, her father was pressing her to marry the man. It was almost an order. The family finances had taken another turn for the worse. He seemed to be in trouble with figures on the mainland, dangerous, powerful individuals. For the first time in her life, she saw him frightened.

One misty February morning, he announced he was flying to Switzerland with her mother in the little Piper he loved so much. An old plane, one not made for winter weather and mountain flights.

It was only later, when she began to understand the tangled web of debts and enmities he'd left behind, that she wondered if he knew and no longer cared.

Wreckage high in the Dolomites, obituaries in the papers that spoke of the fallen count and barely mentioned her mother, a commoner from Vicenza.

Canale was on her in a rush with what amounted to an offer of salvation. She'd just turned twenty-two. He was six years older and had, he promised, the money and the contacts to bury the problems of the Scacchi dynasty along with the broken remains of her parents.

Chas Hawker had three years on Canale and made much the same offer, at much the same price. Submission, obedience, enthronement as the new mistress of the bedchamber in Ca' Scacchi beneath the gaze of a pope's daughter hiding behind those shutters on the wall. Alone, scared, uncertain what to do about her father's financial mess, she knew she had to choose. It might have been a toss of a coin, except it wasn't. The Englishman made her laugh from time to time, while Enzo Canale never did and never would. In the end, it was as simple as that.

They married in Las Vegas at his insistence. A place, a ceremony, a false world of glitter and excess she hated. It went downhill from there.

Pregnancy and the birth of a daughter apart, the path from Nevada to the day her world would fall apart seemed short, predictable, and quite impossible to escape.

Summer was intense that year, steamy, full of sudden storms and thunder. But that was nothing next to the tempest brewing for weeks behind the mosaic walls of the crooked palazzo on the Grand Canal. There, the hasty union of a worldly man from the East End of London and the orphaned aristocrat of a noble Veneto family had travelled far beyond the rocks and was drowning in a tide of hate and fear and fury.

The final straw was Lucia Scacchi's discovery that her husband had been secretly stealing treasures from the palazzo and selling them wherever he could. No word on what he was doing, even though everything in the place belonged to her. No heed to export regulations and the fact they might both end up in jail if he was discovered and she forced to share the blame. It was theft, plain and simple, and his excuses when she confronted him – that the music business had turned sour and he needed the funds to start again – were futile. She could guess where the money was going: on drugs and his ineffectual efforts to rebuild his career, this time in show business, through sharks in TV and the movies, men like him only smoother, smarter. Little Lizzie was caught up in that already, hired out to an ad agency in London selling her innocent and pretty face for TV commercials while Hawker's ageing parents looked after the girl, keeping her apart from Lucia in Venice. No place for the child near a mother who was too bright for her own good, a resentful woman who might put awkward ideas into a fresh and unformed mind.

Chas Hawker had already stolen Lucia Scacchi's independence, and if she didn't act, he would rob her of her daughter too before long. There was only one thing he valued as much as Lizzie: the painting, the damned secret the Scacchi family had been hiding away for years. The Borgia portrait in the master bedroom, the naked woman men lusted after as soon as they'd seen her, the face, the body, the pose they always wanted above them when they came to visit. Chas Hawker adored it. So did Enzo Canale. She'd gone along with their wishes in much, she imagined, the way her mother and countless Scacchi wives had done before. It was a sacred ceremony, for the men at least, hooked as they were on the painting's power. Whenever she looked into the eyes of the Lucrezia portrayed by Bartolomeo Veneto, she saw something they never did: strength, knowledge, determination and no small amount of resentment. All the same, she knew it was priceless, and so did he.

Hawker wasn't the only one. And that just might prove the ticket to freedom she and Lizzie needed.

The night she finally decided to initiate the break, they were alone in the palazzo. Marisol, the pretty Filipino maid, had gone out on a date with the student she'd been seeing. A nice girl, genuinely fond of Lizzie, careful to steer clear of Chas and his louche mates. Lucia waited until her husband had vanished to the *altana* with a bottle of whisky and whatever was the narcotic of the night. Then she walked across the Accademia bridge and met Enzo Canale at his apartment in the Calle Vallaresso, close to the Piazza San Marco. It was a business transaction she sought. She made that clear from the start. Nothing else happened between them, nothing ever would again, however much he pestered. Her purpose was simple: to get the money that would allow her to live independently with Lizzie, set up a new home somewhere well away from Venice, then negotiate a divorce as amicably as she could.

Half the eventual cash she was promised by Canale, in return for Ca' Scacchi and all its contents, might go to her husband. So long as she and Lizzie were able to escape, she didn't care. Whatever the cost, the price would be worth paying. No Chas Hawker squirrelling away precious items from her home, wasted day and night on dope, bellowing in fury at her indifference. No stupid dreams of stardom forced upon Lizzie, a lovable, quick-minded kid who might, given the chance, follow the academic career fate had denied her mother. Nothing was set in stone. Their little world could still be put right. The mistakes of the past would be corrected if only she could prise Lizzie from her husband's clutches and set the two of them free.

It was dangerous. She understood that only too well. Hawker was a man of violence when denied, whether it was a new band, the dope he sought, or a frantic bout of sweating fury in front of the painting in the bedroom. He'd never raised a finger to Lizzie; he surely understood Lucia would bring the whole farce of their marriage to an end the instant that happened. But lately he'd been making threats, saying she'd been cheating behind his back. Two days earlier, he'd thrown at her the accusation that Canale was Lizzie's real father, something she'd denied even though she knew there was every

chance it was true. Theirs was a marriage that fractured early.
The few times she'd been unfaithful were mindless acts of
revenge, retaliation for Hawker vanishing with one of the many
music industry hangers-on he knew from the tours.

When she found out she was pregnant, the question of who
might be the father was one she pushed firmly to one side.
The truth of the matter could stay buried. Only Lizzie was of
any importance, the chance to raise her daughter in something
akin to normality.

That night, Canale agreed to her offer. The down payment
was to be in cash, US dollars, in her hands the following
morning. He wouldn't give up trying to win her back. He
wasn't the kind of man to admit defeat, any more than her
husband. All the same, a deal was done.

It was late when she got back to Dorsoduro, the night dark,
spotted with rain, the air heavy with the harsh stink of sewage
from a nearby *pozzo nero* recently emptied.

She stopped at the iron gate. It was open, though they always
kept it locked in case of intruders. Poor as the Scacchi might
be, the city knew they still owned some family treasures, fewer
now than many appreciated.

There were no lights in the palazzo.

The hairs prickled on the back of her neck. A sudden gust
of wind, it had to be.

Five steps in, she fumbled at the light switch for the courtyard. The thing refused to fall under her trembling fingers.
Then she heard them. Sounds she'd never forget. A woman
screaming, the roar of an angry man, the plashy noise of fists
and metal on soft flesh and brittle bone.

Her fingers tripped along the wall, landed on the right
place.

The light came on, bringing the giant black and white
chessboard across the garden to life.

Blood on the tiles, a dress she knew, a figure there prone
and broken, Chas Hawker bellowing like an animal above her.

'No.' Lucia Scacchi got to her feet. 'Not here. You need to
see. To understand.'

I knew we'd walk into that bedroom. It was one reason

Valentina Fabbri had summoned us to the palazzo. This was where the story began, where it might end too.

The sheets were still a mess from the night we'd spent beneath them. Two half-empty glasses of water by the bed. Lizzie glanced at me for a second and I imagine I blushed. Then I walked over and threw open one of the windows. A lively, humid breeze blew in from the canal.

Lucia cocked her head to one side and gazed at the empty panel where the painting had once hung. A part of me could imagine the missing canvas, re-created from that brief glimpse I'd had when Canale threw off the sackcloth in the abandoned *squero*.

'It was all about possession. Chas owning me. Enzo too if he could. Everyone owning the woman in that painting. So beautiful. So . . . available. Or so they thought. We were just things to them. Marisol too. Chas tried it on with her in here. The usual routine. He showed her the lovely Lucrezia. He did it with every girl we had. I didn't mind. It kept him from me. Marisol just laughed and walked out. He told me all about it. He always did. Thought it was funny. Everything was a joke, you see, me especially. I always fooled myself there was nothing malicious about it. I was wrong.'

She closed the panel. 'The poor girl must have sneaked in here before I left to see Enzo that night. I didn't mind her borrowing things. I just wanted her to ask. That one time, she didn't.'

Lizzie stared across at her, stony-faced. I wondered if that was the cause of her mother's tears, just as much as the vile, unwanted memories, a long-dead agony she was bringing back to life for us to witness.

'It must have been a special boy, I guess. Someone she wanted to impress. That dress was one of my favourites. Perhaps that's why. They gave it to me when I modelled for a charity night in the Excelsior. I forget the designer. If she'd asked, I'd have let her have it.'

'She was a servant,' Lizzie murmured.

Lucia looked right at her, as if seeing a stranger for the first time. 'So was I in some ways. A means to an end. Not like Marisol. Not quite. She was sweet and young, and I was none of that, not any more. We never knew where she came from. Chas found her through one of his drug dealers. Illegal, no papers, no tax, no records. We didn't care much in those days. No one knew she existed, not in Italy.' She blinked. 'Chas was waiting for me to come back, hidden in the dark of the courtyard. He had a hammer. I can still see it. And the blood. He didn't even realise it was her until I found that light.' She groaned. 'I can picture his face. Part of it was shame. Part of it regret it wasn't me.'

'I think you need a lawyer,' I said.

No answer. She walked upstairs and we followed. One glance and a brief, sad smile at the sign on the door, *Lizzieland*, then Lucia Scacchi stepped out onto the flimsy *altana*. There she leaned over the railings and looked down into the courtyard, the black and white slabs of the chessboard, the fractured statues of kings and queens. Someone – Ballarin's men or the Carabinieri – had set up a fresh tarpaulin cover at the entrance to the crypt. The surveyor was still there, hands on hips, supervising.

She pointed at the path from the gate to the giant board. 'It was there. No real light except the moon. He must have seen that dress and assumed . . .'

Lizzie pulled a chair from beneath the table and sat down, arms folded. She was fighting back the tears too.

'I ran at him. Screaming, yelling. Shrieking . . . trying to stop him. Got that damned hammer out of his hands.' A shrug. 'All I could think of was poor Marisol. A silly little kid. Dead because she borrowed a dress of mine the night my doped-up husband decided to kill me. There was nothing I could do.'

Valentina Fabbri looked up from her notepad. 'You could have got out of there and told us.'

A pause, a cold look. 'Even if I made it out of the door, my husband was friendly with the authorities. There was a Carabinieri officer . . . I forget his name . . .'

'Randazzo,' I suggested.

She looked surprised. 'What do you know of that man?'

'Enough.'

'The two of them were thick as thieves.'

'Then . . .?' Lizzie asked.

Lucia Scacchi hesitated for a second. 'Then it just got worse.'

Her first thought was a simple one: how to get out of there alive. Hawker was still furious, still crazed. She'd never seen him that bad. He wanted Marisol's corpse gone, hidden, wiped from his memory, as if that were possible. There was, they both knew, a place for that. When she'd been trying to interest him in the city's history and culture, she'd told him about the crypt, built by the Templars who'd once had a small church on the site. Another Scacchi secret, like the painting by Bartolomeo Veneto. A hidden grave for a corpse he ached to forget.

Obedient, silent, terrified, she took Marisol's feet and left her bloody torso to him. The young woman was heavier than she expected. Perhaps that was what happened to someone when life was lifted from their lungs. Together they carried her battered body down the worn steps, then laid her in front of the altar. There, Lucia Scacchi said a silent prayer, the first since she was a child.

After that, she turned her back on him and, shaking like a leaf, walked upstairs to the kitchen, tried to wash the blood off her hands, her clothes, wondering if the memory of it might ever go away. She was so focused on the task she never realised he'd come up close behind until she felt his breath on her neck, then his hands on her shoulders, roughly turning her round.

He had the hammer still, murder in his eyes.

'I won't tell,' she said, desperate. 'I won't do a thing. Only what you say.'

It all came out in a rush. If she tried to go to the police, he'd kill her before she could say a word. If, somehow, she managed to escape him and reach them, then it was Lizzie who'd pay. Sweet little Lizzie, the innocent who wandered into their ragged, disjointed lives from time to time, eyes wide, astonished, incapable of comprehending what was happening beneath the roof of their crooked palazzo home.

Hawker hit her once, a brutal swipe around the face. She'd

sleep on the sofa in the little study, he ordered. Where she spent most of her days anyway.

Alone, cold with fear, her mind began to race.

The typewriter was there. The story she'd been working on for months, one that came straight out of her somehow and she never knew why. Now she was beginning to understand. It wasn't about Casanova, even the fictional one. It concerned the two of them. Chas Hawker looking for one thing all the time, pleasure. A wife who in some way was willing to placate him, but with a warning too that they were slowly coming apart, walking down a dark path, one steeper and more dangerous than either was to know.

She couldn't let it go. Couldn't get Marisol out of her head, how that corpse beneath the earth was meant to be her. All the things she might have said or done that would have kept the girl alive. She wanted him to pay. And if trying meant he killed her . . . maybe it was all she deserved. Failed wife. Failed mother. Failed . . . everything.

An idea grew, as crazy as anything she'd been through that evening. The old travel book she used to read for fun was on the desk, a reference point for the story. There, she found the secret places she'd add as a riddle to the Casanova tale. Through the night she typed, softly, each letter placed with the utmost care. Then, in the morning, when she heard Hawker leave the palazzo, she took the pages down into the crypt, left them beneath Marisol's body, crept back into the house, prised the Borgia portrait off the wall, put one of his shotguns into a case for protection too. Finally, she tapped out a message for a man she prayed she'd never see again.

You have my silence now, husband. For the Lady L you know where you must look if you dare.

She knew where she was going. The abandoned *squero* in Cannaregio the family had owned for years, a place too derelict to find a tenant even if someone ignored the dark stories the locals told. It was a Scacchi property. Already she'd started to sneak out some precious items from the palazzo, Capodimonte and other ceramics, hiding them there from his thieving hands, hoping he wouldn't notice until she had him out of her life.

At ten, as agreed, she went to see Enzo Canale to get the money. Signed a piece of paper that meant very little. Only a promise to give him first option on the sale of the palazzo her family had owned for half a millennium. He never noticed the difference in her. Just kept trying to persuade her to move in with him, to abandon one possessive man for another. He was happy to think he might be buying his way back into her life. She was quietly delighted she'd be ripping him off with an empty promise.

Cash in a briefcase, the way Enzo Canale liked. Enough to escape. One more night in the *squero* trying to think straight, to plan. Trying to still her mind.

It didn't work. She had the shotgun. She had the painting. A tripod stand the *squero* used, as good as an easel. It wasn't vengeance, not unless he made it so. Lucrezia Borgia had gazed down on a succession of men over the centuries, all fired by her steady blue gaze, not comprehending what might lie behind it. If Chas Hawker came for her, then he could bear the consequences. A jerry-rigged snare, wire and string hidden behind the canvas in a corner, would lie in wait. Whether he had the energy to follow the intricate steps of her puzzle she'd no idea. Or if the trap would work.

Nor did she care. The next morning, she took her money and walked to Santa Lucia station, ten minutes on foot, looking every which way, wondering if Chas Hawker might find her. Wondering, too, whether, if he didn't, he'd trust her typed pledge left in the palazzo, promising silence in return for Lizzie's life.

A train for Naples was waiting, so she took it.

'I hid away in a tiny hotel in Sorrento, buying the papers. Italian. English.' She winced. 'It seemed I was soon dubbed a suicide on Chas's word. It suited me fine.' She leaned back against the railing, folded her arms, tried to smile at her daughter. 'It meant you were safe.'

'It meant you were dead,' Lizzie told her.

She nodded. 'As I was. Lucia Scacchi. I wanted her that way. Maria Baldan was different. A start from nothing. No past. No murderous husband. No old palazzo to worry about.

No lurid, hypnotic painting watching me from the wall. The woman I buried was half crazy, just like the man she stupidly married. What made some kind of sense to her meant nothing to me in Sorrento. Chas was gone. Losing you was the price I had to pay. I had no choice. Can't you see?'

There was no answer.

'Of course you can't,' Lucia said. 'You weren't there. You didn't know the man I did. He made my life a misery the few years we were together. He ridiculed who I was, this city, mocked everything we stood for. He stole what had belonged to my family for centuries and sold it to buy himself a quick fix, a moment out of his misery. He murdered that poor girl thinking it was me. He told me he'd take your life if I gave him up to the police. If ever I tried to prise you from him. To begin with, I wanted him dead. A little while after, I wanted him hurt. In the end, I didn't think about him at all, and that was the happiest outcome of all. I hoped that painting, that gun would be forgotten. All I still thought about was you. And there my hands were tied. Because even when I heard he was dead, I knew you could only hate me.'

'You did hurt him,' Lizzie said in a quiet, troubled voice, almost that of a child. 'I saw it.'

There was the briefest flicker of remorse on her face. 'If you weigh the guilt in the balance, I think I'm on the lighter side. I paid too.' She looked for a fond glance in return, got nothing. 'I never thought I'd see my little girl again. I can live without your forgiveness. But surely you can understand a little of what I went through?'

No answer again, just a strange silence, empty and endless, punctuated only by distant voices, the rattle of boat engines, the whirr of insects and the occasional cry of a bird. The soft, exotic coloratura of a summer night in Venice.

Lucia's hold on herself was breaking as we watched. Slow tears started to run down her cheeks as she leaned back against the balcony and threw out her arms.

'I'm sorry! Sorry for everything. I'm sorry I managed to kill Enzo Canale after so many years. I'm sorry I made a new life for myself.' Quiet then. 'I met a good man. We never married. I couldn't. But we were happy while it lasted. I have two sons, one a doctor, one a lawyer. I imagine I'll be needing him before long. Please try—'

There was a loud crack. Then another. The *altana* had worried me the first time I'd stepped on it with Lizzie. Now, I could appreciate how rickety the ancient structure was. The railing came away behind her, and there was that terrible moment I'd imagined: someone shrieking, trying to balance against nothing, tumbling back into emptiness high above the marble chessboard below.

I leapt off my seat, reaching for her. There was a look on her face I'll never forget. Surprise, acceptance too. If she'd fallen to her death from the disintegrating ledge above Ca' Scacchi's courtyard, it seemed to me Lucia Scacchi would have regarded it as no more than poetic justice, punishment due for the dreadful tale she'd just told us.

All the same, I got there, desperate hands clutching at her waist. The floor was beginning to give. Her eyes seemed to say: *Let go*.

With more than a little force, I managed to drag her back from the brink of the failing timbers. Then Valentina and Lizzie were there, hauling the two of us off the shaky wooden platform, back to the palazzo and the corridor with the sign that still said *Lizzieland*.

There Lucia Scacchi fell to the floor, weeping, lost.

There her daughter came and knelt beside her, crying too.

The *altana* was falling apart behind us, planks and broken railings tumbling noisily down to the courtyard, shattering on the marble slabs.

All the same, I heard.

'It's all right, Mum,' Lizzie whispered, holding her tight.

Fourteen
Epiphany

Summer slipped by as season edged into season. Before long the days turned short, sometimes grey and dull, damp and dismal, then, as the year approached its end, the dazzling brightness of the short winter days emerged, blue sky frosting over lagoon grey.

Christmas passed in a leisurely haze of meals with Volpetti and his friends, Valentina and her many relations too. Capodanno, New Year's Eve, found me happily on my own, lost in the crowd filling the point of the Punta della Dogana as I watched the Bacino San Marco ablaze with fireworks, struggling to dismiss the thought that Eleanor would have so enjoyed this sight.

Then it was 5 January, the day before Epiphany, a winter counterpart to Ferragosto. Once the celebrations were over, and the young busy enjoying their gifts from La Befana, the friendly witch, much of the city would shut up shop until the end of the month. A welcome break after the hectic Christmas season. A time to relax before Carnival, and the return of swarms of goggle-eyed visitors.

An opportunity, too, for a fancy Milanese fashion house to show off what they'd achieved after shipping their architects and designers into Ca' Scacchi to commence the task of bringing the fallen palazzo back to life. Much had happened over the preceding months, little of it expected that day Lucia Scacchi nearly died tumbling from her wreck of an *altana*.

Another depthless Venetian night. There were elegant flood-lights in the courtyard and fiery gas heaters to keep off the bitter winter cold. Beneath them, the pieces, men and women in ornate Renaissance costumes, shuffled around the giant chessboard. A hundred or so guests were flitting between the match directed by two grandmasters through megaphones and the upstairs reception room, where a string quartet was playing a medley of Corelli and Vivaldi. The evening appeared as elegant as a Tiepolo *ridotto* depiction from Ca' Rezzonico: swanky clothes, warm smiles, a constant swell of chatter over glasses of Prosecco and dainty plates of *cicchetti*.

They were all there beneath the glittering restored Murano chandeliers. Valentina in a ballgown alongside her husband, Franco, dressed as an eighteenth-century Italian dandy. Luca wore a purple velvet jacket and cravat as he led one of his lady friends from the university around the room, introducing her to people I didn't know and didn't much want to. Ballarin was accompanied by a whole delegation from the culture department, along with the mayor, all in dinner jackets, a couple with cummerbunds.

Gervaise Lascelles was working the room like a professional, wearing full Highland dress for some reason, Crail jacket, sporran, tartan kilt and even, God help me, a *sgian dubh* dagger tucked into his sock. I, on the other hand, was now quite at one with the idea Italians would never be impressed by what little sartorial sense I possessed. I wore the best clothes I could find: a tweed jacket, brown corduroy trousers, denim shirt and a thick seaman's pullover from a local shop in Via Garibaldi. At least I was warm.

Lucia and her daughter were now formally joint owners of Ca' Scacchi, happy to receive the fashion company's rent and contribution to repairs, along with a substantial donation organised by the council and an international cultural charity. No longer the cursed palazzo, the building was to be both showcase and Venetian outpost for the glamorous brand, a place for fashion shows and public events, while the remainder of the building was converted into luxurious accommodation for visiting VIPs, with the occasional opening for a curious general public.

A happy outcome, it seemed to me, reached in the oddest of ways. On the night she nearly died, Lucia Scacchi was taken into custody, a guest of the women's prison on Giudecca, as a small army of lawyers assembled to decide what to do with the prodigal contessa, newly returned. I'd led Lizzie across the canal to see her there one bright September Thursday. That was when the inmates ran a stall outside the jail, selling fruit and vegetables from their market garden and cosmetics made in the laboratory behind the walls.

The prison governor was a kindly woman, sympathetic to both mother and daughter, and, after a little largely unnecessary translation on my part, happy to allow the two to enjoy a supervised coffee at a nearby bar. I made my way back to the vaporetto stop. They had their private problems to deal with, and I was engaged in business of my own.

I wasn't surprised by Lizzie's sudden interest in her mother. She'd spent her life caring for an ailing parent. The need to support, to protect was in her upbringing from the time Chas Hawker took her away from Venice and made his own sad, failed effort to turn her into some kind of star. Now Lucia Scacchi – she'd reverted to her real name – was the obvious object for her loving attention. Mostly, to begin with, as a shield against the lawyers. The English legal system has always baffled me, though next to its Italian equivalent, the world of wigs and torts back home seems quite rudimentary and straightforward.

After Valentina passed on the case for investigation, the advocates, prosecutors and magistrates lumbered into action, a swarm of black-robed creatures much like the crows we should have been pursuing through Venice all that time. As far as I could comprehend, two factors complicated the question of whether Lucia could be tried for Enzo Canale's death. The first was the statute of limitations and how that might be applied. If the crime of setting up that deadly shotgun trap was judged to have taken place at the moment of its commission, thirty-five years before, then she was beyond the reach of the law. But should the magistrates decide that, in legal terms, the offence occurred the minute Canale ripped Lucrezia off the easel, then a charge might be laid.

The second was Canale's post-mortem. The man had taken a shotgun blast to the face and chest. After that, fire had consumed the *squero*, a blaze so fierce it took the city fire brigade two hours to bring it under control, and a further hour to remove Canale's corpse from the embers. A veritable queue of medical examiners then assembled to decide the cause of death, much as they had done over the corpse in the crypt that turned out to be the unfortunate Filipino servant, Marisol. Was it the shotgun blast that killed him? The blaze? Or a combination of both? In which case, how might the blame be apportioned to Lucia, if the law allowed it to be imposed at all?

Thorny questions I followed in a distanced fashion. By October, as autumn mists began to cast an opaque haze across the city, the picture regarding the future of Lucia Scacchi slowly began to clear.

The catalyst was that powerful weapon public opinion, manipulated, to the surprise of many, by our dogged follower Alf – now Gervaise – Lascelles. Seemingly out of nowhere, he went public, in a very professional and organised fashion, with a series of true-crime podcasts entitled *Death and the Cursed Palazzo.*

Lascelles, to give him credit, could write well when given the opportunity, and came up with a tale that was decidedly less lurid than the title made it sound. It was, in his hands, a story of family tragedy, mistaken identity, traumatic breakdowns, and, in the end, coincidence and rotten luck. The old tabloid hack seemed able to lay his hands on documents that should, Valentina Fabbri complained out loud, never have found their way into the public domain. Historical witness statements, reports from Ugo Abate's time in the Carabinieri, details about the history of the now-vanished Borgia portrait and the copy by Annibale Scacchi that had lain unseen in Ca' Pesaro for decades. The first episode went live a mere five weeks after Lucia was taken into custody. More swiftly followed, reaching an international audience after they were taken up by one of the big audio companies spotting an opportunity to enter what I gather was a burgeoning true-crime podcast market.

By the third, Lizzie was on board, in interviews where she came across as intelligent, caring, highly articulate and very convincing. For the fourth, her mother took part too, recorded in the market garden of the Giudecca women's jail, smiling for the photographer there as she tended to the vegetables, praising the kindness of both warders and her fellow inmates while hoping she'd soon be able to be reunited with her daughter and begin to heal the wounds of the past.

Days after that episode appeared, the medical examiners decided Canale had died of smoke inhalation and a heart attack, rather than the shotgun pellets he'd taken to his face and upper torso. At the same time, as sympathetic international interest in the case grew, the courts determined that any offence committed by Lucia Scacchi had taken place so long ago, she was beyond prosecution.

On a dull November morning, a battalion of TV crews, reporters and photographers waited for her to emerge through the battered green doors of the women's penitentiary in a former convent on Giudecca's Fondamenta de le Convertite. Good news and a moving story were always welcome, and Lucia and her daughter, two smart, attractive women, seemed made for the cameras and the TV interviews. Before long there was talk of a book, a TV series even, all expertly choreographed by Gervaise Lascelles, the proceeds divided between the three.

As if sensing the public mood of support for the women, Ballarin declared Ca' Scacchi fundamentally sound but in need of new purpose and a good deal of investment. The fashion house had been looking for a base in the city for some time and rapidly emerged as a potential saviour. In the space of a few months, Lucia Scacchi turned from unknown fugitive to a heroine who'd stood up to a murderous husband, her daughter transformed from a penniless failed actor into the stalwart supporter of a victimised parent.

I watched, I listened, I read, though much I knew already and what was new seemed mostly frippery. I never made any attempt to talk to them any more than they contacted me. The one time I bumped into Lizzie, while walking to light a candle in memory of my Eleanor on the November weekend of the Festa della Salute, we smiled at one another in the embarrassed way I imagine old lovers do. Not that I fitted the description, in all honesty. That night in Ca' Scacchi was a brief, unconsidered moment of closeness on both our parts, random, unforeseen. An instant, never a beginning.

Then the invitation dropped, and I found myself back in Ca' Scacchi for the first time since that tumultuous summer, listening to a string quartet, awkward among all those elegant, well-connected people. Struggling to strike up a conversation amid the music and the babble of voices – *chiacchiere* in Italian, which, curiously enough, is also the name of a sugary Carnival sweet that was being passed around the room at the time.

I was about to try to sneak out when, from behind, an arm locked in mine and a woman's voice, low, very English and earthy, whispered, hot breath in my ear, 'Not so quick, Signor Clover.'

Lizzie was in an elegant outfit of shiny cream silk, a cocktail dress perhaps, not that I really know what one of those is. A gift from the fashion house along with the loan of a diamond necklace and a matching bracelet. Her hair was up in film star fashion, every strand in place. I was aware she wore subtle make-up and bore the distinct scent of perfume. The same woman, just a side to her I'd never known. I couldn't help thinking Chas Hawker would have been proud to see her like that. This was the daughter he'd surely hoped for: poised, confident, beautiful.

'It was you, Arnold, wasn't it? I'm sure. Don't try to deny it.'

That took me aback. 'I haven't the faintest idea what you mean.'

'Upstairs,' she said, tugging my arm. 'We need to talk.'

Most of the building was still roped off, under the cosh of the builders. There was a new *altana* on the top floor, all fresh timber, bare planks pale under the moon and stars, a floodlight on the trellis edge shining down onto the human chessboard below. Lizzie strode straight ahead. I followed gingerly. The game was mostly depleted of its pieces. It looked as if the black king was close to checkmate.

'Lizzie. You must be freezing.'

'We're English. Aren't we?'

I removed my jacket and offered it.

She laughed, pushed it away and took my cold hands in hers. 'I'm sorry I used you. Then abandoned you.'

'It never felt that way.'

'You don't have to protest.'

'I do. You had a lot to deal with. I was happy to be there when you needed me. Happy – happier, if I'm honest – when you didn't.'

She leaned against the railing and kept quiet.

'The thing is,' I went on, trying to find the words, 'we spend so much of our lives looking forward. For what's to come. What might lie in store. Then, when we get older, it changes. We stop looking forward and begin to look back. You haven't got there yet. You won't for a long time. I have. It changes things.'

She shook her head and snorted. I couldn't take my eyes off her. 'Oh dear. You've such wonderful insights into other people. Their problems and how you might solve them. Into this.' She waved her arm over the rooftops glistening under the moon. 'Your strange new home. I can't help but feel you barely know yourself, Arnold Clover. There, I said it. Me and Mum are leaving tomorrow. First thing. Flight to London, then Miami.'

I didn't know what to say, so I muttered a hopeless, 'Sounds very nice.'

'World cruise. Three months on a liner. Away from . . .' She glanced at the corridor behind us. The *Lizzieland* sign was gone. The place was full of builders' and decorators' material, buckets and ladders, cans of paint. 'Away from all the memories. Good and bad.'

'An excellent idea.'

'I couldn't leave without saying thanks.'

'No need.'

'I still haven't paid you.'

'Consider it a gift. It was just my time.'

She folded her arms and groaned. 'Oh Arnold. We both know it was a lot more than that.'

'I'm sorry?'

'Gervaise would never admit it whenever I asked. I imagine that was part of the deal. You kicked his backside to get him going with the podcast idea. You found him all the stuff he needed for his stories.'

'I really don't—'

'Terrible liar still. That'll never change.'

'The stuff, as you call it, could only have come from a variety of sources, surely. The Carabinieri. The city council. The Archives . . .'

She raised a finger in the icy air. 'Ah. Now I get it. You brought Valentina and Luca and Ballarin in on the act too. And all the while your mate in the Carabinieri was out there shrieking about how shocked she was that all this *stuff* was coming out. God, you're sly.'

'I thought I was a terrible liar.'

'Sly and a terrible liar. Those two aren't incompatible.' She grabbed my arm. 'It is decidedly cold out here. Downstairs. I got them to do it first. There's something you need to see.'

I couldn't begin to guess how much the fashion house had spent on that main bedroom. New silk wallpaper, elegant curtains with the brand's crest, woven by Bevilacqua in their weavers' palazzo by the Grand Canal in Santa Croce.

The bed was bigger, a four-poster, covered with a velvet spread. The bathroom door was open, and I could see one of those fancy rain showers, and sparkling ceramics.

It was hot. Lizzie went to the right-hand window and cracked it open. A sliver of delicious fresh cold air drifted in from the Grand Canal, along with all the noises I recognised from the previous summer, made sharper and clearer by the winter evening.

'We've one month a year to use this place as we like,' she said, her back to me. 'I guess we could stay here. Or let you move in if you fancy a little luxury . . .'

I laughed and said Ca' Scacchi wasn't really me.

'It's not cursed. It never was. A palazzo didn't kill poor Marisol. My dad did. Back when he was mad. Then he spent the rest of his life grieving over what he'd done. I see that now. But I was just a kid. I wanted to believe everything he said. That was what he needed. Something, someone to try to ease the pain.'

'I'm sure you did.'

She half turned and glanced at me, as if to say I didn't understand at all, and never could.

'Trouble is, he was never brave enough to face the truth himself. That was the real horror. All the lies, the deceit, the dishonesty he never managed to acknowledge. It ate away at him. Maybe it killed him in the end. Ca' Scacchi's not full of ghosts. It's full of stories. People. Just like us.'

Not only the palazzo. The city itself was bound together by mud and brick, by history and culture, but just as much by tales of the rich and illustrious, the poor and obscure, high and low, woven together like one of those complex silken fabrics from the Jacquard looms of Bevilacqua that now hung on Ca' Scacchi's walls. Lucia Scacchi knew all this. She was Venetian, born and bred. Myths and fables and outright lies were in her blood. That all came out in her extraordinary story about Casanova, a piece of fiction that, in a few brief hours of misery, she turned into a riddle designed to lead Chas Hawker to face up to the monstrous act he'd committed. To find what he so craved and then to face his death.

'Stories are a way we tell ourselves we're not alone, I suppose,' I said, recalling a conversation we'd had that strange summer.

'And if there are such things as ghosts,' she replied, her back to me, looking out of the window at the black water and the lights of the hotels and palazzi opposite, 'they're the ones who should be scared of us.'

Still she stayed locked to the glittering view. 'And now we've got money. For the first time in my life, I don't have to worry about paying bills. Anything really.'

'That's good.'

She whirled round and leaned back against the expensive wallpaper. 'I suppose so. It just means I've nothing to chase. No one to look after . . .'

'Your mother.'

A toss of her immaculate hair and that snort again. 'Lucia doesn't need me. I know her now. She was never quite the damaged creature Dad said. She's . . . . quite a woman.'

'Runs in the family.'

'Maybe I'll disappear into the jungle in South America. Look for lost treasure. Meet a stranger and marry him on a whim.' She took a step towards me. 'I might never come back. We may never see each other again.'

That, I realised, was the real point of this meeting. A farewell.

'Then I'll always be grateful for those few remarkable days in August.'

She went back to the wall, the space between the windows. I caught my breath. It was where the panel had been. Obvious then. Not so now. The frame was hidden in the pattern, along with two tiny handles.

She threw it open and said, 'What do you think?'

It wasn't the Borgia portrait. No one was ever going to see the likes of that again. No, poor Annibale Scacchi's effort at copying it was there, the elongated Modigliani neck and torso, the lounging pose, the hands at the too-narrow waist. Next to it was a small glass case, inside a hank of hair, the edges charred, almost black.

'Is that . . .?'

'All that's left. Someone checked it against the locks they still have in some museum in Milan.'

'The Ambrosiana? Where Byron said he stole some strands?'

'Same hair.' She smiled. 'The real Lucrezia, I guess. Who's to know?'

The colour of the parts that weren't scorched was quite extraordinary. A shade of blonde close to gold, still almost alive five centuries on.

'I could believe it was her.'

'Me too. Well then.' She coughed, edged closer, turned round and said, 'Zip.'

'Is that Annibale Scacchi's original?'

A quick sigh. 'You do have a habit of asking the strangest questions at the most inopportune moments.'

'I just wondered. If you have all sorts of people coming and going here. Insurance must cost an arm and a leg. Is it safe to . . .'

She marched to the door, locked it, came back and turned around again. 'It's the original, OK? Poor Annibale must have painted it here, in front of the real thing. Now . . . this is my last night here. We've a plane out of Marco Polo at eight fifteen. I may never be back. I'm asking . . . I'm ordering . . . zip!'

It was such a beautiful dress. As I edged the fastener down the gentle ridge of her spine, she uttered a brief and grateful gasp, relieved I guess at being released from such a tight and unworldly gown.

The Scacchi bedroom smelled of something lush and floral, rather than the damp and decay of before. Even a touch over-heated – or perhaps that was me. It seemed delightful. A gift to all the senses.

'What do you think of her?' Lizzie said as she slipped the shiny silk from her shoulders then let it fall to the floor. 'Really? My Lucrezia? She's beautiful, isn't she? Not like the Borgia girl who used to live here. All the same . . .'

A reasonable question in the circumstances.

'I think the lady is quite surplus to requirements.'

And so she was.

The next morning found me watching grown men dressed as witches race along the Grand Canal towards a huge patterned sock suspended beneath the Rialto bridge. Both Luca and Valentina had insisted on it. One of her many relatives, Giorgio, an accountant during the week, a keen rower every Sunday, was a competitor in the Regata della Befana, an Epiphany tradition that had brought crowds to line both sides of the canal. Giorgio wore a long artificial nose, a witch's hat and what looked like a pantomime washerwoman's dress as he sculled his little boat, a broom-stick aloft in the stern, towards San Tomà. There, the contestants, none under fifty-five years of age, would turn round and race back to the finishing line beneath the sock, greeted by rapturous applause from the spectators cramming every inch of the way.

We were drinking warm and spicy *vin brulé* close to the spot where Luca and I had met the previous summer to go through the mystery of Lucia Scacchi's Casanova story, a trail of clues left by a woman we'd then believed dead. Opposite, half hidden by the people five or six deep, stood the palazzo that was once home to an aristocrat named Pietro Bembo. The place he'd hidden the portrait of his former lover, Lucrezia, commissioned by her murderous brother, a token of her affection Bembo surely kept to himself. There was plenty to remind me of Lizzie Hawker everywhere now.

TV cameras were filming from boats along the canal as if this were some Venetian version of the Oxford and Cambridge Boat Race. The day was bright and frosty, the mood everywhere one of joyous relief. After Epiphany, I would subside into an idle lethargy like everyone else. If Valentina and Luca Volpetti allowed. They always seemed to have something up their sleeves.

I was never put out by their antics. The brief distance we'd felt during the Scacchi affair had vanished after they began to feed me information to pass on to Gervaise Lascelles for his true-crime podcast. We all wanted that to succeed, and to spring Lucia Scacchi from prison. Then she and Lizzie picked up the baton and, with the private assistance of Ballarin, found a solution to the problem of what to do with that notorious lopsided palazzo on the Grand Canal. All in all, a satisfactory conclusion, one I could never have dreamt of during that hectic time after Ferragosto.

'Giorgio won't get there first,' Valentina said. 'He never does.'

'Does it matter?' I wondered. 'It's just fun, isn't it?'

'Some men always have to win,' she said with a shrug. 'My uncle isn't one of them. Just as well. Not in his nature. Always wants to take part, but lets others steal the thunder.'

I did wonder if that was aimed at me. Valentina looked very elegant and off-duty in a thick fake-fur jacket. Luca wore his favourite winter outfit, a billowing black *tabarro* cloak, floppy hat and long scarf. They were both staring at me in a way I'd come to recognise: they had something significant to impart.

'Yes . . .?' I said.

'The time has come for plain speaking,' Luca announced rather grandly, genial face dead serious for once. 'We are worried about you.'

'Well, I'm . . . flattered. But no need really.'

'Stop being so English,' Valentina exclaimed, a refrain I seemed to be hearing quite a lot. 'What about last night? All those important people there. Contacts to be made.'

'I've all the contacts I want.'

'You're a solitary man by nature,' Luca declared. 'This is not good.'

'Solitary.' Valentina waved that familiar admonitory finger from side to side, now clothed in a fine leather glove. 'A lonely man who slinks off into the night, vanishing in the midst of an exclusive social occasion that would never have happened without you.'

'Without us,' I tried to correct her.

'On your own! It was a party. There were people we wished you to meet. Influential people.'

'There was Gervaise Lascelles in a kilt.'

'You can hardly blame Italy for that. We'd hoped to expand your horizons.'

'God knows they need it,' Luca added.

I smiled and kept quiet.

Valentina touched my sleeve. 'Arnold. How on earth can we ever bring you out of your shell if you sneak off at the first opportunity?'

I shrugged.

'Female company,' Luca said firmly with a knowing nod. 'Take my word. It always works. Pleasure apart, it brings a man down to earth. Makes him appreciate there's a world beyond himself.'

'My cousin Paola, the librarian at the Querini Stampalia,' said Valentina for the umpteenth time, 'is still in need of English lessons.'

'Then she should find herself an English teacher.'

'Please listen.' She took my arm. 'We're your friends now. Your only friends as far as we can see. I realise this may be against your reclusive English nature. But you're in Venice. What can we do to teach you how to mingle?'

There was the distant whine of a jet in the winter sky, a contrail above the Palazzo Bembo like an artist's fine grey brush sweeping gently across a canvas of perfect blue. A plane headed out from Marco Polo. Perhaps Lizzie and her mother were on it.

'I rather feel I did quite enough mingling for one night, thank you. But I'm touched, deeply, by your concern.'

They didn't seem sure what to make of that. Valentina, in particular, was fixing me with narrowed, beady eyes.

'Anyone for lunch?' I wondered, hoping to redirect the conversation.

'I'm working. I need to change into uniform,' she said.

Luca looked shifty. 'A very quick *ombra* may be possible, but I've an appointment . . .' He glanced at his watch. 'Pushed for time.'

'The lady friend from Ca' Foscari?' I wondered.

'As it happens . . . no.'

His phone buzzed. He glanced at the screen, then held the thing aloft, beaming in the puppyish way I always found both endearing and a little disconcerting. There was a message there it seemed he'd been expecting.

Everyone started shouting, cheering.

'Vienna!' my friend cried as Valentina's uncle finished last beneath the giant embroidered sock. 'The Red Priest! Revelations!'

He was never a chap to shirk the cryptic, or linger over anything, be it puzzles, love affairs, tragedies even, for long. It was clear from his bright and cheery face that he'd moved on from the affair of Ca' Scacchi already. There was, it seemed, another hare to chase.

'Sorry?' I murmured.

He tapped his phone. 'I must speak of it no more. As ever in matters of confidence, I am discretion itself.'

'Ha!' cried Valentina.

He took no notice, just put a finger to his lips then patted my arm. 'You'll love this, Arnold. It speaks precisely to our talents. Apologies. I must away now. More later when I am free to expound upon it.'

'Infants! Beyond hope, the pair of you,' Valentina Fabbri grumbled, casting us both a corrosive glance. She passed her empty plastic cup to a total stranger, ordered him to dispose of it properly, then turned and melted into the fray.

A jaunty Luca trotted off in her wake.

Lost in the laughter and the delight of that happy crowd, I glanced at the sky and those fading paintbrush contrails one last time. Then started out for home.

Author's Note

Ca' Scacchi and the Còrf *squero* apart, the places listed in Lucia's story are real and ready to be found by the dogged explorer. There is no map here, since I feel Venice is best discovered through serendipity, not slavishly following a route laid down by others. But a little research should get you there in the end.

Secret Venice, by Thomas Jonglez and Paola Zoffoli, is a good companion for such a quest, and offers many arcane sights rarely covered by more conventional tourist guides. *Venetian Legends and Ghost Stories*, by Alberto Toso Fei, is another atmospheric introduction to the city's shadowy side. Anyone wishing to know more about Frederick Rolfe, the self-styled Baron Corvo, should seek out *The Quest for Corvo*, a so-called 'experimental biography' by A. J. A. Symons, older brother to the more famous crime writer Julian Symons.

The lock of golden hair reputed to belong to Lucrezia Borgia and seen in real life by Lord Byron, who claimed he stole a sample, remains in the Biblioteca Ambrosiana in Milan, which has owned it since at least 1685. The library also possesses nine letters written by Lucrezia to her Venetian lover, Pietro Bembo. *Lucrezia Borgia, Life, Love and Death in Renaissance Italy*, by Sarah Bradford, is, I suspect, the biography Luca Volpetti would give Arnold Clover as an informative present.

For those wanting to know more about the churches mentioned, I recommend a visit to the Churches of Venice website, http://churchesofvenice.com, an invaluable source of detailed information on places of worship past and present.

As ever, I'm indebted to my local friends and experts, Gregory Dowling foremost, for their advice and encouragement. And I'm grateful to my editor, Simon Thorogood, for his editorial insights and his decision to set this story in a font called Bembo. It is based on the typeface Aldus Manutius commissioned and first used in Venice in 1496, for a book of poetry by none other than Lucrezia Borgia's lover, Pietro.

David Hewson
Kent and Venice, 2022

THE
MEDICI
MURDERS

DAVID
HEWSON

'Character-rich, history-drenched'
Booklist

CANON‖GATE